ARCHANGELS / BOOK 1

HEAVEN'S GATE

Jan Dunlap

FaithHappenings Publishers

FaithHappenings Publishers
7061 S. University Blvd., Suite 307
Centennial, CO 80122

Cover Design ©2016 FaithHappenings Publishers
Book Layout ©2013 BookDesignTemplates.com

Heaven's Gate / Jan Dunlap. -- 1st ed.
ISBN (Softcover) 978-1-94155-509-5
This book was printed in the United States of America.

To order additional copies of this book, contact:
info@faithhappenings.com

FaithHappenings Publishers,
a division of FaithHappenings.com

For everyone who believes that science, as well as faith,

is the dominion of God

"Fight the good fight of the faith. Take hold of the eternal life

to which you were called..."

1 Timothy 6:12

PROLOGUE

He looked beautiful. Even in the darkness, his moonlit face etched in shadows, he could take her breath away.

Temptation, she thought.

No more, she vowed again.

She took a last glance through the side window of the door and placed her hand on the knob. Temptation or not, she owed him this much. She had, after all, been the one to start it, and she wasn't such a coward that she couldn't face him when she ended it.

She could do this.

As she opened the door, a sudden gust of icy wind clutched at her, chilling her to the bone. Shivering, she looked up into his beautiful face.

"It *is* over, Elise," he said, smiling. "In more ways than you can possibly know. And for that, I have you to thank."

He put a bullet between her eyes, and she dropped dead to the floor.

"Too easy," he said, noting a spray of blood on the back of his gun hand. He pulled a linen handkerchief from his overcoat pocket and wiped his hand clean. Then he turned and walked back into the night.

CHAPTER ONE

I *am so close.*

Sitting alone in his darkened lab, Dr. Michael Carilion held his head in his hands, a single high-intensity lamp throwing a halo of light across his broad shoulders and onto the pages of calculations that littered the desk's work surface.

It was almost midnight in the fourth-floor physics lab of Barnet College, the Harvard of Wisconsin, and the rest of his research team had left hours ago. As usual, Michael had remained, wrapped in a world of his own—a world composed of complex mathematical equations, scientific anomalies, wormholes and the mind-bending, multi-dimensional possibilities of String theory, the spoiled darling of theoretical physics. But even though his eyes were aching and his brain literally hurt, Michael wasn't about to call it a day and go home.

Not now.

Not tonight.

Not when he was this close.

And he knew he was close. He was sure of it. So close he could feel it in his bones. So close he could almost taste it, touch it.

"It" being not just another physics theory.

"It" being *the* physics theory—unification, the Unified Field Theory, the Holy Grail of theoretical physics. Also known as the One Theory of Everything, it would explain how the universe ultimately worked, from the smallest subatomic particles to the inconceivably massive galaxies of the universe. With unification, scientists could ask—and finally find the answers to—

the questions that had intrigued humanity since the dawn of time. The answers to "how did the universe begin?" and "how did life start?" would no longer be the raw material of intellectual or spiritual speculation, but instead, footnotes in scientific texts.

In fact, with unification, there wouldn't be the need for speculation of any kind anymore. The mystery of life itself would become an open book that everyone could read. Who knew what might be possible when scientists had all the answers? Would weather be controllable? Could life be extended indefinitely? Would new power sources revolutionize transportation, manufacturing, communication, or even human relationships themselves?

For a moment, Michael allowed himself a reprieve from his calculations. He pulled his time-worn Rubik's cube from his pocket and idly twirled the rows, remembering how he'd once heard a colleague refer to the quest for unification as "the desire to know the mind of God." That was taking it a bit far, Michael thought. Divinity wasn't involved in the equations he attempted; the behavior of physical objects and forces was.

Let the theologians look for the One God.

Michael was looking for the One Theory.

Granted, he certainly wasn't the first. There had been others before him—Sir Isaac Newton, James Clark Maxwell, Albert Einstein. Einstein's theory of General Relativity had even made him a celebrity of the day, making headlines, attracting photographers, attending soirees of the rich and famous.

But Michael also knew that Einstein's career didn't end with the theoretical physics that helped birth the space age. Unknown to many, the scientist with the wild white hair had believed there was a master pattern in the universe, a master equation. His belief became an obsession. The great man had spent the last two decades of his life in his second-floor study, trying to formulate a single theory so powerful it would describe the complexity of the universe. He stopped reading the work of other physicists, unaware of the newest developments in atomic research, focusing only on his quest for unification. He began to spout philosophy, talking about his "cosmic religion," the "big picture," and the "perfect harmony of the universe." Other physicists shied away from him, afraid he was losing his mind. Yet to the very last of his life, he kept searching for the theory.

Michael sighed.

Einstein was the reason he'd gone into the field of theoretical physics more than twenty years ago. Entranced with the man's genius, Michael had not only been drawn inescapably to mathematics, but he had also felt an immediate connection to the man the first time he'd seen a photo of the intellectual giant in his high school physics textbook. Not that there was any physical resemblance between the two—at forty-three years of age, Michael still had the tall, muscled frame of his youth, whereas Einstein had gone soft and bent, with that wild mane of white hair in contrast to the stark black curls that grazed Michael's shirt collar.

"Angel's curls," Elise had called them.

Elise.

He didn't have to look at a calendar to know it had been eight months and six days since her death. Some of those days he couldn't remember now and didn't want to. Other days, he'd thought he would go crazy with anger and confusion and depression and grief. There were nights he couldn't sleep, and the nights when he did sleep, he dreamed dreams he didn't want to have, dreams he didn't want to recall when he woke up.

His friends had been worried about him, and with good reason. Michael had lost interest in his research, dropped too much weight, and taken up drinking. His graduate assistants had done an adequate job teaching his classes during his leave of absence, but the work in the lab had faltered, placing both research grant renewals and the continued allotment of university funding in serious jeopardy—not to mention the future of his academic and professional career.

But fortunately, somewhere amidst the disaster his life was becoming, Michael had heard the One Theory of Everything calling to him, and he'd dried out, hit the weight room, and returned to work. Without Elise, work was the only thing that mattered anymore. He'd pushed hard with this last project—the Strings Project—the past six months, and its results lay thick on his desk. And somewhere among them, he had all the pieces to the puzzle. Unification was within his grasp. He just had to put it all together in the right pattern.

Rubbing his temples, Michael looked again at the papers and photographs strewn across his desk.

The halogen lamp illuminated the mess, making an oasis of light in the corner of the deserted lab. He focused again on the mathematical models of string theory, the theory that had given his project its name, its elegant computations that described the tiniest bits inside an atom as vibrating strings of energy, not particles. As a popular candidate for the One Theory, string theory had been tantalizing physicists for decades, and if it was correct, it was also Einstein's principle of ultimate unification.

The problem was the "if."

Before it could be crowned the One Theory, string theory had two small problems that needed to be resolved. The first was that it predicted eleven dimensions, and though theoretical physicists could find ten, they had yet to locate the eleventh.

The other problem was equally troublesome: with strings being so infinitely small, there was no way to prove they even existed.

Yet Michael was convinced his Strings Project was on the verge of doing both.

I am so close!

"Michael? It is very late. You should go home."

The woman's voice was an unwelcome jolt that shot straight to his nerve endings. Michael abruptly turned in his chair to peer through the dim lab to see a tall, slim woman standing in the open doorway. Backlit by the hallway lighting, her face was indiscernible, but he knew the accented voice.

Unfortunately.

"Khristina," he said, his own voice flat. "What do you need?"

"Nothing," she replied. "It is very late," she repeated.

Michael could feel the annoyance rising in his chest. Khristina Tupikova was the one member of their research team that he'd fought tooth and nail to keep out of his lab. But Lucas Scranton, Michael's unconventional, brilliant research partner, had insisted they needed Khristina to succeed in finding the One Theory.

Because she was a medium.

"I know it's late, Khristina," he said. "I work best when the lab is empty."

He hoped her psychic "sensitivities" picked up his emphasis on the word *empty*, and she would leave, but he'd already noticed in the lab that the nuances of the English language were occasionally lost on the Russian woman.

This time, though, he lucked out. He could see her silhouette shrink back from the door frame.

"Then I will leave you to your work, Michael," she said. "Good night."

He listened to her footsteps receding down the hallway.

"Good riddance," he muttered, turning back to his calculations.

Instead of returning to his mathematical models, though, he picked up one of the photographs on the desk. This was the reason behind Lucas's insistence to bring Khristina into the Strings Project. Taken while Khristina did her "readings," they were a collection of Kirlian photographs that captured incredible images of colored waves of energy emanating from her body. Lucas was convinced that the fluctuations of the magnetic fields documented in the photos would lead them to the One Theory. As intriguing as Lucas's speculations were, though, Michael could only shake his head at the crazy impulse that had forced him to agree to include a psychic in their work.

"There's a key in there," Lucas had argued with Michael. "If we're looking for the Theory of Everything, we've got to turn over the rocks other physicists have missed. You're the one who keeps saying we have to think outside the box, try something new, something creative. You can't deny that something of a physical nature is happening when a medium's magnetic aura changes. You've seen that research. Something's going on. I say we take it the next step. Spectral analysis of the energy. Trace the changes of the emanations to try to find the source of the effect."

And then Lucas had grasped Michael's shoulder, looked directly into his eyes and whispered, "What if the source is the eleventh dimension? The one everyone's been looking for, the one that will prove—prove!—that string theory is the One Theory of Everything? What have we got to lose? It's a whole field of inquiry that has barely been tapped—"

"What have we got to lose?" Michael had scoffed. "Dead people sending messages to the living is going to prove the most sought-after theory in the history of all science? Are you out of your mind? Messages from dead people? We'd be laughed right out of our conference chairs, not to mention any kind of university or research funds."

He'd shrugged off his colleague's hand and rolled his eyes. "Think about what you're saying, Lucas. Our peers wouldn't even let us *in* to the conference if word got out we were using psychic readers in the lab. Gee, maybe that's why the 'field of inquiry' hasn't been tapped. Because it's woo-woo science. Fakery. Fraud. It has nothing to do with legitimate scientific research and certainly, nothing to do with what we are trying to accomplish here."

"But you've seen the aura research. It can't be explained—"

"It can't be explained! You're right! So let someone else figure it out. Someone with the time and money and resources! Not us!"

Even now, six months later, alone in the lab, the argument still rang in Michael's head. Lucas, a natural wizard when it came to applied physics, had become obsessed with the possibility of uncovering the sub-atomic strings of String theory in the electromagnetic auras of human beings. Whereas Lucas couldn't find a single reason not to pursue the idea, Michael, the devoted theoretician, believed it was professional suicide. Finally, in frustration, he'd lost his temper and thrown it right at Lucas.

"What we have got to lose is the one thing we absolutely have to have in this project—complete credibility! Are you nuts?"

But Lucas hadn't backed down, and in the end, Michael had unaccountably caved and told Lucas to go ahead and set up the experiment. By the next morning, Lucas had Khristina Tupikova on her way to their lab. Within weeks, they had reams of psychic reading session transcripts, piles of computerized readouts, and the Kirlian photographs, photos that recorded the variations in the energy waves surrounding Khristina as she delivered messages from the other side of the grave.

Or so she claimed.

Personally, Michael didn't believe there was another "side" to the grave.

Dead was dead, and death was a door that closed shut once you walked through it. The day he watched Elise buried in the ground, he said goodbye.

At least, he had tried to.

Somehow, though, it wasn't enough. Some nights he dreamed of her, vivid dreams that woke him, shaking, imagining he'd heard the gunshot that killed her. Some days, he almost felt her breath on his cheek. That was when he wished, just for a moment, that he did believe in some kind of 'other side,' some place where Elise might still be, whole and happy and knowing he loved her.

But then he'd give himself a mental shake and tell himself to snap out of it. He was a physicist, a man who looked at the reality of the world as it revealed itself through concrete behaviors and physical relationships. As a trained scientist, Michael didn't "believe" in anything he couldn't explain with a formula or mathematical model.

Except for one thing: the Theory of Everything. And he believed he was the one who was going to find it.

He pushed the photos further to the side of his desk and concentrated again on the sheets of calculations he'd been tinkering with all afternoon and into the night.

Some of the mathematical formulas were as familiar to him as his own face, formulas he'd been manipulating ever since he attended the String theory conference back in 1995 at the University of Southern California. Ed Witten, one of the world's greatest physicists, had stood up and presented M Theory, a whole new perspective on String theory, a perspective that not only electrified all the scientists there but reconciled all the existing theories into one simple package, a package that revolutionized the search for the Theory of Everything. It was that package that Michael had torn apart and reassembled almost every day since, every minute he could spare from his teaching duties at the university. It was the motivation for all his research, and since losing Elise, it was the only reason he had for getting up every morning.

Once before, he'd thought he was on the brink of break-through. It was eight months and six days ago.

He'd been working late, as usual, and had managed to isolate some variables in his calculations. All at once, he'd seen the res-olution, the mysterious eleventh dimension unfolding in his head, and he'd begun frantically scribbling down the equations. But halfway to his destination, the phone rang and rang, short-circuiting what was going on in his brain. He'd grabbed the phone in a fury, picked up the receiver and shouted into it, "What?"

It was the hospital.

Elise had been shot.

Stunned, he'd flown out of the office, down the four flights of stairs to the faculty parking lot and then driven without any recall to Johnson Memorial Hospital. By the time he arrived in the emergency room, Elise was dead. The neighbors in their normally quiet neighborhood had heard a single gunshot and called 9-1-1. The first policeman on the scene had found Elise just inside the front door, a bullet lodged in her brain. She'd ap-parently opened the door to her killer, who shot her at point-blank range. There were no leads, no clues, nothing, as to why Elise Carilion was murdered in her own doorway. In the months since, Michael had battled guilt along with grief and depression. If only he'd been home and not working late in his lab . . .

And why did she open the door? Late at night, alone?

Michael shut the thoughts away as he had taught himself to do. It was the only way he could deal with it. At some point, he knew he would have to make peace with Elise's death, but it wasn't going to be tonight.

He ran through the last set of equations he'd written, feeling they were somehow familiar. He'd never been able to recreate the series he'd been working on when the call came from the hospital; when he had finally returned to work, his desk had been cleared off by a well-meaning teaching assistant, much to his dismay.

Actually, devastation would have been a more accurate description of his reaction. If Lucas hadn't pulled him out of reach of the hapless assistant, Michael would have strangled her.

Tonight, though, it seemed like his memory was sharpening, and the numbers and variables began to flow again, bringing him closer and closer to the formulation he'd previously attempted. When he began to reconcile the two sides of the equation, he could feel the adrenaline kick in, his mind working faster.

You are so close.

Michael froze, his mechanical pencil poised on the paper.

It was the voice again. The voice in his head that always spoke up when he did his best work, the voice he hadn't heard since the night Elise died. That year in high school physics, when he'd first heard it in his head, he'd fancied it was the voice of Einstein himself, choosing Michael, of all people, to finish his great work of unification. Later, he'd known that was pure imagination and that the "voice" he heard was his own inner fan club, encouraging him to pursue the intellectual work that only a few of his friends could even begin to understand. Hearing it again tonight, he smiled.

"I'm right where I need to be, aren't I?" Michael asked the empty lab.

No answer came back to him, but as he turned his attention again to the numbers, the edge of his vision caught the Kirlian photograph he'd already pushed aside. There was something about it . . .

There . . .

Michael unfocused his eyes and let his peripheral vision scan the photo, trying to see the big picture of the aura, instead of the details he usually picked out. Then it struck him what was different about the photo. Under the intense light of his halogen lamp, there seemed to be an anomaly—a disturbance—along the edges of the magnetic aura, something he hadn't picked out before.

Yes, the big picture, his inner voice said. *Look at the big picture.*

Michael held the photo away from him, testing to see if the anomaly was only a trick of the lamp.

It was still there.

And suddenly, Michael knew what he was seeing.

He quickly spread out the stack of Kirlians, searching for the same anomaly in each one, finding them exactly where he suspected he would—not in the aura itself, but in the background.

He spun in his chair to face his computer screen and rapidly typed in the commands to access the results of the data analyses of the photographs. He frantically scanned the long columns of numbers until he found what he was looking for—a recurring, tiny blip of data that surfaced away from the main body of the aura measurements. Continuing to scroll through the reports, he found it repeated at the same point in every analysis, virtually buried in the background of the numerical sequences. All this time, he and Lucas had focused on the auras themselves, not the area beyond them. The area beyond in the black background.

The black background with the anomaly that looked and behaved like the faintest echo of a wave.

The wave of an eleventh dimension.

Suddenly, the numbers and variables he'd already worked a thousand times seemed to reassemble themselves in new combinations, in sequences that now displayed a simple elegance that explained the anomalies in the data and photographs. And then his brain took off, and Michael was barely able to keep up with the equations pouring from his pencil.

CHAPTER TWO

I gotta tell you," the bleary-eyed, shaggy-haired man confided to the woman on the other side of the table as he finished off his third beer, "some of those readings were just freaking bizarre."

Lifting his empty glass, he nodded at the waitress at the bar for another drink. It was the end of one more long week working the Strings Project in Carilion's lab and he wasn't planning to get up tomorrow till at least noon. The beer was cold, the booth was cozy, and the woman sitting across from him was hanging on his every word.

Of course, that was her job—Phoebe Dauwalter was the science editor for *World*, arguably the most influential magazine on the planet, and he was giving her the scoop that would land her in the ranks of immortal journalists, and himself, Dr. Lucas Scranton, in the pop-culture world of the obscenely rich and famous.

He smiled to himself, waiting for his beer. He'd always wanted to be a physics rock star, kind of like that mathematician in the film *Jurassic Park*. Only he had something even bigger than reconstituted dinosaurs to tell the world about: he was part of the team that was a step away from formulating the physics theory that was going to blow away every other physics theory known to man. The theory that had eluded the world's greatest scientific minds for centuries.

The One Theory.

When the One Theory was announced, the world was going to become a different place.

And he, Lucas Scranton, was going to be right there in the spotlight to help explain to every man, woman, and child how their fundamental understanding of the universe had just gone the way of the dodo. Scrap all the equations and theories that had described the world as it had been known—a world governed by the laws of relativity and quantum mechanics. Instead, there was a brave new universe of untapped, mind-boggling energy and dazzling discoveries out there, just waiting to be unleashed.

Just waiting until his partner, Dr. Michael Carilion, fit the last pieces of the unification puzzle together into a perfect, unprecedented One Theory.

Until then, the media frenzy that Phoebe Dauwalter's article would cause would have to satisfy his rock star ambitions, Lucas conceded. Maybe he could still do *The Tonight Show*, though. Then, later, after the One Theory was finally published, a PBS special, at least.

"But the content of these readings really don't figure into the Strings Project itself, isn't that what you said, Dr. Scranton?"

Dauwalter's voice broke into his reverie. He shook his head, trying to clear away some of the booze-induced haze, and asked her to repeat the question.

"The readings from the medium—their actual content—aren't important to the scientific calculations themselves, are they?" the editor asked, shuffling back through the notes she'd taken during their conversation. Apparently finding what she was looking for, she underlined something in her little notebook, then pinned her green eyes on his with an intensity that burned right through Lucas's beer buzz.

Man! Lucas thought, mesmerized by the face across the table. Not only was the woman gorgeous, with her sleek black hair and high cheekbones—not to mention those emerald eyes of hers—but there was an aura of determination about her that

Lucas found irresistibly attractive. He shifted in his seat, suddenly aware that he wasn't nearly as mentally, or physically, worn out as he'd thought he was. Maybe this meeting would turn out to be the perfect ending to a long week, after all. A slow smile tipped the corners of his lips as he tried to remember where they were in their conversation.

The woman returned his smile with one of her own, then read back to Lucas the comment he'd made earlier. "It wasn't the content of what the medium was doing that you were interested in, but the physical phenomena that occurred during the reading. Is that right?"

"Yeah," Lucas said, accepting the refilled glass the waitress handed him. "Thanks."

He took a quick sip of the cold beer and watched a thin trail of condensation drip from the bottom of his glass onto the top of the small table. When he set his drink down, he hoped that Ms. Editor couldn't tell it was taking a real effort for him to keep the conversation on the Strings Project, and not on what plans she might have for later in the evening.

"Our lab protocol focused on gathering data from the radiation fluctuations that our equipment recorded when the medium was working," he slowly explained. "We also ran continuous multi-wavelength cameras that filmed the auras around her, so we could match up the video, data, and audio streams to identify when and how the auras shifted."

He drew a finger through the puddle of water that had pooled next to his beer and looked directly into Phoebe Dauwalter's emerald eyes. "The idea is to investigate the interactions of the human body's magnetic field with other sources of . . . input, for lack of a better word."

"Input?" the editor asked.

"Like I said, for lack of a better word . . . at this point."

The woman's smile faded and Lucas thought he could feel, rather than see, her withdrawing from the conversation.

Lucas gave himself a mental kick in the head.

He couldn't blow this interview. He needed to give her the right words—not "input," but "information." He had to tell her exactly what he and Michael suspected was the real source of energy flux, or else she was going to walk out of this bar, convinced she'd wasted her evening on some self-important junior researcher who had delusions of grandeur.

Lucas couldn't blame her. Half the time, he'd have to admit that even to his own ears, the whole thing still sounded more like science fiction or fantasy than hard scientific investigation.

Yet, despite his intention to give this woman the scoop of her career, Lucas was having trouble spelling it all out for her. He briefly wondered if it was some crazy kind of guilt kicking in. He'd spent the better part of the last three days rationalizing why he should tip off the *World* to what was going on in Michael's lab, despite his partner's demand that they keep the Strings Project under wraps a while yet.

"We are at a crisis point here, Michael," Lucas had reminded his partner again just yesterday. "The whole program is on the verge of collapse. The money's almost gone. And we had two more lab assistants leave for other assignments with a lot more job security than we can offer right now."

"This isn't about job security, Lucas," Michael had sighed, his hands twisting and turning that old Rubik's Cube that never seemed out of the man's reach. "If our people can't see that, see what we're trying to accomplish here, then maybe they're better off somewhere else, anyway."

"But *we're* not better off," Lucas had pointed out for what had seemed the hundredth time. "We need these particular assistants, and we need them right now. Otherwise, we're going to have to train new personnel to bring them up to speed, and we can't afford that, Michael. Not now."

For a moment or two, Michael had continued to twist the cube in silence.

"It's me, isn't it?"

Lucas had started to protest, but Michael cut him off.

"The team is questioning my ability, aren't they? They're not convinced I've put Elise's death behind me. They're wondering if I can still lead this team."

Lucas hadn't answered Michael. He hadn't confirmed his partner's fears, though Michael had to know that his erratic behavior after Elise's murder had severely handicapped his team's confidence in his leadership. Instead, Lucas had faulted the failing money for the impasse they were rapidly approaching with the program.

And yet, if Lucas was truly being honest with himself, he also knew that all those justifications paled in comparison to the personal benefits he envisioned for himself as the physicist who broke the story.

He wanted to be a pop culture icon.

He wanted to be rich and famous.

Marshalling his thoughts, he tried again to explain to the science editor.

"The physical data clearly demonstrates that something is affecting the medium's aura during a reading," he said. "Our theory is that some energy source of an as-yet-unknown origin is making itself felt in these experiments."

He lifted his glass in declaration.

"Our hypothesis is that the source has its origin in the eleventh dimension. And once we find the eleventh dimension, we not only have the source, we've also got the One Theory of Everything."

Dauwalter's eyes searched his. He couldn't be positive, but he was fairly certain he saw the pupils of her eyes dilate. He'd recaptured her interest.

"Because then you've resolved the two problems of string theory?" she asked, her voice in a low whisper.

Lucas smiled. The woman had done her homework. She was sharp, intelligent, driven, and she understood his language.

And he liked her voice when it sounded like that. And he really liked the intensity of those green eyes of hers when he had her complete attention.

Yes, meeting Phoebe Dauwalter for a beer tonight had been an excellent idea.

Maybe Jimmy Fallon and *The Tonight Show* wasn't enough, Lucas considered. Maybe he should be thinking the *Today Show*, too. With Phoebe Dauwalter breaking this story, he and Michael were on their way to becoming the newest stars in the physics firmament.

He returned his attention to the editor. "You hit the proverbial nail on the head, Ms. Dauwalter. Make the mathematical model that pinpoints the eleventh dimension, find proof of the same, and bang! Unification. And right now, Dr. Carilion and I are in the home stretch."

CHAPTER THREE

For a split second, Phoebe stopped breathing. Was it really possible? Was this half-drunk junior researcher and his team truly closing in on the One Theory of Everything? Yes, she'd heard a few whispers in the last year that there was a high-powered physics project going on at the local university, but she'd never been able to ferret out any details. Finally, she'd given it up as somebody's pipe dream for more funding. Even while she was driving to the bar to meet Dr. Lucas Scranton tonight, she had convinced herself that her boss, Drake Lamont, the owner of the *World*, must have misunderstood the phone caller, and that rather than a big breakthrough, the physicist had only background information to share.

Now, however, the thought that the most sought-after formulation of physical laws since Einstein published his work on relativity was going to be unveiled right here in town was mind-bending. What were the chances that the search for the Holy Grail of physics was about to succeed right under her journalistic nose? And that she, Phoebe Dauwalter, science editor for the *World*, would be the reporter to announce it?

"Are you saying," she asked slowly, carefully choosing each word, "that you have evidence of the eleventh dimension?"

Scranton leaned across the table and answered her question with a whisper. "It's at the tip of our fingers, Ms. Dauwalter. The 'input' I mentioned is actually hard data."

"Wait a minute," Phoebe said, abruptly leaning back in the booth.

Scranton blinked and Phoebe noticed his eyes drifting down her chest.

Phoebe studied the man sitting opposite her. He was definitely drinking too much, but he clearly knew his science, and she'd noted that his body language was screaming high-voltage tension when he had first walked over to her table an hour ago. She'd figured then that he was nervous about breaking the story because he knew how big it was and what it could mean for his career, not to mention the worldwide scientific community.

She'd also guessed that he was well aware of the professional repercussions he would suffer from his colleague, Dr. Carilion, when the physicist found his well-guarded project splashed across the pages of *World*.

Yet Scranton was the one who had called in, and he had kept his interview appointment. It wasn't Phoebe's problem if the man was jeopardizing his relationship with his partner or his position on the research team. Phoebe was just doing her job, taking the opportunity that had fallen in her lap—an opportunity that, if she played her cards right, might just launch her into the stratosphere of celebrity journalists and give her a crack at that Pulitzer. Maybe that's what Scranton figured he was doing, too—taking a once-in-a-lifetime shot at making all his dreams come true.

From across the table, Phoebe watched Scranton carefully, registering the moment his interest slipped from professional to personal. His reaction to her didn't surprise her. As a matter of fact, she'd been waiting for it. In her eight years of working in the media, she'd already turned down her fill of proposals—indecent and otherwise—from colleagues and the people she interviewed.

Instead of viewing her looks as an obstacle, though, Phoebe had put them to work along with her journalistic talents and quickly ascended the ladder of her profession, landing a job with *World* as the magazine's science correspondent at the ripe old age of twenty-six. Thrilled with her success and determined to please her new boss, Phoebe had devoured every scientific journal she could get her hands on, intent on mastering two things—the newest developments in research and a clear idea of where that research was headed.

As a result, her hard work and intuition had produced a goldmine of important features that had earned her not only the admiration and respect of her journalistic colleagues, but promotions at the magazine as well. Within two years, she'd landed in the editor's chair and set her sights on her next objective: a Pulitzer Prize. That was why, just a few hours ago, when Drake had passed along to her Scranton's phone message, her heart had almost stopped when she saw the words "One Theory of Everything" scribbled on the note.

With a story like that to break, the Pulitzer was only a breath away.

Now, after almost an hour with the physicist sitting at the other side of the little table, Phoebe was thinking that her excitement had definitely been premature.

So far, Scranton hadn't revealed the big breakthrough he'd hinted at in his message, and the stories he was telling her about a medium in the lab were pretty incredible, if not downright unbelievable, and completely useless for her purposes. He'd told her about readings that located family heirlooms lost for generations and double-blind experiments that revealed heart-wrenching personal information. The medium had even foretold the accidental death of a relative of one of the lab employees; Scranton said his colleague was so shaken when her uncle died in a car crash a week later that she refused to return to work until the medium experiments were finished.

Phoebe knew at least four stringers for supermarket tabloids who would kill for those stories, but things that went bump in the night had no place in her high-altitude world of hard science journalism. Voodoo might sell the checkout rags to people seeking an alternate reality, but the reality of impeccable science reporting was what she prided herself on delivering to her readers with every one of her bylines.

Besides, Phoebe had no doubt that if she turned in an article about psychic experiments to Drake, she'd be job-hunting within the week, editor's chair or not. Her boss might be one of the most intelligent and charismatic men she had ever met, but she already knew—from very personal experience—that 'The Gentleman,' as he was referred to around the office, was no gentleman when he didn't get what he wanted. In the offices of the *World*, there was only one commandment: Thou shalt serve Drake Lamont with all thy strength.

No heart allowed. Or soul—let alone dead souls—either.

"Hard data," Phoebe repeated the physicist's words. "Please tell me you're not talking about the Akashic field?" she challenged him. "The pseudo-science, philosophical theory that a cosmic field of information permeates the universe and is the source of all matter, energy, and even consciousness? Is that what this is all about? If it is, you've got the wrong correspondent, Dr. Scranton. Let me give you the number for a New Age publisher, instead."

"No, no, no," he hastily assured her. "I know that's what it sounds like on the surface, but that's not where we're going in this project. You're right—the Akashic field—the A-field—is not rigorous, rep . . . rep," he stumbled over the word, ". . . replicable science. It's a catchall theory for spiritual seekers who are trying to explain away all the unexplainable things in the universe so they can claim oneness. Or something."

The man finished off his beer and signaled the waitress again. He folded his hands on the table in front of him and fixed his attention on Phoebe.

"The point—the clean knife-cut—of what we're doing in our project is to isolate exactly where information—'information' being what we've observed in our experiments to affect our medium and cause the energy flux—is coming from," Lucas explained. "You see, we've got a theory that information is somehow coded into little energy packets, and those packets bombard a medium when she or he does readings, and the physical evidence of that information is being recorded in the lab as units of energy and variations in spectroscopic photography."

Scranton paused, peering at Phoebe.

He was probably wondering if she could make any sense out of his comments, Phoebe reflected. Four beers could muddle reciting the simple ABCs, let alone a cutting-edge physics project. Luckily for the inebriated Dr. Scranton, Phoebe had been chasing this particular story for years.

"The deal here, Ms. Dauwalter," he finally said, "is that we have replicable physical evidence of an unnamed energy. We have photos. We have computer analyses. And as soon as Dr. Carilion—and the man is a genius, I'm telling you—completes the equations, we will have the One Theory."

Replicable physical evidence.

Phoebe realized she'd stopped breathing

The magic words in scientific research.

She drew a quick breath, both stunned and relieved.

Tonight was not a wild goose chase, after all. If she could get access to those photographs and analyses, she was sure that this once-in-a-lifetime opportunity would be more than enough for both her and the young physicist to stake their claims to fame and fortune. Not only that, but in so doing, she could also make Drake Lamont a very happy publisher.

And when Drake Lamont was happy, Phoebe would be happy, too.

Phoebe gave Lucas the most admiring smile she could muster.

"You are a brilliant man, Dr. Scranton. May I call you Lucas?"

CHAPTER FOUR

L ucas could feel his shoulders relaxing as relief poured in. She *got* it! Science editor Phoebe understood the work that had been consuming his life for the last two years. He'd taken the chance of calling the *World*, and though he'd been initially dismayed that the owner had passed him off like a bit player, he wasn't finding any fault now with the woman sitting across from him in the booth.

Far from it, Lucas thought. In fact, it would be a small miracle if he didn't throw himself at her as soon as they left the bar.

To his delight, he also realized he was no longer troubled by any lingering doubts about going public with the research—Michael would be thanking him, eventually, he was sure. Without a doubt, when the story hit the street, new sources of funding would be lining up to share in the last leg of the biggest scientific journey in history. The pressure on Michael to rush the calculations would be lessened, giving him the luxury of doing his best work without the stress of shrinking financial resources. The lab assistants would stay with the project, and the others' concerns about Michael's leadership and mental acuity would disappear. The quest could go on, the lab would forge ahead, and all the positive publicity generated by the magazine article would give them a smooth ride right up to the finish line.

Yes, all things considered, Lucas was now convinced he'd done exactly the right thing for science, along with everyone involved in the Strings Project.

And if prestigious career or lucrative media opportunities came his way because of it, well, he'd feel obliged to consider one and all.

He smiled back at Phoebe.

"Lucas is good," he nodded. "Now I'd like to ask *you* a few questions, if you don't mind. Just curious—why did your hotshot boss pass me off to you when he could've been the one to break this story? Not that I mind having you here instead. In fact," he added, "I'm downright thrilled."

Phoebe laughed.

"You know, I have to say that 'hotshot' is a pretty accurate word for Drake Lamont," she said lightly. "But he's not a writer for the magazine, he's the owner," she clarified. "He's the one who gets to make all the calls. The rest of us just do his bidding."

Lucas leaned forward conspiratorially. "So how exactly does one become the owner of an internationally acclaimed magazine?"

"Opportunity and intelligence, I expect," she replied. "Mr. Lamont attended private schools in Europe and moved to the U.S. to pursue graduate studies. He has masters' degrees in several disciplines. He dabbled in the stock market, did well with his investments, and then launched his publishing empire."

"That sounds like you read it off a conference website," Lucas commented. "No, really, what's he like? I've heard some very interesting things about your boss and where he comes from," he confided. "Have you heard the one where he's rumored to be the illegitimate son of a former American spy chief and a French heiress? Or how about the one that he was born in Australia, but immigrated to the U.S. to escape a murder charge in China?"

Again, Phoebe laughed.

"People are always hungry to know a rich, successful man's past, Lucas," she told him. "They want to hear about a scandalous secret buried somewhere. So when a man like that refuses to share that information, people assume he's guilty of hiding something. Personally?" Phoebe shook her head. "I don't believe that Mr. Lamont is hiding anything that would be valuable to anyone but himself."

Lucas shrugged. "Well, I thought I'd give it a try. It's not every day I get close to people who travel in the kind of circles Drake Lamont frequents."

He shook his head, as though to clear it of thoughts of the *World's* owner, and laid his hands flat on the table.

"So what else can I tell you about the Strings Project?" he offered.

"Whatever you want," Phoebe replied, laying the slender fingers of her own hands across his on the table. "Whatever you want."

The touch of her fingers sent a pulse of electricity through his body.

"I have an idea," he said. "Let me show you the lab. I've got a keycard. No one will be there. It'll just be us," he whispered a bit too loudly. "That is, if you want to go."

"Oh, I do," Phoebe assured him, stuffing her notes into her purse and scooting out of the booth. Lucas slid to the end of his booth bench and stood up. A wave of vertigo washed over him as he fumbled through his pockets, looking for his car key.

"You know, I think maybe I should drive," Phoebe said. "If you don't mind."

He pulled his key ring from his pocket and handed it to her. "I think that's probably a really good idea," he agreed. He waved in the general direction of the bar's door. "After you, Phoebe."

Phoebe stepped past him and started to make her way through the noisy crowd of patrons lining the bar's long counter. Trailing behind her, Lucas remembered another thing he'd meant to tell her.

"Science aside," he said, his words noticeably slurring now, "it was downright spooky to watch our medium produce data.

Gave me the creeps, if you want to know the truth. Really, she's amazing. Did I tell you her name? It's Khristina. Khristina Tupikova. She's Russian."

Lucas grabbed at Phoebe's sleeve and pulled her around to face him, hoping to impress upon her the importance of what he was sharing with her.

"But you can't write down her name," he told her. "It's confidential. Part of the deal we made with her to get her into the lab for the research. Have to protect her privacy, you know. You have to promise me."

"Okay," Phoebe replied. "No problem."

Reassured, Lucas let go of Phoebe's arm and felt his balance shift precariously. He leaned back for support against the polished railing that ran the length of the bar counter, accidentally bumping against a red-haired woman seated there.

"Sorry about that," he mumbled when she threw him a look of disgust. He didn't usually have more than two or three beers all weekend and couldn't remember now exactly how many he'd had at the table. He rubbed the side of his face and suddenly recalled the one lab session with Khristina that had particularly unnerved him.

It had been a double-blind experiment, which meant that the medium and her sitter—the person for whom the medium was supposedly receiving information from the 'other side'— were physically separated from each other.

In this case, in fact, they weren't even in the same state.

Khristina had been given the name of a man, someone she'd never met, as her sitter and simply been asked to verbally record whatever impressions she received while concentrating on the name of the fellow in the solitude of a closed lab booth. Afterwards, the recording was played over the phone for the man, and he evaluated the information's accuracy. Khristina had scored an astounding ninety percent, which indicated that only ten percent of her information was not intimately meaningful to the sitter.

What had shaken Lucas to the bone was that the specific ten percent of the recording that meant nothing to the sitter had meant something very personal to him.

"I have a grandmother coming through," Khristina's voice on the tape had reported. "She is not related to my sitter, but she needs to speak with a Buddy very urgently. She says he will know it is her because he left an animal, I think, an animal toy named Boo, at her home after a Christmas dinner. He was very little then. She is frightened now for him. She says he must stay out from behind bars. I think she means he is in jail? No, that is not right. She is telling me she means bars, like where you drink. Like a café. She is saying something like 'bars will kill you,' I think. I'm sorry, I'm not sure if that's what she means, but that is what I am getting from her. She is very upset, I think. And now she is leaving."

Of course, when the team listened to the tape, they'd laughed, joking that Khristina wasn't telling anyone anything new, that lots of the bars around the university would kill you, if not with cheap booze, then with a diet of deep-fried food.

Lucas had laughed, too, but not in amusement. He'd laughed to cover the churning in his gut that had rendered him speechless.

As a child, his nickname had been Buddy.

And he'd been inordinately attached to a blue, stuffed toy rabbit he'd named Boo, which he'd accidentally left behind at his grandma's house one Christmas.

There was no way on earth that Khristina could have known those things about him, Lucas reminded himself now, as he did every time he remembered the incident. He'd never mentioned anything from his childhood to his coworkers in the lab or to Michael, so it was impossible for their Russian colleague to have picked up the information from an overheard conversation.

Not only that, but even if Khristina could somehow read minds, Lucas himself hadn't even been in the building during her lab reading.

As it continued to do every time he thought about it, the memory of hearing that recording sent icy chills down his spine.

Lucas suddenly realized that he was still leaning against the bar, his hands clutching, white-knuckled, at its rail. He turned to see Phoebe standing beside him.

"This Khristina Tupikova," he told her. "I couldn't believe it when I got her into the study. I'd heard about her. She was the one who got Sherry Smith's $50,000. She knew the code. And her English isn't even that great."

Phoebe gave him a blank look.

"Sherry Smith. You don't know about her, do you?" Lucas asked.

Phoebe shook her head. "I have no idea what you're talking about, Lucas." She nodded towards the door. "You can tell me in the car."

"No, no, no," he protested, accidentally jostling the red-haired woman next to him at the bar one more time. He turned towards her and apologized again. "Sorry."

He turned back to Phoebe.

"You gotta hear this. Khristina was the one who got the code from Sherry after she died." The words tumbled out of him, beyond his control, but he no longer cared. He needed Phoebe to hear it all.

"After Sherry died," he corrected himself, "not Khristina. Sherry was—is—was?—this incredibly talented medium who said that after she died, she would send a secret message to anyone who could get it, and Khristina got it. She got it and took it to the bank in Florida, where Sherry left the money. The message Khristina got from Sherry opened the code for the safety deposit box, so she got the money. Fifty thousand dollars."

He put his hand on Phoebe's shoulder and softly shook her.

"Don't you get it?" he said. "Khristina got information from someone who's dead. That's why I wanted her in our Strings Project so badly. If anyone could receive info packets from the eleventh dimension, Khristina could!"

CHAPTER FIVE

More than a few heads in the bar were turning towards Lucas, whose voice had steadily risen and gotten louder with excitement.

Determined to get him out to the car before they attracted any more attention, Phoebe grabbed his shoulders and propelled him toward the door. She kept a hand on his back to make sure he kept moving forward and mouthed "too much beer" at the bar patrons she passed on the way out. All she had to do was get Lucas some fresh air and into her car, and then they'd go to the university.

Once she was inside the lab, Lucas could pass out and sleep like the dead, for all Phoebe cared. All she needed was access to those photos and printouts as supporting material for her article. With those in hand, she would construct a piece of hard science journalism that would withstand the attacks of even the toughest critics, and, at the same time, bring her the professional acclaim she'd been dreaming of.

The Pulitzer would just be the beginning for her.

Stepping outside, the brisk night air of early October slapped Phoebe's cheeks as she walked a weaving Lucas past two closed storefronts. Suddenly, she felt the fine hairs on the nape of her neck bolt upright just as someone shoved her hard, face-first, into a recessed doorway.

It took only a moment, but by the time she turned back around, all she could see was a long, dark knife blade being dragged out of Lucas's rib cage, blood already gushing across the front of his jacket, his assailant running across the street and vanishing down an alley.

CHAPTER SIX

Skye Hammond covered her right ear with her palm to block out the noise of the sirens while she tried to make herself heard over her cell phone.

"You've got to give me front page in Sunday's edition, Frank," she told her boss, Frank Whedon, editor of the popular daily tabloid *The Midnight Eye*. "I have got the hottest bit of news you've ever seen, and it's gonna sell a million copies."

Skye retreated to a booth near the back of the bar to get further away from the commotion outside in the street. There'd been a mugging, someone near the front door had said, a mugging that apparently had gotten out of hand, and now the cop cars and ambulance had arrived and filled the street with blazing red, white, and blue lights.

It wasn't the street crime that Skye was interested in, though. Muggings and killings weren't her cup of tea, nor were they her readers'. Skye's stock in the journalism trade was the weird and bizarre, and she had a doozy on tap for Frank. Who'd have thought that getting stood up—again—by her as-of-now-former boyfriend would have produced this gem? Jerk that he was, if she hadn't been waiting for Josh at the bar, she wouldn't have heard the story the drunk guy was telling when he bumped into her on his way out. And when Skye recognized Phoebe Dauwalter from *World* magazine, she knew she was on to something good.

"Here's the deal, Frank. There's this woman named Khristina Tupikova, a Russian, who's apparently the world's greatest medium, and this very same Khristina Tupikova was helping a physicist here in town by the name of Dr. Carilion with receiving information from an eleventh dimension by way of talking with dead people!"

Skye smiled, listening to Frank's enthusiastic, characteristically profanity-laced response.

"Yup, you got it, Frank. I'm going home now to do the Internet searches. I'll find out who Dr. Carilion is, see if I get any hits from 'eleventh dimension,' and track down Ms. Tupikova. So do I get front page?"

Twenty minutes later, Skye walked into the second-floor apartment she shared with her two Siamese cats, Mitch and Fitch. It wasn't a big place, just a one-bedroom studio, but she'd managed to make it into a cozy nest with a lot of second-hand furniture and hand-me-downs from her folks when they sold their home and moved into an assisted living community. She'd figured that the apartment was only temporary, anyway. Once she finished her master's degree in English at Barnet next spring, she'd probably look for a good-paying job teaching at a community college somewhere, preferably one located in a warm, sunny climate.

Or she could get serious about journalism and try to find a more respectable employer than a supermarket tabloid.

Or maybe she'd just wait and see what God had in store for her. To be honest, Skye really wasn't sure where she was headed after graduation. She figured she just had to put her trust in the Lord, and everything would fall into place.

Until then, her humble apartment and steady paycheck from *The Midnight Eye* were sufficient, albeit confining. Sure, she'd like to be making more money right now, but between her graduate classes and her part-time hours with the *Eye*, a second job was out of the question. There really were only so many hours in the day.

Two of which she'd wasted tonight, waiting for Josh the Jerk to show up. Although if this story panned out the way she hoped it would, those were two hours well wasted.

She booted up her laptop, again mulling over her chance encounter with the drunk guy and Dauwalter, wondering what significance the guy's story had for the science editor of *World* magazine. *World* was a highly respected publication, only one part of an entire publishing empire, and though she'd never met its owner, the mysterious Drake Lamont, she'd heard impressive rumors about the man's intelligence and professional integrity from some of her instructors and classmates at school. Supposedly, Lamont had advanced degrees in business, physics and theology, a most unusual combination, and his managerial skills and drive were almost legendary, as were his good looks and impeccable GQ clothing style; it was rumored that at the *World* offices, he was referred to as 'The Gentleman' because of it.

It was also common knowledge in the publishing business that he aspired to make his magazine the international standard for cutting-edge cultural reporting and refused to tolerate anything less than absolute excellence from his staff. Based on that information, Skye had to assume that Lamont wouldn't send out his science editor to tap a source unless he knew that source to be solid and reputable.

Recalling the behavior of Dauwalter's companion, however, Skye would say that 'solid' and 'reputable' were questionable characteristics of the inebriated man she'd seen.

Which could only mean that Lamont and Dauwalter knew something she didn't.

Skye decided to go for the psychic first and entered the name 'Khristina Tupikova' into her search engine. While she waited, Mitch climbed into her lap. A second later, her search ended.

"No results found," Skye told Mitch. "Okay, so the lady keeps a very low profile. Maybe she just can't get Internet reception back home in Russia. Or maybe she doesn't use a computer. Maybe she doesn't even have a computer."

Typing again, Skye entered her second lead: 'Dr. Carilion.'

This time, she hit it big.

Really big.

Dr. Michael Carilion's name popped up with a ton of links, including those to multiple academic papers, keynote addresses at physics conventions, journal articles, and Barnet College's own webpages.

"A local guy," she told Mitch. "And a pretty smart one, too, from what these links are looking like. Gee, I hope he doesn't come looking for me when I couple his name in the *Eye* with a lady who talks to dead people. I can't imagine that's going to do a whole lot for his professional reputation, although he just might get all the press attention he ever wanted out of it."

For a moment or two, she hesitated, a wisp of conscience catching at the edges of her attention. What if she did hurt the man's reputation? So far, all her work for the *Eye* had been harmless, which was just the way she liked it.

But to throw stones at another?

Skye shook her head, chuckling.

"Who am I kidding?" she asked the cats. "I write for a tabloid. Nobody believes this stuff, and even if they do, I can't imagine any of them are in a position to threaten the career of a highly regarded physicist."

She rubbed behind Mitch's ears.

"Who knows? Maybe Dr. Carilion can turn the publicity into grant money, somehow. I bet that would make him happy."

Her guilt assuaged, Skye continued to scan down the page of links, until her attention caught on an entry that wasn't related to Carilion's scientific career. Out of curiosity, she followed the link, which led to an archived newspaper article—an article about the unsolved murder of Elise Carilion earlier in the year.

After reading it, Skye leaned back from the computer and sighed.

"Maybe Dr. Carilion has already had all the press he ever wanted, Mitch. How awful for him."

She stroked the cat and scratched behind his ears again, wondering about the man whose wife had been murdered on her own doorstep. According to the article, no arrests were ever made in the case, nor was anyone charged with the crime. Baffled and frustrated by the absence of any leads, the police had finally chalked it up to random and senseless violence, to the evil that seemed to periodically erupt on the streets of every city—even small ones like Litchfield.

Skye couldn't imagine how anyone could accept an explanation like that, but then again, just tonight, she herself had been only steps away from a random act of violence. If she hadn't decided to give Josh another fifteen minutes, maybe she'd have been the one who got mugged outside the bar.

An involuntary shiver rippled over her back.

Life didn't come with guarantees, Skye reminded herself. And evil didn't discriminate, she mentally added, her thoughts returning again to Carilion. Not even the wives of small-town professors were safe when it came to senseless attacks.

With a heavy sigh, Skye picked up the cat and hugged it to her chest.

"I can't do it, Mitch," she said. "My soft spot is showing, I know, but I can't put this guy through anything more. Not right now. He's had enough to deal with. I'll have to do the *Eye* piece without his name in it. We'll just have to go with the ever-reliable and always-popular 'secret project' angle. It works every time, Mitch, and like Frank always says, 'it always sells better with "secret" stamped on it.'"

Skye stifled a yawn and glanced at the time on her computer screen. It was almost two in the morning. She decided to try one more search before calling it quits and hitting the sack.

Typing in 'eleventh dimension,' she figured she'd take a quick look and save it for morning.

She was wrong.

As the computer screen filled with results, Skye had the distinct feeling she wouldn't be going to sleep for at least a while yet, because as she scanned the list of links, she could feel her tiredness giving way to little ripples of excitement, ripples that were rapidly growing into explosions of ideas. She looked again at the links, focusing on words and phrases that seemed to collide together in her head with mounting significance: Theory of Everything, information-energy exchange, and, of all things, soul communication. On top of that, words from her literary theory class were trying to jump into the mix too: words like 'ontology'—the nature of being—and 'epistemology'—mode of knowing.

Concentrating harder, Skye tried to recall exactly what she'd overheard in the bar.

The medium, Khristina, knew how to get information from the eleventh dimension, which, one link explained, was the key to confirming the Theory of Everything. That had to mean that not only was there an eleventh dimension, but that the existence of that dimension was, in fact, evidence of the Theory of Everything. The first conclusion, Skye realized, would be more than enough reason for Dauwalter to be interviewing her source, who obviously worked with Carilion in the research lab, but the second conclusion was the biggest prize of all.

If Skye was right, that meant that Dauwalter and Lamont had the lead on the most important scientific story of the decade—maybe even the century: evidence of the Theory of Everything, the so-called Holy Grail of physics, according to the web link.

But, Skye wondered in mounting amazement, did they realize what else they had?

If Khristina Tupikova could retrieve information from an eleventh dimension which had been scientifically proven to exist, and she said that information came from communicating with dead people, then the eleventh dimension was where dead people lived.

And according to what Skye believed every morning when she recited the Apostles' Creed to begin her day, there was only one place where dead people embraced a new life.

"Oh my," Skye whispered, her eyes flying wide open. "'Scientist Finds Heaven!'"

CHAPTER SEVEN

Scratching his stubbled chin, Michael rolled over in the big king bed and opened one eye to look at the alarm clock on his nightstand.

It read 10:30 in the morning, but it took several seconds for Michael to remember what day it was: Sunday. His grogginess slowly gave way to a dull surprise as he realized he'd been asleep for almost twelve hours; for the life of him, he couldn't recall the last time that had happened. Even in the bad days after Elise's murder, when he'd been drinking himself unconscious on a regular basis, he still hadn't slept more than a few hours at a time.

Michael picked up the cell phone that was lying beside the clock and switched it on. When he'd gotten home in the wee hours of Saturday morning, after working in the lab until he had all the equations finished, he'd turned off the phone, figuring he needed a couple hours of sleep more than he needed to answer any calls that might come in. Then, when he'd gotten back up after a short nap, he'd worked straight through the day, writing the journal article that would introduce the completed One Theory to the rest of the scientific world. Once it was finished, he'd emailed the text to his old classmate Theo LeMay, who for the last five years had edited *Physica, the Journal of Theory and Applications in Physical Science,* the world's pre-eminent physics journal. After that, Michael had eaten some cold pizza left over from lunch and gone back to bed.

Scrolling through his messages, Michael found four missed calls: two calls yesterday from a number he didn't recognize, one call from another unidentified number just an hour ago, and the fourth from Theo five minutes ago. Michael pulled himself up in the bed and tapped in Theo's speed-dial number.

"Let me be the first to congratulate you, Michael," Theo boomed over the phone as soon as the connection was made. "It's brilliant! Absolutely brilliant! You did it, old man! I am the first, aren't I?"

"Ever competitive, Theo," Michael chided. "Yes, you are the first. Even Lucas doesn't know yet. I tried to get him yesterday on the phone, but he never answered. His name is on the article along with mine, but we'd agreed a long time ago that I'd be doing the actual writing if—or rather, when—the day finally arrived. So there you have it in your very capable hands. How soon will the expert panel meet for review?"

"For this, as soon as I can round them all up. We usually review once every five weeks, but I have a feeling that when I tell them we'll be vetting the Theory of Everything, they all just might drop whatever they have on their plates and hightail it out here to New Haven. I'm already imagining the looks of raw and speechless wonder on their faces when they read your paper."

Theo's voice dropped a decibel or two. "Really, Michael, I am in awe of your achievement. Unification. You have done what no one else could do."

"This is where I'm supposed to be modest, right?" Michael laughed. "Like say, 'Oh, it's nothing, I could never have done it without all those who have gone before me.' Well, that may be true, but I fought hard for this one, Theo. Fifteen years, to be exact."

He paused a moment, briefly reflecting on the sacrifices those years had demanded of him.

Long nights.

Failed attempts.

Frustration.

Lost time with Elise.

Elise herself.

When he spoke again, his voice was grim.

"Yes, I had help, but this one is mine."

Theo laughed, too absorbed in Michael's achievement to note the change in his tone.

"Ever egotistical, Michael," his old friend chided in return. "But this time, you're allowed. You're looking at the Nobel, my friend. Fame. Immortal memory. All the funding you can dream of for the rest of your life. Maybe that fellow across town from you will even give you a cover shot on his magazine."

"You mean Drake Lamont? No thanks, Theo. The man might produce an adequate publication for the general reading public, but it's no *Physica*. You're the only game in town as far as I'm concerned. I don't want to show up in anyone's pages but yours."

"Then we'll wait to make the announcement of your accomplishment until the day we go to press," Theo decided. "After that, though, it's out of my hands. Brace yourself for media overload, old man. Better go out and get a haircut while you still can. Once this hits the wires, your days of peace and quiet—not to mention anonymity—will be over for quite a while. And again, congratulations, Michael. You have changed forever how we see the universe."

Michael closed his phone and returned it to the nightstand. Theo's words stayed with him—up until Theo's last comment, Michael really hadn't spent any time considering the full implications of what he had done in the lab. Yesterday, he'd been so focused on writing the article for the review of his professional peers, he'd never stopped to truly appreciate what his equations might mean for anyone outside scientific circles. Now that he had a few moments, he began to marvel at the sheer enormity of what he'd discovered.

An eleventh dimension. Unification. The Holy Grail. Einstein's quest.

You did it!

Michael shook his head. He didn't want to hear any voices this morning. He ran a hand through his tangled curls and thought maybe he'd take Theo's advice and get a haircut. The man was right; once the announcement was made, Michael would be the eye of a press hurricane for at least a short while, so he might as well make a properly professorial impression with a trimmed hairline and maybe even a new suit. Elise had always ensured his suits were clean and pressed when he had conferences to attend and papers to present, but since he'd returned to the lab after her death, he'd barely looked in his closet at all, except to grab jeans and a shirt every day. The thought of posing for the press now set his temper to a slow simmer—he'd had enough reporters hounding him for comments in the wake of Elise's murder that the last thing he was looking forward to was making nice with the local press.

"The cover of *World?*" Michael said aloud to himself, remembering Theo's good-natured jab at his ego. "That's the last thing I need."

A sudden pounding on the front door interrupted any further thoughts Michael might have had about the press and magazine photographs. Pulling on the blue jeans he'd tossed on the floor last night, Michael went down the hall to the entryway. The cool air in the house gave him a chill across his bare chest, but he was too annoyed with the increasing pounding to take the time to go back to his bedroom for a shirt.

"I'm coming, I'm coming!" he shouted, his ill temper growing with every step. Just before he jerked the door open, he glanced through its side window.

Khristina Tupikova was standing on his front step.

Michael grimaced.

"I was wrong," he muttered. "*This* is the last thing I need."

CHAPTER EIGHT

I am so sorry for disturbing you in your home," Khristina told Michael when he opened the door.

Her eyes dropped to his chest.

"You are naked, Michael."

"Khristina, come in," he said, stepping aside and motioning her to come through the doorway. "I'm not naked, but I am cold. Let me get a shirt, and I'll be with you in a moment."

With that, he turned and walked away, leaving her standing in the foyer.

Khristina watched Michael's bare back retreat down the hallway until he turned a corner, disappearing from her line of vision. Unsure if she should venture any further into the house, she pulled off her knit cap, releasing the heavy blonde hair she'd coiled beneath it. Like some of her countrywomen back home in Russia, Khristina typically wore her long hair twisted into a tight braid down her back, but this morning, she'd left her apartment rather abruptly and hadn't taken the time to dress her hair. Clad in a thick fisherman's sweater and jeans, Khristina could easily pass for a born-and-bred Wisconsinite, rather than a Russian immigrant. Other than some stubborn traces of her native accent and a lingering difficulty with some English phrasing, Khristina's assimilation into American culture had been almost seamless since her arrival two years earlier.

Then again, she'd had a lot of help from a multitude of friends.

Since Michael hadn't asked her to take a seat, Khristina waited in the marbled entryway and looked into his living room. After only a quick glance, however, she was uncomfortable. Something about it didn't feel right to her. Even though the overstuffed couch and quilted throw pillows looked comfortable and inviting, Khristina realized that she didn't have any inclination to step into the room. Then, just as she wondered what exactly about the room bothered her, a shaft of sunlight hit the wide surface of the mahogany coffee table, and Khristina knew what was wrong.

The table was covered with a thick layer of dust.

Glancing again at other pieces in the room, Khristina could make out similar layers of dust everywhere. She knew that Michael had lost his wife earlier in the year, and she certainly didn't expect the intensely-driven and focused physicist she had come to know at the lab to be a doting housekeeper, but it still seemed odd to her that any room in a house could sit undisturbed and untouched by the person who lived there.

Especially the front room of the house.

In the front room of the house in which she grew up, her parents made a happy celebration of every guest who entered.

Here in Michael's house, she could sense only emptiness. Even the few framed photographs that she could see around the room were draped in dust.

It is true, Michael, what I have heard in the lab, Khristina thought. *You need a new life.*

Reaching for a shirt in his bedroom closet, Michael had no clue why in the world Khristina Tupikova was standing in his entryway. He'd been cordial with her in the lab whenever she was producing data for him, but her relentlessly cheerful disposition had worn on him badly at a time when his grieving for Elise had made him even more short-tempered than usual. As a result, he'd avoided any additional interactions with the woman and knew next to nothing about her personally. He knew that Lucas had been ecstatic when he had tracked Khristina down and she agreed to come to Litchfield to participate in the study; Lucas said that Khristina was arguably the most gifted medium in the world, since she had claimed Sherry Smith's prize. About the only thing that Michael could remember now about Khristina was his own surprise the first day she showed up at the lab. For some reason, he'd had it in his mind to expect a tiny, old, fragile, soft-spoken, bent-over lady in a babushka who could barely speak English, and instead, there was this tall, thirty-something, striking blonde with high cheekbones, in blue jeans and a T-shirt.

True, her English was still pretty broken at times, but Khristina herself was no shrinking violet when it came to what she did. She gave readings with an imperious authority that made him shut his eyes in disgust. More than once, he'd called Lucas in to take his—Michael's—shift doing the video monitoring of Khristina's sessions because he was mortified to think he'd actually consented to having a medium in the lab.

As far as he was concerned, watching Khristina do a reading was like watching bad theater—she seemed to cry, laugh, lament, and scold enthusiastically on cue. Of course, the cues, she said, were from her 'visitors'—that was the term she gave the energy stimuli to which she was responding and that Michael was tracking with Kirlian photography and sophisticated energy detecting equipment. Regardless of what she called the source, though, he couldn't deny that her data results had been spectacular.

As Michael headed back out to the hallway, buttoning the last buttons on what he hoped was a somewhat clean flannel shirt, he realized it had probably been her data and photos that he had held in his hands on Friday night when the pieces of the unification puzzle had finally fallen into place for him. For that, he could be grateful to Khristina Tupikova.

Other than that, he just wanted her to go away.

As he walked back down the hall, Khristina turned to face him and opened her mouth to say something, but before she could utter a sound, the large picture window in the living room exploded with a shattering crash.

Khristina dropped like a rock to the hard floor of the entry-way.

Without even thinking, Michael dove to cover her body with his own.

Around them, jagged slivers of glass flew through the air like a blizzard of sharp teeth.

CHAPTER NINE

When the last tinkling sound of glass falling on marble had faded, Michael carefully placed his hands amidst broken shards on the floor and slowly lifted himself off his visitor, who was sprawled facedown in the entryway beneath him.

"Khristina, are you all right?" he asked, squatting beside her, laying his hand on her shoulder.

"I think so," she answered. "You are heavy, Michael."

"Wait," he said, placing his hand between her shoulder blades, stopping her as she rose up on her elbows. "There's glass in your hair."

He twisted out two slender slices of glass that had entangled themselves in her thick blonde waves. As he gently worked them out, he felt other soft strands brushing against his fingers and he could have sworn he smelled the heavy scent of honeysuckle.

It was like a punch in the gut.

Michael's fingers stopped moving.

The awareness that he was touching another person swept over him like a flood, tearing away his concentration on his task at hand. The fact that he was touching a woman shook him even more.

When was the last time he'd touched a woman?

It had to have been Elise, the morning before she died. Since the funeral, he hadn't even shaken hands with anyone, let alone touched someone with the intimacy he was now feeling coursing through his blood. He wanted to pull his hands out of Khristina's hair as if they were on fire, but he couldn't do it.

49

Disoriented and paralyzed, he stared at his fingers entwined in a woman's hair.

"Michael?"

He shook his head to clear the thoughts away. He needed to concentrate, not reminisce or indulge in a private pity party. He'd done more than enough of that in the last few months to last him a lifetime.

Right now, what he needed to do was extract glass.

"Working on it, Khristina," he told her, edging a third slice out. "I don't want to tear your hair. Just another minute, here."

He pulled the shard free and tossed it into the living room, then stood up, backing away a little from Khristina as she got to her feet and turned to face him. Still slightly unnerved from the feel of her hair in his hands and his reaction to it, he made sure he put a little space between them. He knew there was no way she could know what had just happened to him, but all the same, he felt better—less vulnerable—with some distance.

Khristina, however, took one look at him and moved closer.

"You are cut," she said, reaching across the space he'd just put between them to remove a piece of glass that had grazed his temple with a jagged line of blood before catching in his dark curls.

Behind him, sunlight poured in through the living room's broken window, framing his head with a halo of light caused by the glinting of other tiny bits of glass trapped in his hair. Carefully picking out the sliver, Khristina took a quick look at Michael's face . . . and froze.

She knew this face.

The hard blue eyes, the dark mass of curls, the grim expression, the intensity radiating from the shoulders, even the track of blood along the hairline—she'd seen it before. Unbidden, the prayer came to her: *St. Michael the Archangel, defend us in the day of battle; be our safeguard against the wiles and wickedness of the devil. May God rebuke him, we humbly pray, and do thou, O prince of the heavenly host, by the power of God cast into hell Satan and all the other evil spirits, who prowl through the world, seeking the ruin of souls.*

"What?" Michael said, touching the now-welling blood where the sliver had cut him. "Is it that bad?"

Khristina closed her eyes, her mind reeling.

It couldn't be. She must have been mistaken. That face belonged to a painting, not a real man.

She glanced at Michael again, almost afraid of what she'd see, but the moment of stunning recognition had passed. Catching her breath, Khristina decided it had just been a trick of the light or a very faded memory. Even so, she could still feel the residue of tremors in her nerves caused by the powerful surge of awareness that had streaked up her spine when she touched Michael's hair—some kind of awareness she couldn't quite name, as well as the sense of utter conviction that had accompanied it.

It reminded her of the feeling she had every time she had a vision.

The feeling of ineffable grace.

But this was no heavenly visitor in front of her. This was Michael Carilion, theoretical physicist . . . and her reluctant employer.

"No, it is not that bad," she told him, dropping the bloody sliver on the living room carpet.

She unconsciously stepped back, restoring the distance between them.

"It was just that, for just a moment, you looked exactly like a painting I know."

"A painting?"

"Yes."

She couldn't help herself; she was still staring at Michael.

"A painting of St. Michael the Archangel."

"St. Michael," Michael repeated.

"Yes," she said again. "For a second, I thought you were St. Michael."

Khristina paused, searching those hard blue eyes, looking for even a hint that he might be willing to hear her out for once.

"He is the defender of heaven."

The defender of heaven.

Great, Michael thought.

He had a crazy woman in his hallway who thought he was an angel.

This was why bringing a medium into his lab had been a major error in judgment, he silently castigated himself once more. Mediums were nuts. They believed they could talk with the dead, and they thought they saw angels. They had no place in scientific inquiry. Even if Khristina's participation in the Strings Project had culminated in his theory breakthrough, he had to believe he would have found it anyway eventually. She'd just given him a shortcut, and the rest was pure science.

He bit back a scathing remark rating angels right up there with postmortem Elvis appearances, and instead turned away to look into the living room. "What a mess."

Everywhere he looked, broken glass coated the carpet and furniture, and the cool October air blowing in through the destroyed window had rapidly displaced any heat the room had previously held. Luckily, Michael had slipped on a pair of loafers in the bedroom before returning to the entryway and throwing himself on top of Khristina. He now walked into the center of the room, pressing bits of glass into the carpet with every step.

"What happened in here?" he muttered, surveying the damaged furniture and splintered window frame.

Khristina, who had followed him into the room, bent down and reached beneath the mahogany coffee table. She picked up a brick, which had a note tied to it with a string, and handed it to Michael.

"What does it say?" she asked.

Khristina couldn't read.

That was another thing, Michael recalled now, that he knew about her. The woman was illiterate. Something about a learning disability that prevented her brain from processing letters into coherent units.

Yet she wasn't ignorant, by any means. On the contrary, she was one of the most educated people Lucas said he had ever met. In her readings with sitters, she was always quoting famous lines of poetry or referring to complex philosophical concepts, not to mention demonstrating a prodigious command of Shakespeare.

When Lucas first informed him about Khristina's disability, Michael was ready to shut the whole experiment down until he realized that the fact that Khristina couldn't read provided an even tighter control on her performance in the lab. If she couldn't possibly know what was in their notes—even the names of the sitters she'd be reading for—there was no chance she was secretly acquiring information to fake her sessions. Of course, the downside of her inability to read was having to take the time to read pertinent materials, like her working contract and session instructions, to her. Thankfully, she had an excellent memory and retained everything on the first pass.

With a quick twist of his wrist, Michael broke the string around the brick and opened the folded piece of paper.

"It says 'God doesn't live in a lab. Or in an eleventh dimension. Burn in hell, atheist.'" He looked at Khristina, his eyes narrowed in suspicion.

"This is about the Strings Project. How in the—"

"This is why I came to see you," she interrupted. "I want to know why my work in the project has been announced without letting me know first."

Michael still held the brick in one hand, the note in the other. He looked at Khristina, uncomprehending.

"What are you talking about?"

"Our confidentiality agreement," she told him. "My name was not to be released without my consent when you and Lucas announced the results of our work."

"There haven't been any announcements," Michael assured her.

At least, not yet, he added silently. Theo LeMay was the only person in the world besides Michael who knew about the success of the Strings Project, and he'd just gotten off the phone with him. Khristina wasn't making any sense, and Michael couldn't figure out what she was trying to say, but all at once, he had a bad feeling about where it was all going.

Tightening his grip on the brick and note, even as he made a conscious effort to keep his voice calm, Michael repeated himself.

"Khristina, what are you talking about?"

"The article in this morning's market rag!" she replied, her frustration evident. "All morning, my phone has been ringing off the table with people who want me to find hidden treasures and give them the winning numbers for the lottery!"

Khristina shook her woolen cap at Michael.

"That is not what I do!" she pointedly reminded him. "I tried to call Lucas and he does not answer, so I came to talk to you. I am angry that my agreement has been broken! I do not know what to do!"

Michael's eyes narrowed even more and his voice was a taut whisper.

"Market rag?"

"At the market, where you buy food," Khristina explained, clearly enunciating each word as if he, Michael, were the one with the language issues.

The physicist in him bristled. Just because he had a cut on his head didn't mean he'd lost his mental capabilities.

"I know what a market is."

"The silly newspapers that talk about aliens and the Bigfoot and the Batboy!" she said heatedly. "They are called rags. I hear people say this."

"The tabloids."

"Yes! The tabloids!"

Khristina threw her hands up in the air.

"It is in the tabloids early this morning about our work. The people who are calling me say they learned about me there, and they want me to work for them to do all these things I do not do."

Michael watched the exasperation and frustration flitting across Khristina's face and felt his own confusion mounting. He had tried calling Lucas all Saturday to tell him about the breakthrough, but he'd never reached him.

Where was he? Out talking with a tabloid reporter?

Michael didn't believe that for a minute. Once they had agreed on the medium experiments, both he and Lucas were fanatical about keeping strict scientific protocol in place to ensure they could use any data that was generated. There was no way Lucas would have compromised the integrity of the work by dropping hints to a tabloid. The stakes were way too high.

Khristina must have gotten it wrong, mixed it up in her head. She had to be mistaken.

"Are you sure this article is about the Strings Project?" he prodded her. "Lucas would never release information without telling me first, Khristina. This has to be about something else. Someone got a whiff of what we're doing and made it all up."

Khristina pointed to the note in Michael's hand, then swept her hand in an angry arc to include the mangled living room.

"And this is a result of a whiff? If it is, I will hate to see what will happen when you do find your theory, Michael."

Michael released the brick and it thumped on the carpet at his feet. His steely blue eyes locked on Khristina's.

"I have found it."

Khristina went still, barely breathing. Her own blue eyes traveled over his face, and again she saw the likeness she remembered from the painting: the set of the jaw, the slight flare of Michael's nostrils, the triumph shining in his eyes. Another frisson of awareness streaked up her spine. When she spoke, her tone was hushed, almost reverent.

"Then the tabloid is correct. It says you found heaven."

"No." Michael laughed and kicked the brick next to his foot, sending it flying against the couch.

"I didn't find heaven," he clarified for her. "I found the Theory of Everything! The ultimate physical expression of the universe. Unification! Not some spiritual hocus-pocus. This isn't about God, Khristina. It's about science."

She opened her mouth to contradict him, but caught the warning look in his eyes that she'd come to recognize in the lab.

He didn't want to hear her opinion.

No, Khristina thought. *He doesn't want to hear the truth.*

Michael ran his hand through his hair, then abruptly pulled it away.

"Ow!"

Khristina put aside her difference of 'opinion' and studied his dark curls.

"There is still glass in your hair, Michael," she said. "Please, can we go to the bathroom and comb our hair out? Then I will put a bandage on your cut and we will figure out what to do. If you did not talk with the tabloid, it must have been Lucas. There is no one else who knew so much about what we were doing."

Khristina was already back in the entryway, heading down the hall.

"Where is the bathroom, please?"

Michael followed his unexpected visitor into the hall, wondering what in the world was really going on.

He couldn't believe that someone—like who?—had leaked the Strings Project to a tabloid, but if that was indeed what had happened, he was positive it would mean bad press and working at damage control. And when Theo got wind of it—and he would—it wasn't going to help with the journal review, which meant his publication, his work, his theory, were all in jeopardy.

Without impeccable credibility, he didn't have a snowball's chance in hell that anyone would accept his unification formulas.

Thinking of a snowball in hell reminded him of the note, still clutched in his hand. Some nutcase was already targeting him for harassment, based on a tabloid?

That was annoying enough, but now that he thought about it, there was something that was disturbing him a lot more: the note had referred to the eleventh dimension.

Only he and Lucas knew the full significance of the medium experiments for investigating a link to the eleventh dimension. Everyone else on the team was focused on the physics of the variations in Khristina's auras as indicative behavior characteristic of the theory's unseen strings.

Which could only mean one thing: Lucas had leaked the story.

Lucas had betrayed him.

Where was Lucas, anyway?

CHAPTER TEN

"The first thing we're going to do is stop at the grocery store and get a copy of the tabloid," Michael told Khristina as he held his car door open for her. "Then we're going to Lucas's apartment and find out what's going on."

"Will your fix-it man be able to finish your new window by tonight?" Khristina asked, buckling her seatbelt.

After cleaning up and changing his clothes, Michael had called his longtime handyman to make the repair while Khristina swept up broken glass from the entry and hallway. She had wanted to vacuum the carpet, too, but Michael had told her to let it go; he figured there would still be tiny bits of glass in the carpet no matter how often anyone cleaned the room. When he had the time, he'd see about replacing the carpet. Since he didn't use the space, it wasn't an urgent concern, he'd explained to her, impatience creeping into his voice.

For some reason, that silenced her, and she hadn't said anything else until now.

"I don't know," Michael replied in answer to her question. "He'll board it up, if nothing else."

"I already tried Lucas's apartment before I took the taxi to come to you, and he was not there," Khristina said.

"We'll try again."

Less than a mile from his home, Michael stopped at a local supermarket. Leaving Khristina in the car, he went in through the automatic doors and made a beeline for the checkout lanes. A quick scan of the tabloids' headlines told him which paper was the culprit. He grabbed it off the rack, paid the cashier, and, mere moments later, he was back in the car, showing Khristina a copy of the morning's edition of *The Midnight Eye*.

"Here it is, 'Scientist Finds Heaven,' just like your callers said." He pointed to the big headline across the front page.

Khristina leaned closer to Michael to see the photograph beneath the bold type.

"Is that supposed to be an angel, do you think?"

Michael took another look at the grainy image.

"I guess so. I know it's not a picture of me. Or of you."

He glanced at the woman beside him and, once again, smelled the ripe scent of honeysuckle. He inhaled it deeply and surprised himself by smiling at Khristina.

"Nice perfume," he said. "It reminds me of summers at the lake."

She returned his smile, and an awkward silence filled the car.

"Thank you, Michael," she finally responded. "Now tell me what the article says."

Though she appeared to be listening as Michael began reading the article aloud, Khristina was having a hard time concentrating on the tabloid's report.

His comment about her perfume had rattled her.

It wasn't like him at all.

From the first time she'd met him, she'd gotten the definite feeling that he didn't like her, an impression that had grown steadily stronger in the course of her work in his lab. She had even heard from a few of the project technicians about how he traded recording sessions with Lucas to avoid her, and suspected it had to do with his opinion of her profession. Why he had ever allowed a medium into his lab, she couldn't begin to fathom, especially since it was common knowledge among the project personnel that Dr. Carilion thought any kind of psychic phenomenon was suspect at best and deliberate deception at worst.

Yet he had been willing to have her play a part in his research and seemed pleased with all the scientific material he had accumulated from her reading sessions.

Whether or not he understood what really happened with Khristina during a reading was questionable, but then, Khristina didn't expect him to. Long ago, she'd come to realize that no one other than another medium could understand what it was like to be in communication with those who had gone ahead. Aside from that, she'd also come to the conclusion that she and Michael were on totally different pages, as one of her favorite American expressions put it. From her limited interactions with him in the lab, and now, those of the last few hours, it was painfully clear to her that even though they were both using English, she and Michael spoke different languages.

Hard science was Michael's native tongue.

Khristina's was faith.

Knowing that, the last thing she would have expected was for him to drop his walls of scholarly preoccupation, even for a moment, to notice her perfume, let alone comment on it. Although, judging from his own discomfort after he made the remark, maybe it was the last thing he would have expected, too.

Beside her in the car, Michael continued reading.

"'Unknown to college officials,'—oh great, that's going to go over real well with the deans at work—'physicists at Barnet College in Litchfield, Wisconsin, have been conducting secret experiments to determine the precise location of heaven.'"

He dropped the paper in his lap.

"I don't think I need to read any more, Khristina."

"Yes, you do," she contradicted him. "I need to know what they write about me."

Michael glanced at her apologetically. "I'm sorry. You're right. This isn't just my problem, is it?"

He picked up the paper again and resumed reading.

"'With the assistance of the world's greatest Russian medium, Khristina Tupikova, information has been secured from the spirits of famed psychologist Sigmund Freud, philosopher Blaise Pascal, physicist Albert Einstein and president Abraham Lincoln. 'The eleventh dimension is now within our grasp,' Tupikova reportedly told the research team. 'We have only to ask and we will have our answers. Once everyone knows this scientific method for contacting those on the other side, we can predict the future and solve problems from the past!'"

"I did not say that," Khristina objected. "And I do not know Freud or Lincoln."

To her dismay, Michael burst out laughing.

"Of course, you didn't say it, Khristina. These tabloids are silly, like you said at the house. They make this stuff up. I can't believe they left out Elvis."

He continued to laugh, and Khristina could feel her emotions sliding from indignation into irritation. Whatever softening towards him and his situation she might have experienced in the wake of his awkward compliment vanished. The man truly was insufferable. And rude. What right did he have to make fun of her gift? She didn't ridicule his work.

"What?" Michael asked.

She was glaring at him, her lips pulled tightly together.

"Oh, I get it," he chuckled. "You're saying you *do* know Pascal and Einstein." He rolled his eyes and shook his head. "Very funny."

"Only to you, Michael," Khristina replied, her voice barely a whisper in the car.

Michael took another look at the woman beside him.

Her blue eyes were startling clear, her skin smooth and unlined. A few wisps of her golden hair trailed across her pink cheeks, and she practically radiated youth and innocence. If it weren't for the murderous glare she was aiming at him, she could have passed for an angel sitting in his Lexus.

She was serious, Michael realized, stunned. She honestly believed she communicated with dead people.

Did she know Pascal and Einstein?

Michael rubbed his forehead with the palm of his hand. *Get a grip,* he told himself. The fact that he'd even have a thought like that was ludicrous. The stress of the day was apparently already getting to him. And being around Khristina was obviously affecting him in more ways than he wanted to admit, and none of them good. He really didn't want to get into an argument with her right here and now about what it was she did—or thought she did—in or out of his lab, so he did the only thing he could think to do.

He handed Khristina the newspaper and started the car.

"We're going to Lucas's."

Twenty minutes later, Michael and Khristina stood outside Lucas's apartment, alternately pressing the doorbell and knocking on the door.

"You see," Khristina said. "He is not here. That is why I come to you."

"Came, Khristina, that is why you came to me," Michael corrected her English.

A dark blush rushed across Khristina's cheeks. "Thank you. You are right. I came to you."

Michael shifted uncomfortably. Ever since he'd laughed at her reaction to the *Eye* article, there had been a definite unease between them, and neither had spoken on the drive to Lucas's. Standing in front of his colleague's door, he was at a loss as to what they should do next, especially since he had obviously just embarrassed Khristina by pointing out her grammatical mistake. He slid his hand into his jacket pocket and wrapped his fingers around the Rubik's cube.

"Perhaps we should call the person who wrote the article," Khristina said, breaking the silence again. "That is the real problem here, is it not?"

Michael turned to face her. "That's a great idea."

"Believe it or not, I am capable of them."

Caught unprepared by her suddenly icy tone, Michael felt his blood pressure jump up a notch.

"Look, I didn't say you don't have great ideas," he told her. "I just—"

"Are you guys looking for Dr. Scranton?"

Michael and Khristina both turned to look at a young woman who had partially opened the door across the hall. She held a sleeping baby on her shoulder and rocked side-to-side on her slippered feet.

"Yes, we are," Michael said. "Do you know where he is, by any chance?"

Her eyes went from Michael to Khristina and back to Michael again. "I guess you don't know what happened, do you?"

"What?" Khristina asked.

"He was killed Friday night, downtown. A mugging, the police said. They were here yesterday checking out his apartment."

Khristina leaned back against Lucas's door, her hand flying up to her mouth to cover her cry.

Michael stood motionless.

"Thanks," he managed to say to the woman. She shut her door softly.

After a moment, he turned to Khristina. Her blue eyes were filled with tears and she looked directly at him while her shoulders silently lifted up and down. He didn't even realize he'd reached for her until he had his arms wrapped around her, feeling her sobs moving against his own heaving chest.

CHAPTER ELEVEN

Over the rim of her wineglass, Phoebe surreptitiously studied The Gentleman as he opened a copy of *The Midnight Eye* to an inside page.

So far, he wasn't reacting.

Phoebe couldn't decide if that was a good sign or a bad one.

When she'd seen the headline on the paper at the grocery store, she'd almost spilled her double mocha latte over the salad greens she was buying for dinner. She hadn't even waited to get out of the checkout line before calling Drake on her cell phone. By the time she'd pulled the Saab into the parking garage fifteen minutes later, his fire-engine red Beemer was pulling in right behind her.

Drake folded the paper together and laid it in his lap. He was dressed casually, but impeccably, in khaki trousers with a white Henley shirt underneath a burgundy sport coat. Reaching for the wineglass Phoebe had poured at his elbow, his face remained blank, and Phoebe braced herself for one of the nasty temper tantrums she'd seen in the course of more than one editorial meeting over the last two years.

But Drake didn't pitch the glass across the room as she had feared he might do. Instead, to Phoebe's relief and surprise, he grinned at her instead, lifting his glass in salute to her.

"Come sit with me," he said, taking a swallow of wine and patting the space next to him on the leather sofa.

Phoebe complied and perched on the cushion beside him. He slid his free hand under her dark hair to take hold of the nape of her neck and gently drew her face to his. His lips brushed hers softly, and then he whispered against them.

"How in the world did the *Eye* get this?"

Phoebe tried to pull back, but his hand held her nape in an iron grip.

"I don't know, Drake. Either Lucas tipped off the reporter before I met with him or someone overheard us at the bar. I think it was in the bar, because a couple of the lines in the article are almost verbatim of what he said to me there."

Drake kissed her then, deeply, releasing his hold on her neck to massage between her shoulder blades. Phoebe could feel her tension diminish, relaxing under Drake's familiar touch. He moved his lips to a sensitive spot under her right ear and nipped at her skin.

Phoebe shivered.

"Phoebe," he whispered, "I believe you. But if you ever lie to me, I promise you will regret it."

For a split-second, the fine hairs on the back of her neck rose up and stiffened in warning.

She shook it off, wondering for how long she'd feel these physical aftereffects, like small recurring tremors of adrenaline, from witnessing a murder. For the past twenty-four hours, it seemed like the smallest things set them off—a squeak from the dishwasher running in the kitchen, a shadow caught out of the corner of her eye. Brusquely reminding herself, again, that she was safely tucked inside her own home and not trapped in some dark alley at the mercy of a murderous mugger, she pushed the thought from her mind and focused on Drake.

"Why would I do that?" she assured him.

She patted his trousered thigh and let her hand linger.

"Not only are you the best boss in town, but nobody offers—ah—perks, shall we say?—like you do."

Drake laughed and took another swallow of wine. "What's for dinner?"

"First you tell me what you want me to do about the story."

"What story?"

Phoebe glared at him. "Very funny. The story that is going to make my career. The Theory of Everything."

"Phoebe, there is no story."

Drake smoothed his streaked blonde hair back off his forehead.

"You told me yesterday that Scranton said a breakthrough was coming, not that it had been made. And now the story's front-page news for a supermarket tabloid. I don't think that's quite the caliber of a research source that the *World* is looking for, do you?"

His silvery eyes squinted as he glanced across the room and into the afternoon sun streaming through the condo's floor-to-ceiling windows.

"It's awfully bright in here. Could you pull the blinds a bit?"

"Don't change the subject with me, Drake," Phoebe said, seriously annoyed with him and unable to keep a hint of anger from creeping into her voice. "And don't patronize me, either. This is a story that isn't going to go away. According to Lucas, Carilion is on the verge of proving String theory. Unification, Drake. The biggest scientific discovery of our age."

"Based on the readings of a medium? I don't think so." Drake finished off his wine and set the glass on the mirrored coffee table.

"But I told you, the readings—the contents of the readings—aren't what's involved here," Phoebe reminded him. "It's the physical evidence the medium generates that validates the theory. The research is replicable, Drake. Replicable!"

Caught up again in her passion for the story she would write, Phoebe pleaded her case. "As soon as Carilion comes up with the equations—"

"And why do you think he will?" Drake coolly interrupted her. He brushed some lint off his trousers. "Physicists have been looking for those equations for decades, Phoebe. What makes you think this man will find them? The word of his drunken associate? Phoebe, listen to yourself. These are scientists turning to a psychic performer to prove their hypothesis?"

He stood up and walked across the room to pull the blinds against the light.

"And as for Carilion, I might remind you that the man was involved in a terrible personal tragedy just a few months ago. I've even heard some speculation here and there that he might not be quite recovered from it, that he doesn't seem quite . . . stable. If I were a suspicious man, I might even think it odd that another person close to him was killed within a matter of months."

"What?" Phoebe thought she must not have heard him correctly. "You're not implying that Carilion was involved in Lucas's death, are you? I was there, Drake!"

"And what did you see, Phoebe?"

Drake pinned her with his eyes.

"You told me it was dark, you never saw the face of the man who attacked you, and before you knew it, Scranton had been stabbed," he recounted. "No clues. No leads. Just like the Carilion murder case, which, I'd like to remind you, was never solved. A common link? Carilion. My advice? Stay away from him."

Drake walked back across the room, which was now shielded from the late afternoon sun, and poured himself another glass of the ruby-colored wine.

Studying the complete self-assurance that seemed to exude from the man, Phoebe decided she wouldn't mention to her boss the fact that she had already tried to call Carilion twice yesterday, or that she had no intention of staying away from what she was convinced was going to be the turning point of her career. Even before Drake had picked her up yesterday morning at the emergency room, she'd already decided she was going to approach Carilion himself about his research and ask for the exclusive.

She'd even beg if she had to.

Drake sat down again beside her and took a taste of his wine.

"I know what you're thinking, Phoebe, but it's time to give it up," he told her. "I know you want to believe it, but let's be brutally honest here: there is no eleventh dimension. Even when I was studying physics all those years ago, theoreticians were talking about string theory and multiple dimensions and at the same time, acknowledging it was totally unworkable. It's an intriguing picture, without a doubt, but, sad to say," he smiled forlornly at her stubborn expression, "unification simply doesn't exist."

Phoebe leaned back against the sofa and swirled the remaining wine in her glass, equal parts of determination and confusion likewise swirling in her head.

She understood what Drake was saying, but she could have sworn that when he handed her the note to meet Lucas on Friday night that he had been eager for her to get the story. If there was one thing she knew for sure about The Gentleman, it was that he lusted for the exclusive. Drake Lamont wanted what no one else could have, and if breaking the biggest story of science didn't fill that bill, then nothing could.

She briefly recalled what she'd said to Dr. Scranton at the bar, that she didn't believe that her boss was guilty of hiding anything, despite his silence about his unknown past and the rumors that constantly surfaced about him.

That, however, had been a lie. Phoebe was sure that Drake Lamont had secrets, and one of them was his obsession with the possibility of finding an eleventh dimension.

Yet now he was casually writing off this unexpected lead as a false one, dismissing her conviction—her intuition—that Carilion really was on to something very, very big.

It just didn't make sense.

She had spent the last two years learning to gauge Drake Lamont's moods and yearnings, and she had been sure that this story was important to him. So why was he now so quick to drop it? Of course, Drake hadn't been there Friday night, she reminded herself, and he hadn't heard the details of what Lucas had been saying.

She bolted upright, almost spilling the remaining wine out of her glass onto the sofa cushions.

"The tape!" she cried.

She'd almost forgotten she had it. She jumped up from the sofa and went to the bedroom to find the micro recorder she'd activated in her jacket pocket in the bar on Friday night. But when she opened her closet doors to find the jacket, she suddenly slumped against the doorframe and groaned.

"No, no, no!"

"What is it?" Drake asked, following her into the room.

"My jacket."

She clutched the doorframe, hopelessness washing over her as she remembered details from the emergency room where she had been examined after Lucas's stabbing. Seeing her blood-soaked jacket, the police had insisted she be checked over at the hospital; on the verge of shock, she had yielded to the nurse's ministrations, even accepting a mild sedative.

"The one I was wearing Friday night. It was covered with blood by the time I got to the hospital. I must have left it there. I don't remember now."

She looked up at Drake, miserable at both the memory of Lucas's dying and at the thought of her lost interview.

"Everything was so awful."

Drake pulled her into his arms.

"I know it was, darling. That's why I came to pick you up from the emergency room as soon as you called. But, I have to tell you," he held her away from him, his eyes pleading forgiveness, "it's my fault your jacket is gone. They offered it to me when I came to get you and I told them to toss it. I didn't think you'd want to be reminded of —well—you know."

Phoebe shrunk against his chest. Without the tape, she had only her notes, her words, to source the story.

And she knew it wasn't enough.

Not with a story like this.

"But," Drake continued, "most fortunately for you, I wasn't traumatized. And I was thinking."

Phoebe pulled back in Drake's arms at his remark and looked questioningly up into his face.

With a theatrical flourish, he slipped his hand into his left coat pocket and pulled out a miniature cassette.

"Your tape, my dear."

For a split second, Phoebe couldn't breathe.

"Oh!" she squealed in pure joy, grabbing it from his hand. "You got it!"

"Of course, I did. I never make a mistake, you know that."

Laughing, she slapped at his chest.

"You are such an egotist. But I don't care. You got my tape!" She snatched a spare tape recorder from her bedside table and popped in the cassette.

"Wait till you hear this stuff, Drake. It will change your mind. You and me and the *World*, we'll never be the same after we break this story. Just listen!"

Phoebe held her breath, waiting to hear her voice and Lucas's on the tape. Her eyes held Drake's in expectation of his response.

A moment passed.

Then another.

And another.

"I'm listening, Phoebe," Drake said, "but I don't hear anything."

"No!" she cried, staring at the small, silent machine, frustration and disappointment rising in her throat, choking her. "It has to be here! Play! *Play!*"

She checked the cassette again. The play button was depressed and the spool of the tape was turning, but not a sound was coming out.

"Phoebe, please don't tell me you didn't recharge the batteries before you met Scranton in the bar."

"I did! I always do! You know that! I don't know what happened! I was sure it was taping!"

In panic and fury, she shook the machine, then tore the cassette out of its cradle and threw it across the room.

"It was my story, Drake! The biggest story of my life!"

She collapsed on the bed, sobbing.

Drake sat beside her and pulled her into his arms again. With one hand, he rubbed her back. Unseen by the distraught Phoebe, his other hand disappeared into his right coat pocket and wrapped itself around a miniature cassette almost identical to the one he'd given her.

This one, however, wasn't blank.

Drake smiled.

Phoebe's taped interview with Scranton was exactly what he had hoped for, and now, it was right where he wanted it.

CHAPTER TWELVE

Are you sure this is where she lives?"

The well-dressed woman peered out of the SUV's passenger-side window to look at the tidy brick house set back from the street on Apple Boulevard. She didn't exactly know what she had been expecting, but this didn't seem to be it. The house looked small and ordinary, like any other 1940s-style brick house in Litchfield. Somehow, she had thought the house would be larger, distinctive in some unique way. She pulled up the collar of her green wool coat.

"I looked it up in the phone book," her companion told her, leaning over the steering wheel to see the house better. He was as well dressed as she, his brown leather jacket open over a lightweight turtleneck. "There was only one Khristina Tupikova listed. This is the address—117 Apple. Do you think she's home?"

"I don't know. It looks kind of empty."

The woman drummed her expensively manicured fingernails against the window.

"No lights on," she observed. "Let's go knock on the door."

Together, they walked up the sidewalk and onto the small front porch of Khristina's modest home. Noting the welcome sign lettered in a flowing, unfamiliar script that hung beside the doorbell, the woman paused.

"I can't read it, can you?"

The man studied the sign.

"No," he finally admitted. "The article said she was Russian, didn't it? It's probably in Russian. Try the bell."

72

She pressed the doorbell button and they listened to the chimes ringing inside the house. After the tones faded away and no one answered the door, the woman sighed in disappointment.

"I don't think she's here."

The man glanced around the yard and the porch. He noticed that the curtains beside the front door were pulled back and somewhere in the back of the house, a light was on.

"Maybe she just went out for a while," he said, nodding towards the house. "She left a light on. No reason we can't wait. Especially now that we know where she is."

He stepped off the porch and pulled out his cell phone. "I'll call the others. They'll want to be here when she gets back. After all, we've been waiting a long time for this."

"Yes, we have," the woman agreed, a note of anticipation and cautious excitement creeping into her voice. "Who ever would have thought that she'd be right here in Litchfield, of all places?" she asked the man, a smile spreading across her face. "The Awaited One herself."

CHAPTER THIRTEEN

Jack Gerrity stepped back from the canvas and tilted his head to a sixty-degree angle to assess the effect of the streaks of stark purple acrylic he'd just applied to one edge of the roiling mass of oranges and yellows that spilled across the five-by-eight-foot frame of his latest composition. Just beyond the canvas, the floor-to-ceiling windows of Jack's studio revealed a wall of brilliant autumn foliage. At first glance, a casual observer would have a tough time determining exactly where Jack's canvas ended and the colors outside began.

Except for the purple streaks.

In the fading afternoon light, the streaks were an ominous presence slipping into the vibrant hues. What had been exhilarating and triumphant was now tinged with foreboding.

"Well," he said. "William was right. It changes the whole feel of the piece."

He laid his brush on the palette and put the artist's tools down on a small bench beside him. He picked up his coffee mug and took a long swig, his eyes glued to his painting.

"Okay, William. What do you know that I don't?"

"Father Jack?"

Startled from his reverie, Jack turned to see a young man timidly peering around the corner of the studio's open door. Fresh-faced and sincere, he had a big smile plastered on his face and even bigger bags hanging under his eyes.

"Our youth group is ready whenever you are for the closing prayer of our overnight retreat," he said. "And we—uh—do have a bus to catch, so if you're ready?"

"Be right there," Jack said. "I'll just grab my stole and we'll get started."

The young man looked relieved and left the doorway.

Heaven save us from the insanities of youth ministry, Jack thought.

At sixty-eight years of age, Jack Gerrity believed that God's greatest gift was a good, long night of uninterrupted sleep. Why in the world youth ministers were so intent on keeping teenagers up all night, he'd never understand. Weren't they already enough of a handful for sixteen hours of the day?

Thankfully, he never had to keep vigil with them through the night, though—that was the job of their bleary-eyed chaperones. Jack's job was to lead some prayers, schedule the catering for their meals, and collect the facility fees. All in all, it was a most agreeable assignment for him here at Sacred Ground, the Jesuit retreat house he'd been managing for almost fifteen years now. He had a beautiful, quiet place to live, a fabulous studio for painting, and with a hundred miles between Sacred Ground and the city, plenty of space for him to make peace with God, if not with his superior who'd sent him out here.

As if either was ever really possible, he pointedly reminded himself.

He draped his green stole over his neck and started down the hallway to the chapel. On the way there, he saw a stack of newspapers lying on the simple wooden bench outside the kitchen door. Catching sight of *The Midnight Eye's* distinctive masthead, he smiled. Mrs. Schneider, his housekeeper, was addicted to the tabloid's outrageous stories. But Jack's stride to the chapel came to a sudden halt when he made out the banner headline on the newspaper. He snatched it up and read through the article rapidly.

What is now proved was once, only imagin'd.

"I'll be a monkey's uncle, William," he said. "Has it really finally happened?"

He looked again at the headline.

'Scientist Finds Heaven.'

Jack snorted.

"A scientist? Saints preserve us. Let's hope he's not an arrogant egghead, because he just might be in for the fight of his life. And that's because," he tossed the tabloid back onto the bench, "if he's really found heaven, then I guarantee, all hell's going to break loose for him. Literally."

He sighed a weary sigh of resignation.

"So much for getting my painting finished."

As he hurried into the chapel, Jack could hear the rustle of dead leaves scuttling against the stained glass windows that formed an alcove behind the altar. He'd always loved the sounds of autumn, the sounds of the earth going to rest.

Too bad he wasn't going to be getting any of that himself.

Rest, that was.

Because now, all of a sudden, he had something much more important to do.

CHAPTER FOURTEEN

Michael wanted a drink, and he wanted it badly.
He tried to remember if by any chance he'd missed a bottle of Jose Cuervo when he'd cleaned out the house after coming to his senses following his drinking binge six months ago, but he doubted it. He'd conducted his reformation with a vengeance that didn't even allow an occasional glass of wine in the house, let alone a bottle of tequila.

Listening to Khristina crying in his arms, Michael felt like he'd had the wind knocked out of him while a yawning black hole opened up at his feet. He recognized the hole as the dark abyss that had almost swallowed him after Elise's death. Lined with unanswered questions, doubts, guilt, anger, loss, and blame, the hole was calling to him, beckoning to him to just slide inside.

It would be easy enough to do, Michael knew. Been there, done that.

Except that this time, he was holding a weeping woman in his arms, a woman whose muffled sobs were bringing other residents of the hallway to open their doors and look out with fear and concern on their faces.

If nothing else, he had to get them out of the building.

Shifting his arm around her shoulder, Michael turned Khristina toward the building's door and steered her outside, back into his car. For several minutes, they sat in the Lexus, Michael absently turning his Rubik's cube in his hand while Khristina's sobs subsided into wet sniffles. He hoped the initial shock was almost over for both of them. Beyond that, he didn't know what to think.

But there was one thing he was sure of—he was going to have questions later.

A lot of them.

Beside him, Khristina wiped her eyes one last time and snapped on her seat belt.

"I want to go home. I will tell you the way."

Without a word, Michael pocketed his cube, put the key in the ignition, and pulled away from the curb. Khristina directed him through residential neighborhoods and past the university, speaking only brief commands to send him turning left or right, since she couldn't read street signs. As he drove, he tried to avoid thinking about Lucas and death and loss and grief. Instead, he found himself wondering how Khristina managed on her own without being able to read; he couldn't imagine what life might be like without literacy skills. You couldn't even microwave a bag of popcorn without reading the instructions on the back.

"How do you do it, Khristina?" he finally blurted out, waiting for a light.

"Do what?"

She wiped her nose with the wad of tissue she held in her hand.

"Anything. Get around town, travel, shop. If you can't read, how do you do those things?"

He accelerated into the intersection, heedless of the incredulous look she sent his way.

"How do I do those things?" she echoed. "You think that reading is the only way to process information? You—of all people."

He risked a quick glance at her, unsure of the biting note he thought he'd heard in her reply.

"What does that mean?"

To Michael's complete surprise, Khristina laughed.

"Michael—do you hear yourself?" she asked. "You are the physicist who has set up a whole research program to investigate exactly that—the alternate ways to obtain and process information. Intangible information. Is that not true? You believe I access 'energy packets,' as you call them, and that somehow I translate that energy into information."

"Yes, that's what I think," he replied, feeling defensive at her lightened tone. "And I call them energy packets, because that is what they are. Packets of energy that behave in a manner extraordinarily consistent with the principles of String theory."

Khristina laughed again, shaking her head.

"They are souls, Michael. Not units of physics. Human souls."

Without warning, he swung the car over to the curb and slammed the gear into park.

Khristina jerked back in her seat, her eyes wide with surprise.

"Look," Michael said, his voice tight, his hands locked on the steering wheel. "I don't want to argue with you about what you think. Like I already told you, I am not interested in religion or spirituality, okay?"

He shot an angry look at her.

"I do what I do because I believe there is one, unifying, scientific principle that explains everything. And I found it. I found it, Khristina! Thanks to Lucas's crazy idea," he swallowed, thinking of Lucas dead in the morgue, "and your work in the lab, I found what I've been searching for these past fifteen years. So thank you very much, but don't expect me to buy any of your soul-talk or use any of your wild explanations for what you did in my lab. It's bad enough that I'm going to have to deal with a tabloid fiasco that makes my work look like it's straight out of LaLa land. I'm a scientist, Khristina, and I interpret the data scientifically. I don't see any of this through the eyes of a . . . medium."

Too late, he heard the unmistakable tone of derision in his own voice, and though somewhere in the back of his consciousness, he knew it was going to infuriate the woman beside him, he didn't care. He wouldn't take it back even if he could. The whole medium thing was a con game. A sham.

No one could talk to the dead.

Not even Khristina Tupikova, and definitely not Michael Carilion.

Khristina leaned toward him, her cheeks flushing bright red.

"Because your eyes are the only ones that see the truth? Is that what you think, Michael? Then I have something to tell you: your eyes can deceive you. Yes, they can! They can deceive even you, the brilliant Michael Carilion!"

Despite the dig of the seat belt's shoulder restraint against her body, Khristina pulled even closer to him.

"Maybe if, for once, you tried to listen to someone else's truth, your eyes might see things differently. You might even be surprised to find out how much you don't know. How much you're missing. Unlike Lucas, you're not willing to listen to someone else's experience."

"Don't bring Lucas into this!" Michael warned her in a low growl, his voice barely containing the grief and anger that was now flooding into him, unchecked.

But Khristina didn't seem able to stop herself, either. The words kept pouring out.

"You want to know how I can do things? How I manage?" Her voice rose to a shout. "I listen, Michael. I listen and learn."

Michael's knuckles went white on the wheel.

It was all he could do not to grab her and shake her. Shake out her insane ideas. Who did she think she was talking to?

Some stupid schoolboy? Some impressionable idiot who believed everything he heard?

Furious, his tenuous control completely shot, Michael spit out the words.

"Who do you listen to, Khristina? Ghosts?"

She didn't flinch.

"I listen to my friends. I use the gift that God has graciously given me, and I listen to the people who are already home. I listen to the Williams and to Blaise and to Catherine and to Francis and to Thomas."

She paused a moment, locking her eyes on his, then whispered, "And to Elise."

CHAPTER FIFTEEN

There was suddenly no air in Michael's lungs. Nor could he look away from Khristina, either. The black abyss tore open right there in the front seat of the Lexus.

Instantly contrite, her anger spent, Khristina reached out to touch his right hand on the steering wheel.

He jerked his hand away.

"Michael, I—"

"Just tell me where to turn," he said, throwing the car into gear to pull back into the street. He wasn't going to talk about it. He wasn't going to think about it. He was taking Khristina home and then he would find a bottle of booze even if he had to buy it from the nearest restaurant.

The abyss was all his.

Khristina sank back against the seat.

She knew she had not handled it well, to say the least. She hadn't even meant to tell him—she knew it was too soon and he wasn't ready for it—but it had come out in her anger at his unbelievable arrogance. How had Elise put up with him? It was one thing to be an expert at what you did, but to hold up that expertise as a barrier against other people and what they experienced was wrong. If she had learned nothing else in all the years she had listened to her friends, both living and dead, it was that life was too big and rich for anyone to think they knew it all.

"Turn right at this next corner," she told Michael.

Now she would have to explain to Elise how she had failed, but she knew that Elise would understand. In the few months since they had become friends, Michael's wife had been a wonderful companion, and Khristina had no doubt that if anyone knew how stubborn Michael was, it was Elise.

Michael made the turn, but immediately slowed the car down to almost a crawl as soon as he was on Khristina's street.

"What is going on?" he asked, peering through the windshield.

Ahead of his sedan, both sides of the tree-lined lane were filled with cars and vans. As he approached the vehicles, Michael recognized the logos of three different local television stations on van panels; two of them already had dishes set up on their roofs for broadcasting. On the sidewalk, a reporter was spotlighted, interviewing a well-dressed, middle-aged woman in a green wool coat. Both of their faces were animated and the woman was pointing at Khristina's house.

"I'm getting a really bad feeling here," Michael said.

He cruised past the camera crew that was filming the interview on the sidewalk. He could feel his heart rate accelerate. He still had bad dreams about the media circus his life had become after Elise's murder, and seeing the broadcasting dishes was like a trigger in his pulse.

"Please, Khristina," he said, his voice low with dread, "tell me I made a wrong turn somewhere."

Khristina didn't answer. She was staring at the throngs of people milling beside the cars and in her front yard.

"What has happened? Why are so many people standing in front of my house?"

Michael rolled to a stop near the end of the block.

"Stay here," he told her. "I'm going to find out what's going on."

He got out of the car and walked back towards a group of men standing along the edge of Khristina's yard.

"Hey," he greeted the men. "What's the big event?"

A man wearing a brown leather jacket turned towards Michael.

"It's the end of the age," he announced, excited anticipation shining in his eyes. "We've found the Awaited One, and now we're waiting for her to lead us into the great Cosmic Release."

"But why are you standing in my yard?"

Michael spun to find Khristina standing behind him.

"Your yard?" the man asked.

Michael grabbed her arm, but before he could take two steps with her, the man had latched onto Khristina's opposite shoulder.

"You're Khristina! Aren't you?"

He turned and yelled to the others in the yard.

"She's here! She's here!"

The yard erupted into motion and noise. People were running towards them. The man on the other side of Khristina jerked her away from Michael's hand and pulled her back towards the house. Camera flashes popped. People were yelling. Reporters elbowed their way through the excited crowd, camera crews scurrying behind them. Men and women of all ages had their hands in the air, reaching toward Khristina, whose face now wore the unmistakable look of a deer caught hopelessly in the headlights.

"Khristina!" Michael cried.

He plunged into the crowd, pushing people out of his way until he was within arm's reach of her. The man still gripped her shoulder. Michael grabbed the leather collar and shoved the man to the side, found Khristina's hand, and yanked her after him into a run.

One more hand reached out to pull him back, and, without hesitation, Michael spun around with his fist leading. He didn't stop to check if he hit a target, but the searing pain in his hand told him he'd hit a bull's-eye. Dodging the glare of television cameras, Michael and Khristina sprinted down the sidewalk and jumped into the Lexus.

"I told you to stay in the car!" he shouted at her, starting the engine and peeling away into the street, skidding wide as he turned right at the corner. "I thought you were supposed to be the one who's such a good listener! What did you think you were doing?"

She didn't reply.

"Khristina!"

"I thought I was going home!" she yelled back. "I just wanted to go in my house!"

Speeding down the street, Michael checked his rear-view mirrors to see if anyone was behind him. He took the next left, then another at the following corner. If anyone was following them, then they had a better sense of direction than he had at the moment, because he had no idea where they were. He just wanted to put as much distance as possible between themselves and Khristina's house. He found a major intersection, checked the street signs, and oriented himself. His thundering pulse began to slow. Risking a glance in Khristina's direction, he saw streaks of tears running down her face. She sat rigid in the passenger seat, staring straight ahead.

Michael kept driving.

CHAPTER SIXTEEN

The cameraman from Channel 9 wound up his cables and laid them in the back of the station's van next to his other equipment.

"Hey, Mara," he called to the blonde reporter climbing into the front passenger seat. "Did you get a look at that guy who took off with the woman?"

Mara Runyon shifted in the seat so she could look back at her colleague.

"Not really. There were too many people between me and them. Why?"

"I thought he looked familiar. I was just coming to catch up with you in the crowd and he pushed past me. Remember that murder case back in February? The one with the woman who got killed in her doorway?"

Mara remembered it very well. She'd practically camped out on Dr. Carilion's doorstep for a week, trying to get an interview with the man, but all he'd done was brush her aside and threaten to get a court order against the station.

"Yes, I remember. What of it?"

The cameraman scratched the beginnings of his five o'clock shadow.

"I think it was him. The guy who took off with the woman, I mean. I think it was the dead woman's husband."

CHAPTER SEVENTEEN

Y ou need to eat something."

"I am not hungry," Khristina sniffed.

Michael read the menu board outside the drive-through window of the corner fast-food restaurant. He was reasonably confident no one had tailed them out of Khristina's neighborhood, but he wasn't taking any chances of sitting down to a meal only to have a contingent of Cosmic-whatever people descend upon them.

"You need to eat," he said again. "I've been down this road before, Khristina. Grief takes a lot out of you. You need calories."

When she still didn't answer, he turned away from the menu to see what she was doing.

Nothing.

She was doing nothing. Except staring at him.

"First you notice my perfume," she quietly observed, "and now you are concerned that I eat. I am becoming a person to you, Michael."

Unaccountably, Michael felt a heated blush rising from the base of his throat. She was right—it was personal. In all the months he'd known her, he'd methodically avoided Khristina in the lab, and when he did cross paths with her, he made only the most perfunctory statements possible. Part of that, he knew, was his professional distaste for her performance—her very presence—in his lab. But it struck him now that in the months following Elise's death, he'd ruthlessly maintained a distance from almost everyone he came in contact with, save for Lucas, and even that relationship had grown strained at times.

What shocked Michael even more, at the moment, was the realization that he'd just referred to his own recent experience of grieving. He hadn't shared it with anyone before now, and the fact that it had slipped out so easily unnerved him. He began to turn back towards the menu, but Khristina reached out and touched him lightly on the arm.

"You are right, Michael. I need the calories. A hamburger would be fine."

He nodded without looking at her and put his hand out the window to press the service button.

"Four burgers, two fries," he ordered and pulled ahead to wait in line for their supper.

"What is that called?" Khristina asked.

He glanced at her face then, only to see that she was watching his fingers nimbly turning the blocks in his Rubik's cube. Although he couldn't recall taking it from his pocket, the cube was in his hand, its squares of color almost completely worn off from his years of twisting it.

"It's a Rubik's cube," he said. "A mind-teaser."

"It is a puzzle?"

"Yes, it is."

"And how do you solve it?" Khristina asked.

Michael studied the old toy in his hand. Memories of countless hours manipulating the sides of the cube washed over him. He'd been thirteen years old when the toy hit the market. One day, he'd come home from school to find his grandfather waiting for him, a brand-new Rubik's cube in his hand.

"Here's a puzzle for you, Mike," he'd said. "As soon as I saw it at the toy store, I thought to myself, 'If anyone can solve that thing, Mike can. The boy's a blooming genius.' Now, do me proud, boy. Solve that thing."

And Michael had. It had taken him three days of spinning the rows every spare moment he could find, but he'd done it. Then he took it to his grandfather and showed him the sequence of moves to solve the cube.

"Never forget," his grandfather had said, slapping him on the back in congratulations, "that this is how you succeed: set a goal, my boy, and never give up. I'm proud of you, Mike."

Four days later, his grandfather was dead.

At the funeral, Michael learned for the first time that his grandfather had been waging a two-year battle with cancer. No one had wanted him to know. But Michael was sure of one thing: his grandfather had never given up.

And neither had Michael.

Not even when his whole world had fallen apart with Elise's murder. Yes, he'd stumbled—fallen flat on his face, actually—but then he'd picked himself up, set the goal and never given up. Finding the One Theory had become his reason to live.

And now he'd succeeded.

His grandfather would be proud.

He set the Rubik's cube on the dashboard in front of Khristina.

"You have to get each side of the cube covered in one color." He pointed at the different colored blocks on the toy. "You twist the blocks in different ways to achieve that effect."

Khristina eyed the cube. "This is quite difficult, is it not?"

Michael shrugged. "It just takes time and determination. When the toy was first available, everybody was crazy for it. Trial and error was the only way to solve it. Nowadays, there are guides to show you how to do it. Believe it or not, there are literally billions of combinations possible for arranging just these twenty-six parts of this one little cube."

He touched one of the colored squares of the toy.

"Pretty amazing, isn't it?"

Khristina considered the cube, then reached out and took it in her hand. Slowly she turned it around, then began flipping its rows.

"A billion combinations?"

"Actually, more like a quintillion, or even a septillion, I think," Michael replied. "For most people, a billion is more than enough."

"Then, in a way, it is like holding infinity in your hands," Khristina noted, continuing to move the rows around the cube's core. "And when you switch the blocks to all these different combinations, it is like 'displaying the infinite which was hid,' don't you think?"

Michael's eyes lifted from the little cube in Khristina's hands to examine her face. In the gathering dusk, her blue eyes looked darker, deeper.

"And is that not what you have done with your theory, Michael?" she whispered. "Displayed the Infinite which was hidden?"

For a moment, Michael was silent, his eyes held by Khristina's.

Then he shrugged again.

"I don't think you and I are talking about the same infinite," he sighed.

Khristina passed the cube back to him.

"Can there be more than one?"

Michael pocketed his toy as the restaurant attendant waved him forward to pick up their meal.

"I have bottles of iced tea at home," he said, changing the subject.

By the time they pulled into Michael's garage, Khristina was ravenous. While she spread out the contents of the dinner bags on the big desk in Michael's back study, he went to the front of the house to inspect the new window. When he returned, she was already digging into her burger and one of the cartons of fries.

"I guess you found your appetite," he said, nodding at the food in her hands.

She smiled around her burger.

"Look, Khristina, I think you should stay here tonight."

She stopped chewing.

"I've been thinking about this and I just don't feel good about you going home tonight," he explained. "For all we know, the Cosmic people could be holding a vigil in your yard right now, waiting for their Awaited One—you—to come back. A hotel is out of the question, too. If anyone recognizes you from the news footage that is sure to be on every station tonight, there's no way you're going to get any privacy, let alone sleep."

He stuck a few French fries in his mouth and washed it down with some tea.

"You can stay right here in the study. You'll be safe," he added.

Khristina finished the burger and wiped her mouth thoroughly with a napkin. Catching himself staring at her full lips, Michael averted his eyes.

"I am not sure this is the right thing to do," she finally said. "But I appreciate your offer, and I am afraid you may be right about my home or a hotel. If you are sure it is not an inconvenience to you, I will stay here tonight."

"Inconvenience isn't the issue, Khristina," Michael pointed out. "Safety is. I feel partly responsible for the mess we're in, and I'm not about to throw you to the wolves."

He held up his hand to stop her when she opened her mouth to protest.

"If you're sleeping here in the study, then that's one less thing I have to worry about. And at this point, one less thing on my plate makes a big difference to me."

He nodded toward the food on the desk.

"Speaking of which, there's another hamburger with your name on it."

Khristina glanced at the hamburger, then back at Michael.

"You really know how to persuade a girl, don't you? Yes, thank you, I will sleep in your study tonight. And Michael," she added, the teasing in her voice suddenly gone, "I have no doubt I am safe with you."

For only a second, Khristina watched a flurry of emotions—relief, grief, and surprise—cross Michael's strong face. The shadow those feelings left behind reminded her that if she were being totally honest with herself, Michael's situation this evening wasn't much better than hers. Yes, his window had been repaired, but that didn't change the fact that his home had been violated with a brick and a threat. Even worse, he'd lost Lucas.

She'd often observed the two researchers in the months she'd spent in their lab, and she knew the men had a close relationship, one from which Michael seemed to derive great satisfaction as the younger man's mentor. She also guessed that their collaboration on the project was a deeply personal tie that bound the men together. For Michael to have to consider the possibility—the likelihood—that Lucas had betrayed his trust, must have been more than painful.

And now, to top it off, Michael had felt compelled by his sense of responsibility to offer his roof to a woman he had intensely disliked, and was, at least in the last few hours, only barely managing to tolerate.

A woman whose safety he now apparently considered one of his professional obligations.

Frowning at the sinking feeling of disappointment that thought gave her, Khristina bit into her second hamburger of the night as Michael turned on the television in the study.

CHAPTER EIGHTEEN

Comfortably settled into his favorite armchair, Drake tapped the remote control for the huge, flat-panel television screen that dominated one wall of his penthouse condominium. He'd left Phoebe after an early dinner to come home for some privacy and quiet. He wanted to think about that *Eye* article and listen again to Phoebe's taped interview with Scranton. He wasn't sure yet what his next move would be, or if circumstances even required him to make any move at all at this point.

As long as Carilion was still fumbling along, nothing had changed. Unification was still unproven. Depending on the repercussions of the tabloid article, proof might be even further away than before—certainly, Carilion's credibility would take a major hit from the project's mention in a grocery store gossip rag. On the other hand, any publicity at all could have the opposite effect: the attention of the media would put unification on everyone's radar.

And that would be very bad for The Gentleman.

Drake checked the time and switched to Channel 9 for their nightly "News 9" broadcast. He wanted to see the sports scores— one of his favorite teams, the Arizona Sun Devils, had played earlier in the day and he'd missed the second half while he was at Phoebe's. While he waited, he muted the sound and read the *Eye* article again, deciding it might be prudent to speak with the Skye G. Hammond whose byline accompanied the article. He'd like to know what she knew about the Strings Project.

He also wanted to find out where she'd gotten her information.

Not that he doubted Phoebe had told him the truth when she claimed she didn't know Hammond or how the reporter had sourced the story. He, of all people, would know at once if Phoebe were lying.

But Drake Lamont hadn't secured his personal kingdom by leaving leads hanging or questions unanswered. And Skye Hammond might just be both of those things.

A waterfall of long, blonde hair on the screen caught Drake's eye, interrupting his deliberations. It was Mara Runyon, Channel 9's on-location reporter, speaking with a woman in a green coat. Obviously taped earlier while it was still daylight, the segment kept focusing on a small brick house, with crowds of people milling around it. When he spotted a copy of the *Eye* held in the woman's hand, Drake turned up the volume.

"And I take it you and your colleagues have been searching for this Awaited One for some time now?" Runyon asked, holding a microphone close to the woman's lips.

"Oh yes, quite a while. All our books of prophecy have been pointing towards the appearance of One who would call us together and lead us to sublime consciousness," the woman gushed. "When that happens, it's the end of the age and the beginning of our transbody fusions, what we call the great Cosmic Release."

"And you think that One is this woman, Khristina Tupikova, who was quoted in this morning's edition of *The Midnight Eye?*"

"Yes, Mara, we do," the woman smiled. "In her interview, she spoke the Key itself. We who have studied our books know she is the One."

A quick cut of the camera showed people running away in a scene of general confusion and noise. Runyon's disembodied voice continued over the visual image.

"But as you can see, joyful anticipation turned to near riot when Tupikova suddenly did appear on the scene a few hours ago. Though our camera crew could not positively identify the man with her, rumors circulated that he was Dr. Michael Carilion, the world-renowned physicist at Barnet College. Calls to both the college administrators and Dr. Carilion have gone unanswered, so at this point, all we have is speculation that there is some kind of connection between the physicist's on-going scientific research and a woman who is being hailed as a spiritual messiah."

The camera returned to the earnest faces of the nightly anchor team, but Drake didn't hear a word they said.

He was too busy laughing.

"This is too much!" he chortled, tears starting to form in his silvery eyes. "I couldn't have done better if I'd orchestrated the whole thing myself! Carilion filmed running away with a medium! Thank you, Mara Runyon."

"You're welcome, Drake Lamont."

Drake twisted in his chair to see the television reporter he'd just been watching on the screen standing in the condo's entrance foyer. He dropped the remote on a side table and rose to greet her.

"I didn't hear you come in," he told her, enjoying the way her shapely hips moved as she came towards him.

"Obviously. You're forgiven, especially since I already had your attention anyway."

She waved at the flat panel of the television.

"Did you see something you liked, darling?"

Drake slid his arms around her and smiled slowly into her exotic, almond-shaped eyes.

"I always see something I like when I'm looking at you, Mara. On or off the screen."

Mara returned his smile with an equally slow one of her own.

"I hate that man, you know. Carilion. He wouldn't give me the time of day when his wife died. So now, it's payback. I'm going to harass him right out of this town and make a name for myself while I'm at it."

Drake's smile widened. "That's my girl."

CHAPTER NINETEEN

Michael and Khristina sat speechless on the couch in the study, staring at the television. They'd just watched their own backs disappearing down a dusky sidewalk.

"They think I am their prophet?" Khristina finally choked out.

"No, they think you're their messiah," Michael wearily corrected her. "A prophet speaks for God, a messiah saves people. There's a difference."

Khristina turned to glare at him. "I did not realize you were such an authority on religious terminology."

Michael sighed heavily.

"Khristina, please, let's not argue. Not right now. We're both too stressed and exhausted for it. Besides, we've got plenty of other problems to deal with that are a lot more serious than my familiarity with a spiritual vocabulary."

He pointed towards the television.

"That woman is one of them. Mara Runyon. She's a viper and she'd like to destroy me."

Khristina glanced back at the television, but Mara's exotic face was gone. Instead, the station's weatherman was predicting a warming trend.

"Why does she want to destroy you?"

Michael toed off his loafers and stretched out his legs. That earlier run down the sidewalk had winded him a little, but his leg muscles weren't feeling any negative aftereffects. At least he could depend on something being normal tonight.

97

"Mara Runyon made me crazy after Elise died," he told Khristina. "Every morning when I left for work—even the mornings I didn't leave for work—she was in her car at the curb, waiting for me. She wanted an exclusive, she said. The 'husband denied justice' story. I told her to get out of my yard. Several times, in fact. I finally called her station and threatened to press charges of harassment. I expect it didn't go over well with her superiors, because I didn't see her on the news again for several months."

"And for this, she wants to hurt you?"

"Well," he said, crossing his ankles, even as he could feel tension returning to his thighs, "that's not quite the whole story. When I saw her again on the news, she was with a different station. The first one fired her. Then, a few weeks ago, I ran into her on campus. I was coming out of the chancellor's office and bumped right into her in the hall. Practically knocked her over, actually. I tried to be polite. You know, let bygones be bygones. All she said was 'Turnabout is fair play, Carilion. One day, I'm going to have your job.'"

Khristina frowned. "How can that be? She is a news reporter and you are a brilliant scientist. She could never do your job. You are the only one, Michael."

Michael absently rubbed his thigh and allowed himself a small smile. For all of Khristina's unusual—and frequently unaccountable—insight, she still had some blind spots with the English language. Or at least American expressions. He was about to explain what 'having your job' meant, but he was interrupted by his inner voice.

Skip the lecture, professor. Just thank her for the compliment.

That was good advice, he decided. Now that he thought about it, the advice his conscience gave him usually was good.

Maybe Khristina was right.

Perhaps he could be doing a better job of listening.

"Thank you," he said. "You're right, Khristina, she couldn't do my job."

But she could make his doing his job a whole lot harder, Michael suspected. Mara Runyon was, after all, in the media business. Her stock in trade was the communication—and manipulation—of information. That made her a potentially powerful enemy.

Michael wasn't fooling himself—more intelligent men than he had suffered disastrous career damage and total character assassination at the hands of self-serving journalists. Look what had happened to Einstein. By the time he died, the press had all but announced he belonged in a mental ward. Knowing that the Channel 9 reporter had a personal vendetta against him, and that she hadn't hesitated to let him know it, didn't leave Michael with any warm toasty feelings towards the woman, either.

No, he decided, Mara Runyon was a loose cannon he couldn't afford to ignore.

"But I am not so naïve to think that she is harmless, either," Khristina insisted, echoing Michael's thoughts. "'Hell hath no fury like a woman scorned.' But seriously," she added, frown lines creasing her brows, "she should not be making statements about you or your work without confirming these things first. This is irresponsible."

"This is television," Michael responded. "It's entertainment, Khristina. Information all dressed up to improve ratings."

"You are a cynic, Michael."

"I am a realist, Khristina."

"'Aye, there's the rub,'" she quoted again, attempting to make her voice deep and rough, while she narrowed her eyes at him menacingly.

Michael laughed.

If she was trying to distract him and lighten the mood, she was succeeding. It struck him that just last week, he would have had a completely different reaction to her theatrics—if he'd seen this same rapid flow of expressive emotion on her face while she'd been giving a reading in the lab, he would have chalked it up to bad performance art. Now, after a day in her company, he realized that the emotional display was genuine: Khristina Tupikova wore her heart on her face. He doubted she could dissemble even if her life depended upon it.

"What? I am turning into a squash?"

Michael was staring at Khristina.

"No. You're not turning into a squash. Or a pumpkin, either, Cinderella. I was just thinking . . . never mind."

"I never told you congratulations, Michael."

Her sudden change in topic took him by surprise.

"Congratulations?"

"The theory," she clarified. "You accomplished your goal. I am no physicist, but I do have an idea how important this discovery is for you. If I am understanding correctly, it will change the way we explain many things in the universe, will it not? In many ways, I think, it will change the world."

Again, she frowned.

"I am hoping the world is ready for that. I hope you are."

Michael had the distinct sense she was once again heading in a direction he didn't want to take—a direction that had nothing to do with scientific data. She was a medium, after all. Not a scientist. With any luck tomorrow, today would be just a bad memory. He'd be back in the lab and she would . . . be doing . . . whatever it was . . . she did.

What *did* she do?

Read tea leaves for paying customers?

Work for a psychic hotline?

She'd told him earlier, rather indignantly, that she didn't help people find hidden treasures or select lottery numbers, but other than her work in his lab, Michael didn't know what Khristina did with her time and . . . skills.

"Do you work out of your home?" he asked.

If that was the case, she was going to have a problem if the Cosmic Release people were still hanging around tomorrow waiting for her. Before she could answer him, though, he had pulled out his cell phone. "We need to ask the police to clear your yard. Maybe post some signs."

The phone rang in his hands.

"Carilion here," he said, flipping it open.

"Michael, it's Stevenson. I realize this may not be a good time, but I wanted to speak with you tonight. I've had a few phone calls of concern from members of the board."

Stevenson Newsome was the chancellor at Barnet. Along with the Board of Trustees, he held the purse strings for all the research programs at the college. Every project not only had to be approved by Newsome for its initiation, but also depended on his continued support for its ongoing existence. The chancellor had been one of Michael's staunchest allies over the years, and even when the Strings Project had been floundering months ago, he'd still been in Michael's corner. The fact that he was calling now, late on a Sunday evening, wasn't promising anything good, however.

Michael groaned inwardly. He was ready to bet the last dollar of his Strings funding that this phone call was a result of the Channel 9 report.

"I think it might be wise if you weren't on campus tomorrow," Newsome said. "There seems to be some wild speculation going on about your research, and I think it would be in everyone's best interests if you were unavailable for comment for a day or so. Let the thing die down of its own accord. You know I'm the first one to welcome good press about Barnet, but this isn't exactly the kind of attention we want, is it?"

"It's a mistake, Stevenson."

"Oh, I know that," the chancellor quickly assured him. "And I'm not throwing any aspersions on your work, Michael. When you're dealing with such esoteric projects as you are, you're bound to encounter ignorant interpretations and misrepresentations of what you're really doing. I'm sure it will just blow over. Give the news crews a day or two and something else will have their undivided attention in no time. I'm issuing a statement in the morning that we do not, as a matter of long-standing policy, comment on articles that appear in tabloids."

Michael ended the call and looked at Khristina, who was gathering up the empty tea bottles on the desk from their dinner.

"The chancellor says I should take the day off tomorrow," he told her. "I'll take you home in the morning, and we'll see what's up with your yard. I know a detective down at the police station, and she could probably tell us what to do if people are still there."

"All right," she said, then left the room with the bottles.

Out in the hallway, her steps on the marble floor told Michael she was headed for the garage. He heard her open the back door and then listened to the familiar ring of empty bottles being tossed into the recycling container that Elise had disguised long ago as an old apple crate. When she returned to the study a minute later, Michael was as still as a stone.

"How did you know where my recycling bin was?"

Khristina hesitated.

"Of course it would be in the garage," she explained. "Where else would it be?"

"In my laundry room. Under the kitchen sink. Outside next to the trash can."

He looked her straight in the eye.

"Not to mention it doesn't even look like a recycling container. So how did you know, Khristina?"

His phone rang again.

He ignored it.

"Khristina?"

"You should answer your phone. Perhaps it is the chancellor again."

Michael snapped the phone open, his eyes never leaving Khristina's face.

"Hello?" he asked, his voice tight with suppressed impatience.

"Dr. Carilion? My name is Phoebe Dauwalter. I've been trying to reach you. Do you have a moment?"

CHAPTER TWENTY

Saved by the cell, Khristina thought ruefully, scanning the contents of Michael's kitchen refrigerator.

She had taken advantage of the cell phone's interruption and walked out of the study to give Michael some privacy and herself a mental reprimand. She would have to be more careful around him, since he had made it amply clear that he wasn't able, or even willing, to accept her unique gift, let alone appreciate it.

In fact, it was obvious that he not only found it disturbing, but totally untenable. In his world, mediums didn't exist.

Nor did life after death.

She took a green-gold apple from the crisper and felt the air shiver behind her.

Someone was coming to visit.

Khristina closed the refrigerator's door and turned around, silently asking for God's blessing as she always did when a visitor arrived.

"It's called a honeygold," Elise Carilion said, nodding toward the apple in Khristina's hand. "They were always my favorite variety. It wasn't really autumn until I had a honeygold."

Her eyes met Khristina's.

"Don't give up on him, Khristina. He needs you, whether he knows it or not."

"Then I feel sorry for him, because I am making a mess of things."

"No, you're not."

"I tell the man I talk with his dead wife, and then I even know where the recycling bin is!"

"That was my fault. Sorry. Old habits die hard, or in this case, I guess they don't die at all. When you picked up the empty bottles, I just couldn't help myself, and I whispered in your ear. I'm still too attached. That's why I asked you to help me in the first place, Khristina. Both Michael and I need to move on."

"Well, my effort today certainly did not contribute to that goal. This is going to take a while, I think, Elise. Michael and I, we are like water and oil. We don't mix at all."

"But you have to. I'm depending on you, Khristina. Michael won't listen to me—he *can't* listen to me. You're my only hope to help Michael through this . . . crisis. He's in trouble, Khristina."

Khristina took a bite of the apple. "Yes, I know. The trouble's name is Mara Runyon, and she is a reporter for the television."

"I'm not talking about Runyon. There's someone else—the Devil, himself. Be very careful."

"And who is this person who is the devil himself?"

"Khristina?"

Michael was standing in the doorway of the kitchen.

"Who are you talking to?"

The air shivered around Khristina.

Elise was gone.

"No one, Michael," Khristina said. "It is just me."

CHAPTER TWENTY-ONE

Drake played the recording again, congratulating himself once more on having had the foresight to affix the high-tech bug beneath the corner of Phoebe's coffee table while she had finished making dinner. It had been a pricey little piece of almost invisible hardware, but as he listened to her phone conversation with Carilion for a second time, he was absolutely convinced that it was worth every penny.

"That little witch," he muttered. "She's disobeying me. She's going after the story even after I told her to stay away from it. After everything I've done for her, all the effort and time I've put into molding and shaping her into the woman she is today, this is the thanks I get."

He punched the recording machine off and jotted down a time and address.

"Big mistake, Phoebe. Very, very big mistake."

He took out his cell phone and hit the speed dial.

"Hello, darling," he said when a woman's voice answered. "I have a favor to ask."

He reread the notes he'd made. "Can you be at Corner Coffee tomorrow morning at ten? I have a job for you."

"Anything you want, Drake," Mara Runyon purred. "You know I live to serve."

CHAPTER TWENTY-TWO

Michael opened his eyes and for a split second panicked, thinking he'd overslept and that Lucas would be on his case for being late to the lab.

Then the scent of roasted coffee beans wafted over his bed, and he remembered that things were very different this morning. For one thing, the college chancellor had specifically requested he not show up at the lab. For another thing, Lucas was dead. And then there was yet another thing: there was a Russian medium apparently making coffee in his kitchen.

As he rolled out of bed, he began making his to-do list for the day in his head. He'd agreed to meet with the Dauwalter woman at ten, so that gave him a couple of hours to run errands first. He needed to take Khristina home and make sure she'd be safe there; if the Cosmic people were still on her property, he'd call Teri Ostrand, the police detective he'd become acquainted with during Elise's murder investigation, for advice on what Khristina could do.

Actually, now that he thought about it, maybe he'd call Teri anyway and find out what anyone knew about Lucas's death. Michael had lain awake a long time last night thinking about Lucas, wondering exactly what had been going on with the younger physicist. The more he had thought about it, the more questions he'd had.

For starters, what was Lucas doing downtown late Friday night?

When he'd left the lab that evening, he'd told Michael that he was exhausted and looking forward to an early bedtime. Obviously, his plans had changed. Had he met someone downtown? Like the *Eye* reporter?

Anger and suspicion welled up inside Michael at the idea. He did a quick timeline in his head. The locally produced tabloid had come out Sunday morning, which meant it could have had a deadline as late as Saturday afternoon. If Lucas had met with the reporter Friday night, that would have given the writer enough time to file the story to make the Sunday morning edition.

But why would Lucas talk to a tabloid reporter, of all people, about the Strings Project?

On the few occasions when the two of them had imagined together what it would be like to announce the project's success, Lucas had insisted they make it a class act, calling a press conference the very day the journal article appeared in *Physica*. Of course, that had been early in the project, when their optimism and funding looked endless.

Had Lucas started to panic, thinking they needed a boost from some good press?

After all, the annals of scientific breakthrough were filled with announcements that a cure, or a discovery, was imminent, and thanks to the enthusiasm the press subsequently stirred up, money always seemed to appear from nowhere just in time to push the programs across the finish line. Look at what happened with the Genome Project: despite the fact that it would take years—maybe decades—to make any substantive use of the information, the announcement that the first phase of deciphering the genetic code was complete generated a veritable tsunami of excitement that launched a hundred new initiatives. Without a doubt, science was as indentured to the media as any politician who wanted to win a seat in the next election.

Still, the *Eye* was no *Physica*, or even Lamont's *World*. What was it that the Dauwalter woman had said to him on the phone?

Oh yes—something about setting the scientific record straight and preserving the integrity of his research in the wake of the tabloid disaster. And, to be honest, after imagining the potential repercussions of that particular disaster, Michael was more than ready to make a grab at any professional lifeline that someone might toss him . . . even if it was thrown by another reporter.

Which reminded him of another item for his to-do list: Skye G. Hammond. He wanted to be sure she knew just what she had set in motion with her *Midnight Eye* article. Maybe he'd even sue her and that rag she worked for to cover the cost of his new front window and the carpeting he was going to order this morning. Not to mention the mess she'd made of Khristina's life.

Yes, he certainly had things to do on his unexpected day off.

Ten minutes later he walked into the kitchen, where Khristina was leaning back against the sink, drinking coffee.

"That smells wonderful," he told her.

"I would have made a breakfast, but there is nothing much in your refrigerator. I like hotdogs, but not for breakfast."

Michael poured himself a mug of the steaming brew and cradled it in his hands.

"I don't usually have company, so I'm a bit understocked in the food department."

He blew on the coffee and took a sip. "It's good. Thanks."

"Did you sleep well?"

It had been a long time since someone had asked him that, Michael thought. He looked at Khristina over the rim of his cup, noting that she looked well-rested and bright-eyed, not what he would have expected of a woman who'd been forced from her home and had spent the night on his study's couch. Her hair was still loose around her shoulders, and it occurred to him that she hadn't even had the benefit of a toothbrush or comb for her overnight stay. Yet she looked as fresh as she had yesterday morning when she turned up on his doorstep.

"I'm afraid I'm not much of a host, Khristina. I didn't even offer you towels last night, let alone shampoo or toothpaste."

He held up one hand to stop her from answering.

"I can see you obviously found what you needed, though, but please, don't tell me how you did it. I don't want to know. And no, I didn't sleep well, but I rarely do."

"And why is that?"

Michael debated whether he should say anything more, but the warmth of the kitchen, the aroma of the coffee, and what appeared to be the genuine interest of the woman standing next to him all conspired to make him lower the walls of his personal fortress, if only for a few minutes.

"I have dreams," he said, softly. "Nightmares, I guess. Ever since Elise died, I hate going to bed at night because I never know when the dreams will come."

Khristina was silent, drinking her coffee.

"What do you think of dreams, Khristina? Are they just Freudian junk rattling around in our heads or do they mean something else? What would a medium say about dreams?"

Khristina tipped her head to the side and considered the man standing before her.

Was Michael seriously asking her opinion or was he baiting her, looking to start a fight after a bad night?

He really was a fighter, she had decided, just before she fell asleep on the couch, wrapped in a blanket he'd found for her in the hall closet. A curious mix of a fighter and a defender, judging from the way he'd taken care of her all day yesterday. Maybe he really was St. Michael, Khristina speculated. Maybe he was her own personal archangel.

"What do you think, Khristina?" Michael asked again, his eyes intent on hers. "I'd really like to know."

"I think," she answered, placing her empty cup in the sink, "that I am not a dream interpreter or a psychoanalyst, but I think dreams can be important if we listen to them with our hearts, not our heads. In every religious tradition, God speaks to people in dreams, so who am I to question God?"

"Even bad dreams, Khristina? Does God want to frighten us? Is that what a loving God does? Is that what your God does?"

She shook her head.

"No. I do not believe that. But there are always at least two sides to a story, is that not true, Michael? Sometimes more than two. Maybe in your bad dreams, you are so focused on the bad, that you cannot see the good that is also hidden there."

She held up her hands in surrender.

"I do not know, Michael. All I know for certain is that there is much that we do not know. A friend of mine says, 'For man has closed himself up, till he sees all things thro' narrow chinks of his cavern.' I think there is great wisdom in this. We all do this, do we not? We decide what we will see—or not—and then we see exactly that."

For a moment, Michael closed his eyes, and Khristina panicked.

Had she pushed too hard at his comfort level? Again?

While she watched, a furrow of concentration crossed his forehead, and then his eyes flew open.

"William Blake," he announced. "You're quoting William Blake."

Khristina smiled, surprised and not a little relieved. She hadn't made another mess after all. And this time, Michael hadn't shut her out and himself down, either. They were still talking and the conversation was continuing.

"Yes, it is William. How do you know him?"

"High school Brit Lit," Michael grinned. "I may be a physicist, but I did have to study a few other subjects along the way. Brit Lit was one of them. Let me see . . . he wrote 'Songs of Innocence' and 'Songs of Experience' and then got pretty weird with elaborate etchings or prints or paintings and a whole poetic world of his own. As I recall, most of his contemporaries thought he was missing at least half of the cards from a full deck. He claimed he saw visions and spoke with angels."

Michael's words suddenly caught in his throat, and his gaze narrowed on Khristina.

Didn't she claim to do the same thing when she acted as a medium—see visions and speak with the dead?

And hadn't she just said, 'it is William,' rather than 'it was'?

Although, now that he thought about it, didn't everyone use the present tense at times when they referred to the work of people from the past? He himself had often said 'Einstein tells us' rather than 'told us' when he was lecturing to students in his Intro to Physics courses at the college. For the first time in his life, he wondered about that little oddity of speech, then abruptly pushed the thoughts aside.

He didn't like where they were going.

Instead, he casually remarked, "After all these years, I can't believe I remembered that."

"Maybe you had a little help," Khristina said. "I mean," she added hastily, too late, "maybe hearing them from me just jogged your memory."

Michael slowly drained his cup and placed it next to hers in the sink.

She just wouldn't let up, would she? Did she really think he was that dense, that he didn't know what she was trying to do? He turned to face her.

"No, that's not what you meant, Khristina. Even after spending just one day with you, I can tell when you're lying—it's written all over you. I know what you meant just now, and it wasn't that you jogged my memory. Yesterday, William was one of the names you included when you were talking about . . . about your friends."

Feeling his jaw beginning to clench, Michael took a deep breath in through his nose and slowly exhaled until the wave of tension lessened.

"And when you talk about these friends, it's always in the present tense," he added. "So I think we need to get something straight here."

He crossed his arms over his broad chest so he wouldn't be tempted to shake her in exasperation.

"I have no doubt that you have some kind of special hypersensitivity to information, coded energy packets from the eleventh dimension—my research proves that. But I do not—I cannot—attribute identity to these packets. It's energy, Khristina. Energy. Not people."

"But, Michael, what is a person," Khristina responded, "if not a bundle of energy? Your own physics theory predicts that energy does not die—it just changes shape. So why can you not accept that human energy does not die, that it, too, just changes shape?"

She braced herself against the kitchen counter, her hands anchored to the solid granite behind her.

"The people we love still live, Michael," she pleaded with him. "They just take new forms when they leave us. They receive their heavenly bodies. They are clothed in Christ! But God has given me a gift: I can see them. I can 'receive' those forms. Call it information if you want, but the truth is that your information packets are souls, Michael. Souls! What is so hard about that?"

Michael's arms flew out from his sides and his voice roared out into the warm kitchen.

"Because people die, Khristina! They're dead! Their 'energy' is gone! Gone! It doesn't exist! They don't exist! And no one can bring them or their 'energy' back! Not me and certainly not some illiterate medium from Russia who thinks she's talking with William Blake!"

"But their energy—their souls—they are not gone!" she shouted back at him, refusing to let his barbed comment deflect her from her argument. "They are just in a different place—a dimension, you call it. The dimension that you've found! Michael, you did find heaven! Now you have to decide what you are willing to see, what you are willing to believe, so you can truly see what is! You need to widen the narrow chinks in your cavern to let more light in. You have to do this. You! No one can do it for you."

Clearly furious, she spun away from him and strode across the kitchen towards the doorway, anger radiating from her with every step. At the entrance to the hall, she stopped and turned to face him once more.

"Not even some illiterate medium from Russia who *knows* she's talking with William Blake!"

She disappeared into the hall, then instantly returned to stand in the doorway for a parting shot.

"And by the way, I did not need help from anyone—living or dead—to find the shampoo and even a spare toothbrush in the bathroom this morning. I did it all by myself. Do you know how?" she challenged him. "I wasn't afraid to look!"

CHAPTER TWENTY-THREE

S kye was checking her office voice mail on her cell phone as she climbed the stairs to her eight a.m. Literary Theory class at Barnet, once again silently thanking her lucky stars she had had the sense to listen to Frank when he'd hired her and instructed her to get rid of her home phone land line.

"When you work for the *Eye*, you don't ever want your personal phone number or address printed in a directory where any lunatic can find it," Frank had explained. "Make all your business calls from the office phone and get yourself a cell phone for personal use. That way, all the alien abduction victims won't be camping outside your apartment to give you the story of the century."

Granted, neither Drake Lamont nor Dr. Michael Carilion were alien abduction victims, but judging from the tone of the voice mails they'd each left on her office phone, they weren't exactly the biggest members of her fan club at the moment, either. So whom was she going to call first after class was over: the man she had scooped, or the man she had inadvertently thrown to the lions?

"Looks like you set off a firestorm, Skye."

Skye dropped her backpack on the seminar room's large round table and pulled off her coat before replying to her professor, a petite brunette by the name of Greta Patocki.

"I'm guessing that means you caught the news on the television last night," Skye said. "I'm not sure if I should be flattered that the television stations picked up my story or if I should be insulted that they didn't call to interview me, too. I'd like to be on television just as much as the next gal."

"Maybe they figured the Cosmic Release people camped on that poor woman's lawn would make a better visual than an underfed, underemployed grad student who's simply trying to make a couple bucks to pay her outrageous tuition bills."

Skye laughed along with Greta, then blew out a sigh.

"But I think I crossed a line I don't like, even if it was unintentional," she said. "I never imagined someone would take it so seriously and track Khristina Tupikova down. I had no idea she even lived here in Litchfield. I'd assumed she was someone they flew in for the project and flew out again. When I heard she was Russian, I assumed she was . . . well, Russian, living in Russia. Now I've violated her privacy and parked a bunch of nutcases in her yard."

She took out her spiral notebook and slapped it on the table.

"And, on top of that, I've got both Michael Carilion and the mighty Drake Lamont ticked off at me. I ask you," she said, pointing a finger at Greta, "is this any way to start a Monday?"

Greta settled into a seat at the table.

"Carilion I can understand, but what's Lamont got to do with it?"

Skye sat across the table from her instructor while another two students straggled into the room.

"I sort of scooped him," she confessed to Greta. "I overheard this conversation at a bar on Friday night and ran with it for the *Eye*. The conversation was between a colleague of Dr. Carilion and Phoebe Dauwalter, the science editor of the *World*. Now I've got a voice mail from Lamont himself asking me to call him as soon as possible. Everything I've ever heard about the man is intimidating—he's very intelligent, very rich, very powerful, and he doesn't suffer fools gladly—or at all. I'm a lowly grad student, Greta. I'm thinking he's going to eat me alive."

"He's right down the hall," the older woman said. "Why don't you go find out?"

Skye looked at her professor, uncomprehending.

"Who's down the hall?"

"Lamont," Greta said. "I just passed the chancellor's office coming in here and saw Drake Lamont standing in the reception area. Believe me, he's impossible to miss." She gave a low, soft whistle of appreciation.

"Why put off the guillotine? You're excused from class—as long as you come right back here and tell me every word he said."

Three more classmates took seats at the table while Skye debated taking Greta's advice. "Alright," she said and pushed her chair back from the table. "I'm going to speak with The Gentleman."

Bolstering her nerve with a quick repetition of the three Bible verses she repeated to herself each morning, Skye walked down the long marble hall to the college chancellor's office.

Greta was right.

Even from a distance, she couldn't miss Drake Lamont's blonde head and the expensive cut of his navy blue three-piece suit as he idly examined the paintings that hung outside the office. Ordinarily, Skye wasn't attracted to older men, but the closer she got to Lamont, the more intriguing he looked. She decided the rumors she'd heard were all correct—even strolling in a college corridor with his hands in his pockets, the man exuded presence, charisma, and sex appeal.

Maybe his eating her alive wouldn't be so bad after all, Skye mused.

"Mr. Lamont," she said, extending her hand. "I'm Skye Hammond. I had a message to call you."

Lamont turned from the painting he was admiring, seeming only a little startled by her intrusion. Smiling graciously, he shook her hand and held on for just a moment longer than she had expected.

"Now, this is a surprise," he said. "Since when does Barnet College employ famous tabloid reporters on its faculty?"

Unable to keep her face from flushing with embarrassment, Skye laughed.

"I'm afraid you're wrong on two counts, Mr. Lamont. I'm not employed by the college, and I'm certainly not famous. I'm a student here in the English graduate program."

"Are you really?"

Skye couldn't stop staring at his eyes. They were the most striking silver color she'd ever seen. She reminded herself it was rude to stare and, with an effort, blinked.

"Yes," she answered. "Just a student."

"How fortunate for Barnet, then, because I think you are a very talented woman. And one day, I wager, at this rate, you'll be one of their most famous alumni."

He carefully placed his hand on the small of her back and turned her toward the chancellor's office.

"I'm sure the chancellor can spare us one of his conference rooms for a chat. Is this a good time for you?"

Oh man, Skye thought, *this man is slick as well as gorgeous.* Not only had he outrageously flattered her and put her at ease within moments of their meeting, but he had managed to convey a subtle sense of physical intimacy with her by touching her back in a near caress.

Get a grip, she told herself. *A guy may be gorgeous, but he can still be a jerk.* If nothing else, she'd learned that much from her experience with Josh.

At Drake's request, a secretary led them into an empty room adjacent to the chancellor's office. As the woman left to return to her work area, Drake asked her to let the chancellor know he'd be with him shortly and thanked her for her help. Then he invited Skye to take a seat in one of the plush armchairs at the table, while he partially closed the room's glass door, leaving it slightly ajar.

"I wouldn't want you to feel trapped in here with me," he explained to Skye, sending her a smile that warmed her all the way to her boot-shod toes.

If only! Skye thought, then gave herself a mental shake.

What was she thinking?

This wasn't speed dating at the corner bar, and the man beside her was no twenty-something college kid looking for a hot date. This man was a local icon who lived, worked, and breathed in a rarefied atmosphere of wealth and power that she couldn't even begin to imagine. His voice message had sounded polite, but filled with an unquestioned authority; the idea had actually run through her head that if she didn't return the call, he would come looking for her. And not for a silly, flirtatious conversation.

She ran through her Bible verses again, waiting for Lamont to get down to whatever business he had in mind for her.

"The reason I called," he finally said, "is that I'm thinking of hiring a new Arts and Literature reporter for the *World*, and it has come to my attention that you are a very resourceful woman who might just fill that bill quite well. What would you think of that, Ms. Hammond?"

Skye couldn't think at all.

A job offer?

It was the last thing on earth she had expected to hear from him. A tongue-lashing, a threat of a lawsuit, maybe even that he'd somehow forced Frank to fire her, she'd been prepared for.

But a job offer?

Not in this life.

Or in the next one either, for that matter, if Dr. Carilion's research really did pan out in the direction she had foreseen.

Besides, given that Drake Lamont could hire any number of well-credentialed Arts and Literature reporters at the drop of his very dapper hat, why would he stoop to pick her up from a tabloid like *The Midnight Eye?*

Sure, every woman likes to think that one day her talents will be recognized and she'll make it to the big time, but Skye wasn't about to fool herself that the owner of the *World* had been avidly following the trajectory of her writing career at a supermarket checkout rag. And this was no beer-bred brainstorming session with Frank, either, but a private conversation with Drake Lamont himself. The part of her that wouldn't mind—okay, was hungry for—a much-improved income and lifestyle shouted at her to take the job and run, but the overachieving, critical, English-literature-grad-student part of her insisted she needed time to think it through, to analyze the setting, the characters involved, and, perhaps most importantly, the plot behind the offer.

Because she was certain, deep down, that Lamont wanted something from her other than her writing skills. Something else was definitely at stake here, and though she was sure it had to do with her article in the *Eye,* Lamont was holding his cards very close to the vest.

Good thing for Skye that Josh the Jerk had gotten her hooked on Texas Hold'em, because she was about to call The Gentleman's bluff.

She folded her hands on the top of the conference table and looked in the silver eyes of the man next to her.

"You're lying, Mr. Lamont. I may write for idiots, but it doesn't make me one. What is it you really want from me?"

Drake hesitated, quickly reassessing the young woman. Was she really thinking she could strike a deal with him? Or was she just enjoying a heady moment in a game that went well beyond her abilities?

Either way, Drake knew that Skye Hammond had no idea what she was getting involved in, or with whom she was playing.

"I'm in the information business, Ms. Hammond," he smoothly reminded her, "and as you—as a reporter—know, information carries with it a certain power. Look what your little tabloid piece did in a matter of hours—it drew a religious cult out of the woodwork and caused a minor media frenzy. It involved an internationally known physicist employed by this college and put a spotlight on Barnet—the type of spotlight, I might add, the chancellor would rather do without."

As he had calculated, Skye's face flushed again in response to his comment. Really, manipulation was so pathetically easy, he reflected. Whereas he had applied blatant strokes to her ego with his earlier remarks, this time around, with hardly any effort at all, he had induced discomfiting feelings of guilt in the young woman.

"I never meant to cause anyone any trouble," she began to explain, but Lamont impatiently cut her off with a wave of his hand.

"I'm not asking for an apology, and I'm not even concerned right now with the irresponsibility you demonstrated in dragging Barnet into this."

He paused and gave her a stern look.

"I'm just illustrating how powerful information can be," he said, "depending on how it's communicated. Or not."

Skye winced, silently admitting to herself that he was right: she'd used very poor judgment in throwing the article together. It had been so early in the morning, and she'd been tired, wired, and foolish . . .

Lamont leaned close, his physical presence demanding her full attention.

"You asked me what I wanted from you, so I'm telling you. I want to be the most influential publisher on the face of the planet. I don't want people to have a single thought that I haven't planted there. But in order to do that, I need the best information possible, as quickly as possible. I need the information that shapes our world, that tells people what to think."

He sat back in his chair, and Skye felt him studying her as palpably as if he were touching her, taking measurements and evaluating her usefulness.

"You're a graduate student in English," he noted. "Have you run across the Grand Narratives yet?"

Skye had. One of her first reading assignments for Greta's class this fall had been a text on literary theory. In the 1970s, literary criticism had entered its post-structuralist phase, attacking Western concepts of identity, being, and truth as mere pawns for capitalism. The work of the critic Jean-Francois Lyotard, in particular, insisted that all thought and meaning was relative and narrational, or a 'story' about the social nature of the world, that was dependent on the agenda of the one telling the story. The Grand Narratives was the name that Lyotard gave to the changing 'stories' that dominated certain cultural eras.

The thing about reading Lyotard that Skye had especially disliked was the critic's negativity about the human spirit or the existence of any ultimate meaning to life. In support of his thesis, the critic had argued that the current Grand Narrative was 'post-modernity,' which blatantly rejected former narratives that perceived society's goal to be the liberation of humanity.

Instead, according to Lyotard, the goal of society was 'cybernetic performativity,' which reduced all human effort to a mindless participation in the smooth operation of a social order in which information was power. Even more disturbing in Lyotard's model, as far as Skye was concerned, was the implication that powerful corporations could virtually dictate what would be considered as real.

And anything they didn't want to be known simply didn't exist.

"So you're saying you agree with Lyotard?" she asked, unsure if she was understanding his point. "That by manipulating the information you give people, you can control what they think?"

"Absolutely," he said, apparently pleased with her conclusion, even as he noticed her beginning to frown in disbelief. "Come on, Ms. Hammond, isn't that what you do when you write an article? You tell someone what to think with every word you write. The pen is still mightier than the sword. The Bolshevik revolution in Russia didn't start with a gunshot, it started with ideas. The possibility of space travel fired the imagination of readers in 1865 when Jules Verne published his novel *From the Earth to the Moon;* it was only a century later when Neal Armstrong planted a flag on lunar soil. And I won't even bother to bore you with all the conflicts throughout history that have been spurred by religious beliefs. Like Lyotard would say, it's all a story and stories are made of information, plain and simple. The key is what you do with it, or what you make other people do with it. It's the way you put it together— you create the reality other people experience. That's the lure of our profession, isn't it? It's all about being 'in the know.'"

Reluctantly, Skye had to agree with much of what the man beside her was saying. Knowing things others didn't was, for her, some of the attraction she found in journalism. It was always a rush to think her writing had the potential to influence other people—it not only made her feel a little superior to others, but it made her feel important, too. Multiply that by a hundred times and maybe that's why Lamont was so passionate about what he did as the owner of such an influential magazine like the *World*. Okay, she could understand that.

But the part about creating other people's reality by manipulating information . . . she wasn't so sure about that, although, she had to admit, all she had to do to find support for that thesis was to turn on her television at night and witness the endless versions of 'reality' shows it featured, not to mention the defining perspectives supplied by evening news anchors.

As far as the media culture went, Skye certainly had to concede that Lamont had a very valid argument.

She might not like it, but she couldn't ignore it, either.

Placing his hand on the armrest of her chair, Drake swiveled her to face him directly.

"I think you've shown you're quite resourceful in taking a lead dropped in your lap by a drunken physicist and a certain careless science editor who works for me, and turning it right around into something that struck a powerful chord in a group of people," Drake told her. "Your instincts are good, and I can use instincts like those at the *World*. In fact, my magazine covets instincts like yours, reporters like you. And the *World* can be very, very good to its employees."

She followed the direction of his gaze, which had dropped to his hand on her chair, very near to her arm. His strong, well-shaped fingers traced a slow line along the edge of the armrest. A shiver ran up her spine. Maybe she was crazy, but she could swear she could almost feel him touching her.

"Think it over, Ms. Hammond," he softly said. "Call me."

Lamont abruptly stood up and walked to the glass door, then turned just inside the door back towards Skye.

"Oh—I do have one question," he added, almost as an afterthought. "Why, in the *Eye*, did you say that Dr. Carilion had completed his research and found heaven, when according to what Ms. Dauwalter told me, Dr. Scranton said they were only very close, but not finished?"

Looking again at those silver eyes, Skye felt a sharp jolt in her gut as the instincts that Lamont had just complimented started buzzing in her head.

This is what he wants.

Skye kept her face carefully controlled, silently acknowledging the inner voice that always seemed to sense the truth before she could even begin to process it. For some reason, the ambitious owner of a publishing empire wanted to know why she had pushed the envelope—no, had ripped out the whole side of it—of what she had overheard in a seedy bar into the realm of religious revelation for the supermarket checkout crowd.

Interesting.

No, more than interesting.

Skye suddenly realized that the invisible hand of poker she was playing with Drake Lamont wasn't yet over, and it was her turn to bid or fold. She could end the hand—and the game—by telling him the truth of her personal conclusions and convictions about the implications of String theory and Dr. Carilion's research, or she could try a bluff of her own, hoping he'd finally give something critical away.

"It was just a wild idea, Mr. Lamont," she casually replied, watching him closely for his reaction. "It's the kind of thing that sells, and it was about three in the morning, and I needed a sensational headline. Why is it important to you?"

He nonchalantly brushed some lint off his jacket lapel, then held the door open for her.

"Because, Ms. Hammond, I happen to have a very big stake in what Dr. Carilion is trying to accomplish here with his Strings Project. You see, I'm his major funding source. Anonymous funding source, that is, and I want it to stay that way, so I'm depending on your discretion."

He smiled his perfectly devastating smile at her.

"The fact is, sometimes donors—especially anonymous ones—are the last to know what's really happening with a research project, and I just wanted to be sure I hadn't been left out of the loop. You probably aren't aware of this, but I also happen to have a personal, academic interest in physics from my own graduate school days. I just wanted to know if, by chance, you knew something I didn't, and if that were the case, believe me, I'd make sure it didn't happen again."

He rested his hand lightly on her shoulder.

Another shiver ran up her spine, but this time, it wasn't seductive at all.

It made her unaccountably uneasy.

"Drake!"

Skye turned around and saw Chancellor Newsome standing in his private office doorway, beaming at Lamont.

"So glad you could make it over this morning," the chancellor told Lamont, moving forward and reaching out to shake the publisher's hand. "I can't wait to introduce our newest member to the Board. Trustee Lamont. How's that sound to you, Drake?"

Lamont's smile grew even wider.

"It sounds perfect, Stevenson. Just perfect."

CHAPTER TWENTY-FOUR

Michael slowly turned the corner onto Khristina's street and dreaded what he might find. After last night, he didn't think he had it in him to run a gamut of reporters and chanting cult members again this morning. If he saw anything suspicious, he was going to keep on driving and not even give Khristina the opportunity to open her door, let alone get out of the car.

To his relief, the street was quiet. Only a few vehicles were parked at the curb, a thick coating of white frost covering their windows and roofs. Smoke curled out of brick chimneys. A pack of elementary-aged school children waited for a bus at the end of a driveway, stamping their feet, gloved hands stuck deep in pockets. The only traces he could see of last night's debacle were some paper cups and cola cans strewn in the gutter in front of Khristina's home.

"They are all gone," Khristina said, happiness flooding into her voice.

Michael took a quick glance at Khristina's face and saw the relief there that mirrored his own. He drove the final half block to her house, where she directed him to pull into the narrow driveway that skirted the side of the property, ending beside a small brick patio off the back kitchen door. Before she could thank him for the ride home, however, he had already pulled his key from the ignition and stepped out of the car. Khristina opened her passenger door and met him on the patio outside the kitchen. He held out his hand for her house key.

"I just want to be sure there are no surprises inside for you before I go," he explained. "It'll just take a minute."

At least he was speaking to her again, Khristina thought.

After she'd stormed from the kitchen, she'd slammed into the bathroom and splashed cold water on her face to calm herself down. When she'd opened the door, he was standing in the front hall in his coat, holding hers for her. She'd grabbed her purse from the study and they'd driven here without exchanging another word. Once or twice along the way, she'd taken a quick look at his face, but he appeared to be totally focused on his driving, so she'd let the silence stand.

She picked out her house key on her key ring and handed it to him.

He opened the door and pulled the key out of the lock, then paused to examine the tin-backed wooden block that was attached to the key ring. He turned it over in his palm.

Painted onto the wood side of the small block in rich colors was the stylized face of a man with dark curls. The tip of a sword was beside his head, and Michael could make out medieval armor on the figure's shoulders. The portrait shimmered with a golden sheen in the bright morning light and Michael's attention was riveted on the man's features. There almost seemed to be a light shining through them. He turned the block back to its tin side and tapped the metal, then placed it picture-side up again in his palm.

"It is an icon," Khristina told him. "In my church, icons are very important. They are holy objects that teach us and inspire devotion, like little windows on our faith. This one came with me from my parents' home and is very small, so I attached my keys to it. This way, I never leave home without it."

She looked up at Michael with a rueful smile. "Like the commercial on the television. Except my faith is much more important than a credit card."

Michael continued to stare at the tiny icon, trying to remember why it looked vaguely familiar to him. After another minute, he gave up the effort and raised his head.

"It's St. Michael, isn't it?"

"Yes," Khristina confirmed.

He turned it over in his hand one last time, then handed the little block back to Khristina.

"I hope this isn't the picture you were referring to when you said I reminded you of a painting of St. Michael. This guy," he nodded at the icon in Khristina's hand, "doesn't look so good. Underfed. Anemic. I hope I look better than that."

"You look much better than that, Michael," Khristina breezily assured him, slipping her key ring back into her jeans pocket. "But the underfed part is true. Please, let me fix you some breakfast before you go. It is the least I can do to thank you for everything you have done for me in the last twenty-four hours."

She walked into the kitchen, tossing her coat onto a chair by the door.

Michael followed her in and stepped past her into the next room. He walked through each of the rooms in the little house, checking for broken windows or anything that might indicate someone had tried to break in. All he found was a pile of notes that had fallen through the old-fashioned mail slot in the lower half of Khristina's front door. He picked up the pile and brought it back with him to the kitchen, where Khristina already had bacon and eggs cooking in a skillet.

"The plates are in the cupboard beside the refrigerator," she told him, taking silverware out of a drawer by the range and laying it on the table. "And there is orange juice if you would like it."

The kitchen phone rang and she picked it up. "Hello?"

There was no reply.

"Hello?" she said again.

"Hang up, Khristina," Michael ordered, putting the plates on the table.

She replaced the phone in its stand and turned to see Michael running a hand through his dark hair.

"Someone is going to show up, now," he said. "They know you're home."

She forked out eggs and bacon on both plates.

"Then we should eat before they get here. Is that for me?" She pointed at the stack of notes.

Michael pushed the pile across the table to Khristina. She looked at him for a moment before he remembered.

She couldn't read.

He picked up the first note and read it out loud.

"'We are so happy to have found you. We don't mean to upset you. Please lead us, Khristina.'"

He took a bite of bacon and picked up another.

"'The Release is near!'"

He read a third.

"'Praise the Cosmos for sending us our Awaited One!'"

"I think I will have to explain to these people I am not who they think I am," Khristina said, finishing her eggs. "I will be sorry to disappoint them, but they will have to keep looking."

Michael leafed through four more notes while he ate, noting that they all repeated the sentiments of the first three. The eighth note, however, was different. As he read it, he could feel a chill spreading across his neck and he was glad that Khristina had left the table to rinse her plate, because he didn't want her seeing his reaction.

God destroys false prophets. Prepare for death.

He needed to call Teri Ostrand. And after he did that, there was no way on earth he was going to leave Khristina alone in this house.

CHAPTER TWENTY-FIVE

It had been a lousy weekend and Monday wasn't looking any better. Not only had she missed the dance recital of her seven-year-old daughter, Bethany, on Saturday evening, but she had spent a cold Sunday afternoon canvassing a crummy section of downtown, trying to find even the slightest lead to Lucas Scranton's murder. Then this morning, her car battery had almost given up the ghost, and her husband Jamie had had to leave for a two-day business trip. It was stretches like this that made her think she should have listened to her mother and become a dental hygienist instead of a police detective. If she had, all she'd be worrying about was whether or not the patient in the chair might bite her finger when she hit a sensitive spot, instead of worrying that someone might pull a gun on her and blast a hole in her head.

But since when had Teri Ostrand ever listened to her mother?

She downed a second cup of coffee and tapped the end of a pen on the edge of her desk, mentally sifting through what little she knew about the murder.

Late night, bad part of town, a visibly drunk victim—according to multiple witnesses, and one witness to the actual killing.

Other than that, nothing.

Except for the details that didn't make sense. It was definitely not a random mugging, since the assailant went straight for a kill. The witness, the magazine editor, said it happened and was over in a second—an unseen approach by the killer, she gets pushed out of the way—convenient for the witness, Teri thought—and a knife goes in and out. No roughing up the victims, no requests for possessions, and no sticking around after the fact. Scranton had absolutely been the target, no doubt about it. But why?

Preliminary background checks had already shown him clean—no drugs, no prior arrests, nothing. The only association that rang any bells for Teri was the name of Scranton's boss: Dr. Michael Carilion.

And all that did was remind her of failure.

Elise Carilion's murder case had been Teri's first one after her transfer into homicide from missing persons. After fifteen years of searching for runaways and abducted children, she'd needed a break, and she figured homicide in a quiet little college town would be an easy beat, giving her more time with Bethany and Jamie, her second husband. Her first marriage had been a casualty of her early career with the force, and she'd promised herself when she and Jamie married that she wouldn't make the same mistake again. For the two years she'd been in homicide before the Carilion case, Teri's biggest challenge at work had been coordinating the department's annual ice-fishing fund-raiser. The utter frustration she'd experienced working Elise's murder eight months ago, however, had more than made up for her two years of idleness.

To now have a second unexplained murder on her hands so soon after the first was just too weird, but try as she might, she couldn't find any connection between the two except Barnet College in general . . . and Michael Carilion in particular.

And that left a really bad taste in her mouth, because she'd spent a lot of time with the guy after his wife's death, and she'd not only come to respect him, but she genuinely liked the man, too. It had been hard on her to hear how badly he'd taken the aftermath of his wife's death—and especially the investigation's being relegated to unsolved limbo status—but Teri had also heard that the physicist had pulled himself back together again and had immersed himself in his research. She didn't even want to think about how this was going to affect him. If nothing else, it was sure to bring back a lot of bad memories.

And Teri fervently hoped that would be the extent of Michael's involvement.

But Teri was also very good at what she did, and because she was, she knew she'd have to consider the possibility that Michael was somehow a connecting link in the two deaths. Scranton's murder demanded that she turn over that rock—she just hoped that she didn't find anything but dirt underneath.

"Call for you, Detective Ostrand," the intercom on Teri's desk announced. "It's Dr. Carilion."

Speak of the devil, Teri groaned silently. She knew she had to speak with him sooner or later, but she'd been trying to delay it as long as possible. Obviously, her stalling tactic was over.

"Michael," she said when she picked up the phone. "I am so sorry about Dr. Scranton. We're doing everything we can."

"I know you are, Teri," he responded, "and I need to talk with you about that, too. But actually, the reason I'm calling right now is about something else. Who do I talk to about a death threat?"

Teri snapped upright in her seat.

"You've received a death threat?"

"No, I haven't, but a friend of mine has. Her name's Khristina Tupikova, and she got a threatening note from some religious extremist. I don't want her to be alone, so I've told her she's got to stay with me for now. What do we do?"

"This is about the cult thing, isn't it?" Teri asked, switching mental gears. "I didn't see it on television last night, but I've heard plenty about it this morning already down here at the station. If you've been threatened, or she has, I think both of you should come into the station and talk to Sam Kittleson. He's a good man, and he can walk you through our standard response and recommendations. I've got my hands full with Scranton's case, so I've got to pass you along to Sam. Sorry."

Teri jotted herself a note to talk with Sam as soon as she got off the phone with Michael.

"Did you say there was a note? Bring it with you."

She switched gears again. "Michael, I know this is a rough time for you, but I've got to come to your lab and look at Lucas's office—look around a little, talk to some of the other lab workers, try to find something, anything, to give us a lead. When's a good time?"

Michael paused. He didn't want to go into detail with Teri about his discussion with the chancellor, or make too much of the political reasons for the lab's temporary closure. He knew she could get a court order to sweep the lab if that's what it took, but he preferred not to have her go that route and he was sure the chancellor wouldn't relish it either.

"We could meet there tomorrow morning," he decided. The chancellor would just have to deal with it. "The lab's locked down today, and no one's in. I can get you a list of lab personnel then, too."

Teri agreed and they set a time. Before he ended the call, though, Michael had one more question.

"Look, Teri, I know you can't really talk with me about an open investigation, but could you confirm one thing for me?" He rushed on, not giving her a chance to refuse. "Was Lucas alone when he was killed?"

The other end of the phone line went quiet. Michael could picture Teri in her office, debating what she could share with him. He knew from his own experience with police procedure that she wasn't at liberty to give him all the details of what she already knew about Lucas's death. At the same time, he reasoned that if Lucas had been killed outside a busy bar, there had to be at least a handful of witnesses who had eagerly supplied information and then gone on to tell everyone they knew about what they had seen of Lucas on Friday night. In a small town, confidentiality didn't last long when sensational news was afoot.

Michael heard Teri's sigh in his ear.

"No, Michael, he wasn't alone."

"He was with a Skye G. Hammond, wasn't he?" Michael's voice went flat.

Teri looked at the phone in her hand and wondered if she'd heard Michael correctly.

Who was Skye G. Hammond, and why did Michael think that was who had accompanied Lucas on Friday night?

Teri had spent a good two hours in the hospital emergency room early Saturday morning, talking with Dauwalter, the woman who had not only accompanied Lucas at the bar, but had witnessed his murder, so why Michael had another name didn't make any sense at all. Especially since Dauwalter had indicated to Teri that she knew Michael and would be speaking with him.

"No, he wasn't," she replied. "He was with a Phoebe Dauwalter. She's the science editor at the *World* magazine. She wasn't harmed. She hasn't talked with you yet? She told me she was going to."

For a beat or two, the phone line was silent.

"Michael? Are you there?"

"Yes," he answered. "Thanks, Teri. Thanks for everything."

Teri replaced the phone in its cradle and tried to identify what she'd just heard in Michael's voice. It had been different from his tone in the rest of their conversation, but she wasn't sure exactly how to describe it.

He had sounded surprised, or confused.

But then it had sounded more like restraint or control.

A vivid memory flashed in her head—a memory of Michael Carilion losing his patience and verbally lashing out at badgering reporters on the steps of the police station. Abrupt and powerful, Michael's anger had played well with the members of the press in their portrayal of the husband seeking justice.

Personally, though, Teri had been glad she wasn't on the receiving end of Michael's temper.

So now she had to wonder: why was Phoebe Dauwalter there?

CHAPTER TWENTY-SIX

"This would be nice in your front room, Michael," Khristina said, brushing her hand over the carpet sample in the Floor Store. "It has warm tones and a nice, thick feel. It would be very good in winter, I think."

Michael swore to himself that he would never be able to figure out Khristina Tupikova. She'd been manhandled by strangers on her front lawn, forced away from her home, routinely yelled at by himself, targeted with a death threat, and still the woman acted like she didn't have anything more pressing to concern herself with than helping him select new carpet for his living room.

Michael, on the other hand, was still steaming from learning that it was the *World's* science writer, Dauwalter, and not the tabloid reporter Skye Hammond, who had been with Lucas when he was killed. Watching Khristina taking her time to thoroughly examine the samples, he decided that whatever his Russian companion was taking to keep calm, he wanted some, too.

"I don't know how you can do this," he said through clenched teeth, watching her finger the carpet.

"You don't like it? Then you should look at others. It's your room."

"No," he protested, closing his eyes in exasperation. "I'm not talking about the carpet, Khristina. I'm talking about you. How do you hold up with everything that's going on? Your life is a disaster right now, but here you are, comparing carpets. I don't get it. What's more, you haven't blamed me once for any of this, when it's my research that has landed you in this mess."

Khristina picked up the sample and handed it to Michael.

"Everything will be all right. I know this. You should see if they can lay your new carpet today."

"How do you know this?" Michael practically hissed at her. "Are your ghosts telling you?"

If Khristina felt any surge of anger at his remark, he certainly couldn't tell from her continued cool scrutiny of the carpet selections. She ran her hand over a new square of tight weave and sighed.

"They are not ghosts, Michael," she replied. "And see, I am not even getting upset with you for calling them that. But at least you are starting to acknowledge them as individuals, and not packets, so I think I should be happy."

Michael opened his mouth to refute her, but she placed her slim fingers on his lips. He was so startled by the intimacy of the gesture, he lost his train of thought.

"You want to know why I am not a wreck?" she asked, holding his gaze. "I am calm because I have faith, Michael. 'Do not worry about your life,' Jesus says in Matthew's Gospel. He promises to care for me. I believe in his promises. How can I not? Every time I receive a visitor, I have proof that God keeps his promises, Michael—eternal life is real. And what is even more comforting is that I have so many of them—my visitors. They are the saints, Michael. Strings of witnesses. Many, many strings of witnesses."

She gently lifted her fingers from his mouth.

"And you have proof now, too, no matter what you call it. You found your eleventh dimension, Michael. That is a scientific fact—a fact that is not altered if I simply give it another name."

"But your name for it implies other things," he argued. "Things I don't accept."

"Because they are not scientific? Because they come from a language of faith, and not a language of mathematical formulas?" Khristina smiled. "'There are more things in heaven and earth, Horatio, than are dreamt of in your philosophy.'"

In spite of himself, Michael returned her smile.

"That's from *Hamlet*. Tell me, do you have a quote for every occasion?"

He tucked the carpet sample under one arm and grasped her elbow, directing her towards the cashier.

"Let's get out of here. I've got a very important date, and I don't want to be late."

He flashed her a grin. "That's from Walt Disney's *Alice in Wonderland*—sort of."

Actually, that was how he was beginning to feel about this whole thing. Ever since he'd completed the equations for the eleventh dimension and proven string theory, it was like he'd been tumbling down an endless rabbit hole. A brick had come through his window, his best friend and colleague had been murdered, his life work had been maligned by a tabloid, he was persona non grata at the college, he'd slugged a total stranger in front of cameras, and now he was buying carpet with a psychic.

So far, no one had offered him a pill marked "Eat me," but at this point, he wouldn't have been completely surprised if someone did. Despite his smoldering anger at Phoebe Dauwalter, he was anxious to meet with her, hoping her answers to his questions would bring the crazy freefall to an end, because he was starting to feel like nothing was what it seemed, and more than anything, he desperately needed to feel solid ground beneath his feet again.

CHAPTER TWENTY-SEVEN

At ten o'clock, Michael was sitting on a ladder-back chair at a small table in the back of Corner Coffee, watching the front door.

He blew on the hot double-shot espresso in his mug, wondering what excuse Phoebe Dauwalter would offer for not telling him on the phone last night that she had been with Lucas when he was killed. The editor had said she wanted to help Michael preserve the integrity of the Strings Project in the face of the tabloid mess, but if she was going to pitch integrity, she'd better have a better-than-good reason for throwing him a curveball of dishonesty last night.

His cell phone rang in his pocket and he dug it out, thinking it might be Khristina asking for instructions about the carpet replacement. Unbelievably, the Floor Store service scheduler had had a cancellation first thing this morning and sent a crew home with Michael and Khristina. Confident that she would be safe in his home surrounded by a carpet crew, Michael had left Khristina to manage the work while he kept his appointment with Dauwalter.

"Yes?" he answered the phone.

"Dr. Carilion?" an unfamiliar woman's voice asked. "This is Skye Hammond, returning your call."

At the same moment, Phoebe Dauwalter walked into the coffee shop. Michael recognized her from the photo that accompanied her magazine column in each issue.

"You've caught me at a bad time, Ms. Hammond. Can I call you back?"

"Yes," she answered. "But please use this number instead. I'll be available the rest of the day."

She gave him the number and Michael ended the call, just as Phoebe recognized him and started towards his table.

"Dr. Carilion," she said, extending her hand. "I'm Phoebe Dauwalter."

Michael shook hands, noting both self-assurance and a certain feminine swagger in her bearing. Phoebe sat down in the chair opposite to his own, her knees almost colliding with his underneath the small table.

"Thank you for seeing me," she said, leaning slightly forward, her green eyes intense on his face.

Michael wasn't interested in any pleasantries.

"Why didn't you tell me last night that you were with Lucas when he was murdered?"

Phoebe barely flinched.

"I didn't think it was the kind of thing you told someone over the phone," she answered. "I'm deeply, deeply sorry, Dr. Carilion, for your loss. I got the distinct impression that you and Lucas were very close."

"Really? And where did you get that impression, Ms. Dauwalter?"

"Phoebe, please."

Michael only glared at her.

She sat back in her chair.

"Dr. Carilion, I was with Dr. Scranton when he was attacked and knifed. I held him while he bled. I followed him to the hospital in a squad car. I will never forget it as long as I live. And I'm the reason he was in that particular place at that particular time, so I am taking a personal blame for his death. Does that make you happy?"

Michael blinked and took a drink of his coffee.

"No, it does not make me happy, Ms. Dauwalter."

He took another sip and his tone softened. "I apologize. I am sure you must be suffering tremendously. Thank you for your condolences."

Phoebe leaned forward again. "I need to tell you why Dr. Scranton was there, and why I called you last night. Will you listen?"

Michael hesitated, then nodded.

For the next thirty minutes, Phoebe reviewed with Michael the notes she had taken during her interview with Lucas, impressing him with her understanding of both the possibilities and problems in string theory as well as her grasp of some of the finer points of M theory, the promising version of string theory that Michael had first heard from Ed Witten at the USC convention in '95. When she mentioned spatial fabric and wormholes, he felt like he was coming home after a long, exhausting trip, and the opportunity to focus once more on the familiar, intricate details of his daily research was like taking a satisfying drink from a clean stream of water after spending a day in what he considered to be the murky chaos of Khristina's decidedly non-scientific alternate universe.

The fact, Michael realized, was that he liked his world in the laboratory just the way it was—grounded in empirical data and mathematical formulas. Having that world challenged by a medium, of all people, had been more of a strain than he wanted to acknowledge.

Here, with Phoebe, though, he was back in his element, and he reproached himself for letting Khristina's crazy perspective rattle him. The work he was doing was worlds away from the superstitions and ignorance that brought clients to a medium's door. Khristina insisted that they were just using different names for the same thing, but after hearing Phoebe translate his work into the language of the reading public, Michael was convinced more than ever that the difference was much bigger than language.

A lot bigger, because ultimately, it was about the nature of reality—a reality that was explainable and understandable, not one that was shrouded in mystical visions.

And what handy quote had Khristina pulled out about that?

There are more things in heaven and earth, Horatio, than are dreamt of in your philosophy.

Michael was suddenly aware that Phoebe had finished talking and was looking at him expectantly.

"Do I have it right?" she asked.

He nodded again, banishing Khristina from his mind and wondering what Phoebe's next move would be. The *World's* science editor certainly hadn't asked to meet with him just to repeat what she knew about string theory. He watched while she carefully folded her notes and slipped them back into her purse. Then she crossed her arms on the table and leaned forward.

"Dr. Carilion," she began. "Your work is, simply, mind-blowing. I've been keeping tabs on research around the world on string theory. I've spoken with physicists at Fermilab in Illinois and with people in the lab at CERN in Europe. Even with their giant atom smashers, they have yet to capture a graviton, which would be evidence of the extra dimensions predicted by string theory. But you've sidestepped them all with your medium experiments. You've taken a completely different approach to the problem, and now you're closing in on the One Theory."

Phoebe stopped talking for a moment, suddenly aware that her voice was rising with excitement.

She glanced around the coffee shop, afraid that her enthusiasm might draw unwanted attention, but only a few customers wrapped in jackets and woolen hats sat huddled over coffee. After the blow of Lucas's death and her resulting panic at the thought that this once-in-a-lifetime opportunity might slip away from her, she was determined that no one else would get near it.

At least not until she had her exclusive.

Satisfied that she had not attracted any interest from the other patrons, she returned her gaze to Michael. "Dr. Scranton thought you were a genius, Dr. Carilion," Phoebe confided. "He convinced me of the same. What I want to offer you are my science journalism skills. When you find conclusive evidence of this theory, I want to be the writer that explains it in layman's terminology so that every person on the face of the planet understands what you've done and what it means for how we understand our world—how we think of life itself!"

She quickly scanned the coffee shop one more time to be sure no one was listening in. As horrible as it had been, Friday night had taught her a lesson she was not going to forget any time soon—the reporter who assumed privacy in a public place was the reporter who's going to get scooped. She'd almost cried when Carilion had insisted she meet him at a coffee shop instead of in the security of his office at the university, but she knew she didn't have a choice. If she wanted to talk with him, she'd have to do it on his terms.

She resumed her pitch to the physicist.

"I have the credentials to do it, Dr. Carilion," Phoebe bluntly informed him. "I've been following string research for years, and I've written award-winning science pieces for the last three years in a row. I've consulted on educational science programs and helped edit the most recent physics-related books for the general reading public. When your journal article comes out announcing your discovery, I want to be publishing the definitive piece about it in the *World*, so that everyone gets the story straight, and you don't have to go through another misinformation nightmare like the one that's happening right now."

She leaned a little closer to him over the table.

"So what do you say?"

Michael studied the intense green eyes of the woman who seemed so jazzed with adrenaline that he could almost feel electricity sparking around her. He didn't doubt her sincerity, because it was plain that she wanted the story. He was also confident, judging from the knowledge she had just demonstrated about the field of theoretical physics, that she was intelligent and about as well versed in string theory as he could hope for in a magazine reporter. And she'd certainly hit the right nerve in him just now when she held out the prospect of avoiding another media disaster at the expense of his One Theory of Everything.

Maybe Lucas had had the right idea, after all, he grudgingly admitted to himself. A good, clean exposition of the Strings Project could only move the work forward.

If only Lucas's idea hadn't cost him his life . . .

With a disciplined effort, Michael pushed the beckoning grief aside and focused again on Phoebe. After what he'd been through since waking up on Sunday morning, he could really use someone in his corner right now, he decided.

Someone who spoke his language.

"What do you need from me?"

It took only a moment for his implied consent to completely register with Phoebe, and then her face lit up like a bank of floodlights. Words started to tumble from her mouth.

"I'd like to see your lab. The Kirlian photographs. Anything. Everything. Notes. Graphs. Formulas. I . . . everything."

With a deep feeling of gratification, Michael watched the woman's excitement grow. She was almost incoherent, barely able to string two words together. For the first time since he'd written those equations in the lab on Friday night, he truly felt the elation of his accomplishment. From Theo, he'd gotten the professional validation. From Khristina, he'd felt the weight of what he'd done. But from Phoebe, he got a dose of pure exhilaration.

"How much time do you need to write the piece?" Michael asked, trying to estimate when the journal article would appear in *Physica*.

Then it hit him like a hammer: Phoebe Dauwalter had no idea that he had solved the equations. How could she? When she'd spoken with Lucas, it had been late Friday night, and Michael had been locked into the lab, making his leap of discovery alone.

Phoebe was still operating under the assumption that the success of the Strings Project was imminent, not already accomplished.

"Why?" she asked. "Is time an issue?"

"Actually it is," Michael told her. "The equations are finished. My journal article is already in the hands of the editor of *Physica*."

Michael watched Phoebe's mouth drop open in shock as she realized what he was telling her.

Across the room, a woman surreptitiously aimed a small camera at Michael and Phoebe and clicked off a few photographs. She wasn't worried that they'd catch her at it, since the two of them seemed oblivious to the rest of the world, grinning at each other like a couple of starry-eyed lovers. For a second or two, it miffed the woman that she could be so invisible—she despised being overlooked even more than she hated being ignored. Then again, with her trademark blonde mane tucked up inside a wool cap and no mike in her hand, not even her most loyal fans would recognize her.

She took a final shot of her subjects, their heads close together over the small table, and walked out the door.

CHAPTER TWENTY-EIGHT

The dirty white van rolled slowly past the house for the second time.

Set near the end of the street, the house looked a lot like the others in the college neighborhood—a neat, traditional one-story with trimmed bushes framing the front walkway to the house door. At the curb, a Floor Store truck was parked while two men wrestled a long roll of carpet out of its back compartment.

The professor was getting new carpet.

The van driver wondered if it had to do with the damage he'd caused yesterday when he'd lobbed the brick through the big front window. He hoped it did. On his first pass by the house five minutes ago, he'd been surprised to see the window already replaced; he'd intended the broken window to be a warning and not just an inconvenient house repair. Now he would have to think of a bigger way to send God's call for repentance to this son of evil.

Then he saw the woman step out the front door and say something to the workmen.

He sharpened his gaze on her face.

It was her.

Last night, after watching the television report, he'd immediately driven over to the site of the demonstration, hoping to exhort all the misled sinners on her lawn to repent and hear the true message of salvation. But by the time he arrived, almost everyone had left. He waited till the last man and woman slipped a note into the front door of the house, then left a note of his own, promising the woman she had a one-way ticket to hell, and he planned to punch it for her.

Now she was here, with the professor.

They were in league with the devil together, and it was his responsibility to purge the earth of their kind.

The work of a prophet is never done, the driver thought, and slowly drove away.

CHAPTER TWENTY-NINE

Mara Runyon practically glided over the thick carpet in the plush executive office suite. She was waved right into the owner's private office by the secretary, an efficient young man with the personality of a palm pilot. Closing the door behind her, she tossed her hat on the armchair in front of the massive cherry desk and slid an envelope of freshly printed photos across its polished surface.

The owner of the *World* carefully examined the pictures and then rewarded Mara with a satisfied smile.

"Just what The Gentleman ordered," Drake Lamont said approvingly.

"What have you got going on, Drake?"

Mara dropped into the leather armchair and shook her head, her long hair straightening itself down her back. "Why am I spying on your science editor? Is she cheating on you?"

"Yes," he answered her, "as a matter of fact, she is, after a fashion."

"Then she's a fool," Mara said. "I mean, the man is gorgeous, without a doubt, but he can't hold a candle to you."

Drake laughed, throwing his head back, his laughter filling the elegant paneled room.

"What's so funny?"

"You, darling," Drake told her. "Your transparency tickles me. You're jealous of Phoebe, you hate Carilion, and yet you're also jealous of Phoebe spending time with the man. If I didn't know better, I'd say you want Carilion for yourself."

"But you do know better. Much better. You're the only man I want, Drake."

"Yes, I do know. And I intend to give you exactly what you're asking for, Mara. But right now, I need you to run a little errand for me."

He took a large brown envelope out of the top desk drawer and slid two of Mara's photos inside. He sealed it shut and held it out to her.

She took the envelope, surprised at its weight.

"What else is in here?"

"Information, darling. Information that is going to ruin the gorgeous man you love to hate."

She turned the envelope over to read the front address and glanced up at Drake.

"I take it you want me to drop this off anonymously?"

Drake nodded and Mara smiled.

"You are so evil, Drake Lamont," she told him. "And when I grow up, I want to be just like you."

"I'm counting on it," Drake told her.

Mara stood up and grabbed her hat. Drake's intercom buzzed and he spoke briefly with his secretary.

"Phoebe's here. You need to run along."

She blew him a kiss as she opened the heavy door. "Later, Mr. Lamont."

Outside the office, she saw Phoebe studying a sheaf of notes in her hand.

"Hello, Phoebe," she said, her voice dripping with false camaraderie. "Having a good day?"

Phoebe barely acknowledged the other woman with a tip of her head.

In her opinion, the Channel 9 reporter was a caricature of all the bad qualities a critical public was eager to ascribe to a female journalist—she flaunted her sexuality, specialized in sensational pseudo-news coverage, was irresponsible in investigating her stories, and unprofessional in hounding sources.

Yet if Phoebe were totally honest with herself, all that paled in comparison to the real reason she hated the flashy reporter: Mara Runyon had made no secret of the fact that she wanted to be Mrs. Drake Lamont.

Granted, Phoebe herself had no desire to marry The Gentleman—she had too many aspirations that reached beyond Litchfield, Wisconsin, to tie herself to any man, even if that man was as powerful and influential as the owner of the *World*. What really rankled her about Runyon, she had to admit to herself, wasn't even Runyon herself, but Drake's response to her. At media events, he seemed to delight in the reporter's abrasive and loud behavior, while at social functions, he flirted shamelessly with her even when Phoebe was standing beside him. The idea that he could be attracted to the woman at all galled Phoebe, but to think that Runyon could turn his head while Drake was conducting an affair with Phoebe was downright insulting. The blonde was a manipulative fake, as far as Phoebe was concerned, and if Drake was going to sink that low, she wasn't going to stand around and watch.

All the more reason to convince her boss that Carilion was the real thing and that the *World* had to have the exclusive—because bylining the science scoop of the century was going to be her express train out of Litchfield and on to much bigger, and more famous, horizons.

Not to mention that Pulitzer with her name on it.

But first she had to get The Gentleman's green light, even though he'd already told her to drop it.

She walked into Drake's office, her annoyance with Runyon's presence already forgotten, and confidently hiked her hip up onto the edge of the big cherry desk.

"Have I got the deal for you," she told Drake. "In fact, it's the story of the century."

Drake sighed in affected boredom and sat back into his deep red leather wingchair.

"Phoebe, if this is about the One Theory of Everything again, I am going to make an appointment for you to see a psychiatrist. We already went over this. There is no eleventh dimension, thus, no story. Can we get back to real work now?"

Phoebe leaned towards him, her fingers splayed against the desk surface to support herself. Her voice trembled with excitement.

"Ah, but there is a story, Mr. Lamont. It just so happens that there is an eleventh dimension, and that Dr. Michael Carilion has, indeed, found it."

Drake went still in his chair, his silver eyes riveted on Phoebe's green ones.

"Say that again," he whispered, barely breathing.

"Dr. Michael Carilion has solved the mystery of the universe," Phoebe announced giddily. "He has the formulations and the evidence to prove string theory. The man has achieved unification."

"You mean he's found heaven," Drake murmured.

Phoebe laughed, delight shining in her eyes.

"Not heaven, Drake! This is the real thing, not a wacko tabloid headline! Carilion's proven string theory! He's got the mathematical models, all the equations, even photos. Scranton was right—the man is a genius. And we can have the exclusive, Drake!"

Phoebe searched Drake's face for signs of an excitement to match her own, but all she found was his blank expression and eyes suddenly emptied.

Why wasn't he jumping for joy with her? The biggest story of the century—of all time!—and he was acting like he'd just learned that his entire publishing empire had been decimated.

"Drake!" Phoebe reached out and shook his slack arm. "What is wrong with you?"

She watched his eyes track down to her hand on his arm, then back up to settle an icy gaze on her face that instantly chilled Phoebe with an awful sense of foreboding.

Startled at the change in him, Phoebe withdrew her hand and straightened up on his desk.

"What?"

He cocked his head and his eyes seemed to wander over her body. When he spoke, his tone was hard.

"Phoebe, I thought I had taught you better than this. Didn't I tell you to give this story up?"

"Yes, but—"

"And you deliberately disobeyed me and contacted Carilion against my wishes?"

"Yes, but –"

"No buts!" he thundered at her. "Have you seen this evidence of his? Have you seen the photos? What do you take me for—a fool?"

Phoebe was lost in his outburst, unable to comprehend why she was being so viciously attacked. Yes, she'd pursued the story he'd tossed away, but her instincts—her excellent instincts—had refused to let her do otherwise.

And she'd brought it back to him, hot and smoking and on fire.

"No, I haven't seen it!" she yelled back at him. "I'm going to his lab tomorrow! And in the meantime, he's already sent the journal article to *Physica*! It's in the mill, Drake. This is already happening!"

Drake was silent again, but this time, only for a heartbeat. Then, without warning, he rose up from his chair and rounded the desk to stand in front of Phoebe. Not sure what to expect, she watched him guardedly, wondering for the first time in her life if she was about to be physically struck.

Instead, to her complete surprise, Drake gently placed his hands on her shoulders and looked down into her face. His voice was filled with warmth and concern and firm resolution.

"Phoebe, I only want what is best for you and this magazine. You can't blame me for wanting to safeguard my life work and my most . . . esteemed . . . and valuable . . . employee. Until I see this evidence, I am reluctant to put any faith in Carilion, even if he says he has completed the work. We both know the man is under great duress right now, judging from last night's news reports, and I have to admit, his credibility seems to have been compromised."

Thanks to Runyon, Phoebe thought. She opened her mouth to object, but Drake shook his head, silencing her.

"We're going to sit on this overnight. Go to the lab tomorrow, see the data, see what you think. I trust your judgment. If you still think this is the real thing, then we'll take it from there."

He slid his thumb delicately along the line of her jaw.

"My thought is only for you, Phoebe. I'm not about to let all the work we've done together making the *World* what it is today come crashing down because of a charlatan's magic trick of physics."

He leaned in to kiss her.

"You deserve so much more than that."

And I'm going to get it, Phoebe thought angrily, her temper still flaring. Whether Drake Lamont wanted this story or not, she was going to break it.

And if that meant she would also have to walk away from The Gentleman and even the *World* itself, she would. Drake Lamont didn't own her, even if he thought he did, she reminded herself. She had talent, a spectacular resume, plenty of writing awards, lots of contacts in the business. Yes, he'd given her the first step up the ladder when he hired her, but she'd come a long way since then, and she wasn't about to roll over and play dead just because he said so. Besides all that, she had the exclusive on the One Theory, the Holy Grail of physics.

If Drake didn't want a piece of that, then too bad.

She had no doubt she could find a home for it—and herself—somewhere else. In fact, leaving Litchfield and everything in it was looking better by the minute.

"You're going to change your mind, Drake," she told him, slipping off his desk and heading for the door. "Mark my words. After tomorrow, you're going to be one of Carilion's biggest fans. So give yourself a head start and start working on the apology you're going to owe me. *Darling.*'

Drake sat silently in his big wingchair, waiting to hear the muffled sound of Phoebe's departure from his suite of offices. When he heard the outer office door close, he pulled out his cell phone, looked up a number in his phone book, and dialed. When the man answered, Drake briefly introduced himself, then proceeded to explain the reason for his call.

"So you see, in light of this most unfortunate and distressing publicity for Dr. Carilion, I have real reason to question the wisdom of publishing any of his work at this point in time. I know I have relied solely on your discretion since my publishing company assumed the operational reins of the journal six months ago, but in all good conscience, I feel I have to intervene for the sake of the journal's professional reputation. Therefore, as of today, Dr. LeMay, I'm suspending publication indefinitely. I'm sure you understand."

CHAPTER THIRTY

Skye double-checked the house number that Dr. Carilion had given her on the phone just a few minutes ago, then pulled over to the curb behind a Floor Store truck.

When he'd finally called her back, she was just leaving campus, so it was only a short drive to his home. He'd said there might still be workmen and that if she arrived before him, she should just go on in, since Khristina Tupikova was there as well. Skye owed Khristina an apology, Dr. Carilion had said, so she had better have one prepared by the time she got there.

Skye resented his tone, but she couldn't deny that she'd majorly screwed up by including Khristina's name in her article. As a rule, she didn't use real names in the *Eye*, but 'Khristina Tupikova' had such a great ring to it, she'd broken her own rule, never dreaming it would bring trouble down on the actual person. She'd explain all that to Ms. Tupikova, of course, but even now, in her own mind, it sounded more than lame. Luckily, she didn't have Dr. Carilion for any of her grad courses. If she had, she was sure she would have been looking at a string of fat 'Fs' on her final grade transcript, judging from how angry he'd sounded on the phone.

Of course, now that she had a job offer from Drake Lamont, she could chuck the whole graduate school routine and take up residence in a cozy office at the *World*. He hadn't jumped down her throat with recriminations or accusations like Dr. Carilion had.

On the contrary, he was so busy flattering her and feeding her lines that the man must have been exhausted by the time he went to talk with the chancellor. He'd said he recognized her journalistic skills and superior instincts and wanted her on staff.

At the time, she'd thought he was bluffing.

Now, thinking it over, she was sure of it.

So what did he want from her?

Apparently, only one thing, from what Skye could determine, and that was information. Lamont had wanted to know if Dr. Carilion had actually completed his research. And then he basically warned her to stay out of the way.

The way of what?

Skye suddenly remembered something else odd about her conversation with Lamont.

She'd expected him to ridicule the conclusion she'd reached based on the scanty information she'd overheard from Phoebe Dauwalter and the drunk guy, but instead, Lamont had kept praising her instincts.

Did that mean he didn't disagree with her thesis, that he thought her connection of heaven with the eleventh dimension was somehow scientifically valid? He was, after all, well educated in both physics and theology, and her own leap of intuition had sent a wild tingle thrilling through her as she had dug deeper and deeper into websites in both of those disciplines. Though she had no training in either field, she'd been repeatedly struck by the parallels between the material she found on the sites—sometimes even the same phrases popped up, like "the New Universe Story," or "holons" or "the process of evolution." If Lamont were familiar with all that material himself, and he did, indeed, find merit in her conclusion, then perhaps she had unknowingly stumbled upon something a lot bigger than a fairy tale headline for a tabloid feature.

Maybe, just maybe, her headline hadn't been that farfetched after all, but instead, had hit the proverbial nail right on the head: Dr. Carilion's research was, ultimately, going to prove the existence of heaven.

Or at least, that's what Drake Lamont thought.

And feared, her instincts told her.

"Feared?" she said aloud. Usually her instincts were right on, but this was going over the top, she decided.

No way was Drake Lamont afraid of a little feel-good, light-hearted, wishful thinking.

"Time for reality check, Ms. Hammond," she told herself. "And right now, reality says 'get out of the car and face the music' for recklessly indulging in that same wishful thinking."

Sighing in resignation, Skye shut her car door and walked up to Dr. Carilion's front entryway. The house door was wide open and two workmen were collecting their tools, tossing scraps of carpet in a heap on the front step. Skye edged around the pile and looked into the living room.

"Ms. Tupikova?" she called out. "Dr. Carilion said I should walk right in."

A tall blonde popped out of the kitchen and came to greet her.

"I'm Khristina," she said, holding her hand out to Skye.

Surprised, Skye shook Khristina's hand.

"I'm Skye Hammond," she explained. "I work for the *Eye.*" Then, because she couldn't help herself, she added, "You're not what I imagined."

Khristina laughed. "I am beginning to think I am not what anyone imagines. Let me guess—you expected me to be about ninety years old, four feet tall, and holding a crystal ball."

Skye's cheeks flushed pink in embarrassment.

"Two out of three," she conceded. "I hadn't thought about a crystal ball."

"Come have some tea," Khristina said, leading her back into the kitchen and indicating a high stool tucked under the breakfast bar. "I would like to hear how I got promoted from being a medium to being a messiah."

Skye sat on the stool and related her Friday night encounter to Khristina while tea bags steeped in the coffee mugs Khristina had found in the cupboard. When she got to the part about writing her story, she apologized profusely for using Khristina's actual name.

"I had no idea you were in town," she pointed out. "I checked the Internet and there were no hits for your name, so I assumed you were long gone back to some mountain village in Russia. My mistake, but you know what they say about assuming."

Khristina gave Skye a questioning look.

"No, I do not know. What do they say about assuming?"

"It makes an ass out of you and me."

"In what way?"

"It's a joke," Skye explained. "You look at the word 'assume' and it breaks down to 'ass' and the letter 'u' and the word 'me.'"

Skye waited a beat, but Khristina still didn't seem to get it.

"I'm sorry, I cannot read," Khristina told her. "I guess I cannot get the joke."

"You can't read?" Skye blurted out, then immediately flushed in embarrassment again.

"I'm sorry," she quickly added. "That was rude."

"It's all right," Khristina assured her. "It does not embarrass me. I have compensated for it in many ways."

Skye eyed Khristina over the rim of her cup. "Is being a medium one of them?"

Khristina took a sip of the hot brew and sighed. "It is a bit more complicated than that, I think, although I cannot really explain the connection, if there really even is one. All I can tell you is that I have many wonderful friends who help me with things I do not know or understand and who have spent many hours reading to me, and because of this, I am well educated. But it makes some things awkward for me, because sometimes, there is no one around me to read when I need it."

A weird tingling sensation crawled up Skye's spine as a flash of understanding hit her.

"These friends," she said slowly, "they're not . . . here . . . are they?"

Khristina looked around the room. "No, not right now," she answered, matter-of-factly. "Generally, the air moves a special way when they come through, but sometimes, they sneak up on me and are whispering in my ear before I even know it. It can be a little surprising sometimes."

Skye convulsively swallowed a big gulp of tea.

'Surprising' wasn't the word she would have chosen.

More like 'totally freaky.'

Yet it was clear to her that for Khristina, life with spiritual companions was nothing out of the ordinary.

If she thought back a minute to her own childhood, though, Skye had to admit that the basic concept wasn't novel at all. In Sunday school classes at the church where she'd been raised, there were always lessons about guardian angels and the good people in heaven, and even now, as an adult, she sometimes carried on conversations in her head with those she had known before their passing.

But that was a far cry from believing, as Khristina apparently did, that people who had died were not only present to her, but actually communicating with her as well.

People who said they talked with the dead were usually mentally unstable, in Skye's experience as a reporter for the *Eye*. True, their tales might make for good copy, but if she had to testify to the mental soundness of most of her sources, she'd definitely plead 'no contest.'

But Khristina was different.

Compared to Skye's typical sources, Khristina's body language was all wrong. Instead of nervousness or insecurity, Khristina exuded calm and confidence. She wasn't desperate to convince Skye of anything and seemed totally uninterested in whether Skye believed her or not. Rather than sending out signals of imbalance and anger, Khristina was radiating peace, Skye realized with a start. But how was that possible, when Skye was absolutely the one to blame for disrupting Khristina's life with a trashy tabloid article that had brought the media and some kind of religious cult down on her head?

If anyone had the right to be angry, it was Khristina Tupikova.

"I don't get it," Skye finally said in exasperation. "You're the second person today who I figured was going to chew my tail, but hasn't. What is going on around here? Why isn't everyone beating up on the stupid reporter who let the cat out of the bag about the Strings Project and then mangled it in the *Eye*? I steal the *World's* thunder and get a job offer. I throw you to the wolves, and you make me a cup of tea."

Skye shook her head. "This is just not making any sense."

"You sound like Michael," Khristina said. "To him, nothing is real that does not make sense. This is not a good perspective, Ms. Hammond. It limits your imagination. It limits your experience. It limits what you can think of as possible. Why limit any of those things? 'No bird soars too high if he soars with his own wings.'"

Skye immediately recognized the quote and couldn't resist adding one of her own. "But," she responded, "'a fool sees not the same tree that a wise man sees.' That's also William Blake. I should know—I'm writing my thesis on him."

She took another sip of the soothing tea.

"And please, call me Skye."

Khristina smiled, and Skye thoughtfully considered her.

"So, if we're both seeing the same tree, Khristina, which of us is the fool and which of us is the wise man?"

Khristina lowered her cup to the counter. "As long as we're seeing the same tree, does it really matter?"

CHAPTER THIRTY-ONE

Michael stalked down the corridor to the chancellor's office. Although he really wanted to wring Stevenson's neck for bowing to pressure from the trustees to close the lab for public relations reasons, he knew that manhandling the chancellor wouldn't win him any points in the long run of getting more research proposals funded. And now, with his work on the Strings Project completed, he could already envision at least four new research projects to pursue promising fields of inquiry into the physics of the eleventh dimension. As a hardened veteran of the money chase in the halls of academia, he wasn't about to jeopardize future grants with a fleeting annoyance at Stevenson.

Besides, he wanted to see the man's face when he told him that the *World* was ready to jump on board with massive coverage of his work. That should effectively undo any lingering doubts the chancellor had about bad press, since Michael knew for a fact that Stevenson held the magazine in the highest regard.

There were also rumors among Barnet's faculty that Stevenson had been wooing Drake Lamont—and his wallet—for quite some time to join the Board of Trustees. As a result, Michael figured that when he told Stevenson that Lamont's magazine was planning to hold the spotlight on Barnet College and its leading-edge physics experiments, it would be a virtual slam-dunk basket for Michael's team. Not only would the chancellor reopen the lab, but he'd probably be there himself to greet

Phoebe Dauwalter with a bouquet of roses when she arrived in the morning for her appointment with Michael.

That would also make it easier for Stevenson to swallow Teri Ostrand's visit to the lab before Phoebe showed up, Michael reasoned. Nobody at a college was happy when the police had to put in an appearance for an investigation, but opening the doors for a detective who was looking for murder clues was going to be infinitely worse. The college would have no choice, Michael knew, and if there was anything he could do to help Teri solve this particular case, he was certainly going to do it, even if he did have to rough up Stevenson's media sensitivity a little bit.

He checked in with the secretary and took a seat to wait for Stevenson's door to open. A few minutes later, he was shaking the chancellor's hand and accepting his expression of sympathy over Lucas's death.

"I know you were close, Michael," Stevenson said. "Such a shock for all of us. Here in a small, quiet community like Litchfield, we think we're immune to senseless violence."

He coughed, obviously uncomfortable.

"And coming so soon after Elise's death, this must be horrendous for you."

Michael felt the usual tension in his jaw come and then go as he deliberately kept his thoughts from Elise and, instead, focused on why he'd come to the office.

"I have some good news, Stevenson," he said. "The *World's* science editor, Phoebe Dauwalter, wants to do a cover story on my Strings Project. She's coming to visit the lab tomorrow morning, so I'll be here on campus to work with her."

After he had agreed to give Phoebe the exclusive, the two of them had debated whether or not to tell the chancellor the extent of Michael's achievement. Knowing Stevenson's penchant for leaking good news to the media, however, they had decided to keep secret the fact that Michael had solved the equations and definitively located the eleventh dimension. With the control of the timing of the article's publication in their hands, there would be plenty of opportunity for Michael to fill Barnet's chancellor in just before the articles appeared concurrently in *Physica* and *World*. For a once-in-a-lifetime breakthrough, neither Michael nor Phoebe were willing to take a chance that an incorrigible publicity hound like Stevenson might ruin the effect.

The chancellor coughed again, and a little flare of unwanted apprehension brought all of Michael's senses suddenly alert.

"Stevenson?"

The chancellor looked at Michael apologetically.

"Well, Michael, this is embarrassing. And inconvenient. You see, I can't let you open the lab tomorrow. This morning, at our Board of Trustees meeting, we had a rather heated discussion about the Strings Project. Our newest trustee is concerned about your credibility after all the trauma you've had to endure in the past eight months—first with Elise's death and now Lucas's. Not to mention your—ah—appearance on the television news last night with a reputed psychic in the middle of a street brawl."

Momentarily stunned, Michael began to protest. "Stevenson, we had this discussion last night. You and I—"

"I know, I know," he said, holding his hands up to placate Michael. "I thought we could just do damage control and it would go away, but our trustees are looking at the big picture, Michael. It's no secret that your work suffered tremendously after Elise died and now with Lucas . . . well, we think the project needs to be rethought. We're concerned that your focus isn't where it should be—"

"Rethought?" Michael's voice went hard. "What are you trying to say, Stevenson?"

The man gave up being diplomatic and looked Michael squarely in the eye.

"It's cancelled, Michael. The Strings Project is over."

"What?" Michael shouted.

Stevenson took a quick step backward, and Michael, suddenly acutely aware of where he was and how his anger would play directly into the hands of the suspicious trustees, turned toward the door and strode out of the office.

He was back in freefall again.

CHAPTER THIRTY-TWO

Teri Ostrand looked up at the quaint wooden sign hanging over the big wrap-around porch of the Dutch Iris Bed & Breakfast Inn.

The drive from Litchfield had only taken about thirty minutes down county highways, and if she'd been making the trip for any reason other than the one she had, Teri would have been charmed with the rolling countryside and the breathtaking fall foliage. As it was, she had spent the drive with her gut twisted in knots, hoping against hope that the typed notes and photos inside the big manila envelope she'd found on her desk was somebody's bad idea of a joke and not the anonymous tip that would finally break at least one murder case wide open.

CHAPTER THIRTY-THREE

G od love a Ford," Jack said as he stomped on his old Ford pickup's parking brake to make sure it held.

The Ford had been with him a long time, almost twenty years now, and it had served him well, carting his large canvases from place to place and hauling the occasional load of youth ministry kids out to the back acreage of the retreat center's property. Today, however, the Ford had only been carrying him, and after the two-hour drive to Litchfield, its motor was sounding a little rough.

"That's okay," Jack told the truck, patting the dashboard. "You're entitled to complain if you want. One of the privileges of age, my friend. Goodness knows, I invoke it enough."

He grabbed his overnight bag from the bench seat beside him and walked up the sidewalk to the front door of the attractive ranch-style house. When a tall blonde answered the door, he smiled broadly.

"You must be Khristina Tupikova," he said. "I'm Father Jack. A mutual friend told me where to find you."

"You know Michael?"

"No, no," he said, shaking his head. "I'm a friend of William's."

Jack held her gaze and watched as amazed recognition flared briefly in Khristina's eyes, only to be quickly replaced with wonder. He guessed it wasn't a line of introduction that she often heard, if ever. He also noted that the woman's eyes darted to his Roman collar inside the throat of his lightweight wind-breaker. The air was surprisingly mild today after the chill of the weekend, making heavier jackets unnecessary.

"I am surprised," she said softly. "William has never been fond of the clergy."

Jack chuckled.

"He makes an exception with me. We share a lot of the same interests, William and I. Mind if I come in?"

Khristina moved aside to let him into the house.

"I'm sorry. Please come in."

She led him to the kitchen where Skye was finishing a second cup of tea.

"Father Jack, this is Skye Hammond. Skye, Father Jack."

At the sound of Skye's name, Jack's face lit up and he stretched out an age-spotted hand to enthusiastically shake Skye's.

"Not *the* Skye Hammond who writes for *The Midnight Eye*? My housekeeper loves your work."

A pink blush rose on the young woman's cheeks.

"Please," she begged him, "my byline has already gotten me into more hassle today than it has in the last three years. I seem to have hit a nerve with yesterday's piece."

"And well you should," Jack agreed. "You went straight to the heart of man's—and woman's—deepest desire: to live for-ever. Who wouldn't respond to that?"

He pointed to Skye's tea mug.

"Have you got any more of that?"

"Of course," Khristina responded. "I am forgetting my manners. I will get you a cup."

She took another mug from the cupboard and filled it from the teapot warming on the stove.

"I am just so surprised to meet you."

Surprised was probably not the right word, Khristina thought as she placed the mug on the counter near Father Jack and met his eyes, not knowing how much she should say in front of Skye.

She had met only a few other authentic visionaries in her life, none of whom communicated with her own spiritual companions. To think that the man before her not only shared her special gift, but that he also knew one of her friends was almost too much to take in all at once. She could think of a million questions to ask the priest, but not in front of Skye. In the short while they'd been talking, Khristina was pretty sure that her new acquaintance was open to accepting psychic talents and spiritual gifts, but she couldn't know for certain how the young woman might react to hearing two mediums compare their very unusual, grace-filled experiences.

Until she knew Skye better, Khristina decided, she would opt for discretion in any conversation with Father Jack while Skye was within hearing distance.

"So, who are you, Father Jack?" Skye asked. "No offense, but it's not every day that I find myself sitting down to tea in a kitchen with a Catholic priest and a Russian medium. Especially when I've just bylined an article about how that same medium has helped prove the existence of heaven."

It was Khristina's turn to blush.

"Please, Skye," she chided her, "I did not prove anything. Michael is the scientist who has accomplished a great task."

She took a quick glance at Father Jack to gauge his reaction to Skye's bluntness, but he seemed totally at ease at the kitchen counter. He took a drink of the tea and set the mug back down.

"I like your style, Skye," he told her, vigorously nodding his head in approval. "No beating around the bush. Curious. Assertive. No wonder you took the bull by the horns and wrote that article."

He smiled widely.

"And that sounds like the beginning of a hummer of a joke, young lady—'a Catholic priest and a Russian medium walk into this bar . . . '"

Khristina found herself smiling, too. It did sound like one of those jokes she'd heard since arriving in America—the ones where people made fun of each other's peculiarities.

"I'll leave it up to you to write the rest of it," the priest told Skye with a wink. "Let's see if I can answer that question for you—who am I? Well," he said, folding his hands in front of him on the counter, "right now I run a Jesuit retreat center out in Blue Springs, called Sacred Ground. It's about two hours from here. Pretty place. Out in the country, quiet, peaceful. I do a lot of painting."

"Painting?" Khristina asked, wondering if that was one of the shared interests Father Jack had alluded to when he had mentioned William. Based on her own experience, Khristina had found that a strong common bond was one of the things that seemed to enable visitors to make contact with receptive people. It also helped explain, she believed, why she had more success as a medium between family members or close associates than she had when she was trying to forge links between people less connected to each other. Ultimately, the connection she felt in the presence of a visitor was always love—and given that Love Himself had bridged the gap between life and death, it made perfect sense to her that love lay at the heart of her gift.

William's own artwork, she remembered, was an impressive collection of engravings, illustrations and paintings, some of which he had publicly claimed to be copies of the visions he had experienced. Unfortunately, most of his contemporaries weren't ready for his unorthodox pronouncement and thought him mad.

Poor William, she reflected. The price he'd paid for his gift had been steep.

Father Jack, meanwhile, was spreading his arms out as far as they would reach, trying to give the women an indication of his preferred scale of work.

"Mostly big canvases," he explained. "Lots of color. Lots of emotion. Keeps me out of trouble, you know."

"And you're here now . . . because?"

"You don't miss a trick, do you, Skye?" Jack said. "A one-track mind. No wonder you figured out where Dr. Carilion's research was headed."

He paused for a moment to throw Khristina a sidelong glance, then refocused his attention on Skye.

"What would you say if I told you I'm here to help Khristina and Dr. Carilion get his work published against all odds? And I mean, *all* odds?"

Skye frowned.

What did odds have to do with it? Was getting an article published in a physics journal that difficult?

Skye had no idea. She expected it would have to be vetted by other experts in the field, but that was the way all academic publishing worked. Sure, string theory was cutting-edge physics, but if and when Dr. Carilion completed his work, certainly he'd have so much data and evidence to back him up, that there'd be no question about publication. So odds had nothing to do with it.

As to why the involvement of a Jesuit priest was required in the process, she couldn't even begin to make a guess.

Unless something else was going on that no one was seeing.

Just like something else was going on with Drake Lamont's interest in the Strings Project?

"I'd say," Skye finally told Jack, returning his steady gaze, "that there was a lot more going on here than one might initially assume."

"You should know," he replied. "You wrote the article."

The sound of a door opening and then slamming shut made all three of them jump. Even the dishes in the kitchen cupboards rattled briefly, jarred by the impact that echoed through the house.

"What was that?" Jack asked Khristina.

"That," she said, "is Michael. I am thinking he is not going to be happy."

Skye swallowed the nervousness that rose in her throat. Relaxed by Khristina's and Jack's easy company, she'd almost forgotten that she had come to the physicist's home to make contrite amends with the world-famous researcher. She gripped her tea mug for support.

A moment later, Michael stormed into the kitchen and came to an abrupt halt.

"Who are these people?" he snapped at Khristina.

Skye jumped to her feet, instinctively reacting to his belligerence with a measure of her own.

"I'm Skye Hammond, Dr. Carilion. You said I should meet you here."

"Who are you?" he turned towards Jack.

"Your worst nightmare?" Jack suggested.

"You're too late," Michael informed him. "My worst nightmare has already happened."

His eyes raked over Skye and settled on Khristina.

"My research project has been cancelled. The Strings Project is dead."

Skye sent a swift glance in Jack's direction. *Is this one of the odds?* she wondered.

He met her eyes, lifted his narrow shoulders in a small shrug. It was almost as if he'd said it out loud—*see, I told you so.*

"What do you mean, it's dead?"

Even though Skye was fully aware that she had no right to ask Michael anything and that he would probably turn on her with a string of expletives to match his obvious anger, she wasn't about to back down, since it was her stupid move that had exposed his work in the first place. She had a serious debt to make up to the man, and she had to start somewhere, so it might as well be right here and now in his kitchen, she decided.

She planted her feet firmly on the tile floor and braced her shoulders for a fight.

"I mean," the physicist growled through his teeth, "that the Board of Trustees doesn't want me around. They think I'm unstable. They think my work is a dead end—a joke that showed up in a certain tabloid and headlined the nine o'clock news!"

"They cancelled your funding? All of it?"

"Give that girl a cigar," Michael announced. "Right on all points."

"But what about Drake Lamont? I just spoke with him this morning—"

"Who is Drake Lamont?" Khristina wanted to know.

"Drake Lamont?" Michael sneered. "What does he have to do with this?"

Michael, Khristina, and Jack all looked at Skye expectantly.

They probably didn't know yet that Lamont was the newest trustee at Barnet, Skye reminded herself. How could they, since she'd heard Chancellor Newsome say he was just about to make the announcement a few hours ago? And they certainly didn't know that he was the anonymous funding source for Michael's work, either, or that he apparently had some pressing personal stake in the work that Skye still couldn't figure out. Drake had asked her to keep that information confidential and then said— what was it?

Oh yeah.

If he found out he'd been left out of the loop with the Strings Project, and that she knew something he didn't, he'd make sure it didn't happen again. And exactly how would he do that— make sure that Skye didn't know something about the project that he didn't?

Two possibilities popped into Skye's head. If Drake thought she knew something he didn't, either he'd make the project go away, or he'd make her go away.

Or both.

Chilled to the bone, Skye swallowed and focused on Michael.

"Dr. Carilion, has there been a breakthrough in the Strings Project? One that isn't common knowledge?"

Michael scrutinized the young woman with the frizzy red hair. If this was Skye G. Hammond, she had already fed him to the dogs once, as far as he was concerned. Why should he give her a chance to do it a second time?

Fool me once, shame on you, he thought.

Fool me twice, shame on me.

"No, Ms. Hammond, there has not."

Out of the corner of his eye, he saw Khristina look at him in clear disbelief. She knew he was lying. Would she keep her mouth shut? Certainly, Michael told himself, she didn't expect him to share his earth-shaking discovery with this sleazy tabloid reporter. He didn't know what they had been talking about before he arrived, but no amount of chitchatting in the kitchen was going to make him forget the disastrous consequences of what the reporter had brought down upon his head.

"Michael—" Khristina began.

"Khristina," he sternly replied.

Their eyes locked and he willed her to stay out of the conversation.

To no avail.

"Yes, Skye, there has been a breakthrough," Khristina told Skye, openly contradicting Michael. "In fact, Michael has completed his work. He has finished his formulas and has proof of the eleventh dimension."

Furious, Michael spun on Khristina.

"What do you think you're doing?" he shouted at her. "This woman is the one who put strangers—crazy strangers—on your lawn and brought you a death-threat in your mail slot! She's ruined my career, not to mention my front window! Why are you telling her anything?"

"Because you have accomplished the greatest feat of science, Michael!" Khristina yelled back at him. "You have stripped away the veil between life and death! 'What is now proved was once, only imagin'd.'"

"Stop quoting to me!"

"Stop lying!"

"I'm not lying!" he roared. "I proved the existence of the eleventh dimension. Nothing less, nothing more!"

What Skye had thought was firm flooring beneath her feet seemed to sag and ripple as her knees began to give way in reaction to Khristina's announcement of Michael's discovery. She fell heavily back onto the stool she had vacated when Michael had thundered into the room, and looked at Jack sitting beside her. The priest seemed unimpressed with the scene transpiring before them.

"Who *are* you?" she whispered to the man.

"Michael's new best friend," he replied. "He just doesn't know it yet."

CHAPTER THIRTY-FOUR

Completely caught up in his shouting match with Khristina, Michael didn't see Jack pull the silver whistle on a lanyard out of his windbreaker's front pocket. Nor did he observe the priest sticking the whistle between his lips. He did, however, pay a lot of attention when the older man blew a lungful of air into the tiny instrument, releasing a harsh shriek that silenced everyone in the room, commanding their attention.

"Who *are* you?" Michael repeated, lightly rubbing his outer ears as the shrill echo inside them faded. He didn't think he'd heard a whistle like that since he'd played his last high school varsity basketball game. Or at least, he hadn't been so close to one that his ears were still ringing a minute later.

"Father Jack Gerrity," the priest said. "Sorry about the whistle, but I thought we were headed for a barroom blow-out here. You've got a temper, son."

"So I hear," Michael replied, his angry outburst apparently having spent itself for the moment. "Or at least, I used to be able to. What's with the whistle?"

"Oh, just one of the tricks of the trade. On occasion, I have to herd around youngsters at our retreat house and this seems to help. Gets their attention, you know." He stuffed the whistle back in his pocket.

"To answer your question, I am here to help you bring your new baby into the world."

Okay, Michael told himself, *Khristina has let a crazy man into my house.*

176

Why did that not surprise him?

He was standing in his kitchen with a woman who talked with the dead, a reporter who wrote stories about aliens, and a senior citizen who dressed like a priest and thought he was making a midwife's house call.

"I'm not pregnant," Michael told Jack.

Jack punched Michael in the shoulder and laughed out loud. "A sense of humor! Saints be praised! Maybe this won't be impossible after all! Tell me, son, do you believe in God?"

Michael opened his mouth to give the automatic 'yes' he'd given since he was a child saying his bedtime prayers, but suddenly stopped, aware that the two women in the room had gone as still as Jack, waiting for his answer, creating a vacuum of noise in the room that seemed to freeze all of them in time and space.

Did he believe in God?

It was a good question, he realized, and one he hadn't seriously considered in a very long time. As a little kid, he'd sucked up all the religious training his parents had given him and never questioned a thing. The big picture of Jesus the Good Shepherd surrounded by white lambs was a permanent fixture in his parents' dining room, and the only image of God he'd ever had in his head depicted a kindly father with a long white beard. His first doubt about the reliability of those images came the year he turned seven. That year, he'd learned that neither Santa nor the Easter Bunny was real, so he'd asked his mother if God wasn't real either.

Clearly charmed with her young son's ingenuousness, she'd assured him that God was indeed real, and then proceeded to share the vignette with her many friends throughout the years. It wasn't a family holiday until his mother told the "Michael and the Easter Bunny" story.

But the truth of it was that he never quite put the same trust or effort into religion again, figuring it was either some kind of orchestrated smokescreen to enforce morally accepted behavior or just one of the traditional trappings of growing up in America. As a teenager, about the only time he thought about God was when he wanted something badly, like making the starting team or a full-ride scholarship to college. If God came through and Michael got what he wanted, he said 'thank-you' and forgot about it until the next thing came along.

Once Michael discovered theoretical physics, however, God dropped totally out of the picture. Mrs. Carilion's little boy was an adult by then, and he didn't need anyone's smokescreens or fairy tales to give him direction in life. He knew what he was doing and where he was going. He believed in science and thought that the way it ordered the universe was a thing of ultimate beauty, a pattern of divine elegance. It was that pattern, in turn, that gave him a purpose.

He was searching for the One Theory, and like his grandfather had taught him, he wasn't about to give up.

Then Elise had died.

Suddenly God had come roaring back into his life with a vengeance—but this time, as the enemy.

For weeks, Michael had railed at God for his loss because he didn't have anyone else to blame, and he desperately had needed someone to blame. Elise's death was inexplicable, it defied everything that was reasonable and made a mockery of Michael's arrogant confidence in predictability and patterns. It was an equation with no solution, a random event that had displaced his previously rational universe.

Yes, he'd gone through the motions of having the church burial service because he knew it was what Elise would have wanted, but alone with his booze, he'd laughed at the absurdity of any faith that claimed that death wasn't final, because he knew just how completely final it was.

Faith wasn't going to make Elise walk back through their front door. Elise had been pushed out of his life and no one was bringing her back.

But what about the recycling bin?

Michael looked at the three faces in the room with him and knew no one had said a word since Jack's question, which meant that his inner voice was back in play and had picked up on the one tiny detail that had unnerved him so badly last night.

How had Khristina known about the recycling bin?

Finding recyclable items laying around the house—items he'd left out—had been Elise's pet peeve, and so she had stashed a bin for them right outside the door that led into the garage from the house. Except that no one else would know what the thing was, since she'd painted the container to look like an old-fashioned apple crate.

But Khristina had known.

Michael looked Jack in the eye.

"I don't know what I believe anymore."

Jack grasped Michael's shoulder and lightly shook it in approval.

"Now here's an honest man," he pronounced. "There's hope for you yet, son."

Then, removing his hand, he added in a hushed whisper, "You know, I've got to say, sometimes I'm not completely sure what I believe, either. Sometimes you just got to go on faith."

Resuming his normal volume, Jack turned to Khristina and Skye.

"I got an idea. Why don't we all just order out for some pizza, and Michael, you can tell us all about your big discovery. If I'm going to help you win this one, I need to know the lay of the land, or, according to you, the strings of it."

"Win this one?" Michael asked, almost afraid the whistle was going to appear again at any moment. This priest, whoever he was, was obviously part steamroller, because none of them seemed able to stop him once he got started. The question was: just where was he going?

"I didn't realize I was involved in a contest here."

"Oh, it's a contest all right," Father Jack assured him. "Make no mistake. And son, I'm sorry to tell you, but you've already got ground to make up. Time's a-wasting."

"Skye," he said, leaving Michael, bewildered, behind him while he took her arm and led her into the living room. "Call that cute little place I passed just around the corner, would you? Pizza Stop or something like that. I like pepperoni. And extra olives. And pop. Lots of pop. How about you, Khristina? Michael? What do you want?"

"Peace and quiet?" Michael muttered wistfully.

Khristina pushed him after Jack.

"He is here to help," she whispered sternly. "Let him do that."

Michael sighed in resignation.

"I don't think I have a choice."

CHAPTER THIRTY-FIVE

This would be easy.

Standing in front of the ivy-covered Physical Sciences Building at Barnet College, the man looked up.

From what he could see on the outside, the fourth floor lab didn't have any special security and it was on the top floor of the building. Inside, he'd only found classrooms and bulletin boards covered with flyers; he'd walked right into the building and up to the fourth floor without anyone giving him a second look. A note taped on the doors of the labs announced that they would be closed indefinitely and questions should be referred to the Office of the Chancellor.

He was glad. He didn't want to involve any innocent bystanders. Accidentally punishing someone who wasn't guilty would be a horrible mistake.

He'd wait for nightfall when classes were done for the day, walk up the stairwell, locate the professor's office, and slide his homemade explosive right under the door. A quick match to the long fuse, and he'd leave the building the way he came. By the time the office blew, he'd be off the campus. Then, with the devil's own research lab gone, he could concentrate on the woman.

She would have to renounce her evil ways.

If she refused, she would have to die.

Retribution was a heavy burden. No one would understand. But then, he consoled himself, prophets are never recognized by the people they've come to save.

CHAPTER THIRTY-SIX

Mara sat in her car a block down and across the street from the Dutch Iris Bed & Breakfast, waiting for the detective from Litchfield to leave.

She'd ditched the woolen cap she'd worn earlier in the day since the weather had warmed considerably and was now pinning her blonde hair up on the top of her head to get some air moving across the back of her neck. According to Art Roberts, the News 9 weatherman, they could expect another two days of unseasonably high temperatures before a cold weather front slammed into them from Canada. And while Mara hated the return of the summer-like humidity that made her neck damp and her hair feel uncomfortably heavy, she hated the Canadian cold even more.

Just as she was deciding to get out of the car and take a stroll down the tiny main street in search of something cold to drink, Mara saw Teri Ostrand exit the inn and hustle down the porch steps to her car. Waiting a few more minutes until Ostrand's car had turned out of sight, the reporter grabbed her purse and headed over to the Dutch Iris. She was betting that the inn's proprietor wasn't accustomed to inquiries from either the police or news reporters and would be unprepared for the attention, making him or her careless about giving out information.

Then again, she didn't need much anyway—it didn't take a rocket scientist to come up with some pretty damaging scenarios based on the photos and notes that Drake had included in the envelope she'd delivered to Ostrand.

It was also obvious to her that the packet was something Drake had been working on for a while. The one photo in particular was from what appeared to be a formal dinner party and showed a glamorous Elise Carilion in deep conversation with a handsome younger man. On the back of the photo, a small label read 'Barnet College Holiday Dinner—Elise Carilion and Dr. Lucas Scranton' and carried a date stamp from the previous year.

Clever man, that Lamont.

If anyone was ever a master at the manipulation of information, he was, and Mara was bound and determined to learn everything she could from him. All she needed was a few well-coached remarks from the proprietor and a 'no comment' from Ostrand, and she'd have her very own Molotov cocktail to toss in Michael Carilion's lap.

Mara had to hand it to The Gentleman—when he set out to destroy someone, he didn't hesitate to kick a man when he was down.

Neither would she.

CHAPTER THIRTY-SEVEN

So let me get this straight," Jack said, leaning forward on the sofa, his elbows braced on his knees, his hands clasped in front of his body. "Thanks to these photos—what did you call them? Kirlian?—of energy emanations from Khristina while she acted as a medium, you were able to figure out the missing part of the equations that not only provide a theoretical basis for your Theory of Everything, but actually spatially locate the eleventh dimension. Is that right?"

Michael nodded. Despite his initial reluctance to explain his work to the motley crew assembled before him, his passion for his research had eventually overcome his hesitation and he'd ended up talking them through some of the more obscure implications of his new formulas. He'd tried to put his work in the simplest terms he could to make it understandable and found the task daunting, but to his surprise, Skye had been a tremendous help in that department. The research she'd done before writing her tabloid article, even though hardly any of it actually appeared in the piece, had gone a long way to making her conversant with the rudiments of string theory. Her translations into simple English of some of Michael's more technical explanations had impressed him, while at the same time, eroded some of the residual anger he felt toward her for putting the Strings Project on the firing line in the first place.

"And this solves the greatest puzzle of modern physics, which was that our understanding of the universe was based on two sets of laws—relativity and quantum mechanics, the subatomic stuff—that don't agree."

"Correct."

"But now that you've discovered the existence of the eleventh dimension that was predicted by the M string theory, you've been able to fit the two conflicting sets of laws together in one big picture, which is unification."

"Yes, Jack."

For a moment, Jack sat silently, his eyes closed, his head bowed. Just like a man in prayer, Michael thought fleetingly. But when Jack lifted his face, he was beaming at all of them.

"Sounds like a thing of beauty to me," he said, reverence evident in his voice, "and exactly what your Einstein was looking for, Michael. The master equation, isn't that what you called it a couple of minutes ago? Who'd have thought it would all come down to tiny bits of energy strings, vibrating in a zillion different and amazing ways. Just like a cosmic symphony, wouldn't you say? The music of the spheres, that's what the Greeks called it. And you've boiled it all down to one principle."

He locked his eyes on Michael's.

"Congratulations, son. I'm no Einstein, only a humble old man, but I know an unprecedented achievement when I see it. You really are going to change our world. So when's the big announcement coming out?"

With a little mental jolt, Michael realized that it didn't matter to him that Jack was just a humble old man—hearing his work appreciated by someone felt amazingly good, just like it had felt when he'd explained it all to Phoebe at the coffee shop. Praise wasn't something he usually sought, but on a day like today, when he'd gotten his own lab doors slammed shut in his face, he had to admit it tempered the blow a little bit.

It was nice—no, it was gratifying—to know that someone believed in his work as much as he did.

Of course, Khristina did, and he knew that, but that was different, because her belief came from another direction and he couldn't quite . . . he didn't even want to start thinking about that again.

He gave Jack the only answer he could.

"Soon, I hope. The journal article is being reviewed this week, so publication should be within the month."

"But in the meantime," Skye ruefully pointed out, "thanks to me, your lab is shut down and your research cancelled."

Michael shot her an accusing look. "If the shoe fits . . . "

"But it is not her fault. Not all of it," Khristina protested, gathering together the empty pizza boxes that lay on the living room's coffee table. She stood up with them in her arms.

"We cannot ignore the fact, Michael, that your work is going to be controversial for a lot of people because of my involvement. There are implications they will assume. Some of those implications will be erroneous, that is true, but some will be correct."

"Khristina," Michael began to warn her, "this is not the time—"

"Yes, Michael, it is," she insisted and looked to Jack for encouragement. His subtle nod was all she needed to plow ahead.

"This is the time. Now, before publication, we all need to face what your breakthrough really means. And I don't mean scientifically. You are the expert on that. But Michael, if you think Skye's article has been disastrous because it made wild claims about your work, how will you handle it when you realize those wild claims are—"

"Real?" Michael interrupted her. "That's what you're going to say, isn't it? Look, Father Jack, Skye, I'm sorry," he apologized to them on Khristina's behalf. "Khristina's got this crazy idea that the eleventh dimension is just what you said it was in your article, Skye: heaven. Heaven where the dead people live. That's her way of—"

"You do not apologize for me!" Khristina bluntly reprimanded him. "There is no need for an apology! It is no crazy idea! It is the truth, whether I have to beat it into your thick head or not!"

Skye sat in the overstuffed armchair, her eyes wide. Now would probably be a good time to leave, but her reporter's instincts were telling her to stay and watch the mounting conflagration. She glanced at Father Jack, expecting to see a similar panic spreading over his weathered face, but, again, he seemed unperturbed by the rising volume level of Michael's and Khristina's shouts. She saw his hand slip into his jacket pocket where he'd deposited the silver whistle earlier in the afternoon, and before he blew it, she had her hands clapped over her ears to muffle its shriek.

"For crying out loud, Jack!" Michael yelled at him over the sound of the whistle.

Without warning, he lunged from his own armchair towards the priest on the sofa and grabbed the whistle out of the older man's hand. He tossed the lanyard around his own neck and glared at him, daring the priest to retrieve it. Skye sunk deeper into her own seat, hoping to become invisible.

"I was just trying to get a word in," Jack said.

"Oh, right," Michael sarcastically agreed.

Jack turned towards Skye and shrugged. "Now, see, this is why I'm here."

Skye smiled hesitantly. She had no idea what Jack was talking about.

Nor did Michael, who threw her a quick glare, then turned again to Jack.

"I thought you were here to help me 'birth my baby' or 'win this one,'" he reminded the priest. "Whatever 'one' you're talking about. Now you're here to break up fights, too?"

"If I have to," he told Michael. "But that's not why I drove here from Blue Springs."

"All right, Jack," Michael said, obvious disdain dripping from every word. "I'll bite. Why in the world did you drive here from Blue Springs?"

Skye watched Jack pick up the crumpled napkins from the table and lay them on top of the boxes still in Khristina's arms.

"To help Khristina beat some sense into your head," he replied. "Actually, it's more revelation than sense. Khristina's right, Michael. Like it or not, there is a heaven, and you found it. My job is to make sure you don't lose it."

"What in the world are you talking about?"

"Heaven, Michael," Jack corrected him. "We're talking about what's in heaven. Or rather, who's in heaven. You could call it the communion of saints, if you prefer—that's what millions of Christians call it every time they recite the creed of their faith. You know—'I believe in the Holy Spirit, the holy catholic church, the communion of saints, the forgiveness of sins, the resurrection of the body and life everlasting.' It's a package deal, son."

Deep in the armchair, Skye felt a ripple of comprehension building at the edge of her consciousness. She'd said those same words countless times growing up, but she'd never really given serious thought to what they might ultimately mean.

Now, searching the faces of the other three people in the newly re-carpeted living room, she sensed a new understanding sharpening itself inside her. While Michael looked as angry as she'd seen him all afternoon, she saw the confidence on Jack's face, the sure smile on Khristina's, and then, like a mighty wave knocking her off her feet, she had her own revelation.

Her wishful thinking when she'd written her piece for Frank hadn't been a wish at all. She'd stated the truth: the eleventh dimension really was heaven.

God's heaven.

Life eternal.

"Oh my word," she whispered in awe.

"Actually, not your word, Skye. God's Word," Jack responded. "He's already been here, done that, you know."

He nodded toward Michael.

"Michael here gets to fight the good fight, but this time around, the playing field's a different place. Forget the hill country of Galilee and the Roman occupation. This time, revelation's in the lab. And since Michael here is the one who's found the way to heaven with the scientific method, he's the one who's got to defend it that way. If he doesn't, his enemy will snatch heaven."

He paused and looked pointedly at Michael.

"*And* the eleventh dimension *and* unification, right out of your hands and tear it into so many tiny shreds that no one will ever believe any of it—or any of your research, for that matter—ever again."

Jack threw a glance at Skye and Khristina.

"We're talking the big one, here, son. It's all . . . or absolutely nothing."

Michael was stunned.

What rabbit hole had he stumbled into now?

He tried in vain to find something to say, some coherent thought in his head, but he couldn't even begin to sort through the jumble of words that were suddenly tumbling around in his mind.

Heaven?

Divine revelation?

In the *lab?*

He looked from Jack to Khristina and back again. They had the same smile on their faces. The word *beatific* came to mind.

Michael shook his head, trying to clear it.

While Khristina was undeniably beautiful and unusually serene—at least when he wasn't arguing with her—she was no saintly painting on the wall of a church, and Michael still didn't know how this Father Jack had turned up on his doorstep. How could a Catholic priest and a medium possibly find common ground in the idea of talking to dead people?

Of course, a priest would believe in heaven—just as Jack had mentioned, that was an article of his faith.

But how many Christians really, truly, believed that, or even considered what the 'communion of saints' might actually entail?

The last time Michael looked—and granted, it had been years—none of the churches he knew of were hosting symposiums featuring heavenly communication strategies. So how could Jack see any validity in what Khristina had to say?

Besides that, he wondered, what was Jack trying to imply about Michael's scientific method?

That it wasn't scientific?

That his work wouldn't stand up to the scrutiny of his fellow theoretical physicists?

Michael knew for a fact that at least one of his colleagues could vouch for the thoroughness—and brilliance—of his work: Theo. And yet the priest had seemed to follow all of Michael's points earlier when he explained the Strings Project. In fact, judging from the brief interaction they'd already had, Michael was convinced that Jack was an exceptionally intelligent man and well educated, which was not really a surprise to him since the Jesuits, of all the Catholic orders, were known for their intellectual pursuits.

But then Jack had mentioned an enemy.

An *enemy*?

Actually, if he were being completely honest, that was probably the one thought to which Michael could attach some meaning. He wasn't naïve—he'd been a college professor long enough to know that piracy existed even in the halls of academia. A high-profile research project was a precious commodity that could attract not only professional jealousy, but actual theft.

"My enemy?" Michael returned Jack's stare. "Are you saying someone is trying to steal my theory? To . . . destroy it?"

Not waiting for a response, Michael looked away and dragged his hand through his hair. The heaven stuff was crazy enough to deal with, but at least he could ignore it and still sleep at night.

But the idea that his work might be destroyed—that was like hearing his own death knell. He couldn't believe he was even considering such a wild speculation, but now that Jack had raised the specter of someone attempting to sabotage his research, the possibility took on a life of its own. True, the work had gone poorly after Elise's death, and he knew some of the team had become disheartened, but to think that any would have leaked—or sold—information to any rival researcher was just too unbelievable. He and Lucas had made careful hires and included confidentiality clauses in everyone's contracts. Yes, contracts could be broken and employers betrayed. That's why high-tech companies walked employees out the door the minute they learned they were leaving for competitors. Secrets were valuable. In the thin air of cutting-edge physics, with whole new technologies waiting in the wings, could someone have been spying on the Strings Project?

Could someone have known success was getting close and then shadowed Lucas and killed him, hoping to slow Michael down, so someone else would cross the finish line of the One Theory ahead of him?

The idea was just too bizarre.

Wasn't it?

Compelled by his own driving sense of rationality to find some sort of order to what was happening, Michael forced himself to consider the unthinkable.

Had Lucas been killed because of their work?

A wave of nausea crept into his stomach and his glance happened to fall on Skye, who had been listening raptly to every word Jack had uttered. Sudden awareness jolted him. If there was a conspiracy against him, Skye seemed to be standing in the middle of it. It was because of her idiot article that his lab was closed and his work was in danger of being labeled lunacy. She'd also been incredibly well informed about String theory, he reminded himself, helping him explain some of its more esoteric aspects to both Khristina and Jack. And she'd admitted to them all that she had been eavesdropping on Lucas and Phoebe in the bar, and that's where she got the ideas for her article.

But what were the chances that an English grad student, a grad student who wrote for a tabloid to help make ends meet, would be so knowledgeable about his research, and in all the wrong places at the wrong times?

Maybe, it occurred to Michael, because she was someone else entirely.

Looking directly at Skye, Michael softly asked Jack, "And who is my enemy, Jack? Could it be a reporter who 'accidentally' tips the press to what I'm doing and manages, in the process, to discredit my work and get my lab closed?"

He took a step towards Skye's chair, cold suspicion rising in him in a palpable rush of energy.

"How much did you get paid, Skye?" he almost whispered. "I hope it was more than enough."

"Michael!" Khristina grabbed at his arm and pulled him away from Skye, who sat wide-eyed, shocked, in her seat. "What are you saying?"

"She was there, Khristina! The night Lucas was killed, she was right there! She just admitted it's her fault the lab is closed, and she knows way too much about theoretical physics for an English grad student!"

He jerked his arm out of Khristina's grasp.

"Who are you, Skye?" he shouted at her. "Who are you working for?"

"Me!" she shouted back at him. "I work for me, not anyone else! I'm a poor grad student, and that's all I am! Are you nuts? I didn't even know Lucas had been killed until Khristina told me this afternoon! How do you think I feel about that? I feel horrible! Horrible! All I wanted to do was write a stupid story that would sell copies and make my boss happy, and I especially didn't want to hurt you! That's why I kept your name out of the article," she added roughly, bright tears filling her eyes.

The sight of the tears washed over Michael like a bucket of cold water.

He looked quickly around him, momentarily disoriented by the sheer force of his unleashed temper.

What was he doing, yelling at this poor kid?

He was suddenly aware of Khristina's hand on his arm and Jack's silence. He looked again at Skye, embarrassed and ashamed of his behavior. She didn't deserve this kind of treatment from him.

A reprimand, maybe.

But browbeating and wild accusations?

He was being a moron. An unreasonable, unthinking moron.

He blew out a long breath and shook his head.

"I'm sorry, Skye," he apologized. "I'm a mess. I'm sorry. What you said—why didn't you want to hurt me? What did I have to do with it?"

Skye swiped the tears from her eyes with both hands.

"I read about your wife, Dr. Carilion. I thought you'd suffered enough."

"Your wife?" Jack's voice seemed to come to Michael from a distance as he stared at the redheaded reporter.

"She was murdered," Michael said, his voice now carefully controlled, his eyes still on Skye. "Right here in my front door-way. Eight months ago. They never found the killer."

"That makes two, then," Jack said.

Michael cut his eyes towards the priest on the sofa.

"Two what?" Khristina asked.

"Two deaths," Jack said wearily. "Lucas and Michael's wife."

"They're not connected." Michael said automatically, his tone flat and empty. Fatigue pulled hard at him.

"Oh yes they are," Jack corrected him. "They're con-nected . . . because of you."

"Random acts of violence, Jack, that's what the police call it."

"Of course that's what they call it. They don't have another word for it. I do. It's evil. Pure evil. Violence, yes. Random? Not on your life."

Michael's phone rang in his jeans pocket.

"Excuse me," Michael said to them, flipping open his cell. "Carilion here."

"Michael." It was Theo LeMay.

Michael heaved a sigh of relief and exhaustion, and with his free hand, rubbed the back of his neck.

"Theo. What's up? I could use some good news right about now."

There was no reply.

"Theo? You there?"

A throat was cleared at the other end of the connection.

"Yes, Michael, of course I'm here."

Another pause.

"I'm afraid I'm fresh out of good news at the moment, how-ever."

Pause.

"Ah, Michael, it's about your article . . . the journal . . . *Phys-ica* . . . what I'm trying to say is that we can't get you published right now."

"What do you mean," Michael asked slowly, "not right now?"

"We've suspended publication," Theo told him. "Effective today."

"For how long?"

Theo's sigh was loud and clear on the line.

"I don't know, Michael. The new publisher says indefinitely, but what it comes down to is that he doesn't want to publish you because of the media attention you're getting right now. It could compromise both of our reputations, not to mention our credibility. *Physica* can't afford it, Michael."

"It was just a blip on the screen last night, for crying out loud, Theo," Michael protested. "It's not like I'm national news."

Another pause. Longer this time.

"I take it you haven't seen any evening newscasts tonight yet. No," Theo added, "of course you haven't. I'm a time zone ahead of you."

A wave of cold ran down Michael's back.

"That local reporter of yours is quite a beauty, Michael. But I get the feeling she really doesn't like you very much."

Michael looked at the time on his cell phone and snapped it shut, turned on his heel and went to the study. By the time Khristina, Jack, and Skye joined him there, he was standing in front of the television set, his eyes riveted on the small screen. The early broadcast was just beginning.

"And at the top of our stories tonight we have a special report from our News 9 investigative team," the perfectly groomed anchorman solemnly intoned. "New leads have come to light in the unsolved killing of Elise Carilion, wife of Dr. Michael Carilion, who just last night was filmed in the middle of a melee at the home of a Russian psychic."

"No," Khristina gasped, her fingers flying to her lips.

Beside her, Michael stood frozen.

The camera panned across the front of a lovely old inn and focused on the striking features of Mara Runyon.

"Eight months ago, the wife of internationally acclaimed theoretical physicist Dr. Michael Carilion was brutally murdered in her own home," Runyon told her audience. "Today, new leads have surfaced linking her to this inn for a mysterious rendezvous. Who was she meeting here? And why? Details coming up."

Michael stabbed the power off switch.

"Your journal article," Jack said, standing in the study's doorway. "It's not going to be published, is it?"

Michael could feel the nerves tighten along his clenched jaw.

"No," he managed to grind out, still staring at the blank television screen.

"It's not."

Behind Michael, Skye exchanged a look with Jack.

The odds were getting worse.

She followed Michael's gaze back to the dark screen.

Much worse.

CHAPTER THIRTY-EIGHT

The front doorbell was ringing.

"You want me to get that?" Jack asked.

"No," Michael replied, then immediately changed his mind. "Yes. And if it's Mara Runyon, tell her I have no comment, except that she can take her microphone and go to . . . " He reached out and stopped Jack before he could leave the doorway. "No. I want to tell her myself."

But it wasn't Runyon on his doorstep.

It was Teri Ostrand.

Michael opened the door and Ostrand stepped inside.

"Michael," she began.

"When were you going to tell me, Teri?"

"Tell you what?"

"You got a lead on Elise's murder."

Teri's expression went slack with surprise, then darkened, frustration flushing her cheeks. This wasn't the way she wanted to play it. She'd wanted to spring it on him, see his first reaction, see if he was the incredibly skilled actor that she had reason to suspect he might be at this point. Now it was ruined, the moment gone.

How did he know?

Barely had she finished the thought when he offered her the answer.

"On the news, Teri. It's the lead tonight. Runyon's ahead of you."

"Runyon?"

So that was where the envelope had come from. The envelope of pictures and typed suggestions that had sent her out to the Dutch Iris. Runyon had put it together.

"What did she say?" she asked him carefully.

"I don't know," Michael responded woodenly. "I turned it off. So you tell me."

Even from two feet away from him, Teri could feel the tension and anger coming off Michael's body in waves. The front hallway seemed insufferably close and hot, so she slipped by the physicist and stepped into the living room. The unmistakable smell of new carpet rose around her and she wrinkled her nose unconsciously, but decided not to mention it. Instead, she went straight to the question she needed to ask him—the question to which she needed desperately to see his response.

"When did you find out that Elise was having an affair?"

To her immense relief, and complete self-loathing, Michael's face went totally blank.

"I didn't," he said, his lips barely moving with the words. "Until now."

CHAPTER THIRTY-NINE

S he was in over her head, and she knew it.

Never mind that she'd never meant for it to happen. Who ever did? When she and Lucas had first put their heads together at the Christmas party, she'd never dreamed it would end up in her having an affair. She loved Michael, she'd loved him through twenty years of marriage. So how this man had blindsided her and swept her up into a betrayal of the husband she loved was still unbelievable, even to her.

She sunk deeper into the tub of hot water and laid her head back on the cushioned rim.

"Okay, Elise Carilion," she announced to the steaming bathroom, "time to wake up. You are a fool, and you have made the biggest mistake of your life. Now it's time to fix it."

She could do it. She would. She'd break it off with him, with this man who had fit himself so seamlessly into her life and then had proceeded to turn it upside down. Oh, she'd had all the best intentions in the beginning. She'd gone to him for help, secretly, to get Michael the assistance he needed. And then he had charmed her, subtly undermined all her defenses, all the while enthusing about the work of her own husband, the fascination of string theory, the lure of learning what no one had ever learned before. He was intelligent, interesting and lavish with the attention she had been missing from Michael. The man was good, no doubt about it. He'd known exactly what to say, what buttons to push, to keep her coming back for more, and it wasn't until this afternoon, when she was checking out of the Dutch Iris for the second time in two weeks, that she'd finally come to her senses.

Acknowledging that the Strings Project was what had brought them together made it even worse. Ironic even, since it was precisely because the project was taking so much out of Michael that she had turned to Lucas for help in the first place.

"He's barely sleeping at night," she'd told Michael's best friend in a quiet corner at the faculty dinner last month. "He's getting close to finishing the formulas, I think, because that's what happens when he's in the final leg of a project. He can't relax. He just pushes and pushes till he's done. Then he drops. All the adrenaline stops flowing and he sleeps for days. It just can't be good for him, Lucas. Isn't there anything you could do to make him ease up? Even a little?"

Lucas had laughed then, taking Elise's hand with his usual companionable warmth and lifting her knuckles to his lips for a quick kiss.

"I could move mountains before I could ever deflect Michael," he'd said. "The man is driven by demons, you know. Theoretical physics demons. Demanding little devils. And he's afraid he won't finish before the funding dries up. So he pushes even more."

Relieved to be finally sharing her concerns with someone else who knew Michael so well, Elise had sighed.

"Okay, I admit it. I'm feeling neglected. Out of the loop. He's so focused right now, I practically have to tackle him to make him remember to kiss me goodnight."

Lucas had leaned back and surveyed her appreciatively from head to toe.

"Now that I find hard to believe. Michael may be focused on work, but he's definitely not stupid."

"You're turning my head," she had teased him.

"I wish," he had replied.

She had been looking almost luminous that night, she remembered, her strapless sapphire cocktail dress revealing the toned and supple lines of her bare shoulders and back. Even Michael had noticed, his attention finally drawn away from the pursuit of extra dimensions and replicable evidence. In fact, he'd even suggested at the last minute, as they were going out the door, that they forego the dinner in favor of an intimate evening at home.

In retrospect, she should have agreed. If she had, then maybe she and Lucas would never have hatched their plan, a plan that had led ultimately to something totally unexpected, like an affair.

As she toweled off after her bath, she practiced telling him that it was over. She had the feeling that it was going to be one of the most difficult things she had ever done, not because she didn't want to, but because he could be so persuasive, as well as seductive.

Her infidelity to Michael was certainly proof of that.

But she would do it, and then she would beg him to never let Michael know, because she knew it would kill him if he ever found out.

And that, without a doubt, would kill her as well.

CHAPTER FORTY

This is going to make things very difficult for Michael," Khristina told Jack and Skye as she closed the study door after Michael went to answer the doorbell. "He is still not coping with Elise's death as it is, and to have anything about it dragged up right now will make it impossible for him to think about anything else."

"And in the meantime, his article is sitting out there in limbo and he's been cut out of his lab," Skye added. "How can this all be happening at once?"

"Very deliberately," Jack said. "Distraction is an offensive play. Someone—whoever produced this 'new lead' in his wife's murder, I bet—is trying to keep Michael distracted from his real work."

"You don't really think his wife's murder is connected to Lucas's, do you?" Skye asked. "That was eight months ago."

"Do you know where he was at with his work eight months ago?"

Skye shook her head.

"I don't either," Jack told her. "But I bet you dollars to doughnuts there's a connection that every time Michael has gotten close to finishing his work, there's been something to interrupt him."

"Except that he's finished the project, now," Khristina pointed out. "Why distract him now?"

"Because it's not published. And because even though he's finished the scientific portion of the work, Michael has one final step left to take—he has to come to the conclusion—the reality—the three of us already know: heaven exists. Souls survive. Call it a leap of faith or the awakening of his spiritual imagination. Either way, he's got to come to terms with what his One Theory has scientifically disclosed."

He sat forward on the edge of the sofa, his hands folded together.

"Like I already said, he found heaven through science, and now he's got to defend it that way. He earned the privilege and got stuck with the responsibility. But in the meantime, for all everyone else in the world knows, nothing has changed. Michael Carilion hasn't proven that heaven exists."

He held out his hands to include the two women.

"We're the only ones who know."

"No, we're not," Skye pointed out. "The editor at the journal knows, though I guess he doesn't count, since he's only interested in the physics part and won't be publishing the article anyway. But Phoebe Dauwalter knows. Michael just told her today."

Khristina nodded.

"That's right. She is going to do the magazine article when Michael makes his announcement. Or at least, that was the plan. But I do not know if she realizes that the eleventh dimension is heaven."

"Well, I hope she doesn't, for her sake. If I'm right, and I think I am, whoever is trying to stop Michael isn't going to leave any loose ends."

He gave each of them a piercing look.

"Do you understand what I'm telling you ladies? Right now, Michael's enemy doesn't know about us, but if and when he finds out, then you and I—we're the loose ends."

CHAPTER FORTY-ONE

O h, Michael. I am so, so sorry."

Teri sat down next to Michael on the living room sofa.

"But I had to ask you. I had to see your reaction, because . . . because . . . "

"You wanted to know if I knew," Michael finished the sentence for her. "You wanted to know if I'd been lying to you back in February when you questioned me as a possible suspect, and I said that our marriage was rock solid. No cheating. No separations. No trouble in paradise."

He dug both of his hands into his hair and bent forward till his elbows hit his knees. He looked at his feet and choked out, "Teri, are you sure?"

Teri swallowed hard. Now that the investigation was reopened, she had to play it by the rules. She couldn't share evidence with him. But she just couldn't leave him hanging with this, either. After all he'd been through with the initial failed investigation, she just couldn't let him wonder about this piece of information. This very rotten piece. Then she remembered what he'd just said about Runyon, and it gave her an idea how she could get around her protocol.

"Are you going to watch the news tonight?"

Michael looked up and said nothing.

"Because if you are, then you'll probably find this out anyway. Although," she warned him, "I have no idea exactly what information Runyon really has, Michael. I think she's the anonymous source of the lead I got, but I can't absolutely confirm that."

She took a deep breath, mentally crossing her fingers that Runyon's report would cover what she was going to tell Michael.

"I have a witness. She's the manager of a bed and breakfast about thirty miles from here, and she helped Elise check in and out of a room on two different afternoons. Elise was meeting a man there."

Before he could protest, she gently added, "The bed had been used, Michael. Both times."

Michael covered his eyes with his hand and sat motionless for a moment.

"Who is he?"

Again, Teri wondered what Runyon would be running in her segment. Would the reporter stop with just speculation or would she try to name names? Teri had some ideas about the unknown man's identity, but as yet, nothing had been confirmed. For now at least, she could be honest with Michael.

"I don't know," she admitted. "The inn's register only had Elise's name. Actually, it wasn't her name at all—she used a fake one. But the proprietor of the inn recognized her from a picture. Unfortunately, she only got a glimpse of the man as he was already walking out the door. She couldn't tell me anything, other than the man had a very nice wool coat and a long scarf tossed over his shoulder."

Michael stood up then and walked across the room, stopping in front of the big picture window, his back to the detective.

"So now what, Teri? Do I get to be the number one suspect again? Obviously I didn't have my story right in February, did I? My marriage was on the rocks and I didn't even know it."

He turned to face her.

"It appears there was a lot I didn't know."

"Michael, the case is reopened," Teri told him. "We're going to canvass the area around the inn, see if we can get anyone to describe the man. I can't lie to you; it's a real long shot this long after the fact, but we've got to try. I've got to consider he might have been Elise's killer."

"Yes," Michael replied mechanically. "There is that."

"There's something else, too," Teri said, dreading the words forming on her tongue, wondering how to phrase what she still had to tell him. "There might be a connection with Lucas."

Again, she watched for Michael's reaction, but he seemed to have regained a rigid control over his emotions. Instead of feeling any heat from him, she was sensing a numbing coldness.

"Lucas?" he echoed.

"The tip I got," Teri started to explain, then hesitated.

For the hundredth time that day, she weighed her trust in Michael against her professional ethics and found herself unable to tip the scales in either's favor. Her gut told her that Michael was innocent of Elise's murder, that he was a victim as surely as if he'd taken the shot in his own head that had killed his wife, and that he'd been nothing but honest with her throughout the time she'd known him. Because of that, not only did he deserve to hear what she had to say, but she was hoping against hope that he would be the one person to make some sense out of the disparate bits of information she'd found in the manila envelope. Even if it had come from Runyon, Teri didn't doubt that the information was accurate—she'd already proven that with her visit to the Dutch Iris Bed & Breakfast. The question now, the puzzle she needed Michael's help with, was how the other pieces of information in the envelope fit together, because she was convinced that if she could just assemble it in the right pattern, she'd have the answer to Elise's murder.

And Lucas's.

The scales tipped in the physicist's favor. "There was the suggestion that Lucas was Elise's lover," Teri told him, "and that you, Michael, had them both killed."

CHAPTER FORTY-TWO

M ichael didn't know what he wanted to do more—shout, cry, laugh or just lay down and die. He even began to think that in comparison to what he was feeling right now, those weeks of drunken stupor after Elise's death were a cakewalk. A downright holiday.

He looked at Teri, stunned, and couldn't think of a single thing to say.

"I don't believe it, Michael," she assured him. "The part about you, I mean. As for Elise and Lucas . . . "

He desperately wanted to tell her it was impossible, but suddenly, he couldn't make the words come.

In a heartbreaking, almost shattering, moment of clarity, he realized that anything was possible, and that he, Michael Carilion, didn't have a clue where the line fell between fact and fiction.

He'd just learned that his wife had had an affair, something he wouldn't have believed possible in a million years. Yesterday, he'd learned that his best friend had gone behind his back to give the Strings Project away to a reporter, something else he wouldn't have believed in a million years. And now, tonight, someone was trying to frame him for the murder of both of them.

Suddenly, Theo's news that the journal was no longer in business was the least of his concerns.

"Michael, did you hear what I just said?"

He looked at Teri, uncomprehending.

"I said you have to think, think hard," Teri urged. "Someone is trying to set you up. Someone hates your guts. Who would that be, Michael? At some point, you made an enemy. Who could it be?"

An enemy?

Jack's words came rushing back to him.

Jack said that Michael had an enemy. But Jack had been talking about the Theory of Everything, about getting it published, not about getting set up as a suspect for murders. Then again, Jack had also said that Elise and Lucas's murders were connected, and Michael had, without hesitation, refused to even consider it.

Now, apparently, Jack was right.

How had the priest known that?

"Someone you worked with at some point?" Teri suggested, obviously trying to jog some memories loose in Michael's head. "Someone you shut down for some reason?"

The words 'shut down' caught his attention, and he had a vivid recollection of the pure hatred he'd felt emanating from Runyon the time he'd almost knocked her over in the corridor outside the chancellor's office.

"Runyon."

"What about her?" Teri asked.

Michael pushed his hand through his hair.

"She hates my guts. She blames me for her getting fired last spring. She's the only person I can think of who'd like to see me go down in flames."

But then he remembered something else and abruptly stood up to leave the room.

"Just a minute," he told Teri, heading down the hall to his bedroom.

He rifled through the drawers in his dresser, trying to recall where he'd stashed the note from the brick. The word 'flames' had reminded him of the writer's suggestion that he burn in hell. In the drawer of his nightstand, he found it, along with the note he'd kept from Khristina's mail. He went back to the living room.

"Here."

He thrust the two pieces of paper into Teri's hands.

"I got this yesterday morning, special delivery, right through the front window. It was tied onto a brick. The other one I found in Khristina's mail, slipped through her front door slot. It's what I mentioned to you this morning."

Death threats.

Michael and Khristina had both received death threats.

Teri read the notes again. Distracted by her discoveries of the afternoon, she'd unintentionally let her morning conversation with Michael slip her mind. Reading the threats now, she kicked herself for her poor prioritizing—she should have insisted he come in to see her right away, and not simply passed him on to her department colleague.

She flicked a glance at Michael, angry at him, too, for not alerting her more aggressively to the potential danger.

She read the notes a third time, her eyes darting back and forth between the two slips of paper, narrowing as she compared the handwriting.

"Yeah, I know," Michael said. "They look like they're from the same person."

Teri sat back on the sofa and laid the notes on her lap. She shook her head and looked at the big picture window while she tried to rein in her own temper.

"How'd you get it replaced so fast? I assume the brick shattered the window."

"I've got a great handyman."

"I guess. Is that what I smell in here? Some kind of adhesive around the window frame?"

Michael pointed to the carpet.

"I had to replace the carpet, too. There was so much splintered glass in the other one, I didn't want to take the chance of cutting my foot some morning."

For a minute, she just stared at Michael.

"Do you have any idea how much danger you are in here?" she asked him. She covered the notes on her lap with her hands. "Not only do you have a crazy person targeting you, but that crazy person knows where you live. Michael! What are you thinking? Did you tell Sam about this? What did he say?"

"He didn't say anything, because I never got over there. It's been sort of busy for me today, you know?" he snapped.

Teri took a deep breath and exhaled, struggling to maintain her composure. Did he have any idea of what kind of situation he was really in here? Sure, the dirt Runyon had tossed at him was bad enough, but it wasn't life threatening. The threats, however, were pure psycho-land as far as she was concerned. What was to stop another brick—or a homemade bomb—from coming through his newly replaced window at any given moment?

"You are so out of here, Michael," she told him, gathering up the notes and rising from the couch. "Until we track this guy down, you're not staying in this house. I've already got two murders on my watch and I'm not taking a third."

She shook Khristina's note at him. "Or a fourth. Where is she? Please tell me she's not at her house."

"She's not."

Teri raised her eyes to the ceiling.

"Thank you, God."

"She's in the study."

The detective tipped her head and shut her eyes. "She's here."

It wasn't a question. It was resignation. The man needed a keeper.

Teri opened her eyes and looked at Michael, her voice commanding.

"I want you both out of here. Now. Stay at a hotel tonight. You'll be all right there, because this doesn't look like the work of any kind of a professional killer here, just a bona fide nutcase. But it will let me sleep tonight. Maybe. In the morning, you come to my office first thing, we'll get the official questioning done about this new stuff with Elise, you talk to Sam about the threats, we'll go to the lab so I can go through Lucas's office, and then we'll see where we stand."

She gave the notes in her hand a look of disgust.

"I can't imagine we'll lift any fingerprints off these except for yours and mine, but I'll have the boys give it a shot. It's a small town, Michael. We'll find this guy. But until then—" she warned him.

"I know. Stay at a hotel."

"Just for tonight. Sam will know what to do when you talk to him tomorrow."

She started for the front door, then turned back.

"I'd like to meet Khristina. You said she's in the study?"

"Yes. She is," he said. "Along with a cast of thousands," he added.

Wondering what he meant by that remark, Teri followed him down the hall to his study near the back of the house. He opened the door and stood back to let her go into the room ahead of him, but she came to a full stop when she saw a familiar face inside the room.

"Father Jack!" she exclaimed. "What are you doing here?"

CHAPTER FORTY-THREE

Classes were done for the day at Barnet. In the late-afternoon sunshine, the leaf-covered grounds glowed golden, and students took their time walking along the campus paths from the classroom buildings to the dorms and dining hall. The unseasonably warm day had enticed the return of inline skaters, who gracefully glided around the campus center, a large, open quadrangle bounded on each end by a circular fountain. The fountains had been turned off the week before as a result of the frigid cold, so the skaters were taking the rare opportunity to skate across the wide, shallow bowls of the empty fountains. Other students were sitting on stone benches watching them, dressed in the shorts and tank tops they'd dragged out of dorm closets for one last day of summer-like temperatures.

He sat on a bench, too, right in front of the Physical Sciences Building that faced the quad. With his backpack and sunglasses, he fit right in with the college crowd. He hadn't taken into consideration that the warm weather would keep the students out in the quad later than usual—he'd hoped to have slipped the device under the professor's door by now and be on his way home. But he had time. He could wait till the students cleared out. After all, his intention was to do no harm to the children. It wasn't their fault that the college had allowed evil on its grounds. By waiting till they'd all gone to dinner or back to their dorms, he wouldn't have to risk debris falling on them in the aftermath of the explosion.

He could wait.

CHAPTER FORTY-FOUR

J ack looked at the woman who had walked into the study. She looked vaguely familiar, but it had been a long time since he'd been waltzing around Litchfield, and the way women changed their hairstyles and hair colors these days, he wasn't about to make any wild guesses. Thankfully, Michael interrupted the woman before he could say a word.

"You know him, Teri?"

The light bulb went on in Jack's head.

Teri Ostrand. Policewoman. Sixteen years ago. She'd been on the team that brought the boy in. A mistake—and one he wasn't going to repeat, his superior had admonished him. As a result, Jack had been treated to years of the mission shuffle, bouncing from one overseas assignment to another, until he'd finally landed in relative obscurity at Sacred Ground.

To heal, his superior said.

To hide, is what he really meant.

He reached out to shake the woman's hand.

"It's been a long time, Teri. How are you doing?"

Teri hesitated only a second before grasping the old man's hand and immediately was struck by how strong his grip was, even though the bones felt fragile beneath the wrinkled skin. He had aged a lot in sixteen years, his salt-and-pepper hair now completely silver and just skirting his bald crown, though his intense, pale blue eyes seemed as sharp as she had remembered. Those eyes had sent chills up her spine once; she was sure they could do that again, given the opportunity.

213

She fervently hoped there wouldn't be.

"You disappeared," she commented.

"Well, yes, the order thought they'd better stash me away somewhere where I couldn't do any more harm."

He shrugged, almost in apology. "The publicity wasn't exactly the kind my order goes looking for. Hard to explain. A real scandal. Easier to just sweep it under the rug. Kind of the standard protocol in that situation, you know. That, and denial."

Out of the corner of her eye, Teri could tell that Michael was confused by her acquaintance with Father Jack. He obviously didn't know about their history together, so she figured she could fill him in later if need be. She turned to Khristina and Skye and introduced herself, then repeated her instructions about getting out of the house for the night and talking with Sam Kittleson in the morning about the threat.

"I thank you for your concern, Lieutenant Ostrand, but I will not be driven out of my home because someone sends me a letter that threatens death because I am the spawn of the devil," Khristina insisted. "I have heard this before. People do not understand what I do, and because they do not understand, they ascribe evil to it. I am not afraid. This will pass, and they will leave me alone."

"But I can't let you take the chance that this time it will be different," Teri argued. "Someone's already thrown a brick through Michael's window. That's a step beyond notes in mail slots. What's next? More vandalism? Personal attacks? Until we know what we have here, or who, I just want to err on the side of safety."

"Come stay with me, Khristina," Skye offered. "I've got room. You're not allergic to cats, are you?"

"Michael, you can bunk with me tonight," Jack suggested. "At the old novitiate in town. That's where I'm staying. Lots of empty rooms these days. Nothing luxurious, but there's always something good in the fridge, and it's quiet. What do you say?"

Teri gave Michael a stern glare.

"Do it," she told him.

Michael looked at the solemn faces of the four people crowded into his study and sighed. Now, on top of everything else, he was getting kicked out of his own home.

"I'll go pack," he said and left the room.

CHAPTER FORTY-FIVE

Drake snapped off the television and tossed the remote control on the seat of the couch.

Once again, he was delighted with Mara's performance. When he'd handed her the sealed envelope in his office that morning, he hadn't doubted for a moment that she'd open it as soon as she was certain that she was alone. She was so predictable that way—hungry and unprincipled.

Actually, it was one of the things he liked best about her. He knew he could always count on Mara to be totally opportunistic.

Phoebe, however, was starting to worry him.

Her success at the *World* had gone to her head. Did she really think she could persuade him to run with the Carilion story, after he'd made it painfully clear what he thought about the man and his complete lack of credibility? The fact that she was challenging his judgment would have bothered him in regards to any potential story, but to have her so insistent that he was making a mistake really rankled him. To top it off, her unabashed admiration for Carilion was making him ill, not to mention how genuinely enthused she had sounded when she told him about her meeting with the man and her faith in his work.

Faith.

Drake sneered and tossed back a glass of neat whiskey.

The only faith Phoebe had had for the last four years was that if she made him happy, both in and outside the office, then life would treat her well.

And it had.

He had.

And she'd been so willing, he thought, just like a malleable piece of clay that begged for him to give her shape. He'd taken her under his wing and taught her every journalist's trick in the book. With his money footing the bills, he'd sent her around the globe to investigate cutting-edge scientific breakthroughs, garnering her professional acclaim and high visibility among colleagues much older and more experienced than she. Unaware of his real motives, Phoebe had kept tabs for him on every researcher who was trying to formulate the One Theory, and by cultivating her own network of lab sources, she'd provided him with an inside track on the progress of every research project.

Except for Carilion's Strings Project.

The good professor had somehow erected an impenetrable wall around his work. His technicians kept their mouths shut. He kept the college administration in the dark, and Stevenson, the idiot, had let him. Phoebe couldn't find a single chink in the wall to spy through. If luck hadn't played heavily into his hands, he very much doubted he would ever have learned how close Carilion was to solving the equations, until it was too late. And then, when Scranton had called him offering the scoop, he was convinced fate was in his corner. Phoebe, of course, had jumped at the chance to interview him. She had made it almost unbelievably easy.

But now, he found himself doing something rather uncharacteristic—he was wondering if perhaps he had made a fatal error in letting Phoebe into the mix with Carilion. Apparently, he had missed something in her before—a hidden, even ruthless, determination that at some point, the student would surpass the teacher and move on.

Ambition, he supposed, or perhaps pride.

Obviously, Phoebe believed her moment had come, convinced that she'd found her great opportunity in Carilion's work, and, if truth be told, she had. But she didn't know that for a fact, or at least, she wouldn't have proof of it until she saw the evidence in Carilion's lab.

Which led The Gentleman to only one conclusion: he could not allow Phoebe to visit the lab. Pride was, after all, one of the Seven Deadly Sins.

He poured himself another drink, called her cell phone and waited for her to answer.

"Phoebe, darling, I was such a pig today," he said smoothly when she picked up. "I want to apologize. Will you be home later?"

CHAPTER FORTY-SIX

What a day, Teri thought, heading home for a late supper. *I got to tell a man his wife was cheating on him before she was murdered, and odds are that she was cheating with his best friend. It just doesn't get any better than this, does it?*

Unfortunately, it probably wouldn't, she reminded herself, because even though she was ninety-nine percent certain Michael hadn't killed his wife and best friend, she would still have to question him in connection with the murders when he showed up at her office in the morning. She had new leads, and she needed to drag out from him whatever information he might have—including things he might not even realize he knew—that could possibly help.

For Michael's sake, she hoped that Lucas wasn't the man that Elise had met at the Dutch Iris, because then he wouldn't have to deal with a betrayal by the two people he loved most. On the other hand, if it was Lucas, it just might make Teri's job a whole lot easier and finally solve Elise's murder. Facts were facts: most homicides were committed by someone known to the victim, and when the victim was a woman, you could almost take it to the bank that the murderer was either the husband or a lover. Elise Carilion had opened the door to her killer late at night, a clear indication she had known who it was, and that, moreover, it was someone she trusted. Lucas would have fit that bill to a T.

As for motive, who knew? In a love triangle, it was generally about passion. Had Elise decided to call it off, and Lucas couldn't accept it? Or was Lucas the one who decided to end it, but couldn't risk Michael finding out and possibly losing his job over it? Committing murder to keep a job was so far beyond any rationalization that Teri could never believe it happened that way, even though she'd heard the stories again and again over the years from her colleagues.

And even if the Elise–Lucas connection accounted for Elise's death, that still left Teri grasping for leads in Lucas's murder. It wasn't like Elise had come back from the dead for vengeance and stuck the knife in Lucas.

Which led Teri to think again about the other picture in that manila envelope on her desk this morning—the photo of Michael and Phoebe Dauwalter, their heads together over coffee.

The typewritten note with it suggested that they looked especially cozy, and that "one good turn deserves another," according to the anonymous tipster. Teri recalled, too, how angry Michael had sounded on the phone this morning when she'd mentioned Phoebe's name to Michael. Now she caught herself second-guessing her initial response that he was angry to learn that Phoebe was with Lucas when he died.

Was he angry, instead, not that Phoebe was with Lucas, but that Teri knew that she was?

That's where that one percent of doubt came in, bred in by years of being a very thorough cop. She was sure Michael hadn't been feigning ignorance tonight when she told him about Elise and Lucas, but then again, she could be wrong. She also couldn't forget that while Michael had a temper, he could also be a very patient man. Despite the frustration of finding no leads in Elise's murder, Michael had never pressed Teri for results during her investigation, and professionally, he was accustomed to projects that ran for years, not just weeks or even months, which meant he was a careful planner. If Michael had been waiting for revenge, a late Friday night, months later, outside a low-life bar, might be the best place for it.

Especially if Michael could depend on Lucas being there, drunk, with a certain science editor.

Teri wondered what Phoebe Dauwalter would have to say about it, as well as what she might say about the coffee picture. In itself, the photo meant nothing. Certainly a well-known physicist would know the local science writers covering the beat.

Phoebe had also willingly cooperated with Teri in the wake of Lucas's murder, explaining that she was working on a story about a project in Michael's lab, so it made perfect sense that she would meet with Michael himself to continue her research. On the other hand, if there was something more sinister going on between the two, maybe Phoebe was a really good actress, too, as well as an ambitious science editor.

And if all that came to nothing, if Teri could prove—and she desperately hoped she could—that Michael was innocent of everything except work-induced tunnel vision, then she had a different riddle to solve: who was setting Michael up, and why?

Teri pulled into her driveway and hit the garage door opener. To her surprise, Jamie's car was already in its stall, his business trip finished in one day instead of two. She sighed in blissful anticipation, already feeling the foot massage her husband would give her before bed. She was going to need all the relaxation she could get tonight, because tomorrow, no doubt, was going to be another exhausting day.

CHAPTER FORTY-SEVEN

Michael watched Skye pull away from the curb with Khristina in the front seat beside her and suddenly realized he had no idea where they were headed, since he hadn't asked where Skye lived. For a crazy moment, he almost felt bereft, like something important had been taken from him, and then the moment passed. It wasn't like Khristina Tupikova had walked out of his life, he told himself, even if he wished she would. They both had a date at the police station in the morning, so he'd see her then.

In the meantime, she'd be safe at Skye's apartment from any cult members or religious stalkers, since no one would know where she was.

Including him.

He had another flash of that weird feeling and realized it was a wisp of loneliness.

Now, *that* was crazy. He'd been surrounded all day by people who apparently couldn't wait to barge into his life. 'Lonely' was the last thing he was.

Or, to be completely accurate, 'alone' was the last thing he was.

But loneliness . . . that was something different. Tonight, he just might be the loneliest man on the planet. He'd just learned that his marriage had been a sham. His wife of twenty years, the woman he'd loved almost from the moment he'd first met her, had been . . . he couldn't even think the words right now. His best friend was dead. His lab was closed down, his theory hung out to dry. And now, for the icing on the cake, someone was trying to frame him for murder.

And that was when he suddenly realized he didn't want Khristina Tupikova to walk out of his life after all. He wanted her to watch television with him and listen to her call Cinderella's pumpkin a squash. He wanted her to quote Shakespeare and Blake and whoever else she wanted. He wanted to argue with her and smell her perfume because she made him feel like he was alive again after being dead with Elise. Eight months of mourning, eight months of working like a madman, and tonight, he had nothing to show for any of it.

Disgusted with the rush of his unexpected feelings, he angrily tossed his packed gym bag in the bed of Jack's truck and stepped up into the cab.

"Hey, I'm not that bad of a driver," Jack protested when he saw Michael's stormy expression. "I know you wanted to take your car, but there's limited parking at the novitiate, and this way, we can talk on the way there."

"It's not your driving, Jack. I'm just having a very bad day."

"Yeah, I can see that. Want to talk about it?"

Michael laid his head back on the headrest and closed his eyes.

"No."

"Okey-dokey," Jack replied, putting the truck in gear. "Let's roll."

Jack turned left at the end of Michael's street and headed towards the college.

"The novitiate's on the other side of the campus, as I recall," he said. "About six blocks down."

He threw a glance in Michael's direction, but the physicist's eyes were still closed.

"Since we'll be passing right by, how about you give me the nickel tour of Barnet?"

Michael still didn't respond.

"I'll take that as a yes," Jack announced.

From the other side of the Ford's bench seat, Michael groaned.

Jack grinned and drove to the college's entrance where he followed the main drive around the administration buildings. "Where's your lab?" he asked.

Michael lifted his head from the headrest and pointed across the quad to a four-story, ivy-covered building.

"There," he said. "Top floor, right side of the building."

Jack pulled into an empty visitor's slot behind the big, shallow bowl of the non-functioning fountain, giving them a clear view of Michael's lab windows.

"Looks pretty quiet out here tonight," he observed. "I always like this time of evening. Like everything's winding down after the sun's set."

He put the car in park and punched down hard on the emergency brake pedal, then turned in his seat to face Michael.

"So how do you know Teri Ostrand?"

Michael looked at Jack in the darkness of the car, the old priest's high cheekbones reflecting light from the streetlamps on the quad.

"I was going to ask you the same thing."

"I asked first," Jack said.

Michael felt a small smile twitch at the corner of his mouth. The old man was incorrigible.

"Teri was assigned to my wife's murder case. She worked her tail off trying to find the killer. I think it was as hard on her as it was on me when she had to give up on finding any answers. That's why she came by tonight," he added. "There's a new lead."

"The stuff on the television?" Jack asked.

"Yeah."

He looked straight ahead through the windshield. He'd told Jack earlier that he didn't want to talk about it, but now he knew he did. It was like he was carrying this unformed lump in his mind, and maybe saying the words would start to give it a recognizable shape, and then he could begin to understand it, fit it somehow into the way he'd pictured his life.

Like reworking an equation with a really lousy variable so that it made sense.

Who was he kidding?

It was never going to make sense, never fit into his life. As a matter of fact, that life had ceased to exist as soon as Teri had said the word 'affair.'

"Elise was seeing someone," he told Jack. "I didn't know."

"Oh, Michael, I'm sorry," Jack said. He reached over and gripped Michael's shoulder.

"Yeah. Me, too."

Jack put his hand back on the steering wheel and looked out at the quad.

"I can't say I know exactly how you feel, son, but I do know how it feels to be betrayed by the people you trust most. It just about kills you, but it doesn't."

His voice grew soft, sad. "You almost wish it would."

The ring of personal experience, the trace of remembered pain, in his voice was unmistakable, leaving Michael intrigued.

"Who betrayed you, Jack?"

In the dim light of the cab, Jack studied Michael.

The younger man looked tired, lines of pain and concern bracketing his mouth and creasing his forehead. He didn't look like a world-famous physicist who had solved the most exotic and elusive equations of scientific history, who had made history himself, who probably had fame and fortune waiting for him just around the bend. Nor did he look like the avenging angel surrounded by shattered glass that Khristina had described to him and Skye in the study earlier in the evening while Michael had talked with Teri in the living room.

He simply looked like a man, a man who had hit the wall of disillusionment one too many times, and as a result, had lost his bearings in the world. Jack remembered what that had felt like and how much he'd needed a friend when it had happened to him. Maybe now, he could be that friend for Michael.

"For a long time," he began, "I kept a secret about myself, about who I was, from my order. I felt like I didn't have a choice. If I told them about it, it would be a scandal, because they couldn't accept it, and I was afraid they'd ask me to leave, and I couldn't do that, because come hell or high water, I love being a Jesuit. It's who I am. You know what I mean, Michael? You find out who you are and where you belong, and that's all there is to it. For me, it was being a priest."

Michael thought it over, recalling his instant attraction to theoretical physics in his high school science class, the fascination, which had only grown more powerful over the years. His gaze slid across the quad to his lab windows.

"For me, it was physics."

"Exactly," Jack agreed, thumping the steering wheel with the heel of one palm. "We all have a calling. It's what we do, who we are. It's God's gift, Michael. Anyway, I tripped up. My secret got out, and the order went ballistic. They couldn't handle it, so they stashed me away. They couldn't accept me for who I really was."

He paused.

"And that hurt. Even when you know it's coming, it can really hurt."

"This has something to do with what you were talking with Teri about, doesn't it?" Michael remembered the odd, brief exchange between the two in his study. "And you said something about publicity. Bad publicity, I think. Teri used to work with missing kids, runaways."

A horrible conclusion began to put itself together in Michael's head. He felt his body automatically shrink from the man beside him. "Tell me you weren't involved in one of those abuse cases—"

"Saints alive!" Jack sputtered. "Of course not. I'm not a pedophile, Michael!"

"I'm . . . I'm sorry, Jack." Now Michael was sputtering, embarrassed at his suspicion. "You said scandal, and I thought—"

"I know what you thought. You thought wrong, son." He took a deep breath and let it out again.

"I'm not a pedophile, Michael," he repeated. "I'm a psychic."

Michael blinked.

"But you're a priest."

"I know that," he assured him. "That was the problem. My order didn't want me to be both. I helped Teri find a child, and it leaked out to the media. Our mutual friend, *The Midnight Eye*, in fact. My superiors were beside themselves. They had a priest who had psychic powers! Now, there's a real vote of confidence in the credibility of the Catholic Church, wouldn't you say? I was right up there with appearances of Elvis, miracle fat cures, and the predictions of astrologers. Believe me, my superiors couldn't get me out of sight fast enough."

Remembering the chaotic aftermath of his brief stint as a psychic child-finder, Jack was tempted to laugh out loud at the memory of the frantic look on the faces of his Jesuit brothers at the city shelter when the tabloid came out. They clearly didn't know what to make of him. Psychic powers weren't one of the seven gifts of the Holy Spirit, and when some of the men staying at the shelter repeatedly begged Jack for a winning lottery ticket number, Jack's brothers decided they had a problem on their hands. Then, when the reporters wouldn't stop badgering

Jack for an interview, the brothers grew alarmed, so they called in for reinforcements: the provincial superior.

"I was an embarrassment," Jack told Michael. "I didn't fit into any bishop's pastoral statements, let alone ministry job descriptions. And it's not like the Church is especially fond of hearing about private revelations or in the habit of giving her stamp of approval to visions too often, either. Look at what's been going on over at Medjugorie in Europe—millions of pilgrims in forty years, reports of miracles, and the Vatican's still thinking it over. Heaven forbid they get it wrong!

"Oh, I know," he said, his right hand stretched out defensively, warding off Michael's protest, "it's not like they haven't made mistakes. What about those Inquisition boys, huh? I guess they must have just slipped in the back door. Anyway, I got pulled off my ministry at the men's shelter and sent to Argentina for a few years. Disappeared, like Teri said. When I got back, they'd figured out what to do with me. I was assigned to Sacred Ground—a nice, safe spot where no one knew about my special gift, and no one ever would. And that, Michael, was a direct order from my superior: hide this particular light under a bushel basket, Father Jack. A big basket. And keep it there."

CHAPTER FORTY-EIGHT

The cold was worse than frigid, and Jack had to concentrate hard to keep the child in his thoughts as he walked the tiny lanes of Pioneer Village, the restored historic town square outside Litchfield. The tourist season had ended with the first of October and wouldn't resume until the first of May, but now, in late January, it was like an abandoned ghost town, the thin clapboard walls of the pioneers' homes gray and sullen beneath a waning moon. If five-year-old Scott Waneke was tucked inside one of those old houses, he wouldn't make it through the night—the windchill was already twenty below zero.

He turned to the young woman, buried deep in her police-issue parka, walking beside him.

"You could wait in the car, Teri. It's brutal out here."

Officer Ostrand's fur-lined hood shook a negative at him, and her eyes, scrunched almost closed against the cold, pinned his.

"Which way?" she asked, her breath forming tiny puffs in front of her lips.

Jack stood quietly for a moment and tried to piece together the images in his mind. The cold seemed to make his thoughts slow. He'd never noticed a temperature effect before. Then again, it wasn't like he did this on a regular basis. Most of the time he was perfectly content just to talk with William and simply ignore the flashes of visions he picked up.

But tonight, when he'd seen that television news report on at five o'clock and the picture of Scott almost jolted him out of his easy chair, he knew he didn't have a choice. The child was going to die if Jack didn't go to the police and tell them where to find the boy.

Of course, that had been easier said than done.

Figuring he'd be passed off as a crank caller, he'd had the foresight to go in person to the station. With his priestly collar plainly showing at his throat, he'd asked to speak to whoever was looking for Scott. He was directed to a young policewoman bent over a map on a table, with a walkie-talkie squawking on her shoulder.

"I know where he is," Jack said to the woman, who looked barely old enough to be out of high school, let alone the police academy.

She straightened and looked him over, her eyes stopping at his white collar.

"Hello, Father," she said, "we could sure use a prayer, here."

Then she realized what he'd said.

"You know where Scott is?"

Jack nodded. "But I don't know exactly where it is until I see it."

The young woman looked confused.

"I'm psychic," he told her. "There isn't much time. We need to go right now so he doesn't freeze to death."

The patrolwoman took a step back. "Wait a minute." She looked at his collar again, pointedly.

"Are you really a priest, or are you some guy who gets a kick out of pretending to be one and saying you're a psychic? Look, mister, we've got teams out right now, combing through Scott's non-custodial father's neighborhood, because that's who Scott was last seen with. I'm holding down the fort. I don't have time for games."

Although he'd really hoped for a better reception than this, Jack knew it had been a long shot. People who professed they had extrasensory skills weren't typically welcomed with open arms by the vast majority of the population. And now Jack knew he couldn't waste any more of Scott's precious time convincing the woman. So he did the only thing he could think of to prove to her that he was a priest as well as a psychic.

He focused his pale blue eyes on her for a moment, then said, "I'm Father Jack Gerrity. I work at the men's shelter downtown; call them to verify. Your name is Teri, your fiancé is Ivan, and, oh my, you bought an early pregnancy test kit today. And your mother would really rather you were a dental hygienist."

He knew what her response would be and he wasn't wrong: her pupils dilated as she instinctively leaned away from him and pulled in a deep breath of amazement.

"I won't tell your mother about the EPT," he promised her in a whisper, then repeated, "but we need to go right now."

Without another word, Teri grabbed her parka and led him out to her car.

Now, in the middle of an empty tourist attraction, he tried to visualize Scott's hiding place. The boy was on a cot. It was in a corner. No windows. Barrels. Not a house.

"We've got to find a storeroom, or a cellar," he told Teri.

"That deadbeat," Teri muttered through chattering teeth. "Of all days to abduct his own kid. And then he gets T-boned in his car bringing back dinner. I hope he rots in prison."

"Teri, please," Jack reminded her, his cheeks stinging from the air's freezing bite while he shielded his eyes with his gloved hand from yet another blast of wind. "I need to focus here."

"Sssorry."

Even with her parka hood pulled tight against her face, Jack knew that Teri could feel the tips of her ears going numb. The temperature was continuing to plummet.

"Come on, Ssscott," Teri pleaded beside Jack. "Tell him where you are. Please!"

They walked slowly past a stable, an old saloon, and two houses, Jack holding the image of the boy's face in his mind, concentrating, while Teri swept her flashlight back and forth across the frozen ground. As they turned a corner, the wind slapped a sign hanging against the side of a building, the sharp cracks loud in the night. Jack felt the cold slicing through his own coat, the air too brittle to breathe. His thoughts were scattering, his pulse racing, whether from the cold or picking up psychic cues, he wasn't sure.

And then he saw it.

The old general store.

He rushed up the wide wooden stairs, Teri right behind him. He reached for the door and it swung open at his touch.

"Scott! Scott!" Teri yelled, dashing into the room, her flashlight sweeping the area before she bolted around a tall front counter to enter a small back storeroom. Barrels were stacked along one side and in the corner was a cot, mounded high with old blankets. Caught in the glare of Teri's light, a small face, eyes wide and frightened, peeped out from beneath the covers. Crossing the room quickly to the child's side, Teri sank to the floor beside the cot and touched the boy's cheek with her gloved fingers.

"Hi, Scott," she said gently. "I'm Officer Teri, and I'm going to take you home.'

CHAPTER FORTY-NINE

Filled with memories, Jack sat motionless in the car. Teri had called the recovery in and an ambulance had met them at the entrance to the village. By the time she drove Jack back to the police station, there had been a press of reporters waiting for them in the bitter January night. He'd tried to slip away, and thought he'd succeeded until more reporters showed up at the shelter in the morning, clamoring for interviews, trying to get film of him. The tabloids jumped on the story, and he'd been called before his superiors.

After the cold of Wisconsin, he hadn't really minded the warmth of a year in Argentina, but the chill of his superiors' rejection of his psychic abilities was something from which he didn't know if he'd ever recover. What was he supposed to do? Deny the gift that God had given him? He had saved a child's life with that gift!

All right, so maybe 'psychic' wasn't exactly included in the list of gifts that St. Paul had listed in his correspondence to the early churches. Then again, 'discernment of spirits' was definitely there. And wasn't that exactly what he'd been doing that night in Pioneer Village—discerning?

"You know, it really is just a matter of language," Jack mused aloud, almost having forgotten that Michael was sitting in the truck with him.

"Language?"

"Yes. As long as I'm psychic, that's a problem. But once you publish your One Theory, I can come out of the closet, so to speak."

Jack laughed at the irony of it—only by stripping his gift of its spiritual dimension could he make it acceptable to his spiritual director.

"I'll finally be legitimate," he told Michael. "I won't be an embarrassment to my superior anymore, because instead of headlining *The Midnight Eye*, I could be featured in a physics journal, processing energy packets of information from the eleventh dimension of theoretical physics. So long, Elvis. Hello, respected science."

Michael turned in his seat to face Jack. "Are you saying you can do what Khristina does? Receive energy packets?"

Jack shook his head.

"No. There's no way I can do what she does. From what I can tell, her gift covers different territory than mine. But basically, I guess, yes, I do the same thing. In your language, I pick up energy. Respond to it. Interpret it. But I'm not very good at it. Nothing like Khristina. It's like I'm only sensitive to a small band of this energy, but Khristina, well, from what I've heard, she's got the best reception of anyone around. Must be ultrasensitive to 'energy forms,' I'd guess."

He spread out his fingers on the wheel. "Well, heck, you probably already know that. You worked with her."

Yes, he had worked with her. But he hadn't pursued that kind of research with Khristina, Michael realized, research investigating sensitivities to different types of energy, sensitivities that might reveal more about how to configure and access the eleventh dimension. Listening to Jack had kick-started his thinking though, and almost before he was aware of it, his thoughts were tumbling around, ideas for new projects forming as fast as he could conceive them. If he could get both Khristina and Jack in the lab . . .

"Would you come into the lab?" Michael blurted out, his excitement growing by the minute as he imagined what two gifted receivers in tandem might be capable of.

Jack threw him a skeptical look. "Right now? It's kind of late, isn't it?"

Michael shook his head. "No, I don't mean right now. I mean later."

And then it hit him again like a sledgehammer: as of tonight, he didn't have a lab to work in.

The Strings Project had been shut down.

He shot his fist into the glove compartment door in front of him. "No!"

He looked out into the darkness of the quad. He had to get his lab back. He had to get his theory published. He turned to Jack again.

"Will you help me, Jack? Will you help me get my work published?"

Jack was just about to remind Michael that he'd already announced that was the reason he'd come to Litchfield, when another thought took its place. A slow smile spread across his face, his eyes lighting in the night while a steady certainty filled him with clarity and wonder.

"That's it," he whispered. "That's the real reason William sent me to you and Khristina."

He thumped the steering wheel in delight as the practical implications of his realization flooded through him. "I help you get your One Theory published, and I'm home free, special gifts and all. Don't you see, Michael?"

He reached over and jubilantly punched Michael's shoulder. "Once the One Theory is out there, and people know all about it, my psychic ability won't be a stigma for the order anymore—it'll be good science!"

"So you'll help?" Michael asked.

"Help? I'll lead the attack myself!"

"And your superiors won't interfere?" Michael pressed. "I mean, they'll be all right with you working on a scientific research team?"

"Michael, son, Jesuits love science. Ever hear of Teilhard de Chardin? One of the greatest scientific minds of the twentieth century? Jesuit. True, Rome had some problems with some of the things he was saying, but they got over it eventually."

"Correct me if I'm wrong, but wasn't he silenced by Rome?" Michael asked. "I seem to recall from my undergrad classes that his pioneering work in formulating the evolutionary sequence of the universe didn't exactly go over well with Church officials, since it conflicted with the party line on creation. He was exiled to China, where he continued to do stunning paleontology fieldwork, even though his own Church forbade him to publish his results."

"But like I said," Jack repeated, "they got over it. His scientific and religious works have all been published now and are still very influential. Some people even credit him with prefiguring global communications and the Internet because of his insistence on an emerging global consciousness. Not bad for a humble French priest.

"The point is, Michael," Jack continued, "the Church has had its share of great scientists. This whole science versus faith debate you hear about is baloney. Kids learn in school about Galileo and assume that every great scientific discovery has been a kick in the seat of religion. Absolutely not true. Look in your own backyard, Michael," he urged.

"What do you mean?"

Jack sat back against the old Ford seat and gave Michael a big smile. "I mean, you've got clerics all over your field of science. Father Georges Lemaitre helped formulate the big bang theory, and Father Angelo Secchi was one of the founders of astrophysics. On top of that, you've got some of today's most celebrated researchers saying that there's no conflict between believing in God and being a dedicated scientist. I've even read that some of them think all their work is slowly converging on one point, that over the last two hundred years in particular, all the really stunning developments in our scientific understanding of the universe seem to be pointing in the same direction, at one unifying idea."

He fixed his gaze on Michael.

"At something called the One Theory. Have you heard about that one, son?"

"Yeah."

Michael returned Jack's stare and phrased his words carefully. "I've heard those speculations, too."

"And you know what that One Theory is, don't you?"

Michael passed his hand over his eyes, not wanting to answer Jack.

"Well?"

"It's God," he finally said. "These particular scientists speculate that the perfect precision of mathematics, the intricacy of the human genome, the big bang theory itself, cannot be explained as statistically improbable accidents, but evidence of a greater intelligence. Evidence of God."

"Michael," Jack quietly asked, "have you considered that your one theory might be, in the end, *that* One Theory?"

But before Michael could even begin to form a reply, the sound of an explosion ripped through the night, and the two men instinctively dropped to the floor of the truck's cab.

"Saints alive!" Jack exclaimed. "What in the name of heaven was that?"

Ears ringing, Michael pulled himself back up to look over the dashboard and out the front windshield.

Directly across the quad, the Physical Sciences Building was in flames. Windows were still breaking, sheets of glass toppling out of twisted frames. Long tongues of fire licked up and down the brick exterior, devouring the brittle vines that had climbed up the walls. From what he could see, the worst of the damage was on the top floor, on the right side.

His lab.

"It's my lab," he said, stunned.

Jack joined him on the truck seat and looked at the blazing building.

"Not anymore."

CHAPTER FIFTY

S kye couldn't stop thinking about it.

From the moment she'd met Khristina that afternoon, she'd been wondering what it would be like to sit for a reading with her, to hear the voice of the dead through a medium.

As a Christian, she knew that only Jesus had returned after his death to communicate with his friends, yet she couldn't help but wonder if perhaps what Khristina did fell into a different category—an unusual category, to be sure, but one that was consistent with the faith she professed.

Christian history was, after all, filled with good people who had experienced heavenly visions or communication of some sort. Who was to say that Khristina wasn't simply following in their footsteps? Maybe what she experienced as a visit from a person who had passed on was actually a type of spiritual communion, some kind of a special gift from God.

Last Skye had heard, no one on earth could announce with complete assurance what God might allow. Didn't Paul say that himself in his letter to the Corinthians?

"No eye has seen, no ear has heard, no mind has conceived what God has prepared for those who love him."

Just the thought of such a gift sent goose bumps rolling over her arms, while another part of her was so curious, she could hardly keep her mouth shut from wanting to grill Khristina about her ability. On the short drive to her apartment, she'd almost blurted it out several times, but the good manners her mother had labored to instill in her had held firm—Skye refused to impose on Khristina, who was now going to be her overnight guest. She unlocked her apartment door and stepped inside, with Khristina following behind her.

"Mitch! Fitch! Mama's home!"

As she flipped on the light switch by the door, she noticed a small envelope on the floor.

"It looks like you have mail," Khristina said, bending down to pick up the envelope. She handed it to Skye.

Skye looked at her name on the front of the envelope, but didn't recognize the bold handwriting. She opened it and drew out a simple, elegant note card with the letter D engraved on the front.

"It looks very classy," Khristina observed, then added, smiling, "A special friend perhaps?"

"I don't think so," Skye replied. She flipped the card open and read the brief message.

Then she read it again.

"It's from Drake Lamont," she said.

"Who is this Drake Lamont?" Khristina asked. "You mentioned him earlier today, at Michael's home, but I do not know him. Michael seemed to recognize his name, and I had the distinct impression he does not care for Mr. Lamont."

Skye had gotten the same feeling, but had no clue why Michael would feel that way.

"Drake Lamont is Phoebe Dauwalter's boss," she explained to Khristina. "He owns the *World*. As a matter of fact, I met him this morning at Barnet. He offered me a job."

"That would be a feather in your hat, would it not?"

Skye smiled warmly at her guest for the evening. "A feather in my cap, you mean," she gently corrected Khristina. "I guess you could say that. It would be a great job with even better pay, that's for sure."

Idly, she wondered where her cats were. They usually met her at the door when she got home.

"I told him I'd think about it, but, in all honesty, he made me really uncomfortable, Khristina," Skye confided. "Like he was trying to intimidate me or something. I mean, sure, the man is rich and powerful and could probably buy and sell a dozen companies, but why waste his time on me? He can hire anyone he wants. *The World* is really a topnotch magazine, and all the editors and reporters are well known in their areas of expertise. I write for a supermarket rag! But Drake insisted he could see I had talent, and that's why he offered me a job. Still, I can't believe he makes a habit of reading tabloids like the *Eye* to discover new writers."

She stopped for a moment, unsure how much more to tell Khristina about her encounter with Drake. So far, she hadn't told anyone about either his financial involvement with the Strings Project or her own growing suspicion that he had been the one behind shutting the project down.

And she had no idea why Michael had seemed so negative when she had mentioned Lamont's name earlier. Her only conclusion was that the two men shared a bad history.

"Anyway," Skye held up the note card, "it's just a note saying he enjoyed meeting me and is looking forward to hearing my response."

"The man is very polite, though," Khristina pointed out. "He took the time to write you a note and have it delivered. Or perhaps he brought it himself to you. Maybe," she added, with a slow wink, "he was hoping to see you again."

For just a moment, Skye let herself remember what it felt like to be the focus of Drake Lamont's attention. It had certainly been a heady sensation, not to mention the purely physical reaction she had experienced, as well. She imagined his powerful presence, standing outside her door, note in hand . . .

He knew where she lived.

The realization traveled in a shiver down to her toes.

Skye was freezing.

What was it about Lamont?

One minute she was imagining him inside her apartment, feeling herself drawn to him like the proverbial moth to the flame, and the next, she was spooked so badly, she wanted to run and hide. Disgusted with her own conflicting emotions, she turned and closed the apartment door, locked it, and threw the deadbolt. She didn't like feeling vulnerable; she especially didn't like feeling exposed in her own home. After taking a breath and telling herself she was on the verge of ridiculous and unreasonable paranoia, she turned to face Khristina.

"Would you like something to drink?"

Walking towards the kitchen, though, she realized something was oddly different: there were no cats winding around her feet, begging for attention, tripping her up.

"Mitch? Fitch? Kitties?"

She turned to Khristina to explain.

"This is weird; they always greet me at the door." She looked into the kitchen again and saw them huddled under the table, wide-eyed.

Following right behind her, Khristina also looked under the table.

"Their fur sticks straight up! See their bushy tails?"

"This is really weird," repeated Skye. "Come on guys, come on out."

The cats stayed right where they were.

"I wonder what got them so freaked out," Skye muttered, grabbing two glasses from the cupboard. She dropped ice in the glasses and glanced out the window over the sink to watch a blood-red sunset.

"'Red sky at night, sailor's delight. Red sky at morning, sailor take warning.' I hope this heat breaks tomorrow," she said, leaving the window to reach inside the refrigerator for a pitcher of orange juice. "It's so unusual to have these high temperatures in

October. It makes me a little nervous, I guess. Like something's not right in the world."

She handed a filled glass to Khristina.

"I had this great-aunt who survived a tornado, and she always had all these little sayings about foretelling the weather. I thought they sounded pretty dumb when I was a kid, but I have to say, some of that old folk wisdom seems to hold up pretty well. Like the 'red sky at night' bit. It really does predict a calm night, weather-wise."

Skye took a drink of the juice.

"I wish I could tell my great-aunt that her sayings weren't so dumb after all. She had some great lines about falling for the wrong kind of guys. If I'd listened to her, maybe I would have spared myself some heartache." Skye laughed. "She would have seen my last boyfriend coming from a mile away, I bet."

"Then you should," Khristina said.

"Should what?"

"Tell her. Tell her she was wiser than you realized."

Skye could feel confusion flooding her face, but Khristina only smiled at her.

"Skye, I will do a reading for you."

Skye almost dropped her glass. A reading?

A reading!

"Really?" she finally managed to stutter out. "You could do that? I mean," she hastily added, "I know you can do that, but you'd do that for me? Like, now?"

Khristina laughed at Skye's reaction. The young woman's excitement delighted and amused her. All day, she'd had an overwhelming suspicion that Skye wanted to ask her to do a reading, but had refrained from asking. She didn't think Skye was being shy, though, and of course, being a reporter, she would have a curiosity about Khristina's abilities.

Finally, on the drive over, she'd decided that Skye was simply being polite. That, along with her generous offer of a place for the night, had convinced Khristina to do a reading for Skye.

Seeing her excitement now made Khristina even happier to oblige her.

Khristina directed Skye to place two of the kitchen chairs at right angles to each other, then sat down in one, while Skye sat in the other. Placing her hands in her lap, Khristina explained how the reading would work, and that she needed Skye to sit quietly with her while she tried to contact her great-aunt.

"Once she is here, you can ask questions and I will repeat them to her," Khristina instructed. "And I will tell you what she says. Are you ready?"

Skye swallowed the knot that had formed in her throat when Khristina had said "once she is here," and the reality of what she was going to do came crashing down around her. Goose bumps raised on her arms. She was going to talk to the dead.

Oh my. Do I really want to do this?

She took a deep breath.

"Yes," she told Khristina. "I'm ready."

Closing her eyes, Khristina relaxed, clearing her thoughts of everything that had happened in the day. She went to the door she always visualized in her mind and waited comfortably for it to open. A silent prayer crossed her lips, and the air shifted around her.

A small, fragile-looking woman approached. She had the same frizzy red hair that Skye wore tied back in a ponytail, and her hands looked roughened and calloused. She had an apron on that covered her chest and the front of her skirt.

"I have a woman coming through," Khristina said, her eyes still closed. "She has red hair, rough hands, and she says she is your great-auntie Edna and that you were right to get rid of the boy. I think his name is Josh, or Jerk?"

Skye nodded, dumbly, totally aware that she hadn't even told Khristina her great-aunt's name, let alone Josh the Jerk's.

"She is saying she has been busy, but she is so happy to have a chance to speak with you. She would not miss it."

"She loved to be busy," Skye said faintly.

"She says she is a farm-girl at heart, but she always liked to visit your family in Litchfield. You liked her homemade pies. When you visited her at the farm, you used to pick blackberries for her, and she would make you your own little pie to eat."

"Yes."

Suddenly, Khristina's eyes flew open and she lifted a finger to scold Skye.

"But it was naughty of you to take the little pie that was meant for your cousin Bradley. And you lied about it, too. You said the goat got loose and came and ate it. Shame on you! But Edna is laughing now about it. She says that Bradley deserved it—he was such a bully to you."

"He was! And everyone knew it," Skye insisted. "And he never believed Edna was really in a tornado, either. Ask her about it."

Eyes still open, Khristina seemed to be focusing on a spot about three feet in front of her.

Skye looked at the spot, too, and a shiver tripped down her spine. Was Edna really right there?

"It had been so hot," Khristina was saying, "almost like the weather we are having now. It was 1948, a muggy morning. Edna says she was helping Papa in the barn when she stepped outside to try to find a breath of fresh air, but there was no air moving anywhere. And then she turned around and she saw it. It was darkness racing toward the barn. Like a wall of boiling dark clouds moving along the ground. She yelled to her Papa and suddenly she heard the noise—like a big train rushing at her."

The words were practically tumbling out of Khristina, and Skye, though she'd heard the story many times from Edna's own lips, felt the awful mesmerization she'd always experienced upon hearing her aunt's frightening eye-witness account of a tornado's destructive fury. She kept her eyes glued to Khristina's expressive face, where she watched a mounting terror consume her features.

"She ran back in the barn and he grabbed her. He wanted to throw her in the southwest corner of the barn, where the floor was sunken, but an old washing machine was in the way! Papa picked it up and threw it aside! You don't know what you can do until you have to do it. Then he pushed me down into the corner and picked up an old wooden door he had been refinishing in the barn. He laid down on top of me with the door over us like a little roof.

"There was a terrible roar! My ears popped. All around us there was the noise of wood cracking, things banging into each other. I thought I was going to die! I could not breathe. But Papa covered me with his body and the old door, and all I got was a big gash in my leg where a milk can was slammed into me by the tornado.

"And then it was over. It was quiet. Papa slid the door to the ground and stood up. He pulled me up and hugged me. 'The good Lord has saved us,' he said. My leg felt wet, and I saw the blood running down my leg where the milk can had cut me. I looked around, and there were no walls left of the barn. We were standing in hay, wood splintered all around us. It was quiet, like there was no sound left in the world. My mother and sister were in the basement of our house, with all the windows blown out, but they were unhurt. We were lucky. Twelve people died in that tornado. Three of them were never found."

Khristina's voice faded away, and Skye thought that her face showed signs of strain. Only then did Skye realize that she'd heard Khristina using the first person as she related Edna's tale; her own attention had been so completely focused on Edna's experience that she'd almost forgotten that her great-aunt wasn't physically present in the room.

"Wow," Skye whispered.

A moment later, Khristina resumed speaking.

"So Edna says to remember, get down as low as you can when a tornado is coming, Skye, and if you can cover yourself, do that. She says this is important to know. Also, trust your intuitions. They are right, she says. They will keep you safe. And now she has to go. But . . . wait. There is someone else coming through now."

Skye watched Khristina's face slowly register surprise, and then a small smile.

"This is someone you haven't met, Skye," she said. "But he apologizes for his rude behavior. He did not mean to bump into you at the bar. He knows he drank too much and he is sorry." Her smile grew. "It is good to see you, Lucas."

Skye's stomach lurched. Her face went white.

"Lucas has come to tell us something important," Khristina continued, oblivious to Skye's response. "He wants me to tell Michael that he is brilliant, that his theory is correct, and that the eleventh dimension exists. But he says that I must convince Michael that the eleventh dimension is also heaven, and he knows a way I can do that. He says we must tell Michael that the little voice inside his head is not his inner . . . what?"

She paused speaking for a moment, frowning, as if she were trying to decipher something she'd heard.

"Oh," she resumed, "Lucas is telling me that Michael calls the voice his inner fan club, but it is really the voice of someone else."

"Michael hears someone from the eleventh dimension?" Skye choked, her eyes darting back and forth from Khristina to the small area in front of her, wondering if . . . Lucas . . . was right there.

Khristina blinked and sighed, leaning back in her chair.

"They are all gone," she told Skye.

"Khristina." Skye drew her own shaky breath.

She wasn't sure exactly what she had been expecting from the reading, but a visit from Lucas Scranton had certainly not been on the list. A dead man had just told her he had firsthand experiential evidence that the eleventh dimension not only existed, but that he himself was in it, and it was heaven. Not only that, but he knew something else his living associate didn't.

Skye's eyes met Khristina's.

"If Michael hears a voice, then he's . . . he's . . . "

"A medium," Khristina finished for her. "But he doesn't know it."

CHAPTER FIFTY-ONE

Drake parked the car a few blocks away and walked the rest of the way to Phoebe's place.

He loved his red Beemer, but he had to admit, there were occasions when he wished it weren't so memorable. Fortunately, for those occasions, he could always use one of his nondescript corporate vehicles. Not only did they give him a certain anonymity, but people hardly noticed them even when they were in plain view, say, parked on a dark downtown street or even tucked into a back parking lot at some out-of-the-way bed-and-breakfast.

Tonight, though, he wanted the car to be seen just where it was, right in front of his favorite bistro. He'd already been inside, made small talk with Leticia, the chatty bronze-headed bartender, and left his drink at a corner table, then slipped out the back door. He estimated he'd be back within the hour to make more small talk with her.

When Phoebe opened her door, Drake put on his best contrite expression and held out a small bouquet of delicate white roses.

"I am a boor and a pig. Will you forgive me?"

Phoebe looked at the lovely flowers in Drake's hand and tried not to smile at the exaggerated hangdog expression on his handsome face.

"That depends," she said, deliberately avoiding his pleading eyes as she lightly stroked one of the tiny petals. She looked up at him again through her lashes, gauging how long she could keep him standing outside her door as punishment for brow-beating her earlier in his office.

Phoebe had spent the intervening hours alternately fuming at and forgiving him in absentia, determined to stand her ground on having the *World* publish Michael's work. The fact that Drake had called to come apologize convinced her that he'd finally come to his senses and that she was on the verge of winning this particular battle of wills. Seeing his repentant expression and the promise of excitement that was already beginning to smolder in his silver eyes, Phoebe felt a ripple of anticipation. Even the hairs on the back of her neck were standing up.

But then, making up with Drake was always frighteningly good.

"Depends on what, if I may ask?"

Phoebe took the roses. "On whether you intend to stay on my doorstep or come into my condo," she told him. "Actions speak louder than words, and I don't want my neighbors getting a free show."

Drake smiled and stepped inside, bolting the door behind him.

CHAPTER FIFTY-TWO

Mara and her cameraman jumped out of the van almost before it had come to a full stop in front of the Barnet College library. Fire trucks and police cars were already haphazardly parked on the quad itself, while two ambulances idled by the dry fountain. Flames were still reaching across the top of the Physical Sciences Building, and big billows of smoke were now rising from portions of the building where the firefighters had aimed their hoses of streaming water. In the middle of the quad, three policemen were stringing a barrier of tape between park benches to keep curious students and other onlookers out of the immediate area around the building. Glass and bricks and other debris littered the sidewalks.

Mara's cameraman let out a low whistle. "Man, I hope there weren't any classes in session when that baby blew."

"Let's find out." She headed for the closest person in uniform. "Mara Runyon with Channel 9. Who's in charge here?"

"Over there," the Barnet security guard replied, pointing to a clutch of men standing in front of the fountain.

Mara hustled across the quad with her cameraman at her side, then skidded to a halt about ten feet away from the men.

She recognized two of the four: the Litchfield fire chief and Michael Carilion. The other two appeared to be a policeman and a priest.

"Start filming as soon as I open my mouth," she instructed her cameraman in hushed tones. Stopping briefly to finger-comb her long hair back over her shoulders, Mara approached the group, her cameraman already angling slightly off to the side to be in place for his shot.

"Mara Runyon with Channel 9," Mara announced, striding up to the men who were engaged in earnest conversation. "Chief Magnussen, what's happened here tonight?"

The four men turned to face her, but Mara kept her eyes on the fire chief, demanding a response.

She could have sworn she felt a tangible wave of hatred rush toward her from Carilion.

"We've had an explosion on the top floor of the Physical Sciences Building, Ms. Runyon. At this point, it's too early to say what caused it or why, but we'll be making a full investigation as soon as we can safely enter the building."

"Was anyone in the building when it blew?"

"Not that we know of," Magnussen told her. "Classes had been finished for the day for a while already, and we think the building was empty. There's a night security guard who makes rounds in the building, but he was on the first floor when the explosion occurred and was able to safely exit."

Without warning, Mara swung towards Michael.

"Dr. Carilion, isn't your lab in the Physical Sciences Building? Do you think there's any possibility this explosion could be connected to the recent controversy surrounding your work with the Russian medium?"

It was all Michael could do to keep from grabbing the woman's microphone right out of her hand and launching it into the empty fountain.

"No comment," he said through gritted teeth and turned to leave.

"Dr. Carilion! Would you care to comment on today's revelation that your wife was conducting a secret affair prior to her death, or on rumors that her lover was your lab assistant who was murdered three nights ago?"

Michael froze. Jack, standing silently beside him, grabbed his arm.

"Don't give her what she wants, son. She's baiting you."

"I'm fully aware of that, Jack," Michael said tightly. "But you're not the one whose life is being shredded and flushed down the toilet right now, either."

In the reflected glare of the flames and fire trucks' lights, his face was hard, steeled for attack.

"No, I'm not," Jack agreed. "But I know a viper when I see one, and she's it. Walk away, Michael. Keep your eye on the prize."

But Mara wasn't done.

"If I were Phoebe Dauwalter, I'd be watching my back right about now," she shouted at him. "People around you tend to wind up dead, Carilion! Funny how that works, isn't it?"

Michael spun to face her again.

"Go to hell, Runyon."

"And find you waiting for me? No thanks, Doctor."

She called to her cameraman. "Skip! Let's try for an angle closer in." And she was gone.

"Isn't Dauwalter the reporter you talked to this morning?" Jack asked. "The one who's going to break your story?"

Michael was staring after Mara, still seething. "Yes. So what does Runyon know about it?"

He was so focused on the reporter that he didn't realize Jack was making a grab for the silver whistle he had taken from him back at the house and then hung around his own neck to keep it out of the priest's hands and lips. When Jack jerked it roughly to the side, however, bringing Michael's head swinging around to face him, Michael's attention abruptly landed on the shorter man's weathered face.

"It's a small town, Michael," Jack pointed out to him. "They're both in the media business. Talk flies."

"I don't like it, Jack. Phoebe and I were discreet. We met in an empty coffee shop and sat at a back table for privacy. We agreed on confidentiality." His eyes narrowed in suspicion. "How does Runyon know these things? She knew about . . . "

He was going to say *Elise*, but couldn't bring himself to say her name.

"The inn," he finished, "before I did. It's one thing for Runyon to hate me, but this—this is something else. It's like she smells blood—my blood—and she's moving in for the kill."

"Then there's only one thing you can do."

Jack released the whistle, and it fell back on Michael's shirt. "Make her your ally."

Michael laughed bitterly. "Over my dead body."

"Let's hope not, son," Jack replied, heading for the truck. "Let's hope not."

CHAPTER FIFTY-THREE

It was just under an hour before Drake slipped back into the bistro. Crowded now with young professionals waiting for dinner, the little restaurant was noisy and busy. Drake edged his way up to the bar and asked Leticia for another drink.

"Alone tonight?" she asked.

"Apparently," he answered. "I think I've been stood up. I've been waiting for the last hour for a friend, but she has yet to arrive."

"Her mistake, Mr. Lamont. Everyone in this town knows you don't keep The Gentleman waiting."

Drake laughed. "Is that what they say?"

Leticia nodded. "Oh yeah. We've got a regular clientele in here from the *World,* and they all agree that what Drake Lamont wants, Drake Lamont gets. And woe to the poor soul who's late to an editorial meeting."

She leaned her elbows on the finely polished bar and brought her face close to his. "They say The Gentleman isn't always a gentleman," she whispered. "They say that sometimes, he's the devil himself."

"And what do you think, lovely Leticia?"

The redhead pulled back to give him an admiring stare. "I think the devil can be downright attractive, given the right circumstances."

Drake tipped his glass in her direction.

"I thank you for your vote of confidence," he said. "It's always nice to hear."

He left a generous tip on the bar and started to walk out when he noticed a small knot of people clustered in front of the flat-screen television in the corner of the bistro's entryway. A burning building filled the screen before the camera swung back to focus on Mara Runyon.

"We've also had it confirmed that Dr. Carilion was here on the campus when the lab exploded," she reported, "despite the fact that his lab had been shut down by the college as a result of his involvement last night in the near-riot at the home of the Russian medium, Khristina Tupikova. Earlier, I had the chance to speak with the professor, but he refused to comment on his presence here, or on the rumors that surfaced this afternoon about his late wife's secret affair."

Mara's image was replaced with a shot of a quaint inn and an inset photo of a strikingly beautiful dark-haired woman.

"A new lead," Mara's voice continued, "in the unsolved murder of Elise Carilion has investigators scrambling tonight as they try to determine the identity of the man she was meeting at this rural inn."

A photo of Lucas was added to the mix on the television screen.

"The most pressing question seems to be if he was Dr. Lucas Scranton, Dr. Carilion's research associate, who was killed this weekend in what was originally thought to be a botched mugging, but has now been tagged as a murder case."

"Sounds like this guy is in pretty deep," a young man standing next to Drake commented. "His wife was sleeping with his associate, they both get whacked, and now his lab explodes? And he's running around with a Russian psychic? This guy's lost it, big-time, man."

Drake's gaze left the screen, where Mara was now interviewing the fire chief. He turned to the man and smiled.

"I think you're right."

CHAPTER FIFTY-FOUR

I told Khristina about you and Michael."

"I know, but I don't know that it will do any good."

"Michael's a brilliant physicist. He can't deny the evidence."

"The question is whether he will believe the evidence. He's not the first stubborn man in the world, Lucas."

"Speaking from experience?"

"Absolutely. Wait . . . someone's coming."

They watched the figure approach. It was a woman.

"Lucas?" she asked.

"Phoebe?"

The fellow next to Lucas extended his hand. "I don't believe we've met. I'm Albert. Albert Einstein."

CHAPTER FIFTY-FIVE

Drake stood on his penthouse balcony and looked out over the sleeping city. Even this late, the air was still warm and laced with humidity, a most unusual condition for October.

Not that he was complaining. He liked the heat. In fact, he positively reveled in it. The years he'd spent in graduate school in Arizona had been some of the best years of his life.

He wondered if Carilion liked heat, too, because if the physicist thought he was in hot water already with the reopened investigation of his wife's death and the rumored connections to his assistant Scranton, that was going to be nothing compared to what was waiting for him in the morning.

In the distance, he thought he could barely make out some traces of smoke lingering over the campus at Barnet College.

He raised his whiskey glass to the night sky. "From whence cometh my help, O Lord?" he sneered. "We both know it wasn't from you, don't we? I'm going to have to find my unknown accomplice and thank him properly, I think. Although his timing could have been a little better, all things considered, I believe he did me a favor tonight. Without his lab, Carilion has nothing left, does he? Such a pathetic man he has become, and so quickly."

He finished his drink, reviewing again how skillfully Mara had exploited the bombing of Carilion's lab. She had practically accused the physicist of blowing up his own lab right on camera. Coupled with her televised implications earlier in the day of Carilion's involvement in a sordid love triangle, her campaign of character assassination was drawing to a brilliant close.

What little professional credibility the professor had had left after his cameo with the Russian medium last night was certainly now dead in the water.

And as soon as the police discovered Phoebe's body in the morning, along with the "evidence" Drake had planted, Carilion wouldn't even have his freedom.

For the first night in a long time, Drake was looking forward to a night of sound sleep, knowing that his kingdom was secure with Carilion and his 'eleventh dimension' irrevocably benched.

It really was too bad about Phoebe, though, The Gentleman had to admit. For her, the bombing had come just a little too late—if Drake had known the lab wasn't going to be there in the morning, perhaps he wouldn't have been so quick to solve the problem of her seeing Carilion's work. Then again, it would only have delayed the inevitable, since she'd made it abundantly clear to him yesterday that she was one problem that was just not going to simply go away. Her determination to bring Carilion's theory to light despite his directive had not only enraged him, it had quite effectively signed her death warrant. He simply couldn't risk anyone else taking a close look at Carilion's claims and following them to their logical conclusion.

Which meant that, tomorrow, he had to start looking for a new science editor.

Stepping back inside, he felt his cell phone vibrate in his pocket. He checked the caller ID and lifted the phone to his ear.

"Congratulations, darling," he said. "Mission accomplished. You should feel incredibly proud of yourself. You made Carilion look like a danger to society."

"He's called a press conference," Mara's perfectly modulated voice purred. "Tomorrow at noon. What do you think, Drake? Is he going to surrender to the police? Admit to two murders and a plot to blow up his lab? I'm going to bring champagne."

A press conference?

Drake felt an immobilizing spear of ice rise up his backbone. There was only one thing Michael Carilion could possibly have to announce to the world, and Drake Lamont knew for a fact that it wasn't a confession of murder.

"Drake? Did you hear what I said?"

Furious, he pitched his empty glass across the room. It hit the stone fireplace and shattered, raining little crystal shards across the black marble hearth.

"Yes, Mara, I heard you."

"And there was this old man with Carilion at Barnet. A priest. Chief Magnussen said his name was Jack Gerrity. Apparently Gerrity vouched for Carilion's whereabouts earlier in the evening when the bombing occurred, so my attempt at nailing Carilion himself for setting the explosive isn't going to fly."

Jack Gerrity.

Somewhere in Drake's memory, the name rang a distant warning bell, but he couldn't place it.

"Did you say Gerrity?" he asked Mara, his voice tight.

"Yes. Apparently he was a big sensation years ago. He helped find an abducted child using psychic abilities, or so the story went. But then he basically disappeared. I guess the Church didn't need his kind of publicity, if you know what I mean."

Drake did know, and now he remembered Gerrity. At a time when the Catholic Church was trying hard to make itself accountable amidst a wave of pedophile scandals, a Jesuit who claimed to be psychic in order to explain how he knew where to find a lost boy was not especially appreciated by his order. 'Inappropriate,' the Church spokesperson had called it. When it had made the news, Drake had counted it as another strike against the Church, with an added bonus tucked inside—not only were priests sexually suspect in the public eye, but the mention of psychic phenomena in connection with priests was doubly incriminating.

Ah, the things you can do with the right spin on information, Drake silently reflected.

Yet Gerrity had obviously survived his superior's censure to resurface with Carilion, and depending on the range of his psychic talents, that could only be bad news for Drake. If the priest was familiar with Carilion's research and had connected all the dots, then Gerrity might be even more of a threat to Drake than an earth-shaking scientific announcement at a noon press conference. Teamed with Carilion, the Jesuit priest might even be the one who could finally bring Drake's whole magnificent house of informational 'cards' tumbling irreversibly down.

In that case, the press conference could be a knockout punch that Drake would never survive.

How quickly things can go from good to bad, Drake thought. Or even worse.

Much worse.

He would have to get rid of the priest.

For that matter, he ought to remove the medium, too. She was, after all, the veritable proof of Carilion's pudding.

"I'll talk to you in the morning, Mara," he said and abruptly disconnected.

He needed to make some phone calls.

CHAPTER FIFTY-SIX

Skye had just handed Khristina a blanket to spread over herself on the living room couch when a sudden pounding on the apartment's door startled both of the women.

Hastily tightening the belt around her terry cloth bathrobe, Skye started towards the door, but before she could cross the room, Michael's voice came booming from the building's hallway, followed by Jack's voice telling him to keep it down. Skye quickly undid the series of locks on the door while Khristina stood up and stepped into her jeans, pulling them up beneath the sleep shirt she'd borrowed from her hostess. A moment later, the two men were inside, both of them buzzed with adrenaline and late-night caffeine.

"I'm going public," Michael announced. "Enough defense! I'm going on the offense. Tomorrow, noon."

Jack held up his hands in appeal to the women. "I can't get him to change his mind," he explained. "I think it's professional suicide, but he's determined to do this."

"I wanted you to know," Michael said to Khristina. "I don't want you to be blindsided again."

Skye winced.

"What are you going to say at this press conference, Michael?" Khristina asked. "Are you going to talk about my work in your lab?"

Michael fell into one of the wooden chairs at Skye's kitchen table. He dragged a hand through his hair, the curls damp on his neck from the still-high humidity.

"I'm not sure. I tried to call Phoebe Dauwalter twice in the last hour to see if she could help me out with this since she's going to do the article for the *World*, and I figure she's got the media savvy to pull this off, but she's not answering her phone. Jack and I have been going around and around with it for the last hour and a half. He's the one who gave me the idea!"

He slapped his hand on the table. "He said I should make Mara Runyon my ally. What better way to do that than let her in on the biggest science story of the century? I called her myself, told her I was going to make a surprise announcement, and if she wanted to be the one to carry it to the national networks, she'd better bring her cameraman. "

"You're going to announce the existence of the eleventh dimension," Skye guessed, a sense of vague dread welling up inside her.

"I just wanted to know if, by chance, you knew something I didn't, and if that were the case, believe me, I'd make sure it didn't happen again."

Why did she keep remembering Drake's comment?

"That's right," Michael said.

"Without any support from the scientific community," Skye added, a note of question entering her voice.

"Now, see?" Jack dropped his wiry body into another chair at the table. "This is what I keep saying. If you are dead-set on doing this, you have got to get another physicist in there. Credibility, Michael. You've got to have it. Backup. Otherwise, Runyon is going to eat you alive, son."

"No, she's not!" Michael slapped the table again. "Phoebe is going to handle her. This is Phoebe's big break, too, and she won't let Runyon or anyone else take this away from her. She gets it, Jack! She's got a reputation to protect, too. She's got the respect of science journalists all over the world, and they're not going to dismiss her without looking at the evidence. Even Theo—" Michael broke off abruptly.

He pulled out his cell phone and punched in a number. While he waited for it to ring, he threw a glance at the other three.

"Theo knows what I've got. If anyone can back me up . . . Theo?"

As he listened to Theo's initial protest at the late hour, Michael's eyes fastened on Khristina's face. Even in the midst of his intense concentration on the task at hand, he noted the calmness in her eyes, her complete self-possession. What he was going to do would probably change her life—again—but the only feeling he got from looking at her was a swell of reassurance and the conviction that she trusted him.

Completely.

And somehow, that made him feel . . . invincible.

"Theo," Michael finally interrupted his friend's lengthening tirade, "you know that I have never presumed on our friendship before to ask you to take a professional risk, but I am asking you now. I know that *Physica* has suspended publication, and you're bound by your contract not to comment on anything under consideration, but I really need you to support my findings . . . tomorrow at noon . . . via a broadcast link. I'm making the announcement, Theo."

Michael listened for a few minutes, focused and frowning, then ended the call.

"He needs a little time to think it over," he told the others in the room. "He said he'll call me back within the hour. But I think he's going to do it."

Skye let out the breath she'd apparently been holding.

"I'm making coffee," she said and headed for a kitchen cupboard.

"All right," Jack said, clasping his hands on the table in front of him. "Assuming Theo says 'yes,' that takes care of my first objection. What about my second, Michael?"

"What is that, Jack?" Khristina asked, taking the third chair at the table.

"I think that you need to be in on this, Khristina, and not just as a footnote." Jack glared at Michael. "Give credit where it's due, Michael. Khristina is the key to your equations, and you know it."

Michael stretched his long legs out beneath the table and blew out a sigh of exasperation.

This was another point that he and Jack had been circling for the last few hours. The man just didn't give up.

Just like my grandfather, Michael suddenly realized. *Set a goal, my boy, and never give up.*

How many times had he relied on that advice over the years? How many times had he imagined his grandfather's face, smiling with pride at the way that grandson of his solved problems of ever-increasing complexity?

He slid a look at Jack.

We're a lot alike, you and I. Who would have thought?

He turned to Khristina. "I am giving you credit," Michael explained to her. "I'm going to detail your role in our energy recording experiments and how the anomalies in your magnetic readings were the final piece of the whole strings puzzle."

He looked back at Jack for a moment, then returned his attention to her.

"But I can't talk about the info packets you receive having 'personality,' Khristina. That part of your work I can't talk about. It's not scientific. It really has nothing to do with physics and the Theory of Everything."

"Saints alive!" Jack exploded. "It has everything to do with the theory!"

"Jack—" Michael warned him.

"No, Michael! Call a spade a spade, for heaven's sake! Hah! 'For heaven's sake.' This is exactly what you've got here."

Jack pushed himself out of his chair and paced the small room, his arms swinging in agitation.

"You scientists! You want to find the One Theory of Everything, then when you do, you turn around and take it back. No sooner is the word 'everything' out of your mouth than you take it back, you qualify it. 'Well, not everything. We only meant some things.' Here you have the One Theory in your hand, Michael, and you squeeze the awesome majesty out of it until it fits into your little preconceived notion of what 'everything' is."

Jack whirled on Michael and shoved his closed hand almost in his face.

"This is your everything, and you've already decided what it includes and what it doesn't. What about all this stuff out here?"

He waved his open hand around his closed one. "Isn't this space out here part of everything, too? Who says you get to decide, anyway? Who made you God, Michael? 'Everything' means 'every thing'—seen and unseen alike. Can you see an atom? No. Do you include it in your definition of everything? Yes! Could Einstein see relativity? No. Do you think it's real? Yes! Then what's the problem? Here you have proof of the survival of consciousness after death—heaven itself—thanks to Khristina's work, and you're saying it's not real? Proof, Michael! What more do you want?

"It's not physical science, Jack."

"Yes, it is! You yourself said it—Khristina responds to unique energy units from the eleventh dimension. You've recorded the physical effects of that energy and even located the source with mathematical equations. That's good science, Michael!" he assured him, bringing his palms together in a single clap. Then he pointed his joined hands at Khristina, his eyes still on the physicist.

"Khristina just has a name that you don't approve of for that source," he reasoned, "because it isn't what you call 'scientific.' Nor is her name for those energy units—she calls them 'visitors.'

People! And why does she call them that? Because when she unpacks those energy units, when she 'reads' the information that is encoded in them, it is personal, son! They're memories, they're relationships, they're communication from people's hearts to other people. It's not collections of numbers or physics equations! Bottom line here, no matter what you call it, you're dealing with energy. Human energy, Michael! And what is physical science if it's not about matter and energy?"

"It's not about dead people talking through mediums!"

"Why not?"

"Because that's not the way I define science!"

"Then change your definition!" Jack shouted back at him. "Copernicus did! Galileo did! Einstein did! And the world and the human mind have never been the same again."

He dropped back into his chair and leaned across the table towards Michael. "This is your chance to change the world, Michael. Isn't that what you wanted to do with your Strings Project in the first place? Change the world and the way we think? Well, you got it. You just didn't know there were heavy responsibilities that came along with it, did you? Like, Michael Carilion would have to change, too, and admit there is more to 'everything' than he ever imagined!"

Braced for Michael's angry response, Jack was taken aback by the intense silence that suddenly filled the room. He glanced into the kitchen and caught Skye's eye as she stood motionless, holding a carafe of coffee, her body tense with apprehension, likewise waiting for Michael's stormy reaction. Khristina, at the table next to Jack, seemed practically shell-shocked, her gaze fastened on Michael.

No one, it seemed, was breathing.

"After everything that's happened today, Jack, I don't know that I even want to think anymore, let alone imagine," Michael finally said, his voice hardly a whisper. "At this point, the only option I can see is to go forward, ready . . . or not."

Actually, there had been another possibility to consider, but Michael had refused to even acknowledge it. He'd already been down the road to oblivion once after Elise's death, and he'd sworn he'd never take it again, no matter how bleak his life looked. Glancing around Skye's little living room, he wondered if he would have made that vow of sobriety had he known what was lying in wait for him just months away.

Because here he was, on the eve of making one of the biggest announcements in the history of science, and the only people he could count on being in his corner were a tabloid reporter, an illiterate Russian medium, and a psychic Jesuit priest.

What a joke.

Except it got funnier.

Or worse, depending on how you looked at it.

The reporter, the medium, and the psychic priest were sure he had discovered heaven, and they were trying to convince him of the same.

If anything could drive a man to drink, that would certainly do it for him. He wondered if Skye had any tequila squirreled away somewhere in the apartment, because right now, he could almost make himself forget he'd sworn off alcohol for the rest of his life.

Instead, Skye held up the carafe.

"Coffee?"

At the same time, his phone rang.

Theo.

"I'm sorry, Michael. I can't do it." His voice on the line was heavy with regret. "I've got to consider Louise and the kids. I can't forfeit my job. Not even for you."

Michael let out a long breath and nodded. "I understand, Theo. I do. But I had to ask."

"If only Lamont weren't so concerned about appearances, *Physica* would be publishing you tomorrow, Michael."

"Well, it's . . . " he started to say, but then belated recognition hit him and brought him forward in his chair. "Lamont? Did you say Lamont?"

Next to him, Skye's grip tightened on the carafe.

"Yes, he's the new publisher. Drake Lamont. He's the one who shut us down. Why?"

"Thanks, Theo. I've got to go." Michael closed the phone with a snap. He looked at the three faces around the table. "Drake Lamont is the publisher of *Physica*."

"He is the one who has blocked your journal article, then," Khristina said, echoing his thoughts. "But why would he do that, when his own reporter is going to publish it in the *World?*"

"Actually, that isn't a given either at this particular moment." Michael admitted hesitantly. "Phoebe's ready to go to press, but she told me that Lamont was playing the devil's advocate with her, saying she needed more confirmation, more validation of the work. We were hoping her visit to the lab in the morning would take care of that. But now . . . "

"Wait a minute," Jack interrupted. "This is the same man who owns the *World?* The pop culture magazine? What is he doing with a theoretical physics journal?"

"Not just any physics journal, Jack. The preeminent physics journal on the face of the planet," Michael corrected him. "It's the theoretical physicists' bible."

"He's also the new trustee at Barnet," Skye added. "And the trustees just shut down your Strings Project." She shook her head in confusion. "I don't get it. It doesn't make any sense."

"What doesn't?" Khristina asked, recalling Skye's earlier comments about her encounter with Lamont that morning. "Did he say something to you about Michael's work?"

"You talked with Drake Lamont?" Michael pressed her.

Skye set the coffee carafe on the table and met his eyes. "Yes. Yes, I did. He was at Barnet this morning and offered me a job."

"What?"

"I know, I thought it was incredibly weird, too. I mean, out of nowhere, this man wants to hire me. I'd never met him, never applied for a job at the *World*, nothing."

She crossed her arms over her chest and rubbed her arms. "He said he saw my article in the *Eye*. The one about your project."

Michael's face darkened and a nerve twitched in his jaw.

"What is it?" Khristina laid her long fingers on his arm, her blue eyes searching his face. "What is this bad blood between you and Drake Lamont?"

Michael looked at her fingers, focusing on a memory that had remained sharp and clear in his mind for almost two years. It had been at a reception hosted by Stevenson to drum up funding for the new library wing. The pleasure of the company of all the college department chairs and their spouses had been requested, and since Michael still had another year of his term to go, he and Elise had both been in attendance.

As had Drake Lamont, the very wealthy empire-building publisher of the *World*.

"We really want him on board," Stevenson had quietly informed Michael over a glass of wine, nodding across the room at Lamont. "The man has more money than a Saudi prince, and I can think of hundreds of ways we could put it to good use. Why don't you go tell him about the Strings Project and promise him eternal fame if his name is associated with Barnet? From what I hear, he's got an ego to match his bank account. Tell him we'll put his name on anything he wants if he'll toss a big check in the kitty."

Elise had laughed. "I thought this was a fundraiser for the library, not for Michael's lab, Stevenson."

The chancellor snagged some shrimp toast from a passing waiter.

"It is, Elise," he said. He popped the appetizer in his mouth, chewed and swallowed. "But let's face it, being a part of the biggest breakthrough in theoretical physics sounds like it would be a bit more enticing to a man of Lamont's stature than paying for some new bookshelves. Besides, if Lamont funded Michael's work, then I could reallocate some monies left in the budget towards the library wing."

He finished his glass of wine.

"That way, everybody wins."

Elise stretched up on her toes and grazed Michael's jaw with a kiss. "One for the gipper, darling."

Michael reluctantly smiled, rolled his eyes and started across the room towards Lamont.

Deep in conversation with the head of the English Department, the publisher looked like a man of prestige and wealth to Michael. Tall, tanned, and trim, Lamont wore an expensively tailored suit and a heavy gold wristwatch. His confident stance alone marked him as a man accustomed to authority, and though he was probably about his same age, Michael guessed, Lamont wore his blonde-streaked hair in the style of a younger man. As he got closer, however, Michael could see deep lines etched around the publisher's eyes, lines that resembled his own.

"Mr. Lamont?" Michael held out his hand. "I'm Michael Carilion. I'm the chair of the Physics Department."

Lamont took his hand in a firm shake.

"You're being modest, Dr. Carilion. I happen to know you're much more than that. In fact, didn't I just read somewhere that you've been called 'string theory's brightest hope'?"

Michael smiled in acknowledgement.

"Don't believe everything you read, Mr. Lamont. I'm afraid that's a little bit of journalistic license operating there. There are several researchers working today who are making great strides in resolving string theory's contradictions."

"Yes, but you're one of them, Doctor," the publisher smoothly noted. "And you're right here in Litchfield. Barnet should be proud to have you—and I expect they show that appreciation very generously when it comes to supporting your work. I know I haven't had any invitations to donate to the physics lab."

"Proud is a relative thing when it comes to the college budget sweepstakes, Mr. Lamont. The projects that get funded first are the ones that produce results, or build new library wings, while projects like mine are long-term commitments," Michael pointed out. "Thankfully, the Barnet trustees have a lot of confidence in my work, and yes, they have been generous."

"And well they should," Lamont responded. "Cutting-edge science eventually benefits everyone."

He took a drink from his glass and studied Michael.

"Though I have to tell you, I think the notion of an eleventh dimension is just a bit too farfetched, even for string theory."

Michael felt a frisson of irritation ripple beneath his politely attentive demeanor. This was exactly one of the reasons he hated these functions—having to listen to the opinions of potential donors who really knew nothing of what they were talking about.

"Really," he said in the noncommittal tone he'd perfected for just these occasions.

"Yes," Lamont continued. "Actually, I hold a master's degree in physics myself and considered a career path into research, but decided my heart—and checkbook—really belonged in the world of corporate enterprise. And so here I am—owner of the *World* itself, with 'a finger on the pulse of humanity,' as we like to say in our publicity materials. And as an observer of that same humanity, I can tell you quite plainly, Dr. Carilion, the existence of an eleventh dimension is totally . . . irrelevant. Ridiculous, really."

He smiled broadly. "Nothing personal, you understand."

Michael laughed, not out of humor, but as a way to cover his mounting temper. He wasn't going to let anyone, especially a self-impressed CEO of a popular culture magazine, bait him into arguing the merits of the esoteric nature of theoretical scientific inquiry, let alone discuss the intricacies of his own research. If Stevenson wanted donations from Lamont that badly, he could do the stroking himself, because there was no way that Michael was going to spend another minute with this pompous egotist.

He raised his glass to toast the publisher. "Thank you, Mr. Lamont, I will certainly keep it in mind."

"Mr. Lamont."

Michael turned to find Elise beside him, extending her delicate hand to the publisher.

"You've made my husband laugh, so you must be quite the wit, since Michael isn't exactly known for his jolly temperament, I'm afraid. I'm Elise," she added.

Lamont held onto her hand and gave her a slow, warm smile.

"Charmed, Mrs. Carilion. If your husband hasn't been jolly, then he's obviously not spending enough time in your company, because you are a vision to lighten any man's mood. And please, call me Drake."

Elise returned the smile. "You're very kind," she said, withdrawing her hand, which she then tucked into the crook of Michael's elbow.

She glanced up at her husband. "I'm so sorry to interrupt, but we need to be going, Michael."

She looked again at Lamont in apology. "We have theatre tickets tonight, and we don't want to be late. It was a pleasure, Mr. Lamont."

As she steered Michael to the door, he leaned over to whisper above her ear. "You are such a liar. We don't have any tickets."

"Then we'll get some," she answered. "I could see your jaw clenching from across the room, so I decided I would intervene before you spoiled any chance that Stevenson might have with romancing Lamont."

"He said my work is ridiculous," he told her.

"Michael." She stood before him and shook her head. "Since when do you care what anyone else thinks about your research? You know where you're going with it, and that's all that matters, isn't it?"

He looked down at her lovely face and noted the fine lines around her own eyes, wondering when they had appeared and when he had ceased to pay the kind of attention to his wife that Drake Lamont just had.

It was true—his work consumed him, and his quest for the One Theory was the driving force that kept him in his lab for far more hours than any wife should have to tolerate. And yet Elise had tolerated it, had always accepted his professional obsession and been his staunchest supporter. Until Lamont had held her hand and made that remark about the two of them not spending time together, Michael hadn't even considered she might be feeling some loneliness or that she might respond to some other man's attention. Now that he had thought about it, he realized he needed to make some amends.

He took her face in his hands and kissed her.

"You matter, Elise."

CHAPTER FIFTY-SEVEN

M ichael?"
Disoriented, he looked at the three people in the room, each of whom were watching him intently. Khristina's fingers gently brushed his arm.

"You went somewhere," she said softly.

He held her eyes for a moment or two. Elise's eyes had been a rich brown color, and it was painfully obvious to him now that he hadn't spent nearly enough time looking into them. He'd made amends all right, for about a week, and then he'd gone right back to burying himself in the lab.

And Elise had taken a lover.

"I was a fool," he told Khristina.

She reached out and laid two fingers across his lips. Her eyes told him that she didn't know exactly what he was referring to, but that she somehow sensed it had to do with him and Elise.

Am I so transparent? he wondered, feeling a vulnerability and pain that pierced his heart.

"It's all right, Michael," Khristina softly reassured him, her eyes still holding his. "It's all right."

And then, for the first time in a very long time, Michael let himself believe it.

It would be all right.

His eyes locked on the woman whose fingers still lay on his lips, a fine tremor coursing through his whole body as he felt the weight of his grief for Elise lifting up and away. In its place, the beginnings of a warm, bone-deep fatigue settled in, and along with it, a certitude that, tonight, Michael would sleep, his bloody dreams finally gone.

Never taking his eyes from Khristina's, he covered her fingers with the palm of his hand and lightly kissed her fingertips.

"Thank you."

"I will pass it along," she told him.

He looked at her, confused.

Somewhere behind him, Jack noisily cleared his throat.

"Michael? I think you were going to tell us something about Drake Lamont?"

A quick rush of blood colored Michael's cheeks as he suddenly remembered that he and Khristina weren't the only people in the room. By the time he turned to answer Jack, though, Michael's voice had regained its hard tone.

"Two years ago, I met Lamont very briefly, and he was an insufferable boor. He told me in no uncertain terms that my work was both irrelevant and ridiculous."

"Well, that would do it," Jack agreed. "I can definitely see why he's not on your favorite person list."

"He said that?" Skye asked, obviously struggling with Michael's perception of the *World's* owner. "But he . . ."

She stopped, her sentence left hanging.

"But what, Skye?"

Skye almost cringed at Michael's harsh tone, tinged as it was with impatience and a little edge of anger. And why shouldn't he be impatient and angry with her? She was the one responsible for setting this catastrophe in motion with her article in the *Eye*. Sure, she'd apologized repeatedly to him and Khristina both over pizza earlier, but that didn't change the results of her story's publication. And the real irony of it all, Skye reminded herself, was that she deliberately had kept his name out of it from the beginning, because she had felt sorry for him and had decided he had already suffered enough with his wife's murder.

So much for good intentions.

And so much for Drake Lamont, she decided.

Determined to redeem herself in Michael's eyes, Skye could think of only one way to do that in the current situation, and if breaking Lamont's trust was what it would take, so be it. She owed the publisher nothing, but she owed Michael his mangled career.

"Drake Lamont has been anonymously funding the Strings Project for the last nine months, Michael," she said. "He told me himself and asked I keep it confidential. So I don't understand why he would tell you it was irrelevant and ridiculous, then turn around and fund it, and then turn around again and shut you down."

She paused a moment to catch her breath.

"And he wanted to know everything I knew about the project and if you'd had any breakthroughs, and he said if I knew about it before he did, he would make sure it wouldn't happen again."

"He was threatening you?" Jack asked, incredulous.

"This was how he made you uncomfortable," Khristina murmured.

"I don't get it, Michael," Skye repeated. "Why would he torpedo work that could make him even more famous than he already is?"

Fueled by Skye's revelations, Michael's mind was spinning, trying to fit the pieces together, searching for a pattern, a formula that would explain what was happening. Somehow, it all hung together. It could all make sense. If he could just get it into an equation, he could understand it. If he could understand it, he could control it.

And right now, more than anything, Michael needed some control.

The data wheeled in his head. Lamont had mocked him, then funded him, then shut him out from publication of the biggest discovery of the century. Why would he do that? If the project succeeded, there was prestige to be claimed by a donor, but Lamont didn't need prestige. If the project failed, the money was written off as a loss, and usually the researcher's reputation got written off along with it.

But if Lamont didn't think the project was feasible in the first place, why would he have contributed the funds? To watch Michael make a fool of himself in the eyes of the scientific community? That was a pretty expensive proposition just to help someone humiliate himself.

Besides, Lamont had specifically told Michael it was "nothing personal."

But what if Lamont had had a change of heart and realized that Michael was on the right path to the One Theory?

Then, by being a donor, he could have that vicarious thrill of being in on the big discovery—the man had even made a point of making sure Michael knew he had that physics background, Michael reminded himself. But if that were the case, why did he fund the Strings Project anonymously? Why not get out in front and milk it for the press? The logical answer to that, of course, was that if the project failed, no one would know Lamont's involvement, and he'd be spared the embarrassment.

But the project had succeeded, and Michael had solved the equations. Michael had formulated the Theory of Everything.

And now Lamont didn't want anyone to know about it.

Michael's mind spun harder, patterns trying to emerge in his head. The patterns shifted, rearranged themselves, just as his final calculations for the One Theory had seemed to almost take on a life of their own before suddenly falling into place. He was getting closer to the answer. He could feel it coming.

You are so close!

Michael's thoughts froze at the echo in his head, the inner voice that had pushed him on in the lab last Friday night. It hadn't failed him then, and he was sure it wouldn't now, either; yet something about the voice bothered him.

And then he knew what it was.

Until this moment, he'd only ever heard his inner fan club when he'd been working on a physics project, trying to solve equations or analyze mathematical probabilities. He'd never heard it in regards to his personal life. Not even once.

But that wasn't right, either, he realized now. He'd heard it before he'd said something to Khristina earlier today. How strange. Had he heard it other times and not noticed?

Dismayed at his own distraction, he pushed away that train of thought and concentrated harder on the matter before him.

Maybe Lamont was trying to dissuade you in the first place because he knew where your work was headed. And he didn't want you going there.

Now, that was an odd idea.

He turned it around in his mind and tried to look at it from different perspectives. Why would Lamont not want Michael to solve the equations? Like many researchers, Michael believed there was no downside to developing new scientific theory, since it increased the store of knowledge. Yet he also knew that in some cases, it could outdate or outmode how certain things were done, and that could trigger a resulting financial blow to certain corporations or manufacturers. But the idea that string theory might have an impact on the operation of a publishing empire was so totally ludicrous, it was truly laughable.

So there had to be something else that Lamont believed gave him a stake in Michael's work.

Taking a different tack, Michael wondered if Lamont was simply a control freak. That was why some donors donated, Michael knew. They wanted to feel they were involved somehow in the direction of the research. That way, it became personal, and they could get a better-than-vicarious thrill from the success of the project.

Was that what Lamont was doing? Had he wanted to feel in control of the project once he recognized its implications and possibilities? That would certainly explain why he must have been more than annoyed when he couldn't find out how the research was going, because Michael had kept a tight lid on every development in the lab right up until Elise was killed.

And then it had all gone to pieces and was dying a slow death.

Until Lucas brought in Khristina.

Which no one knew about.

Or at least, no one did until Lucas called Phoebe.

And Phoebe worked for Lamont.

And then Lucas was murdered the same night. But unknown to Lucas and anyone else, the work was already finished, and nothing could stop its publication.

Unless his credibility was suddenly called into question, Michael reasoned.

Or was ruined.

Professionally.

Personally.

Or *Physica* was shut down.

All three of which had happened.

What were the odds of that? Coincidences didn't just 'happen' when it came to calculations, Michael reminded himself—they were inherent in the formula. And if Michael took those 'odds' one step further, could Lamont have been behind the other two, if he had been responsible for even one?

Michael felt ice spreading up his spine.

Could Lamont have been behind the whole chain of events, including the senseless murder of his wife and best friend?

"I'm going crazy here," he whispered desperately to the others, repeating to them his suspicions. But when he was finished laying out his thoughts, there was only silence.

"Tell me I'm wrong," he begged. "Because this is the raving of a paranoid! Why would Lamont target me? What did I ever do to him?"

He pounded his fists on the table, the vibration shimmying down the legs onto the floor.

"He told me it was nothing personal!"

Skye swallowed hard. "He told me it was all about information, Michael. That he was in the information business and that information was power. He said he wanted to tell people what to think and that if he created their reality through the information he supplied, he could control that reality and what people do. He called it his Grand Narrative."

She looked at Khristina and Jack.

"I just thought he was psycho or something, that he wasn't really serious. I mean, come on! Who thinks they can control the world?"

Khristina exchanged a long look with Jack, then turned to Skye.

"If Michael is right, and Lamont is trying to control the One Theory now by keeping it away from everyone else, because he could not stop Michael from finding it, this is not about the world at all, Skye. It is about heaven—Michael's eleventh dimension."

"The eleventh dimension? Why would Lamont care about that?" Michael demanded. "How is that information going to allow him to 'control people'? I'm sorry, but this whole conversation is insane!" He buried his face in his hands. "This is it. I really am going crazy, aren't I?"

It was Jack's turn to lay his hand on Michael's arm.

"No, son, you're not. Think about it. Just for a minute, play this game with me, all right? If people knew—really *knew*—there was a heaven, which you and Khristina have proved, wouldn't it change their lives? The way they acted. What they considered to be important. The way they treated other people. It would be different, Michael. The world would change."

He gave Michael's arm a squeeze.

"Now, if the world changes from a place where people are self-centered to a place where everyone is genuinely caring for others, from a place where people lie, cheat, steal and kill, to a place of justice and peace, who stands to lose the most? Who loses his tight-fisted hold on people's minds and spirits if everyone knows there's a heaven?"

Michael looked blankly at Jack.

Next to Khristina, Skye took the last empty chair at the table and abruptly sat down.

"Oh my," she breathed. "You're talking about the Devil. And he was here. No wonder the cats were so spooked. Somehow, they knew."

Michael blinked and stared at Jack. His voice came out totally flat. "You want me to believe that Drake Lamont is the Devil?"

"It's not a question of belief, Michael," Jack argued. "I think we have to accept that it's a fact. He told Skye flat-out he wants to dictate to people what to think. Look at his publishing empire! Thanks to the incredible amount of influence he wields through his media outlets, he's basically telling people what their priorities should be, how to succeed, how to perceive events. It's manipulation, pure and simple."

He shrugged. "Well, not pure, but simple, yes. The Devil's favorite strategy has always been deception—from the moment he convinced poor Eve to take a bite of that bright, shiny apple—and how much simpler can deceiving be when he's got his audience already hanging on his every word because he's the reigning cultural authority?"

Michael shook his head in disbelief and glanced at Khristina and Skye.

"Let me guess. You both agree with him, don't you?"

Their solemn nods answered his question. He ran his hands through his hair in frustration. "This is totally crazy."

Yet at the same time, his gut was telling him that it would be a fatal mistake to discount the disturbing way Lamont's name continued to come up, no matter which way Michael turned, as he tried to make some kind of a coherent picture of the last few days.

Lucas and Phoebe, who worked for Lamont.

Theo and Lamont.

Barnet and Lamont.

Elise and Lamont.

The sudden realization that he could even link Lamont to Elise seared through him like an electric shock and for a split second, he couldn't breathe. Elise had met the publisher at that same cocktail party. He'd taken her hand. Said her name. Asked her to call him Drake. Michael was immediately aware that the others had fallen silent and were watching him closely.

He swallowed past the anger that had lodged in his throat.

"I will say one thing, though," he assured them now, his voice cold and hard, "and that's whether Lamont is evil incarnate or the Easter Bunny, if he's responsible in any way, shape, or form, for Elise's murder, or for Lucas's murder, this is definitely not 'nothing personal.'"

Jack patted his arm again. "You're absolutely right, son," he sadly affirmed. "Evil is never 'nothing personal.'"

CHAPTER FIFTY-EIGHT

Freddy Glass shifted in the driver's seat of his little black Volkswagen bug. It was about three in the morning, and there hadn't even been a high school joyrider come down the quiet residential street for the past two hours. Middle-of-the-night surveillance jobs always dragged after an hour or two, but the pay was good for a minimal expenditure of energy.

Beside him on the passenger seat, his cell phone chimed. He checked the caller and picked it up.

"She's not home," Freddy told his employer, "but there's an old van sitting a few houses down on the street. And there's some guy sitting in it. Every so often he looks towards her house, like he's looking for her, too. You want me to check him out?"

"Yes," said his employer. "I think that would probably be a good idea. I'd like to know who else is looking for Ms. Tupikova, especially at three in the morning. Let me know when you have something, Freddy."

"Will do," he replied, closing the phone.

He squinted through the darkness at the van, trying to read the license plate, but he couldn't make it out in the shadows of the night. Since the figure in the driver's seat hadn't moved in the last hour, Freddy decided he'd take a chance that the guy had fallen asleep and wouldn't notice him walking past the van on the sidewalk. Slipping out of his own vehicle through the passenger's side door, Freddy moved soundlessly to the sidewalk and walked towards the van.

Sure enough, the guy at the wheel was passed out, his head back on the headrest, his chest moving rhythmically in a deep sleep.

What an amateur, Freddy thought. He hoped the guy's client wasn't expecting much, because this idiot apparently didn't know the first thing about surveillance, if that's really what he was doing here. Freddy noted the big wooden crucifix hanging down from the rear-view mirror, and a collage of decals plastered on the side windows of the van, most of which seemed to be warnings about Satan and the end of the world.

"You're supposed to be innocuous, buddy," Freddy quietly commented as he passed the length of the van. "Not making a statement."

He pulled a pad of paper out of his pocket and copied down the license plate letters and numbers. As soon as he got back to his office, he'd hack into the Department of Motor Vehicles' files and get the guy's ID. By the time his employer got up in the morning, Freddy would have a full report for him on the van man.

As for Tupikova, she was definitely a no-show. There was no car on the property, and her mail slot on the front porch had papers jammed in it, which convinced Freddy that the woman hadn't been home since at least the afternoon. It wasn't much to relay to his employer, but then again, he didn't know what the man was looking for, either, other than the woman. Was she his employer's errant lover? A partner in crime?

Freddy had no idea, and as always the case when he worked with this man, the less he knew, the more he liked it. Whoever he was, the employer Freddy knew only as The Gentleman was an easy client to please, and he certainly paid well. The only thing Freddy ever had to do for him was watch women, learn their routines, and keep his mouth shut.

Even when they turned up dead, like that one back in February.

That time, he was really tempted to call the cops, especially when that $10,000 reward for information had been offered by the dead woman's husband. But The Gentleman called him up and made him a better deal: $20,000 for saying nothing. Of course, even if Freddy had called the cops, all he could have given them was the cell phone number of The Gentleman, which changed with each assignment, anyway. So he'd taken the $20,000, along with the next two jobs that came along: the magazine editor and the hot television reporter.

He had to say one thing for his employer. The man sure knew how to pick great-looking women.

Tonight, though, the Gentleman had asked him to do something different: he wanted him to track two women at the same time. Since the Tupikova woman had a house, he'd decided to start with her, seeing as it was easier to check out a single house than an apartment inside a building, which was where the other woman lived.

As he got back inside his car, he figured he could be parked down the street from that building by sunrise. Then all he had to do was wait for a redheaded grad student to walk out and hope it was Skye Hammond.

CHAPTER FIFTY-NINE

K hristina lifted her arm to check the time on her antique wristwatch. She might not have been able to read words, but she had learned to tell time by the position of the arms on the face of a clock.

By the moonlight pouring through the open kitchen windows across the room, she could just make out that it was four in the morning.

She was wide awake.

Someone was coming.

"It's okay to be attracted to him, Khristina. In fact, I hope you fall in love with him."

Khristina sat up on the couch and drew the blanket around her as she felt her skin react to the shift in the air. Elise Carilion was sitting at the table.

"I think I have been already a little in love with him for a long time, Elise," she said. "Perhaps ever since you came to me in Florida and told me he needed my help with his research. But he is not the easiest man to deal with, as you know. He has a temper and he can be very—how do you say, small-sighted?"

Elise smiled. "I think you mean he has tunnel vision."

Khristina thought about the words. "Yes," she agreed. "Definitely tunnel vision. But I understand that. My father had tunnel vision. When he played Stravinsky, he was oblivious to everything else. My mother thought it was his curse, but I understood it was his liberation. When he made music, he could forget how little money we had to live on. He could forget that instead of playing in the orchestra, the only job left for him after the government collapsed was to clean offices. Every time he picked up his violin, his life was new again, and everything was possible."

She smoothed the blanket over her lap and sighed. "In these last months, I think Michael's research has been his liberation, also. He has been grieving for you, but I think he is ready to let go now."

Elise nodded. "Especially now that he knows that I was unfaithful. That should definitely make it easier for him, don't you think?"

Her light tone grew serious. "I couldn't tell you, Khristina. I'm sorry. I had to wait until he knew, to see his reaction. I'm afraid I wasn't who he thought I was."

Khristina studied the soft lines of regret on Elise's face. "I think, he didn't know who he was, either, Elise. But I think now, too, he has forgiven you. And perhaps forgiven himself."

She remembered Michael's lips against her fingers, the shadows of regret that she'd felt around him, and the lightening of those shadows that she had sensed when he had kissed her fingertips. "He is going to make a new life, Elise."

"I know," she said. "Thanks to you."

Khristina shook her head. "I am not so sure about that. He is much stronger than he realizes, and he does not need me to tell him what to do."

"I beg to differ, Khristina," Elise said. "He does need you. He needs you to show him heaven."

Again, Khristina shook her head.

"I have tried. Jack has tried. Michael cannot see that heaven is his eleventh dimension. Lucas said I should tell him where his inner voice comes from, that he himself is a medium, but I don't know why he would believe me. I just don't know how to open his mind to heaven, Elise."

She wiped away the tears that were forming in the corners of her eyes. "When I came to the project, I wanted very much for Michael to be able to understand what I do and acknowledge the validity of my profession, but that is not the most important thing to me anymore," she confessed. "Now the important thing—the critical thing—is that Michael acknowledges heaven, because without that, without his recognition that his eleventh dimension is really heaven, his work is just another formula, but not evidence of eternal life. If he does not see what he has found, Elise, he cannot know how to protect it, or himself, from the evil that Jack and I see coming closer. He has to make a leap of faith, Elise, and I cannot do it for him."

Elise reached out as though she would touch Khristina in comfort.

"He'll see it, Khristina," she promised her. "And he'll do it. When the moment is right, he will do it."

Elise turned to leave, then hesitated, turning again to face Khristina one more time. "Do you want to know?"

"Know what?" Khristina asked.

"The name of the man I slept with?"

Khristina's breath rushed quietly out of her lungs. Her eyes searched Elise's and found sadness there, along with lingering regret.

"No," she answered. "That is your cross to bear, I think."

Elise nodded.

"Yes, it is. But one day soon, I am going to be able to lay it down. Now that Michael has forgiven me, the only thing left for me to do is forgive myself."

She raised her hand in farewell.

"Give him my love, Khristina. And yours."

CHAPTER SIXTY

H e ought to be sleeping.
He needed to sleep.

But Michael could only lay awake on the narrow bed in the spartan room at Novice House, replaying the day in his head, desperately trying to make everything fit together.

He'd found the eleventh dimension. He'd formulated the One Theory.

And his lab had been blown up.

He'd written the article, sent it to Theo.

And *Physica* was shut down.

Professionally, he was shut out.

Meanwhile, at the moment of what should have been Michael's great success, Lucas was killed, and someone was trying to frame him for not only Lucas's murder, but for Elise's as well.

And he'd learned that there was a chance that Elise's murder was not a random act of violence at all, but something very cold and very deliberate—and something over which he'd had no control at all.

Elise had taken a lover, and he hadn't known a thing.

In the privacy of his borrowed room, Michael wept—for Elise, for the marriage he'd thought he'd had, and for the life he'd imagined he'd been leading.

He really hadn't known a thing. His life had seemed perfect until he closed in on the One Theory.

And then his life had shattered, just like his living room window.

And somehow, Drake Lamont was behind it, he was certain.

Which, if he subscribed to Jack's and Khristina's and Skye's version of what was going on, would make perfect sense. Because according to their worldview, their paradigm, Drake Lamont was the Devil, and he wanted to destroy Michael's work because it proved the existence of heaven and even God himself—so what better place to trap Michael in than a hell on earth?

Jerking himself up to sit on the edge of the bed, Michael held his head in his hands, appalled that he would let his thoughts wander even as far as they had.

What had happened to his celebrated, rational scientific mind?

He walked across the room to lean his forearms on the open window, trying to catch even the faintest breeze stirring the night, but it was no use. The air was still. The night too warm.

And yet, try as he might, he couldn't push the crazy thought away: Lamont was the Devil. Nothing else Michael could think of could come close to explaining why these things were all happening to him. As insane as it was, it was the only theory that could account for all the data, and as a scientist, a researcher, it went totally against his training to dismiss it out of hand. The fact that it rested on an assumption he couldn't accept—that his eleventh dimension was, in reality, heaven—well, maybe he needed to take another look at his own paradigm. He had, after all, been terribly wrong about Elise and his marriage, so why was it so inconceivable that he could be terribly wrong about this as well? Was he really infallible?

Unbidden, Jack's words came back to him as he stood at the window, looking out at the darkness.

"Who made you God, Michael?"

The question was eating him alive. He thought about twenty-plus years in the lab, the growing recognition he'd received in his profession, about the authority he knew he could exercise in the rarefied air of the world of theoretical physics.

He'd extended that self-confidence from his work into his personal life, and now all he had left to show for it was a career teetering on the brink of ruin and the shredded memory of a marriage.

"I did," he finally answered, his heart aching. "I guess I did, Jack."

The silent reply came so softly, he wasn't sure he heard it at first.

Don't we all?

Michael allowed himself a bitter laugh.

"I suppose we do," he told his inner voice, "but once you do, it's awfully hard to give it up."

He turned then to go back to bed and try to get a little rest before morning, but a glint on the wall opposite the bed caught his eye. Hanging near the door was a small, simple, gold crucifix, a shaft of bright moonlight illuminating the peaceful features of the man on the cross.

It reminded him of Khristina.

Khristina, who always seemed at peace, even with chaos at her heels.

Khristina, whose fingers had touched his lips in forgiveness and whose simple words of reassurance had been a balm for his conscience.

For some reason, whenever he was around her, he felt like life was flowing into him. That life would, indeed, go on. And wasn't that ironic, especially since she professed a talent for communicating with dead people?

Michael sighed.

Maybe that was why her presence affected him so much— maybe he was actually one of the walking dead, and so she knew exactly what he needed.

Or at least, he had been, until she showed up at his door on Sunday morning. Since then, he'd had a crash course in getting to know her, her emotional honesty, her unfailing optimism, her unshakeable belief in eternal life. And that was a problem for him, because Khristina believed she spoke with dead people and that his work could virtually open the doors of heaven to those left behind.

It was a problem because he wanted to get to know her better, he realized.

Much better.

But he also refused to lie to himself—what kind of a relationship could he possibly hope to have with a woman who believed those kinds of things?

Stretching out on the bed again, Michael closed his eyes. He would never see the world as Khristina saw it. Not in this lifetime. He could let his imagination run as wild as he wanted it to tonight and concoct scenarios straight out of all kinds of supernatural fantasies, but he knew that in the clear light of the morning, he'd be back to banging his head against that metaphysical wall whenever Khristina talked about her 'visitors.'

"An alternate universe, Khristina," Michael sighed in frustration. "That's what it would take for you and me to agree on this one."

Tomorrow, he would end this maelstrom that had swallowed him whole. He would announce the One Theory to the world and see where it led.

An alternate universe.

He bolted upright in the bed as his own words came rushing back at him.

It was one of the more mind-bending predictions of string theory. There were alternate, or parallel, universes to our own. If his theory were correct, and he already knew it was by virtue of his discovery of the eleventh dimension, then there might well be parallel universes sitting right next to the one we knew, universes stacked up like slices of bread in a loaf, or like sections of an orange fitted together.

Universes with their own kinds of energy systems that reflected ours.

And if that were the case, wasn't it possible those universes could support the same kinds of life-forms as this universe? Didn't there have to be something holding that loaf, those orange membranes, together?

Michael's mind wheeled.

The big picture! Look at the big picture!

Like a basketball player making a clean break for the winning shot of the game, Michael could feel his brain racing, his thoughts realigning themselves, his conceptual frameworks becoming elastic, stretching and reshaping themselves, like a million tiny strings—the millions of tiny strings of string theory—into new configurations of possibilities.

What if the eleventh dimension was really a gateway between those parallel slices of the loaf or the contact point between the membranes of the orange slices?

What if its energy packets really were human?

What if it really was what Khristina called heaven?

Michael broke out in a cold sweat.

Then Drake Lamont might well be the Devil himself.

CHAPTER SIXTY-ONE

Jack was finishing his second cup of morning coffee at the long wooden table in the cavernous dining room of Novice House when a freckle-faced Jesuit stuck his head around the doorframe.

"Phone call for you, Jack," the younger man said. "You can take it in the kitchen if you want. Line three."

Jack lifted his cup in answer and wondered if he'd ever been that young as a Jesuit, or if he had simply jumped into advanced maturity as soon as he took his vows. God had given him a great ride in the order, Jack knew, even if his career hadn't followed the arc he had anticipated back when he was a novice. On fire with his faith, he'd been convinced that he was called to create glorious artwork to help teach others to appreciate the ineffable nature of God's presence in the world.

The memory of that presumption alone was enough now to make him laugh. It had taken years at the men's shelter, then years in South America, and, finally, years at Sacred Ground, for him to realize that God laughed at man's presumption even while handing him other things to do. And yet, at the same time, God had never completely dismissed those presumptions, or those gifts, but simply left them to ripen till the time was right.

Just as the time had been right for him to find that boy all those years ago.

Or like now, when it was time for him to help Michael.

Jack walked into the empty kitchen and picked up the phone. "This is Father Jack."

295

"Jack! I caught you!"

Oh no, I hope not, Jack thought automatically as he recognized the voice of his superior, the Jesuit provincial. Brenden Sheerin might have been an excellent strategic administrator of his province, but when it came to thorny personnel issues, his heavy-handed management style had often sidestepped any collegial niceties. In other words, Brenden had stepped on many of his Jesuit brothers' toes over the years, and he didn't care who knew it.

He had also been the most vocal critic of Jack's public display of his extrasensory ability fifteen years ago and most assuredly was the man responsible for Jack's speedy change of assignment that sent him out of the country. The fact that Brenden was aware that Jack was even in town and had tracked him down so quickly didn't bode well, and Jack wondered how in the world his superior had been tipped off.

"Brenden," Jack said. "What can I do for you?"

"Well, Jack, to get right to the heart of the matter, I'm hearing some rather upsetting noises about an association you seem to have developed with Dr. Michael Carilion."

Jack's gaze had wandered to the windows over the kitchen sink. The skies were the color of lead and filled with banks of clouds. He vaguely remembered hearing a weather report that had predicted the possibility of strong storms by noon. With how high the humidity had stayed throughout the night, he wasn't surprised.

"What about it?"

"Ah, then it is true," Brenden said. "I was hoping I was misinformed. Look, Jack, you have this penchant for bad publicity, you know? We did the best we could with damage control for the little lost boy thing, but I can't have you linked with this man, Jack. For the good of yourself, as well as the order. I think the kindest thing we can say right now is that the man is unstable, possibly dangerous." He paused. "I want you to go home to Sacred Ground, Jack. Today. For your own safety."

Jack studied the cracked yellow linoleum on the kitchen floor and carefully considered what to say. No matter how nicely Brenden put it, Jack was under no illusion whatsoever that his personal safety was the driving issue here, but that the reputation of the order was. Brenden was, if nothing else, a company man. That being the case, what exactly did Brenden think was going to come from Jack's 'association' with Michael?

Jack looked out the window again at the thickening clouds.

"I'm curious, Brenden. What are these 'noises' you've heard about Carilion? That he killed his wife? That he killed his colleague? That he's a lost soul? And where did you hear these things? From the media? And we all know, they've always got their facts straight," he added with more than a touch of sarcasm.

"But, Brenden," he barged on, "even if that is the case, even if Carilion is a homicidal maniac—which he definitely is not, by the way—shouldn't we be offering him forgiveness and healing and redemption, instead of condemnation? Why shouldn't I be associating with him, Brenden? I'm a priest! The man is certainly needy, wouldn't you agree?"

The provincial's voice lost its genial tone.

"Jack, this isn't about ministry."

"Obviously," he said bitterly. "So why don't you just spit it out, then. What is it about, Brenden?"

For a moment, there was only silence on the line.

Jack waited.

"Jack," Brenden began, his voice low and obviously strained, "you have never appreciated the position you put our community in when you helped find that boy. Whether you want to believe it or not, you publicly embarrassed us. People heard about the Jesuit priest who used telepathy to find a child and laughed at us. 'What kind of head cases is the Church taking on as priests?' people were thinking. Not to mention the humiliating jokes—'If you want to find a little boy, ask a Jesuit.' Jack! How many years do you think it takes for the Catholic Church to recover from a scandal? Decades! We're still dealing with the fallout from the child abuse of more than twenty, thirty, years ago! What does that do for us? For all the good and honest and hard-working Christians who just want to do the Lord's work? It undermines us, Jack! It undermines the faith!"

Jack could hear his superior pausing to audibly catch his breath.

"So I won't have you back in the news with a man who not only is having a very public meltdown, but who is keeping company with a medium, of all things. I am telling you—I am ordering you, as your superior to whom you owe a vow of obedience—to step out of this and go home. Just do it, Jack."

The pain in his voice was clear even across the phone line.

"Or I will have you removed from this order."

Jack realized his head was pounding. He took a moment to breathe deeply through the tension and consciously rolled his shoulders up and back.

He understood what Brenden was telling him. He had unintentionally caused heartache for his brother Jesuits, and for that, Jack was heartily sorry and would devoutly repent.

But he could not, and would not, let that past mistake deter him from the task he now saw so clearly before him—helping Michael announce the One Theory.

Jack made the effort to keep his voice level and calm. "What if I told you, Brenden, that Dr. Carilion has done the unthinkable and scientifically proven the existence of heaven?"

Silence again stretched out on the phone line before Brenden answered. His voice sounded tired, even though it was only seven in the morning.

"Listen to yourself, Jack. Scientific proof of heaven? You're right," he conceded, "it is unthinkable. Not to mention impossible, because the last people scientists want to get into bed with are theologians. You need to go home. We're all too old for this."

Jack rubbed his temples and realized that Brenden had been right from the very beginning of the conversation: he was caught. Why would anyone listen to him, a crazy old priest who claimed to be psychic and who had been safely hidden away at a remote retreat house where he couldn't be a public relations liability?

When he thought about it that way, Jack had to admit that perhaps Michael's chances of getting his theory successfully into the public eye might be better without him, even if Michael were facing the Devil himself. Michael was already besieged with credibility questions, and the last thing he needed was a priest by his side who was in danger of being defrocked.

Maybe Jack Gerrity was not the best man for this job, after all. Maybe William had been mistaken in sending him to help Michael. And maybe Jack was still presuming as much as he had when he was a freckle-faced Jesuit novice himself.

"All right, Brenden," he conceded. "I'll go home. But, just out of curiosity, tell me who blew the whistle on me this time."

Jack could hear Brenden's sigh of relief over the phone line.

"A good friend called me late last night. He's been a loyal supporter of the work we do for many years, and I value his opinion. He said you were on the Barnet campus last night after the bombing with Dr. Carilion. Drake was concerned about the media linking you—and, by extension, our community—with the firestorm that he expects will erupt around the professor today. He didn't want to see us faced with the repercussions, and figured if I could get you out of the picture as soon as possible, we'd have a much better shot at staying out of the whole thing."

Jack's gaze focused on the floor. "Drake as in Drake La-mont?" he quietly asked.

"Yes." Brenden sounded surprised. "You know him? He owns the *World*."

The pounding in Jack's head got worse. "Yes, I'm beginning to believe that."

He returned the phone to its cradle and looked up to find Michael standing next to him. He was holding out Jack's silver whistle.

"I forgot to return this to you last night," he said. "And I didn't intend to eavesdrop, but it sounds like Lamont has some-how taken you out of the game."

Jack met his eyes and was startled to see a steely intensity that hadn't been there yesterday. Combined with his disheveled hair, unshaven cheeks, and the wrinkled, unbuttoned shirt that lay open on his chest, Michael looked like a different man this morning, the planes in his face hard and harsh under the kitchen's florescent lights, a far cry from the exhausted and beaten researcher that had returned with Jack to Novice House less than six hours ago. With his artist's eye, Jack envisioned waves of stark energy gathering around the man, feeding him, making him stronger. If he could paint a portrait of Michael at this very moment, Jack would put a bright sword in his hand and a shining shield on his arm.

And a halo on his head.

St. Michael, pray for us.

Shaken by his vision, Jack took the whistle from Michael's outstretched hand. He weighed it in his own palm, along with his vow of obedience to Brenden.

To whom did he really owe his allegiance?

To his superior, who, out of necessity of minding the earth-bound Jesuit store, had been wooed by Lamont's wallet and de-ceiving good-intentioned concern?

Or did Jack have a greater Master, one who had given him this unbelievable opportunity to stand by a man who could throw open the very gates of heaven?

He looked again at Michael's formidable face, determination etched in every line.

Jack closed his fist tightly around the whistle.

"Lamont's not calling my plays, son. Nor is Brenden. Not by a long shot."

CHAPTER SIXTY-TWO

This absolutely could not be happening, Teri thought. But it was.

All around her, conversations flowed and ebbed as the crime scene team of investigators took photos and dusted for prints. At the polished cherry dining table, another detective was sitting with Phoebe Dauwalter's housekeeper, encouraging her to drink some water in hopes it might cut into the torrent of tears and cries the woman was issuing.

Although if Teri had been the one to find Phoebe Dauwalter's body as the housekeeper had, she couldn't imagine that any amount of glasses of water would have had a calming effect on her.

Stripped to only her red lace underwear and her high-heeled sandals, Phoebe's body lay twisted in front of the leather couch, her eyes wide open in alarm, and her throat neatly slit. Her killer had used a razor-thin wire as a garrote, and though the blood was profuse and dried, it looked now almost like a black scarf laying across her neck, draping down the sides and spilling onto the carpet and mixing into her dark hair.

On the coffee table nearby, a single glass of water stood half-empty next to a cut-crystal vase filled with delicate white rose buds. A florist's card lay on the table as well. It was one of those stock cards a customer might pick up to include with a bouquet. It read "Thanks for everything."

And it was signed.

With the letter M.

CHAPTER SIXTY-THREE

The tapping sound on the window beside his ear woke him up. Startled and groggy, he realized he'd fallen asleep again after the last time he'd moved the van just after sunrise. Thankfully, the man outside the car door wasn't wearing a policeman's uniform, because he certainly didn't want to be asked to produce either a valid driver's license or proof of insurance, especially since he currently had neither.

He carefully rolled down the window. "Yes?"

The gentleman outside was noticeably well dressed.

"Forgive me for intruding, but your decals caught my eye. Especially the one about false prophets and Satan. Are you, by any chance, waiting for the woman who claims to be the Awaited One?"

Just the mention of her heresy brought him fully alert, making him look at the stranger with sharp interest.

"Why do you ask?"

The stranger rolled his unusual silvery eyes up towards heaven. "Because she must be punished and I am called to do this."

The man laid his hands on the open window frame.

"Will you help me, brother?"

CHAPTER SIXTY-FOUR

Thisis insane, Teri, and you know it."

Virtually vibrating with anger, Michael sat at the scarred metal table in the police station's interrogation room. Seated across from him, Teri rubbed her fingers across her lips and chin, desperately searching for the answers that would make this whole nightmare go away. Ever since Michael had walked into the detective's office with Khristina at eight o'clock on the dot to talk about the new evidence relating to Elise, she felt like she'd been trapped in a room with a tiger on a chain. The fact that she'd had to immediately pull him into an interrogation room to question him about a murder that was barely hours old hadn't made any improvements in the situation.

"I do know it, Michael, but right now, it's out of my hands," she told him again, pointedly. "The commissioner himself wants you off the street, and it was all I could do to even get this much of a concession from him—to do an unofficial questioning instead of serving you with a warrant for arrest. So let's just finish this, all right?"

"I did not kill Phoebe Dauwalter," he said, his voice hard. "I was with Jack all evening, and then we joined Khristina and Skye at her apartment for a few hours. Ask them. They'll tell you. And I didn't send Phoebe any flowers, and I certainly didn't send her a florist's card with my initial on it. Do a handwriting analysis, Teri. It's not from me."

He pinched the bridge of his nose and squeezed his eyes shut. When he opened them again, the blue in his eyes was covered with a fine sheen of tears.

"Teri, I'm a walking curse. I spent part of last night trying to get hold of Phoebe to talk to her about today, about a press conference, and now she's dead."

"We've got her cell phone," she informed him. "We know you were calling, Michael, but that doesn't prove anything other than you were leaving messages for her. No good for an alibi."

"I don't need an alibi, because I didn't kill her!"

"I know. I know."

Teri tried to defuse his anger, while her own frustration mounted. "Khristina's already confirmed you were with her last evening, and we'll get Jack and Skye in here, too. Michael, I believe you, but you've got to understand you're in deep here—"

"Are you saying I need a lawyer?"

"No, that's not what I'm saying. But I am saying we need to step very carefully here."

She took a deep breath and willed herself to calm down.

"Take a look at what we've got, Michael," she said. "If someone wanted to build a case against you, it wouldn't take much. Your wife is murdered by someone whom she knew well enough to open the door to late at night. You go on a drinking spree and almost tank your career. Next thing we know, your best friend and research partner is killed, we've got a lead that suggests Elise and Lucas were having an affair, and the woman with Lucas the night he's killed is murdered. The same woman who was supposed to show up in your lab this morning to finish her story on your research project. In the meantime, you're involved in a street brawl on behalf of a psychic, and then your lab blows up with you parked in front of it."

"You left out the part about my window getting smashed and Khristina's death threat," he reminded her.

"Which could be your own attempt to mislead the investigation!"

Teri wanted to reach over the desk and shake him. "You didn't report the broken window, Michael, and, for all I know, you or Khristina wrote out the threats! How much of a stretch would it be for a prosecutor to say you're a brilliant, totally stressed-out scientist who completely snapped when he found out his wife was cheating on him with his best friend, and so you killed them both—or had them killed—along with the woman who helped you set it up?"

She splayed her fingers out and pressed them hard against the surface of her desk.

"And then you blew up the lab to destroy any evidence that might be there to connect you to any of it. It might not be the truth, but it sure could be played that way," she warned him.

"Khristina has nothing to do with this, Teri," Michael told her. "She's caught in the crossfire. She's a target because of Skye's article."

"I know that!" she shouted, then dropped her volume. "But I can't prove it," she added raggedly. "Someone is trying to put you away, Michael, but I don't have a clue who that someone is, and until I figure this out, I don't know what to expect or even who to protect!"

"Look at Drake Lamont, Teri."

She cocked her head in question.

"What?"

"Look at Drake Lamont," Michael repeated. "You told me there was no sign of a forced entry, so Phoebe knew her killer. She knows Lamont."

"I'm sure she knew lots of people, Michael. Lamont is— was—her boss."

She looked at her hands still lying on the table. "He's also a very influential man," she pointed out. "A pillar of the community. An international player. You better have a really good reason to ask me to take a look at him."

"They were arguing over Phoebe doing an article for me, Teri. An important article. One that could shake the scientific community—maybe the whole world—to its very foundations."

Michael shifted forward in his chair. "That's what she told me over coffee yesterday morning when I gave her everything on the Strings Project."

Teri held up her hand for him to stop. She didn't know anything about scientific foundations, but she did know about a certain photo of him and Phoebe. Silently, she debated whether to tell him about the photo she had of them at the coffee shop.

The photo that carried a typed caption on the back that read, "Scientific research as payoff for services rendered?"

The photo that someone had anonymously left for her, along with the others in the envelope, suggesting that Michael and Phoebe had plotted together to have Lucas killed, giving Michael a betrayed husband's revenge and Phoebe the biggest story of her career.

The photo that undeniably linked Michael with a murdered Phoebe.

The photo that she knew in her gut was evidence that someone was working very hard at framing Michael Carilion for at least one murder, if not three.

"All right," she said, "tell me about Lamont. He and Phoebe were arguing?"

Now it was Michael's turn to hesitate.

He genuinely liked Teri, and it occurred to him that he didn't want her approaching Lamont and running the risk of inadvertently exposing herself or her sympathies for Michael, especially not after what had happened to Phoebe. True, Michael's own suspicions about the man hadn't fit themselves into a working model yet, but here was one more factor—a fatal one for Phoebe—for which he had to account. Thanks to Skye, Michael had proof that Lamont was secretly connected to his research work, and thanks to Theo, he knew Lamont had canceled the journal, but until Phoebe's murder, Michael had only had the uneasy, unsubstantiated, suspicion that a link might exist between the powerful publisher and the violence that seemed to be closing in around him.

But Phoebe's death had changed that.

Now there was something stronger than a link.

Now there were the beginnings of a pattern.

Michael ran through the sequences he'd built in his head last night and slipped Phoebe's murder into his equation.

When he did that, Lamont's name now turned up in connection to two murders—Lucas's, and now Phoebe's. What were the odds of that?

Not to mention that during their conversation over coffee, Michael had picked up definite hints from Phoebe that an intimate relationship existed between her and her boss, and it had become obvious to him that it was that relationship that Phoebe had been counting on to help her sway Lamont's decision to print the article.

Phoebe's body had been discovered unclothed. The door unforced. Michael closed his eyes, guilt and reproach crowding in on him. Lamont had been in Phoebe's apartment last night, Michael was certain.

He opened his eyes and wondered if the man he'd met two years ago at the chancellor's cocktail party was a cold-blooded killer.

Or the Devil himself.

For a mindless moment, Michael caught himself actually considering if Jack and Khristina and Skye were right, and he was wrong.

Could Lamont be evil incarnate, orchestrating even murder to irrevocably bury Michael's Theory of Everything?

Michael shook his head, willing away the encroaching absurdity. Lamont was a man, not a theological concept, and whatever his agenda might be, or however he played into the insanity that had suddenly engulfed Michael's life, he wasn't going to stop Michael's triumphant announcement. In another two hours, Michael was going to be standing in front of a microphone, introducing the equations that would rock the world. He just had to keep focused a little while longer.

His eyes on the prize, as Jack had said.

But once that announcement was made, he was going to find out why Drake Lamont wanted to ruin Michael Carilion's life.

"You know, Teri, you're probably right," he said, deflecting her question. "Phoebe knew lots of people."

He injected what he hoped sounded like a contrite note into his voice. "I'm sorry if I sounded like I was trying to tell you how to do your job. I'm having some really bad days here. Forget I said anything about Lamont."

Teri looked at the lines of strain in Michael's face. She could only imagine how bad the last two days had really been for him.

But she wasn't imagining the naked hatred she'd heard in his voice when he had suggested she look at Lamont as a suspect in Phoebe's murder. Nor was she imagining his poorly disguised attempt to distract her from pursuing her line of questioning.

For some reason, Michael didn't want to talk about Drake Lamont.

Was Michael targeting Lamont because Phoebe had told him that she and her boss had argued about her article on Michael's work?

How important was this article, anyway?

Could it possibly be important enough to qualify as a motive for murder?

Teri flipped over a new sheet on her notepad.

"Michael, maybe you should tell me what you told Phoebe about your Strings Project."

CHAPTER SIXTY-FIVE

It was almost nine-thirty in the morning by the time Teri finished questioning Michael and released him with his promise to stay in town and call her immediately if he had anything else to add to his statements. He'd been very patient explaining his research to her and trying to make it understandable, but Teri still felt mentally fried by the sheer enormity of what his work addressed.

"Parallel universes," she murmured, underlining the words on her notepad. "Energy packets. Membranes. And all because of little strings of energy. Okay, I can grasp the idea that this is going to change how scientists think, but really, what does it have to do with the rest of us?" she asked the empty room. "If these strings of energy can carry information, what good does it do us, unless we know how to reach out and read that infor . . ." she trailed off as a memory of Jack Gerrity's face, rigid with concentration on a frigid night, rose in her mind.

"Jack can read energy," she whispered, knowing immediately that was the reason the old priest was here in town with Michael.

And Khristina. Khristina could read energy, Michael had told her.

But Khristina was a medium. She talked to dead people. Did dead people have energy? Then they weren't really dead, were they? Energy was a sign of life, wasn't it? So Michael's new theory had proven that the energy of people survived death?

No way, Teri thought as the truth of what she'd learned almost knocked her from her chair.

Michael had turned heaven into a fact, and he was going to announce it at noon.

"Okay," she thought out loud again, "now I understand why Phoebe's article was important, but how could it possibly be a motive for murder?"

In total frustration, she laid her head on her notepad and closed her eyes.

Eager to collect Khristina from where she'd been waiting down the hall in Teri's office, Michael turned the corner in the corridor and nearly collided with the man turning in the opposite direction. Instinctively, he grabbed the man to steady him and keep him on his feet. Only when he opened his mouth for an apology did he realize he was looking directly into the strange, silver eyes of Drake Lamont.

"Here to make a confession, Dr. Carilion?"

Michael released the publisher as if his hands had been burned.

"What are you doing here, Lamont?"

Lamont turned his attention to his jacket and brushed his sleeves as if he were flicking off dust. He returned Michael's cold stare.

"Making sure this police department doesn't let a dangerous man walk the streets of this fair city for another moment."

He leaned slightly towards Michael and dropped his voice to just above a whisper. "What in the world made you think you could get away with killing Phoebe, Carilion? Or did you simply hire it out while you were busy blowing up your lab?"

Michael's eyes went even colder. He felt his jaws clench tight. When he answered Lamont, the words spit out of his mouth. "I know you're making all of this happen, Lamont. I don't know why you're doing it, but I know you're the one pulling the strings."

"Interesting choice of words, Doctor. You said it yourself: strings."

He dropped his voice to a dark whisper. "Strings explain everything, don't they? Once you solved the equations, you knew that. Strings are the agents of unification. The One Theory. But I'm willing to wager you had no idea what you were really dealing with at that point. You're a man of science, after all. Proving that life continues after death certainly wasn't on your agenda, was it? What a surprise it must have been to you to find that the most coveted scientific principle of all time is also the elegant articulation of the existence of heaven, of the mind of God himself."

The quest for unification is the desire to know the mind of God.

The words of his fellow physicist from years ago came crashing in on Michael, even as he stared at the growing rage blazing in Lamont's eyes.

And then it hit him.

Hard.

Lamont had just agreed with Jack. And Skye. And Khristina.

He was talking about the eleventh dimension.

As heaven.

Beneath his feet, Michael could almost feel the ground shifting.

Outside the corridor windows, the wind picked up and began to howl.

"Or don't you believe your own evidence?" Lamont's eyes narrowed into slits. "Is that why Gerrity showed up? To help you leap the chasm between science and faith? Tell me, did he succeed?"

He searched Michael's stony face again, and, apparently finding his answer there, suddenly laughed. "My, my. I do believe you haven't quite solved this particular equation to your satisfaction yet. Here I thought I had to deal with Gerrity and the medium, and it looks like I've jumped the gun."

He leaned towards Michael.

"Did they tell you who they think I am? The Devil himself? But isn't that who all the frauds and psychic priests blame when their own deceptions are found out?"

Lamont took a quick glance back down the hallway towards the police station reception desk before continuing. "Of course, on the other hand, maybe I'm just a controlling, power-hungry egotist who's toying with you, feeding your delusion. After all, what man in his right mind would say that the Devil even exists? Superstitious paranoids, maybe. Religious extremists. Bona fide mental cases, perhaps. But an internationally respected physicist? The man who keeps trying to formulate a Theory of Everything?"

Michael found himself paralyzed, mesmerized by the man's hatred that was as palpable as if it were a thing that Michael could see and touch.

Lamont continued, his voice a rasp in the empty hallway.

"If that man thought Drake Lamont, a man of equal international reputation and respect, was the Devil, he'd better be careful with whom he shares those observations, because he really doesn't need to give the police one more reason to lock him up right now and throw away the key."

He tossed one last glance over his shoulder at the reception desk.

"So, Carilion, I'm curious. Who do you say I am, really?"

The steel in Michael's voice was honed sharp as he leaned into Lamont's face and said in a tone pitched only for him to hear, "You're a lying killer, and make no mistake, Lamont, that is one thing I am definitely going to prove to the world."

Lamont made a sound of disgusted dismissal in his throat and moved to step around Michael, but Michael matched his step and blocked his way.

"Just one thing, Lamont. Devil or not, if you didn't want me to solve the One Theory, then why didn't you just take me out of the game permanently, instead of paying my salary all these months?"

The Gentleman's eyes narrowed again. "That little witch. She couldn't wait to tell you, could she? Her mistake. One, I promise you, that Skye Hammond will regret."

Again he tried to sidestep Michael, and again Michael blocked his way.

"Tell me."

Lamont met his eyes. "It's simple, Carilion. Kill the messenger and it merely brings more attention to the message itself—a mistake I won't make twice. But discredit the messenger, and the message is discredited along with him, and then no one will want to touch it with the proverbial ten-foot pole. I wanted you to find the theory, so I could be right there to crush it. I've worked a long time to establish my empire, to shape my world, Carilion, and in my world—this world—there is no heaven. And I'll do whatever it takes to keep you or any of your friends from even beginning to suggest anything otherwise."

A blast of rain slammed into the building, pouring down the windows. The lights in the hallway flickered.

"You killed her, didn't you?" Michael accused him, thinking of Phoebe's determined promise to persuade Lamont to publish his work.

"Yes, I did," he admitted in a whisper for Michael's ears alone. "And, by the way, I think you should know—she never called me a lying killer. Not even once. Not even when I showed up at your door and put a bullet in her head."

Michael was motionless for only a split-second as the meaning of Lamont's words sliced razor-sharp through his consciousness. He swung his fist, but Lamont had already spun back towards the reception desk.

"Someone lock this man up!" he shouted, pointing to Michael. "He's a madman!"

"Michael!"

Teri had appeared from nowhere and caught his arm in a death grip. "What are you doing?"

Almost blind with anger, he shook her off.

"I've got to get out of here. Where's Khristina?"

"She left a message with the front desk. Said she took a cab to her place to change clothes and you should pick her up there."

Teri threw a glance at Lamont, who was loudly demanding to see the police commissioner. "What's going on here?"

But Michael was already furiously tapping in Khristina's home phone number on his cell phone. Then, in a flash of terrifying clarity, he recalled Lamont's words just moments ago that he thought he had to "deal with" Jack and Khristina.

Jack's superior had ordered him to leave town . . . at Lamont's urging. It had been the publisher's veiled attempt to remove Jack from the equation.

As for Khristina . . . she'd been here in the police station waiting while he'd talked with Teri.

Safe.

But now she had gone home alone, unaccompanied for the first time since Michael had found the death threat under her front door.

And Lamont had just admitted to killing Elise.

"Pick up, pick up!" he breathed into the phone as it connected to Khristina's, feeling a cold sweat breaking out across his forehead. Why hadn't she waited for him? Why hadn't someone told him she was leaving? How long had she been gone?

"Be there, Khristina. Just be there," he begged her, his lips forming the words silently.

The phone continued to ring.

"Hello," Khristina's voice came over the line.

Michael let out the breath he'd been holding.

"I am not at home right now."

"No!" Michael cried in desperation. He saw Lamont across the room, watching him.

The man was smiling.

"Hello? Michael, is it you?"

It was Khristina, cutting into her answering machine's recording.

"Khristina! Yes, it's Michael. I was worried . . . " He swiped the sweat off his forehead. "Stay there, I'll be over in a few minutes."

"Michael, the rain is coming down in sheets. The radio says we have a severe thunderstorm warning and a tornado watch. You should stay there where you are safe, off the road. We have plenty of time until we have to be at the television station for the press conference. I can wait."

He looked up again at Lamont, who was vehemently arguing with Teri, threatening to have her removed from the force if she didn't immediately throw Michael in jail for assault.

"I can't," he told Khristina, already heading out the door into the lashing rain. "I'm on my way."

Khristina hung up the kitchen phone and thought she saw something moving through the driving rain outside the window. A van had pulled up in the driveway. While she watched, a man jumped out from behind the wheel and made a dash for her back door, where he pounded on the doorframe and yelled loudly for help.

Khristina pulled the door open. The man stumbled into the house and grabbed for her right arm to steady himself. By the time she saw him place the small black gun against her left shoulder, it was already too late.

CHAPTER SIXTY-SIX

Khristina had been right when she'd said that the rain was coming down in sheets.

Michael had to slow down almost to a crawl at least three times before he reached Khristina's neighborhood because the visibility was so bad he couldn't see the road. Pulling into her driveway, he honked the car horn to let her know he had arrived, and once he slammed the gearshift into park, he sprinted out of the car to her back door.

Which was standing ajar.

"Khristina!" he shouted, hustling in out of the rain. "You've got rain coming in!"

He closed the door and went over to the kitchen sink, where he shook off the water clinging to his hair and brushed rain off the arms of his jacket. He grabbed a paper towel and went back to wipe up the water on the floor.

As he leaned over to wipe, he spotted a small square of tin on the floor. He picked it up and turned it over in his palm.

It was the icon of St. Michael. Khristina's key chain.

"Khristina?" he called again.

The house was quiet.

She must be upstairs, he thought, changing her clothes, and she couldn't hear him. He walked through the little kitchen and glanced into the front living room. He saw a small stack of mail lying on the foyer floor beneath the mail slot. She obviously hadn't had time to pick it up yet. Michael wondered how long she had waited in Teri's office before getting a cab to come home. He started up the steep, narrow staircase to the small upper floor and wondered why he didn't hear even the sound of her floorboards creaking.

And then a heart-stopping panic grabbed him by the throat.

"I thought I had to deal with the medium and it looks like I've jumped the gun."

He took the stairs three at a time.

CHAPTER SIXTY-SEVEN

Jack and Skye sat in the living room at Novice House, the television on and the sound up while the local weatherman repeated a litany of storm watches and warnings. Yet neither of them was paying much attention as the newest advisories scrolled across the bottom of the screen, since they were both still mentally fixed on the newsbreak that had preceded the return of the weatherman.

Phoebe Dauwalter had been found dead. Murdered. In her own home.

Jack had offered a prayer for her soul.

Skye had put her head down between her knees to fight the rush of nausea.

Even the Channel 9 reporter had looked shaken as he made his report standing before Phoebe's condominium building, sheltered from the rain by a wide roof that covered the front entrance. He hadn't had a lot of details to share, since the police team of investigators was still processing the crime scene, but what he did tell his viewers was enough to get Michael's name mentioned yet again in connection to a murder.

"What is especially disturbing, Chad," the reporter pointed out to the morning news anchor, "is that this is the second murder in just a matter of days that has a link to the controversial research being conducted at Barnet College under the direction of Dr. Michael Carilion. Our sources tell us that Ms. Dauwalter was with the first murder victim, Dr. Lucas Scranton, a colleague of Carilion's, at the time of his death, and that she was currently working on a story about the progress of the research.

Whether or not Dauwalter's involvement with the research team played a factor in her murder has not yet been determined, but I can guarantee that investigators are going to be taking a very close look at what's been going on in that college lab."

Pulling herself upright again, Skye turned to Jack.

"Michael has to know about this, right?" she asked. "When I dropped off Khristina at the station, he was waiting for her out front for their appointment with Teri, so someone had to have told him by now."

Jack nodded. "I'm sure he knows. I expect that by now, he's already been questioned about it."

"But he was with you all night," Skye protested. "They can't possibly think that he . . . "

"Who knows what anyone thinks?" Jack interrupted her. "There'll be as many versions of what might have happened as there are people to think them."

He looked at Skye's stricken face and softened his tone.

"Yes, he was with me all night, and I'll be the first to tell Teri that," he assured her. "Teri's a good cop, Skye, and she knows that someone is trying to set up Michael, but she's also a good cop who has to cover all the bases. So she'll question Michael and try to find the thread that's going to lead her to the real killer, to the truth."

He waved his hand at the television.

"This is all media spinning. Suggesting scenarios. But it contributes to what people perceive as the truth, whether it is or not. And what is perceived is powerful."

Skye gave him an odd look. Drake Lamont had used almost the same words describing his work to her.

"It's a Grand Narrative," she said, her voice filling with realization. "That's what it is, isn't it? It's exactly what Lamont was talking about—creating reality. Whoever controls the information, controls what people think."

She pointed at the television screen.

"Make enough suggestions, show only what corroborates your story, and voila! It's real. Because people accept as truth whatever is presented to them as 'information,' even if it's not. So how—"

Her cell phone rang. She looked at the caller ID. "It's Michael," she told Jack, hitting the speakerphone button so they could both hear him.

"Khristina's gone!" Michael's frantic voice shouted over the line. "I don't know where she is! Somebody's grabbed her, I'm sure of it—I found her icon on the kitchen floor and she never leaves the house without it. And the back door was open when I got here. And he was smiling! Lamont was smiling! He's got Khristina!"

Jack grabbed the phone out of Skye's hand. "Michael, son, say it again. Khristina's gone?"

"Yes! She's gone, Jack! He's going to kill her!"

For only a moment, the old man was as silent as a stone. Skye felt the air shifting around her, and when she looked again at Jack, his eyes were unfocused.

No! she thought. *He's having a stroke! Please, dear God, no!*

"Jack!" she cried, reaching for his arm.

But then Jack came back to life and put his mouth close to the phone.

"We're on our way, Michael. We're coming to pick you up. I know where she is."

CHAPTER SIXTY-EIGHT

It was hard to keep the old Ford truck in sight in this rain, so Freddy closed the distance to a half-block. At least he was moving again, after sitting in his bug for the last two hours, waiting for Skye Hammond to come back out of the dormitory or whatever it was. When she finally had reappeared, a small man had accompanied her, and the two had run through the rain and hopped into the truck parked next to her car, then taken off like a bat out of hell.

And now—wasn't that a surprise?—they were turning into the driveway of the Tupikova woman's house.

Freddy pulled into the driveway of the house next door, but before he could back out and park on the street, the Ford came skidding back out with three people in the cab, and it looked like a big, dark-haired man was driving. The truck shot off into the storm.

Freddy stepped on the gas to follow.

CHAPTER SIXTY-NINE

Drake held on to the wheel and fought the mud catching at his tires as he bounced over the rutted tracks to pull around behind the old barn. The torrent of rain had finally stopped and the clouds lifted some, though he could see another line of dark clouds racing in from the southwest even as he ducked out of the car and made a dash for the barn door. The humidity was still oppressive, but at least the lashing winds were gone. He pulled open the door, calling out as he did so.

"It's me! Where are you?"

Illuminated only by the weak light that came through the small window near the back wall, the cavernous barn was littered with dark shapes that slowly took on more recognizable forms as Drake's eyes adjusted to the dimness. A collection of antique hand plows stood in the middle of the floor, their steel and copper blades still intact. Along one wall, an assortment of farming implements—shovels, scythes and hoes—were propped beside a rusting horse-drawn plow, and standing in front of the big barn doors stood a hay wagon with "Pioneer Village" stenciled across its side. A loft sat above the front third of the barn, its platform empty of any hay bales, though hay lay thickly scattered across the barn's floor.

"Over here," a man's voice answered from behind the wagon. "I think she's starting to wake up."

Drake picked his way around the hand plows to the wagon, feeling sweat running down inside his shirt collar. The heat in the airless barn was almost unbearable. He needed to get this done and get out. The stupid fool hadn't even waited to check and make sure that it really was Drake calling to him.

"Where did you park?" Drake asked, coming around the corner of the wagon. "I didn't see your van."

Sitting on a bale of hay with Khristina lying at his feet, her mouth, hands, and ankles bound with silver duct tape, the Prophet smiled at Drake.

"The stun gun worked great," he said. "Thanks for letting me use it. It made everything a lot easier."

"Yes, it did, didn't it?" Drake agreed. He stepped next to Khristina's captor, pulled his gun from his inside coat pocket, and shot the Prophet in the head.

Khristina was confused.

Her ears were ringing from an explosion, but she was sure she heard a man's voice speaking. Rough straw scraped her cheek. She couldn't move her hands or feet, and she was lying on her side. Her vision seemed blurred and her mouth was taped.

" . . . very helpful, Freddy," the man's voice said somewhere above her. "Why don't you call it a day and go home? Get out of the storm. I don't need anything more on Skye Hammond for today, anyway. Your check will be in the mail, as usual." There was the sound of a cell phone snapped shut.

Then someone grabbed Khristina's arm and jerked her up to her feet.

She stood unsteadily, her balance hampered by her taped ankles. When she looked up into the face of the man who had lifted her, her stomach clenched in a terrible and sudden spasm of recognition, despite the fact that she had never seen him before. Even in the semi-darkness of the barn, she could see clots of wet blood clinging in his light-colored hair, streaking his cheeks and staining the front of his white dress shirt. The smell of gunpowder hung thickly around them, mixed with the growing odor of sulfur.

As Khristina watched in horror, the man's facial features shifted, flattening to lose their previously handsome definition. But it was the eerie silver of his eyes that told her exactly who he was—eyes that were now focused on her with undisguised hate and unmistakable triumph.

He tore the tape from her mouth.

"Hello, Khristina," The Gentleman's voice rasped as the shrieks of thousands of demons filled the barn. "Welcome to my world."

CHAPTER SEVENTY

S kye knew she was going to die. If Michael didn't roll the truck because of the madman way he was driving through a deluge of blinding rain, then a wall of wind was going to slap them right off the road. She glanced at the speedometer and saw the needle pushing past ninety miles per hour as the rain unexpectedly quit, giving her a clear look through the windshield.

Ahead of them was a sign pointing to the entrance for Pioneer Village. Jack yelled at Michael to turn, and he spun the wheel, throwing Skye first against Jack on her right, then against Michael on her left as the old Ford clipped part of the entrance gate as it barreled into the park. Gripping the dashboard in front of her, Skye leaned forward to peer at the storefronts on either side of the gravel street, which was riddled with puddles and running streams, as Michael slowed the truck to navigate the mud.

"Jack!" Michael shouted over the noise of the engine and the grinding of the wheels. "Where is she? Which building?"

The truck roared past a short block of houses, and then Jack saw it behind a restored farmstead.

"The barn!"

Again, Michael spun the wheel and Skye bounced off the men, the truck rocketing over potholes and deep ruts. Slamming the truck into park, Michael shot out of the cab while Jack and Skye tumbled out the other side and ran after him.

But Skye ran only a few steps before she realized something was wrong.

Terribly, terribly wrong.

The sky was green.

The air, motionless.

And there wasn't a single noise, almost like a vacuum had sucked all the sound out of the world.

She turned back around and watched a black funnel taking shape in the distance, dipping down from the wall of clouds racing toward them. Even as she watched, both fascinated and terrified, the wind picked up again, dead leaves already fallen beginning to stream past her.

"Oh my," she whispered.

And then Jack grabbed her arm and started running with her, the distant roar of a freight train in her ears.

Michael tore the back door of the old building open and threw himself into the barn.

"Khristina!" he bellowed. "Khristina!"

The sound of a gun firing above him brought his head up, just as the first blast of wind shook the side of the barn, sending the old farm implements crashing into each other on the floor.

It took only a split-second for his eyes to find her in the dimness. Fourteen feet above him, Khristina was sitting on the very edge of the loft, her ankles taped and her hands behind her back.

Standing behind her was Drake Lamont, holding a gun, still smoking, to her head.

"I've decided it's not enough to destroy every bit of your credibility," Lamont shouted at Michael from the loft. "I need to destroy your evidence, too. And that," he added, digging the muzzle of the gun into her temple, "would be Ms. Tupikova."

Another blast of wind hit the barn, rattling its walls and sending its beams creaking.

Michael's heart pounded, sweat pouring off his forehead. The interior of the barn was unbelievably hot, and pieces of straw swirled in the air, partially obscuring his vision. He quickly estimated the distance to the loft. With luck—a lot of it—he might be able to jump just high enough to reach Khristina's feet and pull her off the ledge, down and away from Lamont's gun. But with a gun to her head, Khristina would be dead before he'd even left the ground.

Or if Khristina could throw herself off the ledge, he could dive for her at the same time and try to cover her body from the bullet . . .

He needed to get closer.

"Let her go, Lamont!" he yelled, stepping nearer to a spot just under Khristina's feet.

He caught Khristina's eye and held it for only a second, while he made the old 'bring it' motion from his basketball days at Lamont, hoping desperately that Khristina got his message to shift closer to the edge of the ledge.

"Shoot me instead! I—"

"I already told you that doesn't work for me, Carilion!" Lamont shouted back over the rising sound of the storm. "But I am The Gentleman, and I'm always willing to strike a bargain. I'll get out of your way, you can announce the One Theory, and Khristina lives. You get your place in history, Carilion! Your precious life work gets published! One condition, that's it!"

Michael was almost under Khristina now. He could see her leaning forward, mouthing the word "no," begging him to refuse Lamont's proposition.

Above them, a piece of the roof suddenly screamed and buckled, wrenched from its timeworn supports by the pummeling winds.

"The condition!" Michael yelled, already knowing he would agree to anything Lamont asked in order to save Khristina. "What is it?"

Lamont pushed the gun against the back of Khristina's head, forcing her head down so she was gazing directly at Michael, while with his other hand, he shielded his face from the splinters of wood whistling past him.

"You announce," he yelled back over the rumbling sound that was shaking the rafters above him, "unequivocally, that heaven has no place in the Theory of Everything. It's a pipe dream, Carilion, and I want you to make sure everyone knows it!"

"No, Michael!" Khristina cried. "It's a lie! You found heaven! Believe it!"

Lamont pushed Khristina's head further down with his gun.

For an awful moment, Michael hesitated.

Did he believe it?

And then it didn't matter what he believed, because suddenly Lamont was right in front of him, swinging his fist into his jaw.

Michael staggered from the blow, tripping over a rusted plow on the barn floor. He caught himself before he fell and swung his body low to regain his balance, twisting back to face Lamont.

"A pipedream, Carilion! Heaven doesn't exist!" Lamont kicked out a leg to knock Michael to the ground.

Michael saw the leg coming and turned his body to avoid the blow, shooting out his hand to grab Lamont's ankle. He pulled it up, tipping Lamont back, but the man's balance was uncanny. He slipped his ankle out of Michael's grip and pivoted on his heel in the straw to land a vicious kick to Michael's right shoulder, sending him sprawling on his back across the floor.

Lamont leaned over him, rage consuming his features and grotesquely contorting them into a hideous mask.

Hate was there.

Unchecked savagery.

Evil.

"Announce it, Carilion!" Lamont demanded. "Heaven is a fairy tale and science is the only god!"

"No!" Khristina screamed. "Don't do it, Michael! Believe! *Believe!*"

He could make this deal with the devil himself, he thought desperately. Khristina would live and his theory would survive. Wasn't that enough? Wasn't that what he wanted? Heaven, God, salvation—it meant nothing to him. Ever since Elise had died, the only thing that had meant anything to him had been proving the One Theory.

Finding the answers man had sought from the dawn of time.

But then he looked again into the eyes of the woman in the hayloft—the woman who had a confidence in him that he couldn't understand and answers he couldn't accept. She had eyes that saw people on the 'other side.'

Eyes that, last night, had finally released him from his guilt and grieving. Eyes that had brought him peace.

Eyes that saw heaven.

And in that moment, Michael knew he wanted to see heaven, too.

He believed.

Behind him in the straw, his right hand grasped the edge of a long blade that had broken from an ancient plow. He wrapped his hand around it, and with a roar blasting out of his lungs, Michael surged to his feet, the blade raised high over his head.

In the same moment, a single shaft of unearthly light suddenly speared through the hole in the roof, illuminating the fierce determination on Michael's face and the deadly edge of the makeshift sword in his hand.

He blazed with light.

Lamont froze.

"No! It can't be!" he hissed.

He stumbled backwards, eyes fixed on his enemy, recognition and fatal realization stunning him, racing through him like a consuming fireball.

"It can't be you!" he shrieked. "Not here. Not now!"

Michael swung the blade in an arc of brightness, then aimed its tip directly at The Gentleman.

"Oh, yeah," Michael snarled. "It is me. Right here and right now. And I'm sending you back home where you belong."

He lunged straight forward.

"Go to Hell, Lamont!"

The barn exploded.

CHAPTER SEVENTY-ONE

Khristina wasn't afraid of dying as she floated in the air. She knew her friends would all be waiting for her, and she'd never have to deal with the tiresome face of skepticism again when it came to her special talents. It would be an enormous relief, really, to no longer have to cover up how it was that she knew all the things she knew.

Things like all the lines of the poetry of William Blake. Things like directions to the homes of physicists she only knew on a professional basis. Things like where Elise Carilion kept her recyclables.

Gradually, the floating sensation faded away, and Khristina felt the warm wings of an angel wrapped securely around her.

Except that the wings were rough against her skin, prickling and chafing her.

And the angel was heavy, lying on top of her.

She opened her eyes to a dim light and carefully studied the features of the sleeping angel's face. His chin was bruised and swelling. A cut just below his right eye had left a swath of drying blood across his cheekbone. The silver strands that flecked his dark hair were wet and matted against his temples.

He was beautiful.

Her own St. Michael, defender of heaven.

She reached up to brush her fingertips lightly against his closed lips, and he stirred, and opened his eyes, then lifted his head just enough to stare down at her.

"Hello, Michael," she said. "I think there is a barn door leaning on your back."

He slowly raised himself up on his elbows, his shoulder muscles straining against the heavy wooden panels until they began to slide off his back. As they did, clear light slid in around them, and overhead the sky was a bright blue mottled with trailing wisps of white clouds.

They were lying in mounds of hay in what had been the barn. Scattered around them were the smashed remains of antique hand plows and broken blades and pieces of barn siding. Gritting his teeth against a jolt of sharp pain in his right arm, Michael reached behind his back with his left hand and shoved the panels completely off his back, freeing both of them from the pinning weight. Only then did he carefully roll off of Khristina and help her sit up, strip the tape from her wrists and ankles, and pull her close in mind-numbing relief.

"Khristina. I'm so sorry," he whispered into her hair. "You were right all along. I couldn't see it. If I had, it wouldn't have come to this. You wouldn't have been in that loft, his gun to your head. None of it would have happened."

"You do not know that, Michael," she said, pulling back just enough to look into his troubled eyes. "One way or another, I think it would have come to this. He wanted your theory, yes, but even more, I think he wanted your soul. You did not give it to him, Michael. You stood firm. You did the right thing."

Again, he pulled her close. He wanted to believe her about this, too, but he knew that the image of her at the feet of Lamont, a gun to her head, was going to stay with him until the day he died.

And maybe even after that.

With a final brush of his lips against her temple, he released her a little, and the two of them sat in the hay, surveying the devastation around them. Ten feet away, the old wagon was upside down, two wheels completely gone and the other two slowly spinning to a halt. The horse-drawn plow was standing on its narrow end as if a giant hand had staked it into the ground, and just beyond it, some of the massive beams of the barn's roof lay snapped in half like so many toothpicks.

Nothing moved anywhere amidst the debris. It was as quiet as a tomb and almost as eerie.

Except for the muted shrill of a whistle.

"Jack!" Michael cried, pulling himself to his feet. Another wave of agony crashed through his arm, and he tucked it tightly against his body, his mouth a grim line of pain, even as he held out his left hand to help Khristina up.

"They came with me," he hastily explained, already turning in the direction of the whistle. "Jack found you with his . . . his—"

"Gift," Khristina finished for him, as they both awkwardly picked their way over the splintered wood and metal shreds that littered the barn floor.

Once they were clear of where the barn had stood, Michael grabbed Khristina's hand with his left, his right arm still held tightly against his side, and together, they stumbled across the slippery wet ground to where the old Ford had apparently been tossed like a toy and was now laying on its side. Turning the corner of the bed of the truck, Michael found Skye huddled in a ditch not four feet from the overturned truck, Jack's whistle in her mouth and tears rolling down her face. Beside her, Jack was slumped unconscious in the mud, red blood seeping from around a scythe blade buried in his thigh.

"I was afraid to move the blade," Skye said between soft sobs, her words barely audible. "I'm afraid the bleeding will get worse."

Khristina scrambled down into the ditch and took Jack's hands in her own.

"Stay with us, Jack," she urged. "Stay with us."

She closed her eyes to concentrate. The very air around her seemed to still. But then her eyes popped open to look desperately at Skye, then at Michael, who had slid down behind her.

"I cannot get any help. No one knows what to do. He will die without help."

She fastened her eyes on Michael's own pain-stricken face.

"You have to do this," she whispered, begging him. "Please, Michael. Do this."

"Do what?" he asked in despair, kneeling next to her in the mud, his own grief beginning to form a familiar black hole around him. "I don't know what you're asking me to do, Khristina!"

But Skye did.

"Ask your friend!" she commanded Michael. "The one who talks to you!"

He looked at Skye's panicked face.

"*What?*"

"Ask your inner fan club!" Skye was shouting, paralyzed with fear at the moments that were passing as Jack continued to bleed out in the ditch. "Just listen to it, Michael! Don't think! Just listen to your inner voice!"

Total confusion raced across Michael's face, but then, clear as a bell, he heard it.

Make a tourniquet.

"We need a tourniquet," he said, repeating the words ringing in his head—words that were tumbling unbidden into his consciousness. "It's Jack's femoral artery—he'll bleed out if we don't tie off between the gash and his body."

Skye already had her belt whipped off from her jeans, and she and Khristina were sliding it under Jack's leg, tying it in a tight knot, each of them pulling an end as tautly as they could.

Khristina's eyes ran with tears, her attention completely on Jack, while Skye focused on Michael's face.

"Now what?"

Pray, Michael.

"Now we pray, Skye," he repeated. "Pray hard."

He reached out his hand and laid it on Jack's shoulder, while forgotten words from a childhood prayer tumbled from his lips.

"The Lord is my shepherd . . . "

And then the blare of a siren sliced through the silence.

Michael turned his head, and there, barreling through the soggy ruts of what was left of Pioneer Village, was a police car, followed by a medical emergency vehicle. He bolted upright, and pain shot through his injured arm, almost bringing him back down to his knees. He waved his good arm and shouted, and the police car plowed a path to the Ford.

"We need the medics!" Michael yelled as Teri practically vaulted out of the squad car. "It's Jack! Over here!"

Three emergency medical technicians jumped out of their vehicle and were kneeling in the mud with Jack, a stretcher beside them. Khristina and Skye handed over the ends of the belt they still gripped in their fists and fell wordlessly back, watching the technicians cut away Jack's pant leg to get a closer look at the blade embedded in his thigh.

Skye choked at the sight of the blood pooling on Jack's pale skin and turned away, nausea finally defeating her. Teri held the younger woman's shoulders until the spasms of retching subsided, then gently folded her arms around her, rocking her on the muddy ground.

"You did great, Skye," she assured her. "That was smart—sending me the text message when you were heading here. We came as fast as we could, but the tornado . . . it held us up, you know?"

She glanced at the overturned truck sitting a few yards away.

"I can't imagine what this must have been like. To have a tornado blow over your head."

"I thought I was going to die."

Skye heard again the terrifying roar of the twister in her head, remembered the popping of her ears, as she had cowered in the ditch, with Jack covering her body with his own.

"The good Lord has saved me," she whispered, wonder mixing with awe and gratitude in her voice as she echoed the words she'd heard last night from Aunt Edna. She turned her tear-swollen eyes towards the paramedics who were strapping Jack onto the stretcher, an intravenous tube pumping fluids into his arm. "But will He save Jack?"

CHAPTER SEVENTY-TWO

Now, this was different, Jack thought.

He was standing off to Khristina's left, looking at himself on the stretcher as the emergency crew secured his body. White light suffused the scene, but he didn't find himself squinting at the glare. Two angels knelt on the ground beside his body, while a third held a bag of fluid that was being hooked up to one of the IVs.

"It makes quite a picture, doesn't it?"

Jack turned to find William beside him.

"I don't think I want to paint it, thanks," he told his old friend. "I'll stick with my big canvases of color. Death scenes don't appeal to me."

"It's not a death scene," William corrected him. "It's the depiction of a thin place—one of those wonderful spots in life where the veil between our worlds—dimensions, as your Michael calls them—become almost transparent, and for a brief moment, we see clearly what truly is and who we really are."

"I'm not dead?"

"Not yet, Jack. Michael bought you some time, with a little help from his friends."

The old priest looked again at the tableau before him and nodded at Michael kneeling in the mud.

"Does he know who he is?"

"I'm not sure. But I think he'll start to suspect it. Facing down the Devil tends to do that to a person—self-examination is a powerful agent for self-understanding, you know."

Jack knew. He'd spent years searching his own heart for answers while he'd been in exile out of the country, only to finally realize he'd never have them all. And then it had taken years more to be at peace with that truth before he could hand it all over to God and live in the peace that really did pass all understanding.

He glanced again at Michael. "That right wing of his is going to give him some trouble. It looks pretty ragged."

"A battle wound, nothing more. He'll only feel it in his arm, and that will mend."

"The two other angels," Jack said, his vision dimming, "one of them is—"

And then there was only darkness.

CHAPTER SEVENTY-THREE

Michael watched the ambulance skillfully negotiate the ruts of the road as it left with Jack and Skye tucked inside. With his good arm around Khristina, and his injured one in a temporary sling, he led Teri back towards what was left of the barn and stopped short when he caught sight of two more vehicles almost buried beneath uprooted trees.

One looked to be a white van.

The other was a red sports car.

They were both smashed through the roof with only a few shards of glass remaining in the window frames.

Teri ran ahead and climbed over the biggest branches to peer into the vehicles' interiors, but by the time Michael and Khristina had reached the tangled mass of tree limbs and metal, she was turning back to them.

"No one inside. That's the good news," she reported.

She studied the piles of rubble and debris strewn across the site.

"The bad news is, where are they now?"

CHAPTER SEVENTY-FOUR

Khristina was asleep, her head on his left shoulder. Michael shifted a little on the minimally padded couch to better arrange his bandaged right shoulder against the armrest. He didn't want to wake her until the doctor had something good to say about Jack. They had been waiting for hours now in the family lounge while a team of surgeons had worked on Jack's sliced leg. So far, the only report they had was that Jack's vital signs were improving and that he wouldn't lose the leg. About an hour ago, he'd been moved into an intensive care recovery unit, and Skye had persuaded the nurses to let her sit at his bedside, leaving Michael and a sleeping Khristina in the lounge.

With nothing to do but think, Michael's thoughts kept returning to two things: the moment in the barn when he leaped to his feet with the old plow blade in his hand, and the words of his inner voice telling him how to save Jack's life. As he'd grasped the blade, he'd felt a rush of power and certainty he'd never before experienced in his life. Even the eerie transformation of Lamont's face into pure evil hadn't shaken him; on the contrary, Michael had had the feeling that he'd been expecting it. And when he'd aimed his weapon at Lamont's heart, he hadn't doubted for a minute that he'd kill the monster, though he had no memory now of anything that happened after that instant.

Nor could he remember catching Khristina in his arms, which he must have done when the tornado hit the barn, throwing Khristina out of the hayloft and collapsing the doors on his back. What he could recall, though, was the look on her

342

face when he refused Lamont's offer and charged him, even though it meant Michael had forfeited her life to defend heaven.

She looked . . . he struggled to find exactly the right word . . . beatific.

Like she had looked when she and Jack tried to convince him that he'd found heaven.

Like she looked right now, composed and completely peaceful, sleeping on his shoulder.

As for his sudden inspiration about tying Jack's leg, Michael had no idea where it came from. He'd never taken an interest in anything medical beyond learning to follow the doctors' instructions for caring for sprained ankles or tendons when he'd played basketball. A deep leg wound with a severed artery was well beyond his repository of general knowledge.

And yet he had known exactly what to do. The paramedics had even told him as they put Jack in the ambulance that his quick thinking had probably saved Jack from bleeding to death.

Kneeling in the mud, Khristina had asked Michael for help. Skye had shouted at him to ask 'his friend'. And then he'd heard it—directions to save Jack's life.

He'd *heard* it.

It hadn't been his own voice at all.

It belonged to someone else.

Michael laid his head back on the couch cushion and closed his eyes.

"The big picture just keeps getting bigger, doesn't it?" he whispered to the empty room.

Yes, it does, the voice answered.

"Michael?"

He opened his eyes, surprised to find he had dozed off on the couch with Khristina.

It was Teri. She pulled up a chair and sat down, her knees almost touching his.

"How's Jack?"

Michael scrubbed his knuckles against the five o'clock shadow beneath his chin. "He's through surgery. Other than that, I don't know anything."

Khristina stirred on his shoulder, woke, and blinked against the bright lights of the lounge. She sat upright and brushed away from her face blonde strands of hair that had fallen loose from her braid.

"What is going on?" she asked him. "Jack is all right?"

Michael squeezed her knee in reassurance. "He's in recovery, Khristina. Skye's with him. We'll hear something soon, I'm sure."

"I wanted to tell you a few things. Both of you," Teri clarified. She glanced back over her shoulders, and Michael guessed she was checking to be sure they were alone in the room.

"I had the canine unit go over the area around the barn," she said. "The dogs found a body."

Khristina's hand covered her mouth, while Michael's hand kept its grip on her knee.

"It was under the old hay wagon that was overturned. There was identification in the wallet. His name was Edward Iverson. It was his white van under the trees. We ran the plates."

"Not Lamont," Michael said.

Teri gave him a sharp look. "Not Lamont."

"This was the man who kidnapped me." Beside him, Khristina drew a deep breath. "I only had a brief glance at his face before he knocked me out, with a stun gun, I think it must have been."

"I think so, too, Khristina," Teri agreed. "We found the stun gun in the van, along with a roll of duct tape and some other things."

She turned her attention back to Michael.

"There was a box of materials that are used in home-made explosive devices. According to our experts, they're identical to the materials used in your lab's bombing, Michael. And we found some notes he'd made about timing devices. I had the lab check Iverson's handwriting against the threatening notes you two received." She nodded her head. "Perfect match."

"So we can go home," Michael concluded, "and not worry about bricks sailing through the front windows. Or worse."

"I would think so," Teri agreed again. "I had a couple of officers do some investigating and it appears that Iverson believed he was some kind of modern-day prophet with a divine mandate to rid the world of false prophets. Apparently, when you and Khristina made the Channel 9 news the other night, he thought it was a sign from God. At least that's what his landlady said he told her right before he peeled out of her driveway on Sunday night."

Khristina covered Michael's hand on her knee with her own.

"I am sorry, Michael. Your window, your lab—all because this man was so misguided."

"There's something else about Iverson," Teri said before Michael could respond to Khristina. "We checked his phone log after we found his cell phone in the van, and it looks like right after he grabbed you, Khristina, he called Drake Lamont."

She paused, again checking that they were alone in the lounge. "And Iverson wasn't killed by the tornado," she added. "He was shot in the head. We're assuming by Lamont, because we found the gun under the old horse plow. It's registered to Lamont, and two bullets were missing."

"That must have been the explosion I heard when I was waking up in the barn," Khristina told them.

She looked at Teri with fresh tears in her eyes. "He must have been standing very close to me when he was shot," she said, shuddering. "When I looked at Lamont, his face, his hair—he was covered with blood."

Michael felt the shiver run through Khristina's body and immediately moved his arm to circle her shoulders, drawing her close to his side.

"Michael," Teri said, "there's one more thing. The ballistics test on the bullet that killed Iverson—it matches the bullet that killed Elise. After you told me to look at Lamont this morning in connection with Phoebe's murder, and then that scene with you two in the corridor at the station, a wild hunch told me to run the tests."

She leaned forward, excitement and satisfaction in her voice. "I've got the evidence, Michael. It was Lamont's gun. I'll have a search warrant for his office and home tomorrow to see what else we might find. If I can tie him to Phoebe's, or Lucas's murder, I'll do that, too. I don't have the whole theory hammered out yet, but I think a pattern is starting to emerge."

A pattern, Michael thought, and he smiled. Patterns, he understood.

Voices in his head—not so much.

But he could begin to try.

Teri stood up to go.

"I'm going to solve these cases, Michael," she promised him. "I can feel it in my gut. If, by any chance, Lamont survived that tornado—and I don't see how he possibly could have—he's going to wish he hadn't."

She offered her hand to Michael.

"Thanks, Teri," he said, maneuvering his right hand awkwardly in his sling to shake hers. "I owe you a lot."

"No, Michael," she replied. "I owed you for Elise. We're even now. I'll be in touch."

She started for the doorway, then turned back.

"By the way, I figured out what was so important about your One Theory, although it's hard to believe that someone would go as far as committing murder—multiple murders—to keep evidence of heaven from becoming public. I mean, for all the people who already believe, it's not going to make a difference if there's proof. As for those who don't believe," she shrugged, "well, who's to say that even scientific evidence will convince them? Ultimately, it's a matter of heart, I think. And faith. And that's something I don't think science can ever replace. At least, I hope not."

With a final wave goodbye, she was gone.

For several moments, neither Michael nor Khristina spoke.

"Do you think she's right?" Michael asked, his gaze fastened on a spot in the lounge carpeting where a single loop of thread had loosened.

Idly, he wondered how long a string the loop might become if he leaned over and pulled on it. Would the whole carpet unravel at his feet?

Or was it simply nothing more than a single loose thread in a tightly woven whole?

"I think she is right that science should not replace faith," Khristina finally answered, bringing his brief contemplation to an end. "But I think we need them both, because together, they give us more than one way to look at, and think about, the world. Faith is about the heart, Michael, and science is about the intellect. But they are not enemies—they are allies."

Michael lifted his eyes to meet hers.

"And what about my theory making a difference, Khristina? Do you think it will?"

For a long moment, silence hung in the lounge, Michael waiting for Khristina's reply.

"I think," she slowly said, "that Teri has an opinion shared by many people—that you either do or you don't have faith, and no amount of evidence will change what you think either way."

She raised her hand to trace the small bandage below his eye where he had been cut during the tornado.

"But you and I know there is at least one person who holds a very different opinion about that."

Her eyes returned to his.

"The Devil hates the light that truth brings, Michael. He knows it can defeat all his deceptions, and because of it, he loses his power over people. You found the truth, and he feared what it could do."

She withdrew her hand and pulled a little away from him, a smile tugging at the corners of her lips. "And since when does the world-famous physicist ask an illiterate Russian medium for her opinion?"

Michael felt the beginnings of a smile tugging at his own mouth.

"Since he learned that she saw a lot more than he did," he answered. "Thanks to her, he's finally found heaven."

He cupped her cheek in his hand and brushed his thumb over her smiling lips.

"Hey, you two," a tired—but obviously happy—Skye said from the doorway of the lounge. "Jack's awake, and he wants to see you."

Layered in bandages and sheets, the priest looked small and frail in the hospital bed with a colorful assortment of monitor wires and IV bag lines crisscrossing his chest. Khristina went immediately to his side and laid a soft kiss on his weathered cheek.

"Is this what I have to do to get a girl in this town?" Jack asked her with a wink, then settled his attention on Michael. "It's good to see you again, Michael, though I have to say you're looking a little ragged around the edge of your wing there. Is it broken?"

Michael lifted his sling an inch or two.

"Dislocated shoulder. I think it was the barn door that hit me in the back when I wasn't looking. It's going to put me on the bench for a little while, Coach. How about you?"

Jack waited to answer till the nurse checked his pulse, jotted the numbers on his chart, and was gone.

"The doctor says I'll have some permanent nerve damage in the leg, but with physical therapy, I'll be walking again," he told them. "I may have to use a stool for sitting while I paint, but I can live with that. I'm thinking of taking a sabbatical from Sacred Ground while I go through therapy here in town. I'll tell those freckle-faced kids at the Novice House they have to put up with the old man for a couple of months."

"You can stay with me, Jack," Khristina offered. "I would love to have your company."

He patted her hand that lay next to him on the bed. "That's sweet of you to say, but no. My goodness, what a scandal that would be—living with a beautiful young woman, let alone a beautiful young woman who hears voices from heaven! We all know how the Church feels about that, don't we? Although, just between you and me, how come St. Clare and St. Therese and St. Catherine, among others, could hear voices, and the Church says that's okay, but it's not okay for you, too?"

He shook his head in bemused frustration. "Gotta love that Church of mine. Full of both the wise and foolish."

He glanced at Michael, a sly smile playing across his face.

"Besides, I plan to be busy. I hear there's this hotshot physicist over at the college who's going to be looking for some lab rats once he gets his new lab up and running. I've been told I've got just the combination of talents he's looking for." He winked at Michael. "I figure it's my chance to get into *Physica*, you know, and I sure can't turn that down. A fellow my age doesn't get too many opportunities to be a rock star in the world of science."

"Oh no!"

Jack, Khristina and Michael turned to look at Skye, standing at the foot of Jack's bed.

"The press conference! I totally forgot about it! Michael, did you . . . announce?"

Michael shook his head.

"There will be a better day for it, Skye," he said. "But I did call Runyon and tell her I'd give her the interview of the century in another few weeks or so, after *Physica* publishes my theory. With Lamont gone, there will be a new publisher, and I really want to do this the right way. I talked with Theo and he's already got my article in the hands of the reading panel."

He slid a look at Khristina.

"At this point, all that remains is for me to make a few—well, not exactly minor—changes in what I want to say to the press when the theory is published."

He returned his gaze to Jack's face. The old man's eyelids were getting heavy and his breathing deeper. "And Coach, just so you know, I'm thinking it just may be that particular One Theory after all."

Jack smiled, sleep gently pulling him under. "I know you do, son. Take care of that wing, now, you hear?"

CHAPTER SEVENTY-FIVE

The doorbell was ringing.

Michael rolled over in bed and picked up the alarm clock on his nightstand to check the time.

It was ten in the morning.

He sat up groggily, ran his hands through his hair and picked up his jeans from the floor.

The doorbell continued to ring.

"I'm coming!" he shouted as he dressed, trying not to jostle his sore shoulder too much.

Padding down the hall barefoot and bare-chested, he couldn't help himself from taking a quick glance into the living room.

"No shattered window," he muttered. "It's going to be a good day."

A brown-clad UPS driver was standing on the front step when Michael opened the door.

"Good morning," the driver said. He held out a small package and a clipboard. "I need a signature for this. It's a certified delivery."

Michael signed the verification form and took the package.

"Have a nice day," the man said and returned to his truck.

Michael closed the door and turned the package over in his hands. It felt like a book.

He turned into the living room and momentarily paused, enjoying the feel of the thick new carpet under the soles of his feet. Dropping onto the couch, he tore the wrapping off the package and found a receipt addressed to Elise.

"Thank you for your advance order of *Einstein: The Search for Unification,*" he read aloud. "We hope you enjoy this new release and look forward to doing business with you again."

Beneath the receipt was the book. Elise must have pre-ordered it last winter, Michael realized. He'd heard some early buzz about the manuscript from Theo and had mentioned to Elise he wanted to buy a copy once it was published. She'd obviously tracked down the publishing house and placed the order, perhaps hoping to surprise him.

Unlike him, Elise had been paying attention.

Almost without thinking, Michael's eyes sought out the photo of his wife on the fireplace mantel.

"Forgive me," he whispered. "I never meant to lose you."

Michael wiped a tear from the corner of his eye and began to thumb through the book. Browsing through the text, he noted a section that drew on the physicist's previously unpublished personal correspondence. In fascination, he read part of a letter that the great man had penned to an associate, recalling an incident at his father's manufacturing company when he was still a child.

One of the massive spools of cable that was going to be used to light the Oktoberfest in Munich suddenly came loose from its bindings on the truck upon which it had been loaded, and the heavy cable began to unwind, but at a truly frightening pace. It snapped like a living thing at the men who were loading the truck, whipping the air like a cat-o-nine-tails. My father shouted at the men to move away, but one man was not quick enough, and the cable sliced across his thigh, cutting clean to his bone and through his femoral artery. The blood rushed out of him like a geyser with every beat of his heart.

Fortunately, there was another worker there who had trained at one time in a hospital, and this fellow knew to cut off the injured man's circulation between his heart and his wound so as to prevent him from bleeding to death there on the street. This particular fellow saw me standing by my father, my mouth open in horror at the sight of the gushing blood, and yelled at me to bring him my schoolbag, which had a long strap attached to it. I did, and the man tore off the strap, then wrapped it very tightly around the man's leg, just below his torso. To finish the tale, the injured man lived, though he lost his leg, and I decided that medicine was not the field for me, despite our good friend Max's encouragement that I follow him into medical school.

I did, however, upon witnessing this devastating demonstration of what sheer energy could do, develop a rare appreciation of the relationship between mass and energy, and well, my dear friend, you know what that led to.

Michael closed the book, his hands not quite steady.

Albert Einstein had learned what to do when a man's femoral artery was cut.

The voice Michael had heard . . . had heard all these years . . . was it possible?

And if it were, then there was only one way Michael could imagine that happening.

Like Khristina, he could access the eleventh dimension.

Like Khristina, he would have to be a medium.

And that would mean he had a spiritual gift.

Michael leaned his head on the back of the sofa and laughed in pure delight.

After a moment or two, he dug his old Rubik's cube from his jeans pocket, turned it in his hand and tossed it high up in the air, its colored blocks spinning out an infinity of breathtaking patterns.

"This big picture just keeps getting bigger and bigger."

AUTHOR'S NOTE

When I set out to write this book, I wanted to give readers an opportunity to reflect spiritually on the nature of reality as seen through the lens of contemporary cutting-edge physics research.

In other words, I wanted to synthesize science and faith in speculative theology.

To that end, I immersed myself in research ranging from the work of Albert Einstein and Brian Greene to Francis Collins' Humane Genome Project to theories about the Akashic field. I read biographies of Romantic poet William Blake and modern-day mediums and the life-after-death stories of ordinary people. I spent weeks mulling over the Apostles' Creed and other Christian doctrines. Time and again, I was struck by the convergences of Christian faith with scientific discovery—convergences which seem to be occurring with more frequency as we have entered the twenty-first century (or perhaps, it's just that we're now learning to recognize those occurrences, and so it seems there are more of them!). For all these sources of material and contemplation, and for God's mysterious grace that allows me to write about it all, I am grateful, awed, and humbled.

In addition, I've recently come to the realization that every story I write is a chronicle of not only my characters' journey, but also my own. Some of the minutia of my life shows up in my books, as well as my own deepening understanding of what it means to be a Christian in today's world. Not only that, but I have been granted the blessing of wonderful companions while I have undertaken these twin journeys, and it is to these people that I owe a debt of gratitude for everything from inspiration to encouragement, from the stratosphere of ideas to the concrete realities of getting housework done, from text revision comments to the examination of my Christian faith.

For this book, in particular, I want to thank my son Tom for introducing me to the work of Dr. Gary E. Schwartz, one of his professors during his undergraduate career at the University of Arizona and the author of "The Afterlife Experiments." Our conversations on the topic produced the seed that grew into this book. To Joan Timmerman, my first professor in my graduate theology program at St. Catherine University, a blessing for inspiring me to write fiction as a way to explore theology. To my daughter Nicole for her special enthusiasm in helping me complete this project, my deepest thanks. To my agent Greg Johnson, unending gratitude for finding the right publishing home for the Archangel series. And to my husband Tom for being the most patient, faithful, generous man in the whole world, my love and thanks forever, because without you, none of this would be possible.

ABOUT THE PUBLISHER

FH Publishers is a division of FaithHappenings.com

FaithHappenings.com is the premier, first-of-its kind, online Christian resource that contains an array of valuable local and national faith-based information all in one place. Our mission is "to inform, enrich, inspire and mobilize Christians and churches while enhancing the unity of the local Christian community so they can better serve the needs of the people around them." FaithHappenings.com will be the primary i-Phone, Droid App/Site and website that people with a traditional Trinitarian theology will turn to for national and local information to impact virtually every area of life.

The vision of FaithHappenings.com is to build the vibrancy of the local church with a true "one-stop-resource" of information and events that will enrich the soul, marriage, family, and church life for people of faith. We want people to be touched by God's Kingdom, so they can touch others FOR the Kingdom.

Find out more at www.faithhappenings.com.